"I won't let this wedding happen."

Caden stalked toward Lucy, crowded her back against the mantel, trying to use his size and his anger to intimidate her.

But he realized his mistake at once. This close, the scent of her perfume wound around him and he could see the freckles dotting her cheeks. He wanted to trace his fingers over the pattern they made, feel her softness against his rough skin.

And there was something more. A sorrow in her eyes—a loneliness that called to the empty space inside him and made him feel a little less like the outsider he knew himself to be.

He gave himself a mental head shake when her gaze softened and she swayed toward him. What was it about Lucy Renner that broke through his defenses like they were made of air?

A Christmas change of Heart

MICHELLE MAJOR & BRENDA HARLEN

Previously published as *Sleigh Bells in Crimson* and *Bring Me a Maverick for Christmas!*

HARLEQUIN

If you purchased this book without a cover you should be aware that this book is stolen property. It was reported as "unsold and destroyed" to the publisher, and neither the author nor the publisher has received any payment for this "stripped book."

Special thanks and acknowledgment are given to Brenda Harlen for her contribution to the Montana Mavericks: The Lonelyhearts Ranch continuity.

HARLEQUIN®

Recycling programs for this product may not exist in your area.

ISBN-13: 978-1-335-50012-0

A Christmas Change of Heart

Copyright © 2020 by Harlequin Books S.A.

Sleigh Bells in Crimson
First published in 2017. This edition published in 2020.
Copyright © 2017 by Michelle Major

Bring Me a Maverick for Christmas!
First published in 2018. This edition published in 2020.
Copyright © 2018 by Harlequin Books S.A.

All rights reserved. No part of this book may be used or reproduced in any manner whatsoever without written permission except in the case of brief quotations embodied in critical articles and reviews.

This is a work of fiction. Names, characters, places and incidents are either the product of the author's imagination or are used fictitiously. Any resemblance to actual persons, living or dead, businesses, companies, events or locales is entirely coincidental.

This edition published by arrangement with Harlequin Books S.A.

For questions and comments about the quality of this book, please contact us at CustomerService@Harlequin.com.

Harlequin Enterprises ULC
22 Adelaide St. West, 40th Floor
Toronto, Ontario M5H 4E3, Canada
www.Harlequin.com

Printed in U.S.A.

CONTENTS

SLEIGH BELLS IN CRIMSON 7
Michelle Major

BRING ME A MAVERICK FOR CHRISTMAS! 203
Brenda Harlen

SLEIGH BELLS IN CRIMSON

MICHELLE MAJOR

To my readers.
I'm honored and grateful that you make a place for me
and the stories I write in your lives.
May your holidays be filled with peace, joy and so much love! XO

Chapter 1

Lucy Renner pulled her compact rental car to a stop in front of the enormous barn on Sharpe Ranch outside Crimson, Colorado.

If Norman Rockwell and John Denver had looked down from the afterlife to create their perfect town, she figured Crimson would fit the bill to a T. She'd made a pit stop at a local bakery, Life Is Sweet, on her way through the picturesque mountain community. She had been greeted like an old friend even though she felt like an outsider in every way that mattered.

The woman who introduced herself as the shop's owner, Katie Crawford, had not only added an extra shot to the espresso Lucy ordered but then insisted she sample a fresh-baked cookie, still warm from the oven, all the while asking about Lucy's visit to Crimson and plans for the holidays.

But as kind as Katie Crawford seemed, Lucy didn't trust people who were too nice. It meant they wanted something. At least, it did in Lucy's world. Definitely in her mother's world, which was why Lucy's scam radar had gone on high alert when her mom called three days earlier "just to chat."

Her mother reached out only when she needed something. Despite Lucy's resolve not to get mixed up in any more of Maureen's romantic schemes, she'd never been good at saying no.

Now she'd been summoned to the quaint Colorado town that looked like it had puked Christmas cheer all over the place. Much like the rest of downtown Crimson, the bakery had been decorated with festive lights, greenery, ornaments and other vestiges of Christmas, all coming together to make Lucy feel even more grinch-like than normal.

She didn't do Christmas, didn't go in for the magic of the season. She'd worked retail long enough to know that Christmas spirit was a ploy to get consumers to part with their hard-earned cash. She'd had plenty of experience as a kid watching her mother *make spirits bright* in order to further her agenda of the moment. Lucy wanted no part of it any longer. Her plan for the holidays was to survive both the visit and her mother so she could retreat to her boring, quiet life back in Tampa.

Unfolding herself from the car into the biting winter air, she pulled her thin jacket tighter around herself. A two-story farmhouse sat beyond the big barn, situated in the center of a copse of trees, the naked branches swaying in the cold breeze. A cozy stream of smoke rose from the redbrick chimney, and Christmas lights twinkled from a front window as the afternoon light began to gently fade while she stood watching.

She couldn't quite force herself to face her mother yet, not when Lucy's life had become collateral damage in the fallout of Maureen's last romantic catastrophe. Not when she would have to spend the next two weeks playing a role that made her stomach pitch and twist if she couldn't convince her mom that whatever fantasies she had about being some sort of modern-day frontier wife weren't going to hold up for the long term.

A startled cry escaped her throat as something brushed against her leg. An orange tabby cat wound its way between her ankles then trotted over to the barn and disappeared through the slightly open door. A soft whinny broke the quiet a moment later, followed by an excited yip. Lucy followed the noises and slipped into the barn. Her mother was expecting her in time for dinner, but she had a few minutes to spare and couldn't resist exploring.

She'd taken horseback riding lessons briefly as a girl, paid for by her mother's husband number three. The smell of a barn—the heady mix of hay and animal—had quickly become her favorite scent in the world, and it had broken her heart when she'd had to say goodbye to the leased horse she'd considered hers.

That was when she'd been young and not so careful with her heart, but the smell of the barn still made her happy. It was warmer than she expected thanks to two industrial-sized heaters mounted on the far wall.

This barn was even larger than the one at the farm where she'd taken lessons, with stalls lining either side and a packed dirt floor in between. A horse leaned its head over a stall door and snorted in greeting.

"Hello, there," she said, glancing around but not seeing any sign of human life inside the barn. "Aren't you gorgeous?"

The lights were on overhead and to her right was the open door of someone's office. She peeked her head in at the meticulously ordered desk, but other than stacks of papers, there was nothing in the space to indicate who used it.

Was this the office of her mother's fiancé, Garrett Sharpe, the wealthy rancher who owned the property? She assumed someone with as many business dealings as Sharpe employed a ranch manager, so maybe the office belonged to that person.

Whoever ran the barn was clearly quite tidy. Even the horse

tack hanging on pegs in one corner was lined up evenly. Lucy could barely remember to put her wet towel on a hook after each shower.

She spotted a basket of apples sitting on a shelf outside the office and grabbed one, then moved across the barn toward the horse. She heard the stamp of a hoof, and the animal bobbed its head as if calling her closer. He'd clearly noticed the apple.

She held it out in an open palm and the horse snuffled, then took it from her hand. She slid her fingers along the underside of his jaw and up to his neck, loving the feel of the bristly hair under her hands. A high-pitched bark had her turning her attention to the next stall and, suddenly, as if she'd just been discovered, a cacophony of noise broke out across the barn.

She heard barks and yips and a low, mournful yeowing sound and quickly realized each of the stalls was occupied. There were four more horses and at least a dozen dogs, mostly in pairs. She went from stall to stall, visiting with the animals, reaching through the slats of plank siding to pet the ones that came forward to greet her.

At the end of the row of stalls were two rooms that had been built along the barn's outer wall, and she held her breath as she carefully opened one door. The walls of the room were lined with wooden hutches, and a myriad of twitchy noses and bright bunny eyes greeted her.

"What kind of ranch is this?" she asked in a hushed whisper, but the bunnies only hopped back and forth in response.

She reached for the other door, curiosity building in her chest. What was next? Llamas? Alpacas?

Cats.

The second room was filled with cats.

Well, not exactly filled, but there were more than she would have expected, and while she was counting, a small black kitten darted out through her legs.

She closed the door and leaned over to pick up the wanderer, but he crawled under a wide wood shelving unit and out of her reach.

Lucy felt like she'd stumbled on something private here, the animal version of a secret garden or some fairy-tale beast's private castle. She was no Beauty, but whatever this place was or whom it belonged to, she had a feeling she wasn't supposed to be here without permission.

Still, she couldn't leave until she saw the kitten safely back to his cat room, so she got down on her hands and knees and peered under the shelf to the corner where the kitten had lodged himself.

"Here, kitty, kitty," she crooned. The little cat's green eyes focused on her for a second. Then he lifted a leg and started grooming his man parts, which seemed to interest him far more than she did.

"Time for that later," she told him and wedged herself farther into the space. "You look too tiny to be away from your mama, little guy."

"He's seven weeks," a deep voice said from behind her. Startled, Lucy both cried out and lifted her head, banging it hard enough on the shelf above her to see stars.

The kitten dashed past as she struggled to wriggle out from where she'd squeezed herself. Head pounding and blinking away tears, she managed to back into the open space of the barn again. Still on her hands and knees, she looked over her shoulder to find the biggest, baddest-looking cowboy she'd ever seen staring down at her with a deep frown.

The wayward kitten was cradled in the crook of his elbow.

She hadn't heard the man enter the barn but could see the play of light and afternoon shadows from the open door at the far end. Heat colored her cheeks as she realized that the whole time he'd been walking the length of the middle row, she'd been giving him a prime view of the faded jeans that covered her backside.

Way to make a first impression, Lucy.

"Hi," she said, scrambling to her feet and holding out a hand. "I'm Lucy Renner. I'm—"

"The gold digger's daughter," he interrupted in a tone that reminded her of gravel crunching under tires. "You look like her, only not yet as ridden hard and put away wet."

Lucy felt her mouth drop open as her protective streak exploded like a powder keg. Yes, she had problems with how her mother cycled through men, but this would-be Marlboro man, handsome as sin and clearly twice as dangerous, was way out of line.

The man nudged her out of the way as he opened the door to the cat room and dropped the kitten to the ground. "You're also trespassing in my barn."

"You're rude," she said through clenched teeth.

"Doesn't make the words less true."

Dusting off the front of her jacket, Lucy threw back her shoulders and glared at the man. "I don't think Mr. Sharpe would appreciate you speaking about his soon-to-be bride that way."

He started to turn away, and she grabbed his arm, refusing to be intimidated by his hulking physical presence. If there was one thing Lucy could do, it was appear more confident than she was. She had fake conviction to spare, and no way was she allowing some ranch hand to bully her or her mother.

"What's your name?" she demanded. "I'm going to make sure this is your last day working for Garrett Sharpe."

The man stared at her fingers, the pink polished nails so out of place on the dull brown canvas of his heavy coat. Then his gaze lifted to hers, those piercing green eyes as hard as granite.

"Caden," he said so quietly she almost didn't hear him. "My

name is Caden Sharpe. Garrett is my—" he paused as if the word was stuck on his tongue "—my father," he said after an awkward moment.

"I thought Garrett's son died a few years ago?" Lucy regretted the question when Caden flinched. Maybe her mother had gotten the story wrong or played fast and loose with the facts to elicit sympathy when she was trying to convince Lucy to make the trip to Colorado.

Family is important to Garrett, her mother had said. *He was devastated by his son's death, and I want to show him I value family the way he does.*

"Tyson." Caden's lips barely moved as he said the name. "Tyson was my brother."

Then, as if her touch was physically painful to him, he shrugged it off and stalked away.

Chapter 2

Caden forced himself to walk out of the barn at a measured pace, even though sweat rolled down between his shoulder blades and his hands shook like the leaves of an aspen tree in a strong wind.

He'd been back on the ranch for almost two years and was so used to everyone in town knowing his story that Lucy Renner's question had caught him off guard.

It brought back all the regrets he had about his relationship with Tyson and how he'd failed the very people to whom he owed his life.

Two years of trying to make up for who he was and who he could never be to Garrett. Trying to keep the old man on track when he would have spiraled into depression after losing his flesh and blood.

A month ago, Garrett had returned from a business trip with Maureen Renner on his arm, a flashy peacock of a woman, so different from Garrett's first wife, Julia, and ridiculously out of place on the ranch. Caden had been suspicious from the start, and when they'd announced at Thanksgiving that they planned to be married Christmas Day, he'd had no doubt Maureen was more interested in Garrett's bank account than his life as a high-country rancher.

He had two weeks to convince Garrett to call off the wedding, and nothing was going to stop him from that goal. Certainly not a petite, chestnut-haired beauty who smelled like expensive perfume and looked like she belonged at one of the swanky lounges in neighboring Aspen, rubbing elbows with the rich and famous. She did not belong in Crimson and definitely not in Caden's world.

His reaction to her had been unexpected and wholly unwelcome. As much as he wanted to blame it on the view she'd inadvertently given him of the most perfectly rounded hips and butt he'd ever seen, there was something more to it than that.

Caden hadn't felt the powerful pull of attraction in years, not since his desire for a woman had driven a wedge between him and Tyson. Nothing was worth what he'd lost because of love. Or, more likely, it had been lust, which was even worse. Caden had sworn he'd never let another woman affect him that way.

But the immediate wanting—yearning—he'd felt when Lucy lifted those big brown eyes to his had been like an explosion going off in his brain. He didn't want it, couldn't handle it, and it only made him more committed to getting Lucy Renner and her mother away from the ranch for good.

His world would undoubtedly be turned upside down by those two women. He had a routine at the ranch—a mostly solitary existence, especially through the winter—that kept him busy. If it weren't for the barn full of critters that made up his animal-rescue project, Caden could have gone for weeks without seeing anyone but Garrett and the other ranch hands.

In the waning light of afternoon, he checked the outlying cattle troughs, then returned to the barn to feed and water the rescue animals. Lucy's scent still lingered in the air, and his body hardened in response. He forced the image of her out of his mind, focused on his routine and the animals he cared for. Next weekend he was opening the barn for a pre-Christmas adoption event, and he was way behind on preparations for it.

Erin MacDonald, the kindergarten teacher who also ran an after-school program for kids in the community, had convinced him to work with the local humane society to introduce more people to the animals he rescued. He hadn't actually planned on running a makeshift animal shelter. Hell, keeping the ranch going was more than a full-time job. But it seemed as though Caden had been collecting strays since he was a boy.

Maybe because he'd been one until Garrett and Tyson had come into his life.

Once he was certain she'd gone to the house, he finished with the animals, taking time to give some attention to each one. He let the dogs out into the big fenced pen connected to the barn to run and play and couldn't help but smile at their antics.

A light dusting of snow covered the hard ground, and a big storm was forecast for early the following week. Winter on a mountain ranch was a constant battle against the elements and nearby predators, and Caden took seriously the protection of every animal under his care.

Stella, the ranch's cattle dog, had taken on a maternal role with a few of the younger pups, and she nipped at ankles and herded the group of rescue dogs as they ran through the cold evening air, oblivious to the dropping temperature.

Once he had all the animals safely back in the barn, he headed for the main house. Tension knotted his neck and shoulders with every step. He would have much preferred to hunker down in the bunkhouse as a way of avoiding another run-in with Lucy, but he'd promised Garrett that he'd make an appearance at this family dinner.

Golden light spilled from the windows as he approached the main house. Maureen had hung thick swaths of pine rope from the porch railings, decorated with glittering red bows that seemed to draw more attention to the faded gray siding and dull paint of the black trim. He'd climbed those front porch steps thousands of times over the years, but since Tyson's death he'd never been able to step foot in the house without regret washing through him.

"It's about time." Garrett's deep voice boomed from the family room as soon as Caden stepped into the house. "Come in here, Caden, and see how Maureen has transformed this place into a winter wonderland."

Caden sucked in a breath as he entered the family room, with its muted-yellow walls and well-worn furniture. He almost had to shade his eyes at the garish display of Christmas lights strung above the windows and shimmering garland covering the mantel.

"It's pink," he said in horror. It looked like a five-year-old girl obsessed with princesses had decorated the space, not a thrice-divorced woman pushing sixty.

His eye caught on the box marked Decorations that he'd brought down from the attic now shoved into one corner. That box held all the decorations he, Garrett and Tyson had used each year. There were ornaments whittled out of tree branches from the woods on the ranch's south border, along with the small nativity set Tyson's mother had painstakingly painted the year before her cancer diagnosis.

Caden had come to live on the ranch only months after Julia Sharpe's death, and although he'd never met her, he'd felt her presence like a warm blanket at night. In the twenty years since Julia's death, little had changed in the house from how she'd arranged it.

Until Maureen Renner descended on Sharpe Ranch.

"Mom loves pink," Lucy offered from where she stood just inside the room. Color was high on her cheeks. If Garrett didn't know better, he would have guessed she was as put off by the whole display as he was.

"It's a vibrant color," Maureen purred, nuzzling Garrett's shoulder and tracing a manicured hand over his heart. "Bright and alive. This place needed some life breathed back into it."

Caden's adoptive father chuckled as he grinned at Caden. "I suppose you and I have gotten set in our ways living the bachelor life out here. We need a little infusion of spark and color, right?"

"Where the hell do you even find pink Christmas decorations?" Caden asked the room in general.

Garrett laughed again and Maureen darted a dismissive glance toward Caden, then beamed at her daughter. "Remember all the years we decorated for Christmas? You loved putting the star on the tree."

Lucy made a noise that sounded suspiciously like a gag, then cleared her throat. "Sure, Mom. But you're missing a tree."

Maureen opened her mouth but Caden spoke first. "Dad and I will cut one down next weekend." No way in hell was he giving that woman a chance to bring in some fake tree covered in more gaudy lights.

"About that, son." Garrett smiled gently. "Maureen hasn't had much luck finding a wedding dress around here, so I'm going to fly her to New York City for a few days to do some prewedding shopping."

"What?" Caden and Lucy spoke at the same time.

"I need to put together my trousseau," Maureen said, planting a smacking kiss on his father's mouth, "and pick out something special for our honeymoon."

"It's your fourth marriage. What the hell could you possibly need?" Caden pinned the overly made-up woman with a look that let her know exactly what he thought of her, not that it was any secret.

"Caden." Garrett's voice was a warning growl. Caden had heard the tone enough growing up. He'd always been a button pusher and for years had more temper than sense. Tyson had been the one to soften his sharp edges. His brother was always good-natured and smiling. Up until the one fateful argument that had severed their bond.

He wondered what Tyson would have thought about Maureen Renner and her tempting daughter. Well, he could guess what Tyson would have thought about Lucy. She was the type of woman to make a man melt into a puddle at her feet with one glance.

It only made Caden dislike her more.

"Lucy will help you," Maureen offered, her typically brilliant smile tight. "The two of you can put up the tree. She loves Christmas. Traditions are so important to our family."

Another muffled snort from Lucy. "Mom, I came out here because you told me you needed help planning the wedding." Lucy's voice was calm and slightly amused, but Caden noticed her hand was clenched so tightly at her side that her knuckles had gone white. "I can't stay here if you're gone. I need to get back to my life."

Maureen's glossy lips turned down at the corners. "I *do* need you, Lucy-Goose. Especially since we'll be in New York." She placed her fingers on Garrett's cheek and gave him another deep kiss. "My teddy bear and I need a getaway."

"You've got a two-week honeymoon cruise planned," Lucy muttered.

"I've always wanted to see the Rockettes' holiday show," Maureen insisted. "Don't ruin this for me, honey."

Caden saw Lucy's chest rise and fall, as if she was struggling to keep from losing it. "I've got a life in Tampa. I can't ignore it until the new year."

Maureen rolled her big green eyes. "Don't be silly. You haven't had a decent job since you got fired six months ago."

"And whose fault was that?" Lucy snapped.

"It was a misunderstanding that got blown way out of proportion." Maureen gave her daughter a quelling look. "I know you don't blame me."

The air crackled with tension between the two women. "I blame myself," Lucy said after a moment. "For so many reasons."

"I can put you to work," Garrett offered, pulling Maureen even closer, if that was possible. "Maureen said you're real good with finances."

Lucy gave a slight nod. "I have an accounting degree."

"I've been looking for someone to put the books to right on the ranch. Nothing's been the same since Tyson..."

His voice trailed off and Caden closed his eyes, unwilling to bear witness to the pain he knew he'd see etched in his father's gaze.

"Oh, my Lucy's a whiz with numbers," Maureen said, throwing her arms around Garrett's neck. "That would be perfect."

"Not for me," Lucy protested, and Caden felt a strange connection to this beautiful, prickly, unreadable woman. In the barn she'd been fiercely protective of her mother, but here it felt like she was as opposed to this whole charade as Caden.

"I'm happy, Lucy-Goose." Maureen stepped away from Garrett and walked toward Lucy. An image of a coyote approaching a defenseless and cornered jackrabbit sprang to Caden's mind.

He could almost feel Lucy shrink back, although she remained ramrod still. He had the strangest urge to step between the two women and shield Lucy from whatever invisible power her mother was aiming in her direction.

"You want me to be happy. Right, sweetie?"

There was a fraught moment when Caden wasn't sure how Lucy would respond. He could feel the emotions swirling through her from where he stood. Then her shoulders slumped and she whispered, "I do."

Maureen wrapped Lucy in a tight hug and murmured something in her ear that Caden couldn't quite make out. Then she bounced back to Garrett's side.

"I have a lasagna in the oven. Shall we have our first family dinner together?"

"Sounds good to me," Garrett said.

"I have a headache after traveling all day," Lucy told the group, all the spunk and sass he'd heard earlier in the barn gone from her voice. "I think I'm going to head up to bed."

"Take care to drink enough water," his father told her, moving forward with Maureen at his side. "It's easy to get dehydrated at this altitude, especially coming from sea level."

"I will," she whispered. "Thank you, Mr. Sharpe."

"Call me Garrett," his father said with another chuckle. "We're family now."

Not yet, Caden thought. There was still time to turn around this sinking ship, and based on the exchange between Lucy and her mother, maybe an unexpected ally had just arrived on his doorstep.

"You'll join us, Caden," his dad said.

He wanted to refuse, but there was so much hope in his father's eyes. He couldn't disappoint the old man again. Not after everything Caden had put him through in the past and his secret determination to run off Maureen Renner.

Guilt stabbed at his chest when he thought of how sad his father would be when his engagement ended. But Caden had to believe it was better to end things now, before Garrett made things legal. He knew what could happen when his father's heart was truly broken, and he couldn't allow that to happen again.

"I just need to wash up," he told Garrett and earned another wide smile.

Maureen led Garrett out of the family room, toward the kitchen. Caden expected Lucy to move toward the stairs, but instead she walked forward and touched the tip of one finger to several of the brightly colored Christmas lights.

"You can help me stop this," he said into the quiet.

Her shoulders stiffened and she gave a slight shake of her head but didn't turn around.

"Come on," he coaxed, moving closer. "You have to see this for the farce it is."

"Your father seems happy."

Caden opened his mouth to argue, then shut it again. He couldn't deny his dad's upbeat spirit since Maureen had come into his life. In fact, Caden couldn't remember the last time he'd heard Garrett laugh and smile the way he did when Maureen was near.

But that didn't matter. It wasn't real. It wasn't right. And he sure as hell didn't believe Garrett and Maureen were meant to be.

"It won't last," he answered instead. "With her track record, you know it's true. You could talk to her."

She turned to him now, her eyes flaring with emotion he didn't understand. "Does my mother seem like the type to be influenced by anyone else's opinion?"

"She's going to hurt him," he said quietly.

"You don't know that," Lucy shot back, but her gaze dropped to the floor.

Caden muttered a curse under his breath. "*You're* going to hurt him," he accused, lifting a finger and jabbing it at her. "A gold digger and her accomplice daughter. And now my father wants to give you access to his finances." He blew out a breath. "Hell, was this the plan all along? Are you two professional grifters or something?"

"Of course not," Lucy answered, but there was no force behind the words. None of the anger he would have expected at his bold accusation, which made him understand how close he'd come to the truth.

"I won't let this happen." He stalked toward her, crowded her back against the mantel, trying to use his size and his anger to intimidate her.

But he realized his mistake at once. This close, the scent of her perfume wound around him, and he could see the freckles dotting her cheeks. He wanted to trace his fingers over the pattern they made, feel her softness against his rough skin.

And there was something more. A sorrow in her eyes—a loneliness that called to the empty space inside him and made him feel a little less like the outsider he knew himself to be.

He gave himself a mental head shake when her gaze softened and she swayed toward him. What was it about Lucy Renner that broke through his defenses like they were made of air?

She was dangerous to him and, more important, to his father. The thought of how broken Garrett had been after Tyson died brought Caden back to reality like a bullet piercing his skin.

"I'm going to make sure this wedding doesn't take place,"

he said through clenched teeth. "Even if my father can't see you for what you are, I do."

Lucy's head snapped back like he'd slapped her. "You don't know me," she whispered.

"But I'm going to," he promised. "Every detail until I expose you and your mother. Mark my words, Lucy Renner. You will not survive me."

Before she could respond, he turned and stalked out of the room.

"You have to let him go." Lucy sat on the edge of the bed in the master bedroom of the main house the following day. "Stop it now, Mom, before it goes too far."

Maureen pulled a dress out of the closet and turned to Lucy, holding it in front of her chest. "For our New York trip, Garrett made reservations at Tavern on the Green. I've always wanted to eat there. It's a landmark, you know? One of the Real Housewives even renewed her vows there. What do you think about this? Too fancy or not enough?"

Lucy sighed. The dress was perfect. It was a deep forest green color with a scoop neckline, fitted without being slutty. Maureen would be stunning in it. Lucy should know. She'd helped her mother pick it out back when Maureen was trying to catch husband number three. "Why Garrett Sharpe, Mom? He isn't your type. Fitting into his life is a stretch, even for you." She pointed to the mounted caribou head above the bedroom's stone fireplace. "Are you going to start wearing camo now?"

Maureen grinned. "Do you know they sell pink camo at the sporting goods store in downtown Crimson?"

"That's not the point and you know it."

"I love him, Lucy-Goose."

The words made Lucy's stomach roil. "I told you after last time—"

"It's not the same," her mother insisted as she folded the dress and placed it in the open suitcase on the bed.

"Of course it's not. Garrett has a son who is both overprotective and beyond suspicious. It's a terrible combination for you. When he finds out—"

"Garrett knows I've been married before."

"That's not what I'm talking about."

Maureen slammed the suitcase shut. "You have to make sure it isn't an issue."

"How am I supposed to do that? The man trusts me even less than he trusts you."

"Don't underestimate your charms, sweetie."

Lucy groaned. "This isn't like when I was a kid and I could be cute or invisible, depending on what your man of the hour wanted. It makes it sound like you're trying to pimp me out."

"Of course I'm not." Maureen gave the suitcase's zipper a hard pull, then let out a little cry. "The dress is caught in it. I've ruined it." She turned and dropped to the bed, covering her face with her hands. "Caden Sharpe is going to ruin everything."

"Don't cry," Lucy said when her mother's shoulders began to shake. She'd always hated her mother's tears. As a girl, she'd done everything in her power to keep Maureen's spirit lifted. It was no easy task, especially after a breakup with whatever man Maureen had fallen in love with in any given month.

Lucy had too many memories of her mother in a weeping puddle on the bathroom floor, but even worse were the times when Maureen was quietly despondent. Those periods of depression had terrified Lucy because she never knew what her mother might do to end the pain.

Maureen was emotionally stronger now—at least, Lucy liked to believe she was. But the sound of quiet sobbing still tore across her chest, and she couldn't seem to stop her panicked reaction that if things got bad enough, her mother might try something desperate.

Lucy gently pried the zipper open and smoothed her hand over the delicate fabric of the beautiful dress. "It's fine. Not even a snag."

"You don't believe I love him." Maureen kept her face buried in her hands.

"I believe you," Lucy whispered. She believed her mother had convinced herself she loved Garrett Sharpe. But Lucy had seen Maureen head over heels too often not to have doubts about how this would end.

Maureen lifted her head and swiped her fingers across her cheeks. "I don't care about his money."

"We both know that's not true."

"It's real this time, sweetie. I promise."

"Have you told him everything?"

Maureen blanched. "I can't. Not yet. He might not understand."

Of course he won't, Lucy thought. A year ago her mother had barely avoided a bigamy lawsuit when it was revealed her third divorce had not been finalized on the eve of what was to be her fourth wedding. Unfortunately, her wealthy boyfriend also happened to be the uncle of Lucy's fiancé.

Lucy still blamed herself. She'd been in love with Peter Harmen and had erroneously thought Maureen would finally step into the role of supportive mother, allowing Lucy to have the happiness and security she'd craved for so many years. That didn't happen.

Maureen had met Peter's uncle, a famed fashion designer and owner of the exclusive boutique Lucy managed in Florida. After a whirlwind courtship even by Maureen's standards—a whole eight days—the two had planned to be married, much to the consternation of the rest of the family.

Then the fact that Maureen was still legally married to Bobby Santino, her third husband and a former professional hockey player, had been revealed. Lucy had never liked Bobby, who had ended up being more of a scam artist than her mother in Maureen's darkest moments. He'd returned before the wedding, attempting to extort money from Maureen to grant her the divorce she'd thought was finalized a year earlier when she'd sent her ex the papers to sign.

Her fiancé had ended the engagement, much to his family's delight, but that hadn't been enough. Peter's cousins had wanted to make a public spectacle of Maureen, making an example of her to warn off any other potential women who thought their father might be an easy target.

To save her mom, Lucy had taken the blame, claiming she'd orchestrated the whole scenario by introducing her mother to the fashion designer and encouraging the courtship as a way to take control of the Harmen fashion dynasty. That couldn't have been further from the truth.

The family had been happy to condemn Lucy as well, and Peter had been pressured to break things off with her by his uncle and cousins. She'd been fired from her job and blacklisted in the retail community. Lucy's burgeoning career had been ruined, but she wouldn't have changed her actions even to salvage her relationship with Peter.

Her role had always been protecting her mother. If she could eke out a bit of happiness or contentment during the times when Maureen was settled, so be it. Otherwise, she was constantly on call, ready to catch Maureen after her many inevitable falls.

Lucy had vowed that the fiasco with Peter would be the last time, but here she was, freezing her butt off in the high mountains of Colorado, the glass eyes of a stuffed caribou gazing down on her as she packed the rest of her mother's things.

"Talk to him," she said softly when she had the suitcase zipped up tight. "Garrett seems like a good man and he clearly adores you. Maybe—"

"Not until after the wedding."

"Has Bobby signed the divorce papers?"

Maureen bit her bottom lip. "He will. He promised."

"Mom, he's a snake."

Maureen stood and walked into the bathroom connected to the bedroom. Lucy heard the sound of drawers opening, then water running from a faucet. When her mother reappeared, a fresh coat of lipstick brightened her smile and she was pinching her cheeks to bring the color back into them. "Help me with Caden." Her voice had returned to its normal raspy, girlish tone, somewhere between Marilyn Monroe and Betty Boop.

"Why didn't you mention him to me before I got here?" Lucy asked, even though she knew the answer. "You made it sound like Garrett's only son had died."

"His older son, Tyson, was killed in a rock climbing accident two years ago. Apparently Caden had been estranged from them both before that."

"Why?"

"An argument over a 'no-good woman' is all Garrett would say about it. I think he was ready to sell the ranch before that, but now that Caden's running things, he feels like he has to stay out here."

"Maybe he wants to stay," Lucy offered.

Maureen shook her head. "He's tired and this was the house he shared with his first wife. She died twenty years ago, and nothing has changed in all that time." She glanced up at the mounted animal head and shuddered. "He needs a break."

"With you?"

"I *love* him."

It was difficult for Lucy to believe her mother could truly

love anyone except herself. But there was no sense in arguing about it now.

"Promise me you'll tell Garrett everything *before* the wedding, Mom. You can't get married until Bobby signs the divorce papers."

Her mom made a face. "Bobby's my past, sweetie. Garrett is my future."

"You can't have a future until he knows. If your love is real, it will survive the truth."

Maureen blinked. For a moment, her eyes lost their guarded quality, and Lucy could see so much hope and vulnerability in them. Her breath caught.

"Do you think so?" Maureen whispered.

"There's only one way to find out."

"You're my best thing, Lucy." Maureen stepped forward and wrapped her arms around Lucy's shoulders. "It's the two of us against the world."

Lucy sighed. "The two of us."

Chapter 3

"She's using you." Caden lifted his father's duffel bag into the back of Garrett's hulking silver truck.

"Have a little faith," Garrett said, clapping a big hand on Caden's shoulder.

"I don't want to see you hurt again." Caden shook his head. "After Tyson—"

"I'm better now." Garrett's blue eyes clouded but he kept his gaze firmly on Caden. "You don't have to worry about me anymore, son."

Son.

That word was like a knife slicing across Caden's gut. Garrett and Tyson had rescued him from the foster-care system and given him the family he'd always craved. But he'd been an angry and stupid kid, constantly pushing boundaries and testing his adoptive father's love because he never truly believed he deserved the happiness he found on the ranch.

He slammed the truck's tailgate shut. "I watched Tyson self-destruct because of a woman and have to live with my part in that. I pulled you back from the brink after his death, and I'm not going to lose you to someone like Maureen Renner." He sucked in a breath when emotion clogged his throat. Then he whispered, "I can't lose you, too."

"You're not losing me." Garrett reassured him in the same gentle tone he'd used when comforting Caden after the nightmares he'd woken from for several months after he'd come to live at Sharpe Ranch. Caden hadn't been willing to let his new father nearer than the foot of the bed at that point. So Garrett had sat on the edge of the sagging twin mattress and talked—telling stories about his childhood or his blissful marriage to Tyson's mother—until Caden had been able to fall back asleep.

Garrett's deep voice had been a lifeline in the dark all those years ago. Now Caden had to squint against the bright morning sun, even though a wide-brimmed Stetson shaded his eyes. It was a perfect Colorado day, with the expansive sky already deep blue. Although the temperature still hovered in the high teens, the sun seemed to warm everything, and the cattle were grazing contentedly on grass and hay in the far pasture.

Caden's heart remained frosty. He'd seen firsthand how much damage a scheming woman could do to a gentle man, and Garrett was one of the kindest souls he'd ever known.

"Think of it as gaining a family," Garrett continued as he hit the remote start on the key fob he held. The diesel engine of the truck roared to life, muffling Caden's disbelieving snort.

"I don't need a family," Caden muttered, and although his father didn't argue with him, they both knew it was a lie. As was true of many kids with tumultuous early lives, Caden craved security and stability like a junkie craved his next fix.

"Tell that to your barn full of rescues," was Garrett's only response. The man never tired of teasing Caden over his penchant for attracting stray animals.

"I'm going to look into her past," Caden said, ignoring the flash of anger in his father's eyes.

"I don't give a damn about her past. She makes me happy, Caden. You should try a bit of happiness on for size. You'd be surprised what a comfortable fit it becomes."

"I'm happy," Caden lied again.

Garrett stepped closer until the toes of their boots touched. At six feet, he'd seemed such an imposing figure the first time Caden had visited the ranch. Now Caden was at least three inches taller than him, but Garrett still remained a force to be reckoned with. "You *deserve* to be happy."

Caden tried to hold his father's gaze but turned away after a moment. How could Garrett say that, let alone believe it, when Caden was the reason Tyson was gone?

"Take care of Maureen's girl while we're away."

Caden swung back, grateful to have a reason to let his temper fly. "She doesn't belong on the ranch, and she sure as hell doesn't need access to your finances."

"I met with her this morning. She's got a good head on her shoulders. I've lost track of the business side of things recently. That's the part Tyson handled and—" The old man pursed his lips and ran a hand through his thick crop of silver hair. "Anyway, it's good to have fresh eyes reviewing things."

"More like a fresh attitude." Caden kicked a toe into the dirt. "I don't trust her, either."

"Give her a chance," his father coaxed. "It makes me feel better to know you won't be out here all alone."

"Chad's here," Caden said, referring to the young bull rider who worked winters on the ranch. "He's company."

"Chad's too busy in town chasing women." Garrett wagged a finger. "You could stand to go in with him a time or two. It's amazing what a difference it makes having a woman in your bed at—"

Caden held up both hands. "Stop before you make my ears bleed. I don't want to hear about my dad's romantic escapades."

Garrett chuckled. "You could learn something, young man. Be nice to Lucy. She's important to Maureen which makes her important to me."

Caden's jaw tightened at the thought of spending any more time than necessary with Lucy Renner, but he nodded. He'd learned from a young age there was no point in arguing with Garrett Sharpe when the man had his mind set on something. Caden was just going to have to prove what a mistake marrying Maureen would be. And he had two weeks to do it.

Later that afternoon, Lucy stood looking out the main house's big picture window, taking in the snow-covered peak of the mountain looming in the distance and the expanse of open fields that surrounded the property. She'd lived in Indiana until the age of eleven when Maureen had transplanted them to Florida for husband number two.

Lucy liked the change of seasons, but the thick white snow that blanketed everything for miles was a revelation. It was difficult to believe animals could survive outdoors in this climate, although the serenity of the scenery spoke to something deep in her soul. Colorado felt fresh, clean and full of new promises, which she assumed was part of the allure for her mother.

Maureen loved nothing more than to reinvent herself with each new adventure that came along. Lucy found herself reluctantly smiling at the thought of her mom herding cattle or churning butter or whatever it was ranch wives did these days.

It had been hours since the happy couple had driven off toward the regional airport, where they'd board a private plane to take them into Denver to catch a commercial flight to New York City.

"First-class," her mother had whispered into Lucy's ear as

they stood in the driveway earlier, saying their goodbyes. "I haven't flown first-class since Jerry." Maureen's marriage to husband number two, Jerry Murphy, had lasted only a few months, but Maureen had made the most of her time with the wealthy restaurateur from Naples, Florida.

Lucy had seen Caden's shoulders stiffen and guessed that he'd overheard Maureen. Great. One more reason for Caden to mistrust them. How could Lucy explain her mother's childlike immaturity when half the time Lucy didn't understand it herself?

Garrett seemed to take it all in stride, and Lucy got the impression he tried to be purposely over-the-top to illicit a reaction from Maureen. There was something inherently magnanimous about the older rancher, as if he enjoyed having someone with whom to share the trappings of his wealth.

As soon as the truck had disappeared down the long, winding drive that led to the highway, Caden turned and stalked away.

Lucy returned to the main house and wandered from room to room, imagining life here before the force of nature that was her mother descended. How did a father and son, a widower and a bachelor surrounded by the memories of a beloved wife and brother, spend their evenings?

From Garrett's effusive compliments about her mother's cooking, he wasn't accustomed to home-cooked meals. Lucy could relate to that. The only time her mother had ever cooked when Lucy was growing up was when Maureen was trying to impress a new boyfriend.

She moved toward the bookshelves in the family room, which were filled with volumes on outdoor life and classics she'd expect a man like Garrett to read—Hemingway and Twain—with the occasional modern thriller thrown in for good measure. A collection of framed photos took up an entire shelf, and she could piece together the Sharpe family history from the faces smiling out at her.

There was one of a beautiful young woman holding a toddler, who grinned widely and wore cowboy boots a size too big for him. The woman's hair was pulled back into a low ponytail and she wore no makeup, but she didn't need any. She stood in front of a split-rail fence with a dozen cattle grazing behind her.

The next photo showed the same boy, who Lucy assumed was Tyson Sharpe, as a gangly adolescent with his arm slung around Caden's shoulder. Lucy could easily recognize his mutinous scowl, although in the photo he was all gangly arms and skinny shoulders. He was glaring at the camera, a fact that his brother seemed to enjoy immensely.

Another photo showed both Tyson and Caden wearing graduation gowns and caps, Garrett with an arm wrapped around each of them. Caden had started to grow into his body by that point, and Tyson had also become a wildly handsome young man with thick blond hair and a careless grin so different from that of his brother's tight smile.

Lucy's breath caught at the final photo. It showed Tyson and Caden at the base of a sheer cliff, both wearing climbing gear. Caden was a few inches taller than his brother, but what punched at Lucy's chest was the pure joy displayed in the photo.

Caden's head was thrown back in laughter, and Tyson was grinning and looking at Caden with a good bit of love and adoration. The bond between the brothers had clearly been solidified at that point. At least in the second the photo was snapped, Caden had dropped his defenses to revel in whatever moment they were having.

She couldn't help but be curious as to the circumstances of Tyson's death and why Caden seemed to take the blame for it.

She wished she'd asked her mother for more details, although there was a good chance Maureen wouldn't be aware of the situation since it didn't affect her directly.

The sound of the front door opening and male voices coming closer interrupted her musings. She whirled away from the bookcase and took two hurried steps toward the middle of the room, feeling somehow like she'd been spying on Caden by looking at the photos.

He appeared in the hall a moment later, and color rushed to Lucy's cheeks as his stark gaze landed on her. She cursed her pathetic and weak body, which reacted to the way he was studying her with an involuntary shiver.

How was she supposed to keep her distance from this man when she could almost feel the current of attraction pulsing between them?

"Are you casing the place now that my dad's away?" he asked drily, offering an acute reminder of why it would be easy to stay away from him.

Because he was a jerk.

"You must be Maureen's daughter," the other man said and strode forward to take Lucy's hand. She guessed he was younger than Caden by at least five years. His light blond hair fell over hazel eyes that were wide and welcoming. "Your mom is awesome. She's pretty hot, too. A real MILF—"

"Chad." Caden's voice was like a slap, cutting off Chad midsentence. Lucy had to admit she was grateful. She should have been used to how men both young and old reacted to her mother. Yet it still made her as uncomfortable now as it had when she was a kid. There were many years she'd lied to her mother about school activities just to avoid Maureen showing up in her plunging necklines and thigh-grazing hems to flirt with unsuspecting teachers or the fathers of Lucy's few friends.

The younger man chuckled. "Sorry," he said, although

he didn't look the least bit apologetic. "But, sweetheart, you clearly inherited your looks from your mama."

"I'm not your sweetheart," Lucy said softly, earning another chuckle from the man.

"Not yet, anyway," he said with a wink.

Lucy rolled her eyes but felt the corners of her mouth curve up. There was something so inherently charismatic about Chad, not to mention how handsome he was. In his tight jeans, cowboy boots and fitted flannel shirt, he reminded Lucy of a young Brad Pitt circa *Thelma and Louise*.

Not that she had any intention of driving her car over the edge of a cliff or getting involved with an obvious player like Chad. But it was fun to be on the receiving end of that thousand-watt smile, especially when Caden was looming at the far end of the room, glowering at the two of them.

"I'm Chad Penderson and I work here at Sharpe Ranch."

"I'm Lucy Renner."

"Pleased to make your acquaintance, Miss Lucy." He took a step back and gave her a courtly bow. "If you need anything while you're here, just let me know." He straightened again and wiggled his brows. "I do mean anything."

Lucy heard something that sounded like a growl from Caden, but Chad's grin only widened. "How long are you staying at the ranch?"

She shrugged. "The plan is for me to stay through the wedding. Garrett has asked me to go over the books and—"

"Not necessary," Caden interrupted, stepping forward.

She bristled at his dismissive tone. Lucy had spent too much time being dismissed to ever let it pass without a fight. "That's not what your father seems to think."

"We have a financial manager who's taken over the accounting since..." He paused, then said, "For the past couple of years. He's immensely qualified."

He didn't add the words *unlike you*, but Lucy felt them linger in the air just the same.

"You can hang out with me," Chad offered. "It's quiet around here in the winter but there's plenty of work to go around. You know how to ride a horse?"

"Not really," Lucy admitted.

"Then I can teach you."

"She's not learning to ride with you," Caden said, his voice pitched low.

"Listen to Mr. Party Pooper back there." Chad hitched a thumb in Caden's direction. "Speaking of parties, I'm meeting some friends in town tonight for a little pre-Christmas bash. Why don't you join us?"

Lucy shook her head. "I don't think—"

"Come on," Chad coaxed. "You'll have more fun with me than stuck out here with Caden." He threw a glance over his shoulder. "No offense, boss, but you're about as much fun as mucking a hog pen."

"She's not going with you. Grab a cup of coffee and let's finish fixing the heater before the water freezes."

"As in, we won't have running water?" Lucy asked, trying not to sound panicked. She was by no means spoiled but definitely enjoyed a hot shower on a cold morning.

Chad winked. "We have to keep the water troughs heated for the cattle."

"Can't they eat snow?"

"No, darlin'. One of the biggest threats to livestock in the winter is the cold. The snow lowers their body temperature, which could be deadly. Our job is to keep them warm and safe."

"Oh."

Caden folded his arms over his big chest. "Your job is not

standing in the house jawing all afternoon, Chad. You wanted a cup of coffee. Get it and let's go."

"If you change your mind about tonight, I'll be leaving here around seven." Chad pointed out the window toward a smaller structure about ten feet behind the main barn. "I'm out in the bunkhouse." Another wink. "For your information."

"She's not going," Caden repeated, glaring at Lucy over Chad's shoulder.

If there was one thing Lucy hated, it was being told what to do. By anyone. It had led to some monumentally stupid decisions on her part, but it was a part of herself she couldn't seem to rein in.

"I'd love to go to your Christmas party," she told Chad, offering a slight smile.

"Hot damn," the young cowboy said, slapping his knee. "I've got me a date."

He shot Caden a gloating smile. "You hear that, old man? Miss Lucy here is going to be my date for the evening."

Caden said nothing, but Lucy could almost see the smoke curling from his ears.

"I'll see you later, darlin'," Chad crooned before leaving the room.

Caden didn't move, just continued staring at Lucy.

"Of course it's not a date," she said after a moment, pulling at the hem of the pale pink sweater she wore. Having lived in Florida for so many years, she had very little in the way of warm clothes and wondered if there was any discount shopping to be found in Crimson. "He's far too young for me."

"That won't matter to Chad." Caden spoke through clenched teeth. "Don't let the aw-shucks act fool you. That boy is a player."

Lucy wasn't sure whether to be offended that he hadn't denied she was too old for Chad or flattered that Caden was, in his own awkward way, trying to protect her from being hurt. "I'm not in the market for getting played. You don't need to worry about me."

He looked as though he wanted to argue, but said, "I wasn't kidding about the ranch finances. One of Tyson's friends from high school who's a CPA has taken over since…"

"Since your brother died?" she asked gently.

"Yeah."

"My mom told me it was a rock climbing accident. I'm sorry."

Once again, Caden's silence stretched so long she thought he might not respond. He looked past her, out the window into the darkening night. His green eyes filled with so much sorrow that Lucy felt an answering pull of sadness in her chest.

"I'm the one who's sorry," he said finally. "His accident was my fault."

Lucy gasped, and Caden's gaze shot to hers. All the vulnerability that had been there moments before was gone, his expression carefully blank.

"You don't belong here," he said, his voice so low she had to strain to make out the words. "I'll hurt you whether I want to or not. It's what I do."

Then he turned and walked away.

Chapter 4

Caden pulled open the door of Elevation Brewery later that night, the heat and noise of a festive bar crowd spilling out into the cold. He took a deep breath, then walked in, scanning the faces of the people without making eye contact with any of them.

"Caden!"

He stifled an amused sigh and turned to the dark-haired, dark-eyed woman waving to him like mad from a seat at the bar.

"Caden, over here!" she shouted as if he hadn't heard her the first time.

Out of the corner of his eye, he saw Lucy Renner glance over her shoulder. But he ignored both Lucy and Chad, who were huddled together near the pool tables at the far corner of the bar, and moved toward the woman still feverishly waving at him.

"He sees you," David McCay, the bar's owner, told Erin MacDonald as Caden approached. The tall brewer with the overly long blond hair and a good two weeks of beard leaned forward to plant a kiss on the mouth of his fiancée.

"I didn't think he'd come," Erin said against David's lips before swiveling her chair to face Caden. "I'm so glad you finally took me up on my offer."

Caden blinked, looking around like one of the other bar patrons might be able to shed some light on what the sweet-tempered schoolteacher was talking about. Because he sure as hell had no idea.

David gave a soft chuckle. "He's not here for you, darlin'."

"I texted you about meeting here to talk about the animal-adoption open house next weekend." Erin pointed a finger at him. "You've ignored my invitations to hang out with David and me for weeks. I figured bringing the animals into it might motivate you to agree. That's why you came tonight, right?"

"Um, sure." Caden's gaze strayed to Lucy, who was leaning over the pool table to set up a shot. Several of the men standing near her were watching her with interest, but Chad had his arm draped around the shoulder of a buxom blonde.

He started when Erin placed a hand on his arm. "I'm not going to be offended that you ignored me once again because this is even better. You're here for a woman."

"I'm not," he answered, but Erin was craning her neck to get a better look at Lucy.

"She's pretty. Not from around here, I'd guess. Tell me all about her."

Caden shot a help-me glance toward David, who gave him a you're-on-your-own shrug.

"There's nothing to tell," Caden said with a sigh.

"Come on." Erin grinned up at him. "You never come into town, especially on a Friday night. She must be special."

"She's here with Chad. It's not a big deal."

"I don't think she's leaving with Chad," David said, inclining his head toward the back of the bar.

Caden turned to see Chad and the blonde in the midst of a

hot and heavy makeout session. Lucy was on the other side of the pool table, talking to a group of men, some of whom Caden recognized as locals. A moment later Chad and his new woman came up for air, then quickly headed for the bar's entrance. His ranch hand disappeared into the night without sparing another glance at Lucy.

"Damn," he muttered. "I tried to warn her."

"Were they on a date?" Erin asked, sympathy lacing her voice.

"I don't think so. Maybe. Hell, who knows with Chad? But he was definitely her ride home."

"So now you'll take care of her," Erin said matter-of-factly. "And you can tell us all about how you two met."

"It's not important."

Erin let out a sigh. "Fine. If you won't share, maybe she will." She stood on the stool's footrest and waved Lucy over when she glanced up, presumably looking for Chad.

Caden saw confusion darken her eyes, and then something else crept in when her gaze landed on him. But she moved toward them, weaving her way through the brewery's high-spirited patrons.

Several male heads turned as she passed, but she didn't slow her progress.

"She's not my responsibility," he said quietly.

"*She's* the reason you're here," Erin responded. "Gosh, she's even prettier than I first thought."

"Not nearly as pretty as you," David whispered.

"You're sweet," Erin told her fiancé, but Caden barely registered their conversation.

He couldn't take his eyes off Lucy.

Her dark hair fell over her shoulders, and she wore a burgundy-colored sweater with the fabric cut out at both shoulders, giving him the most tantalizing glimpse of bare skin.

It was totally inappropriate clothing for a December night in Colorado, and Caden thanked his lucky stars that Lucy came from a warmer climate.

"So you're not a party pooper after all," she said as she came to stand directly in front of him.

He cocked a brow. "I told you a date with Chad was a bad idea."

"I told you it wasn't a date."

"Obviously not since he just left with another woman."

"Oh." Her glossy lips formed the syllable and Caden's body tightened in response.

"He ditched you, Lucy." Caden knew he was being purposely cruel, but he couldn't seem to help himself. It bothered him on some primal level that she'd gone out with Chad, and he certainly planned to have a serious conversation with his ranch hand about how to treat a woman.

"Was it the cute little blond-haired woman?" Lucy asked.

"Yeah."

"Good for him," she said, a slow smile lighting up her face. "Her name is Jessica and he has such a crush on her. All I heard about most of the night was how she's been dating some guy who doesn't treat her right. She finally broke up with him last week. Tonight was Chad's big chance but he was so nervous. I gave him some tips and—"

"You and Chad were over there talking about how he could put the moves on another woman? The last thing that boy needs is more moves."

"He *really* likes her," she said. "I get that he seems smooth, but it's different when the woman means something, you know?"

Caden wasn't sure how to answer that. He thought he'd been in love once, but that experience had not only torn apart his heart, it had done some major collateral damage to his relationship with his brother.

"I know exactly what you mean," Erin said from behind him. She nudged his shoulder and he stepped to the side so that Erin could pull Lucy closer. "Why do men act like idiots when they have real feelings for a woman?"

"I wasn't an idiot," David protested gently.

Erin rolled her brown eyes toward the ceiling. "You were a total idiot." She reached for Lucy's hand and pumped it enthusiastically. "Hi, I'm Erin MacDonald and this is my fiancé, David McCay." She leaned in closer and added, "He's a reformed idiot."

"Can I get you a beer?" David asked Lucy with a chuckle.

"He also owns Elevation Brewery. We're friends of Caden's."

Lucy gave Caden a funny look out of the corner of her eye, as if she found it difficult to believe he actually had friends. "Nothing more for me," she told David. "I had a couple of pints of the wheat beer earlier—which was amazing, by the way. But I'm definitely feeling the altitude."

"The alcohol hits you hard up here," David confirmed.

"Caden was just about to tell us how the two of you met," Erin said.

Lucy arched a brow in Caden's direction. "Really?"

"It would probably be better coming from you." Erin placed a hand on Lucy's arm like they were old friends. "Our Caden is kind of the strong, silent type, if you know what I mean."

"My mother is marrying his father," Lucy said, thankfully not commenting on what she thought about his "type."

"Maybe," he muttered, earning a frown from both women.

David handed him a tall glass of dark beer. "You look like you could use this."

"I've seen her around town," Erin told Lucy. "She and Garrett seem so happy together. She's really pretty. You look like her."

Lucy's gaze strayed to Caden once again, her eyes narrowing slightly as if she was thinking about the rude comment he'd made when they first met.

Then she smiled at Erin. "Thank you. My mom and Garrett left this morning for a prewedding trip to New York City."

"How romantic," Erin breathed.

Caden snorted, causing beer to slosh over the side of the pint glass. David handed him a napkin.

"Will they be back for the adoption open house?" Erin asked, turning to Caden.

"Doubtful. I'm guessing Maureen will want to stay in the city and spend as much of Garrett's money as she can manage."

Erin gasped. "That's a rude thing to say, Caden. And unlike you. You know better than most people what it's like to be judged unfairly. I'm disappointed you'd stoop to that level, especially talking about Lucy's mom when she's standing right in front of you."

"Sorry," Caden mumbled, feeling suddenly like he was a kid being reprimanded by his favorite teacher. He could only imagine how bad the kindergarteners in Erin's class felt when they messed up. Erin might look like she was as harmless as a kitten, but she definitely had sharp claws.

David covered his mouth with one hand to hide a smile while Lucy raised a brow and moved slightly closer to Erin, as if her new friend would shield her from Caden's wrath. He gave himself a mental head shake as guilt pinged through him. Still, he hadn't said anything about Lucy's mother that wasn't the truth, and they both knew it.

He placed the glass of beer on the bar. "We should head back to the ranch."

Lucy crossed her arms over her chest. "What's the adoption open house?" she asked Erin, ignoring Caden.

"Have you seen Caden's pet-rescue operation?" Erin rolled her eyes. "When he's not being Mr. Rudepants, Caden takes in unwanted animals from around the county."

"The ones in the barn?"

Erin nodded. "They're animals no one else wanted. He rehabilitates them, does training and then matches them with forever families."

He saw Lucy's mouth drop open. "Seriously?"

"Did you think I was selling them to some kind of lab for experiments?" he asked, not caring that the words came out a growl.

"No," Lucy answered after a moment. "I thought you were a pet hoarder."

"Are you kidding me?"

She flashed a grin that made his heart stutter. "Yes."

She turned back to Erin, who was watching him with a gleam in her eye Caden didn't trust in the least.

He picked up the beer again and took a long drink.

"Erin's onto you," David said quietly as Erin explained more about the open house to Lucy. "You need to get a better poker face, bud."

Caden stepped closer to the bar. "I don't know what you're talking about."

"You like this one."

"She's a pain in my—"

"Right." David laughed. He made a show of wiping the already-gleaming wood counter when Erin shot him a questioning glance. "You should probably stop staring at her like she's on the menu and you're starving."

"I'm not staring."

"Erin has been wanting to fix you up for months. She fancies herself a matchmaker."

Caden groaned. "I'm trying to convince my father to call off the wedding. That's not exactly going to endear me to Lucy."

"Doesn't change the fact that you like her," David said with a shrug.

Before Caden could respond, Erin turned and grabbed his arms.

"Great news," she shouted over the din of the brewpub. "Lucy's agreed to help with the adoption event."

Caden shrugged off her hold and shook his head. "I didn't ask for her help."

Erin frowned. "Don't be rude again."

"I'm not—"

"You need her."

"I don't," he said through clenched teeth.

Erin pointed a finger at him. "How much of the marketing plan I created have you implemented at this point?"

"I've been busy on the ranch."

"Exactly. Lucy has retail experience in sales and marketing. She's going to take over for you to make sure we have enough publicity for the event."

Caden looked over Erin's shoulder to Lucy. "If you don't want my help," she muttered, "it's not a big deal."

"It *is* a big deal," Erin insisted. "Ever since word got out that Caden would take on stray animals, people have been bringing them to him left and right. It's too much. An adoption event right before Christmas is the perfect way to find good families for your sweet babies."

Caden felt color rise up his throat when Lucy's mouth kicked up at one corner. "I wouldn't call them my sweet babies."

Erin threw up her hands. "You have a certified therapy

bunny, Caden. Play the hardened cowboy all you want, but we know you're a big softy at heart."

"We do," Lucy agreed, her eyes dancing with amusement.

"I don't even know why I agreed to open the barn. I can find homes for the animals on my own."

"The adoption event is happening, and Lucy's going to help," Erin said in the same tone of voice he imagined she used to quiet a room of rowdy five-year-olds.

Caden looked at David. "You've got your hands full."

"Wouldn't have it any other way," David answered.

"I'm so glad we met tonight," Erin said to Lucy as she pulled her in for a tight hug. "I have a feeling we're going to be great friends."

Caden's focus sharpened as he watched Lucy go stiff. All the humor disappeared from her gaze, and instead she looked like someone had just punched her in the gut.

"It was…um…nice to meet you," she said quickly. "But I'm kind of jet-lagged, so I should probably head back to the ranch. Have a good night."

She turned and fled, weaving through the crowd so quickly that Caden lost sight of her within a few seconds.

"Was it something I said?" Erin asked quietly.

"Nah, honey." David reached across the bar to smooth his fiancée's hair away from her face. "You were brilliant. I'm just not sure Caden's Lucy is used to having someone as sweet as you offer to be her friend."

Caden felt his jaw clench. "She's not mine."

"Not if you don't catch up to her," David agreed.

Caden knew the smart thing to do would be bellying up to the bar and ordering another beer. Lucy Renner seemed plenty capable of taking care of herself. He sure didn't need her infringing on his life, his friends or his animals. He needed her gone.

He took a breath and turned to find Erin and David staring at him with equally knowing looks on their faces.

"Damn," he muttered and took off toward Elevation's front entrance.

It had started snowing while Lucy was in the bar. Big, fluffy flakes streamed down from the sky, glowing in the light of a nearby streetlamp and lending a sense of peace to Crimson's Main Street. Lucy would have stopped and tipped up her face to catch a snowflake on her tongue if she wasn't in such a hurry to get away.

She felt like a fool rushing out of Elevation and away from a woman who'd been nothing but kind to her. When was the last time Lucy'd had a girlfriend?

She almost laughed out loud at the thought. Her mother had always taught her that other girls, and later women, were to be viewed as competition and not to be trusted.

As much as Lucy knew her mother's ideas on female friendships were wrong, some part of the message had sunk in and she'd never seemed to be able to make lasting friendships. Maybe because whenever another woman made a friendly overture, she freaked out like she did with Erin.

At least Caden was probably happy she was gone.

Of course, she had no idea where she was headed. She needed to get her bearings and find a taxi or Uber to get her back to the ranch. But it was hard to slow down when it felt like running away was what she did best.

Heavy footsteps sounded on the sidewalk behind her, and she glanced over her shoulder to see Caden approaching. She hated to admit how happy she'd been to see him at the bar.

Chad and his friends were fun, but they were immature boys compared to Caden. Even though he'd never been anything but gruff and rude with her, she felt an odd sense of comfort when he was around.

As usual, he was scowling when he caught up to her. "Where's your jacket?" he demanded.

She looked down at the thin sweater she'd chosen for the night, along with skinny jeans and ankle-high boots that allowed a tiny strip of skin to show below the hem of her jeans. It was amazing how cold that little bit of exposed skin had gotten already.

Caden, in contrast, wore dark jeans, well-worn cowboy boots and a heavy canvas jacket that looked deliciously warm. She shivered as his gaze raked over her, and she wasn't quite sure whether it was in response to the cold or the intensity of his green eyes.

"I didn't wear one."

"Are you trying to catch your death of cold?"

Lucy clapped a hand over her mouth when a giggle bubbled up unexpectedly. "You sound like a grandma."

"At least little old ladies have the common sense to wear a coat in Colorado in the middle of December."

She shrugged. "We were going to a bar in Chad's heated truck. I didn't think I'd need a coat." At the mention of heat, her body seemed to register the below-freezing temperature of the winter night. A shiver coursed through her and her teeth started to chatter.

"Let's go," Caden ordered, unbuttoning his heavy coat and wrapping it around her shoulders. She almost sighed as the residual warmth from his body enveloped her.

"You don't have to do that," she said even as she pulled the jacket tight around her.

"My dad will kill me if I let you freeze to death." He took her elbow none too gently and began to steer her toward a dark gray truck parked next to the curb.

"I'm fine on my own. I can call a cab."

He laughed. "In Crimson?"

"Or I'll Uber a ride."

"Don't read too much into this. We're going to the same place. I can drive you back to the ranch. I'm not asking you to wear my high school ring."

Caden held open the truck's passenger-side door as she climbed in. He might not like her, but this cowboy was a gentleman. Lucy couldn't remember ever being with a man who had such decent manners.

"Do boys still give their girlfriends a class ring to wear?" She pulled the seat belt around her and giggled again. "Or letter jackets? Is this canvas coat like the ranch version of a high school letterman's jacket?"

Caden leaned closer and stared into her eyes. "Are you drunk?"

She pushed him away. "No. I had a couple of beers when we first got to Elevation."

"Talking nonsense is a symptom of hypothermia." He slammed the door shut before she could respond. A moment later he climbed into the driver's side and turned on the car.

"I'm not hypothermic," she said through her teeth as he cranked up the heat and adjusted the vents to blow on her. "It was a joke."

His hand stilled for a moment, and he glanced over at her as if he was unfamiliar with the concept.

"Chad shouldn't have left you," he said, pulling out into the middle of the deserted street.

"I haven't seen snow like this for years," Lucy told him, ignoring the comment about the young ranch hand. Truly, she was happy Chad had made the connection with the girl he wanted. There was something about the snow that made the night feel particularly intimate, and someone should be taking advantage of it.

"How long have you lived in Florida?"

"Mom and I moved from Indiana when I was eleven."

"Why?"

She hesitated, then admitted, "She'd met someone at the restaurant where she worked. Jerry had come to Indianapolis for business."

"Husband number two or three?" Caden asked quietly.

"Two." Lucy sighed. "He was a good man. He treated me like a real daughter."

"But it didn't last?"

He asked the question casually, but she couldn't help but wonder if he was digging for information to use against her mother. "They wanted different things from life."

Caden arched a brow but didn't say anything else. She pressed her fingertips to the side window, then to her cheek, hoping the cold would calm the blush she could feel rising to her face.

As much as she didn't want to admit it, on the surface Caden was right in so many of his assessments of her mother. But what he didn't see was that Maureen never went into a relationship with malicious intent. At least, not as far as Lucy had ever been able to tell. Her mother always seemed to believe she was head over heels in love with whatever man she'd set her cap for in the moment. Unfortunately, that didn't make Maureen's romantic history appear any less dubious.

"Are you a Crimson native?" she asked, needing to fill the silence between them and distract Caden from whatever thoughts he was having about Maureen. Lucy could tell by the set of his jaw that they weren't positive.

He gave a brief shake of his head. "I moved here when I was ten."

"To live with Garrett?"

"I was with a foster family after my mom died."

"I'm sorry."

One big shoulder lifted. "It's not a big deal. She wasn't much of a mother, anyway."

Barely slowing, he turned off the highway and down the long gravel drive that led to Sharpe Ranch. Lucy grabbed hold of the door handle when the truck's tires slid on the snow-covered road. Clearly Caden was more affected by his mom's death than he professed to be.

Lucy wanted to push him for more, intensely curious as to the circumstances that had made him Garrett Sharpe's son. As a girl, she'd entertained embarrassing fantasies about being adopted by a wholesome, all-American, network-sitcom-type family. A family where the mom baked batches of homemade cookies instead of spending hours dolling herself up for whatever man she was trying to impress that week.

Guilt lingered over the daydreams that had made her feel disloyal to her mom. In her own needy and immature way, Maureen loved Lucy to distraction. But Lucy had always wondered what it would have been like to get a do-over on her tiny dysfunctional family.

Caden had been given that gift, but she guessed it had come at a steep price. Besides, it was dangerous to know him better. Her feelings for him were already a jumble when she needed to stay clear as to her purpose at the ranch. The task her mother had given her.

She couldn't fall for him and still do her job as Maureen's faithful lackey. And even though she hated that role, it felt as much a part of her as her own skin.

He pulled to a stop in front of the main house. The porch light glowed in the dark and snow swirled around her as she climbed out of the truck. The air felt even colder now that she'd warmed up a bit, but she couldn't stop herself from lifting her face and catching a few icy flakes in her open mouth.

She opened her eyes to find Caden standing directly in front of her. "Snow tastes like a fluffy winter cloud," she said, feeling like she owed him an explanation for her behavior.

A layer of white dusted the brim of his Stetson and his wide shoulders. He didn't seem to notice the frigid temperature at all, even though he wore only a thin navy-striped Western shirt tucked into his dark jeans.

Lucy'd met a lot of men in her life, but this surly rancher was her first bona fide cowboy. She'd never fancied herself a fan of the John Wayne/Clint Eastwood cliché, but the butterflies dancing across her stomach as Caden's eyes darkened in the soft light told a different story.

Apparently she had a thing for cowboys.

That generalization was easier to swallow than admitting the low hum of lust buzzing through her was a response only to Caden.

"You're an odd one," he said quietly, but his mouth curved into a slow smile, making the words feel like a strange sort of compliment.

"One of a kind," she agreed, trying to make her tone sunny. "That's me."

He gave a slight shake of his head. "I don't want you here."

The desire whirling through her deflated like a day-old helium balloon. "Well, that's just too bad for you, then." She made to move past him, but he grabbed her arms.

"But I do want you," he whispered. Before she could react to that revelation, he lowered his head and claimed her mouth.

Despite the gruffness of his tone, the kiss was shockingly gentle. A hopeful exploration. A question that she was happy to answer with a resounding yes.

His mouth was soft against hers and need shot through her,

hot and sharp like a match set to her skin. The tiny part of her that wasn't lost in the moment did a little jig at knowing she wasn't the only one unable to douse the spark that flickered between them.

She swayed closer, feeling his grip tighten on her arms. It was as if he was trying to resist pulling her tight against him, and the truth of that was like a face-first fall into a snowbank.

Of course he was resisting. He'd just said he didn't want her here. Lucy knew all too well that lust wasn't a dependable emotion. It could be used to manipulate someone far too easily. Carelessly.

After a few too many painful lessons dealt by life, she'd promised herself never again to be careless with her body or her heart.

She broke away, stumbled back a few steps and raised her hand to her mouth. The still-falling snowflakes seemed to sizzle against her heated skin. "And you were worried about Chad taking advantage of me?" she accused. "Pot, meet Kettle."

Caden took off his hat and slapped it against one thigh, ran a hand through his hair. "I'm not…"

"No," she interrupted. "I'm not going to let you hurt me or whatever else you think is within your power. And I'm sure as hell not going to let you chase me away."

He laughed harshly. "Is that what it felt like I was doing?"

"Good night, Caden," she said instead of answering. "Thanks for the ride."

Then she turned and rushed toward the house.

Chapter 5

Caden climbed the steps to the main house the following afternoon, massaging his knuckles against his aching back.

He'd slept on the lumpy sofa in the barn's office the previous night, a kitten nestled against his hip while another purred contentedly on his chest. It had been cold and uncomfortable, with only a horse blanket as a cover, but he'd figured it was better than following Lucy into the house.

Not when his need for her had burned away what he believed about her motives for being in Colorado to a pile of useless ashes around his feet. There was something about the woman he couldn't seem to resist. It went beyond her physical beauty, although that was lethal in and of itself.

He couldn't deny the immediate connection he'd felt to her. As much as he wanted to sever it, the more time he spent with her, the stronger it became. Having her smile up at him as she caught snowflakes in her mouth, perfectly enjoying the quiet moment, had made his heart ache with longing to feel that kind of simple joy. So he'd kissed her. He'd tried to claim some of that pleasure through fusing his mouth to hers.

Damn if it hadn't worked, too. As soon as his lips grazed hers, a feeling of euphoria had rocketed through him like he'd just taken a hit off some kind of crazy, powerful drug. It wouldn't take much for him to become addicted to the feel of Lucy in his arms, and he realized he owed her a debt of thanks for pulling away before he forgot himself and let things go too far.

The one other time Caden had let his heart lead him with a woman, he'd ended up destroying his relationship with his brother. And Tyson had ended up dead as a result.

For that and so many other reasons, Caden needed to stay as far away from Lucy as possible.

He found an old jacket in the barn to wear for morning chores and grabbed a granola bar from the tiny kitchen in the bunkhouse. Chad pulled up just as Caden was heading toward the barn to feed and water the animals. The young ranch hand was still wearing the same clothes from the night before and sporting a quarter-sized hickey on the side of his neck. He looked like the cat that swallowed the proverbial sexual canary.

Caden wanted to punch him.

"I'm in love," Chad proclaimed at the top of his lungs, doing a few fancy dance moves as he caught up with Caden.

Caden's gaze strayed to the second floor of his father's house—to the room where he guessed Lucy was still fast asleep in the wee morning hours.

"Keep your voice down."

Chad lightly punched him in the arm. "You and Luce have a late night?"

"No, but you shouldn't have left her stranded at Elevation."

"I didn't strand her," Chad argued. "I saw you come in and knew you'd take care of her."

"She's not my responsibility."

Chad laughed. "You make everyone your responsibility, boss. Want to hear about my night with Jessica?"

"Hell, no."

Chad told him anyway, peppering in enough sappy details to make the granola bar he'd eaten threaten to make a repeat appearance. He'd finally managed to shut the kid up by sending him out to the far pasture to make sure the cattle had enough food and water.

Caden kept himself busy the rest of the morning and did his best to pretend he wasn't regularly checking for activity in the house.

Despite her claim that he wasn't going to chase her away, he'd half expected Lucy to pack up her compact rental car and take off for town. And as much as that would have simplified his life, he feared it would have also been a big disappointment.

He liked the way she stood up to him. He was accustomed to intimidating people with his size and silence and was a master at using both as an excuse to maintain his solitary lifestyle.

But after only a day and a half, Lucy's presence on the ranch suited him in some strange way. Garrett had always warned him that being alone and being lonely were two distinct beasts. For the first time, Caden understood the message his dad was trying to convey.

Which was why he'd decided to take his lunch break in the main house. He could scrounge together a meal from the bunkhouse kitchen, but he could no longer resist the urge to check in on Lucy. Part of him hoped he'd find her lounging on the sofa reading a gossip magazine or doing her nails or whatever gold-digger daughters did when they were trying to pass the time.

Instead, as he walked into the house, the distinct smell of lemons and oil soap hit him. The cherry table that sat in the entry, the one that Tyson had told him came from his grandmother's house in Kansas, gleamed in a way Caden had never seen before.

When Tyson and Caden were young, Garrett had hired a local woman to be at the house when they came home from school and he was out working. She made simple meals and did some light cleaning but had quickly tired of the two Sharpe boys' antics and quit.

Garrett had immediately put both Tyson and Caden to work, giving them enough chores around the ranch to keep them exhausted and out of mischief. Caden still found plenty of trouble, despite Tyson's efforts to keep him on a straight path. Garrett hired a housecleaning service to come through once a month, so even with three men living on the ranch, it was never too disgusting. Now Caden realized how much they'd been missing all those years without a woman's touch.

He was even more shocked as he stepped into the living room to see Lucy balancing precariously on a kitchen chair that she'd pulled up to the edge of the brick fireplace surround. She was reaching out to place a string of holly across the picture hanging above the mantel.

The chair had two legs on the ground and two on the higher brick and teetered back and forth as she stretched forward. A sudden vision of Lucy crashing her head on the brick had his heart pounding.

"What the hell are you doing?" he bellowed as he rushed toward her.

Apparently yelling was the exact way to make his vision a reality. She gasped, then turned to him. As the chair rocked, she tumbled backward with a yelp.

Caden caught her before she landed, his heart racing as he hugged her tight to his chest. Immediately she squirmed in his arms and he set her away from him.

"Are you trying to kill me?" she demanded as soon as her feet hit the floor.

"Why would I need to when you were doing a fine job of it yourself?"

She shook the strand of holly in his direction. "I had everything under control until you scared the pants off me."

"Hardly," he muttered, taking in the fitted jeans that hugged her curves. She wore a flowing, flower-patterned blouse over them and her feet were bare. He took in the bright pink polish on her toes and his gut reaction felt akin to a matador waving a red flag in front of an angry bull.

He pointed to her feet. "You're not wearing shoes."

"Thanks for the news flash, Captain Obvious."

"It's the middle of December."

"I'm in the house." She threw up her hands. "I don't like wearing shoes in the house."

"You should put on socks." He raked a hand through his hair. "Or slippers. Something."

"Are my feet so offensive to you?"

He almost laughed at the absurdity of the question. On the contrary, her bare feet were some sort of peculiar, diabolical temptation. They made him want to see the rest of her body. To lay her across his bed and peel off her clothes until every inch of her was exposed for his eyes only.

Coupled with the way his body had roared to life just by holding her for a few seconds—her soft curves pressed to him—Caden was reminded why he'd slept in the barn last night.

"The chair was tipping," he muttered instead of answering her question. "You were going to fall."

She stared at him for a few moments, then let out a breath. "Hold it for me while I hang the holly."

Without waiting for a response, she climbed onto the chair

once more, and Caden gripped the top rail to keep it steady. Unfortunately, that put him at eye level with her perfectly rounded back end, and he forced his gaze away from her.

He didn't understand why Lucy made him feel like a randy teenager instead of a full-grown man in control of his faculties. There was no control around her.

So instead he focused his attention on the rest of the room. The gaudy, over-the-top Christmas trimmings Maureen had strewed across every surface had been replaced with Julia Sharpe's understated—and in many cases homemade—holiday decorations.

The bubble of happiness that rose in him, light and luminous, was a surprise. Something about seeing the house decked out in the Christmas finery he'd come to love over the years gave him a feeling of deep satisfaction. Caden would have never described himself as the sentimental type, and yet...

He took in the little folk Santas and the snowman candles that cheerily decorated the bookshelves. Across the back of the upright piano, Lucy had spread a quilted runner in checkered patterns of red and gold. She'd arranged the ceramic nativity scene that had always been Garrett's pride and joy on top.

"You can change it if that's not where it goes," Lucy said softly. He jerked his head around and realized she'd finished with the holly and was standing next to the chair in front of him. "I know families have certain traditions about decorating. The nativity set looked right there to me, but—"

"It's right," he interrupted. "That's where my dad always put it."

She walked over to the piano and picked up one of the ceramic sheep. "I love how it's painted. The details and color for each figure are perfect."

"Julia painted it the Christmas before she was diagnosed with cancer."

Lucy lifted her gaze to his, her whiskey-colored eyes gentle. "Julia was Garrett's wife?"

He nodded. "She died a couple of months before I met Tyson. That's why the counselor made him be my tour guide when I first came to Crimson Elementary. She thought we'd have something in common because neither of us had moms."

"That's a tragic common denominator," Lucy whispered.

"Our situations were totally different, anyway. From everything I ever learned about Julia Sharpe, she was the perfect mother. The exact opposite of mine." He moved forward and took the figure from her hand, returning it to its place on the back of the piano. "My first Christmas on the ranch, I was screwing around with the nativity scene and broke off the donkey's ear."

He ran a finger along the barely visible seam where Garrett had glued the animal back together. "I did a lot of stupid things when I was younger, especially when I was trying to test Garrett and see what it would take to make him send me away. But I've never seen him as angry as he was in that moment."

"Do you really think he would have sent you away once he claimed you?"

He stilled and fisted his hand at his side. How could he admit that she'd just voiced his most secret fear? The one he couldn't quite release?

Even after everything they'd been through and the love and devotion Garrett had shown him, Caden was still waiting for the day it all ended. He wondered if he'd ever be able to trust himself not to ruin the good things in his life.

"Your mother isn't going to be happy that you took down her Pepto-Bismol-colored winter wonderland in here."

She shrugged. "My mom means well, but Christmas is about tradition." She laughed, as if surprised to hear those words out of her own mouth. "At least, that's what I'm told."

"You didn't have traditions?" As much as he didn't want to be curious about this woman, he couldn't help wanting to know more about her.

"Not really. Nothing lasting."

"Sort of like your mother's three marriages," he blurted before thinking about it.

He regretted the words immediately. Lucy's gaze hardened and her full lips pressed into a thin line. She went to move past him, but he placed a hand on her arm.

"I'm sorry, Lucy."

"I doubt that."

"It's the truth." He bent his knees so he was at eye level with her. "I appreciate what you did in here."

"I meant it as an olive branch," she said, her gaze steady on his. "I'm not the enemy, Caden."

He toyed with the idea of that for a moment and found that it felt right. True. "I know."

"And neither is my mom," she added.

He couldn't allow himself to believe that but didn't argue. For once in his damn life, he was tired of arguing.

"We need a tree," he told her, gesturing to the box of ornaments still shoved in the corner. "There's enough time to head up into the forest and get one now."

"I thought you and your dad were going tree hunting when he got back."

"He won't mind if we take care of it." Actually, Garrett would probably be thrilled if Caden and Lucy dealt with hauling a tree back from the forest surrounding the ranch. The old man had seemed to age decades since Tyson's death. He could no longer spend long days working the ranch. After a few hours on horseback checking the fence line, Caden would often find that his father had retreated back to the house and his comfy chair in front of the fire.

It was difficult to know whether time or grief was the hardest on Garrett, but Caden imagined his father would appreciate a reprieve from their annual trip into the forest to cut down a tree.

She crossed her arms over her chest and studied him before answering. "I can't decide if you're extending your own olive branch or trying to lure me into the woods to have some kind of high-altitude Tony Soprano moment."

Caden felt his mouth kick up and found it odd that even when she was challenging him, Lucy could make him smile more than he had in years. "Let's call it an olive branch." He lifted a brow. "For now, anyway."

She laughed, as he'd hoped she would. "I'll get ready."

"Meet me out front in twenty minutes," he told her, then cleared her throat. "Unless you need more time?" When he'd been with Becca, she'd taken close to an hour to get ready no matter what they had planned for the day. It still blew his mind that once upon a time he'd fallen for such a high-maintenance woman. And it made his stomach clench that he hadn't realized the twisted game she was playing with him and his brother until it was too late.

Lucy only shook her head. "I just need to find warmer clothes. It won't take long."

He nodded, and she left the room. He waited until she was up the stairs before he blew out a breath. An olive branch or rope to string up his heart once again?

It was difficult to know exactly what he was offering when Lucy had his emotions so jumbled.

Fifteen minutes later, Lucy walked out onto the front porch. She shielded her eyes from the sun reflecting off the snow that blanketed the ground. Although the air was cold, the sky was a swath of brilliant blue as far as she could see.

The white-capped peak of Crimson Mountain loomed in the distance, like a benevolent ruler presiding over its kingdom.

"I definitely won't lose you in that coat," Caden called from where he stood in the gravel driveway.

Lucy smoothed a hand over the down jacket she'd found in her mother's closet, the hue a shade of pink that seemed more appropriate for Miami Beach than the Colorado mountains.

"It's the warmest thing I could find," she answered and pulled the coordinating knit cap farther down around her ears.

She'd put on athletic leggings under her jeans to act as another layer of warmth and tucked her jeans into a pair of fleece-lined snow boots.

She'd told herself it didn't matter how she looked because she wasn't trying to impress Caden. Of course, that hadn't stopped her from applying a fresh coat of gloss on her mouth. But only so her lips wouldn't chap.

Not because she wanted Caden to notice them. Not because she couldn't stop thinking about his mouth on hers the previous night.

But if she had been thinking about the kiss they'd shared, she'd have to admit she'd never felt anything like it. Lucy couldn't remember ever responding to a man the way she had to Caden. The featherlight touch of his mouth had made her body zip to life like some kind of fancy race car with the pedal slammed to the floor. Then he'd deepened the kiss and the rush of desire made her feel as if she was hurtling over a cliff with no parachute.

At that moment she would have done anything he asked. She wanted everything he was willing to give, which scared the hell out of her. Wanting made her weak. Needing something she wasn't meant to have was a sure path to heartache.

Only her finely tuned self-preservation skills had forced her to break away and retreat to the house. She'd lain in bed in the small guest room she occupied, waiting to hear his footsteps on the stairs, her body still humming with desire even as she recited in her head all the reasons Caden was bad news for her.

But when she'd awakened in the morning, early enough to watch the sky beginning to turn from gray to orange, something had pulled her out of bed and to the window just in time to see Caden walking from the barn, still wearing the same clothes as the night before.

Apparently she wasn't the only one who realized how dangerous their connection could prove to be. She'd made coffee and a bowl of oatmeal, hurrying in case he made a morning appearance to get his own breakfast, but the house had remained quiet.

After a shower, she'd slipped into the chair behind Garrett's oversize cherry desk in the second-floor office and powered up the computer. She'd spent the next couple of hours poring over ledgers and spreadsheets, increasingly baffled as to the ranch's financial records.

She'd gotten her associate's degree taking evening classes over a three-year span of time and had kept the books for the high-end boutique where she'd worked in Florida. Secretly she dreamed of going back to school for a full-fledged business degree, although how she'd find the time or the money to make that a reality wasn't clear.

But while she'd always had a knack for numbers, the Sharpe Ranch books made her feel like a second grader struggling with the fundamentals of adding and subtracting. There were several spreadsheets dealing with day-to-day ranch operations, expenditures and income from hay and grain. Then she found the accounting records that covered Garrett's other holdings, from business investments to a few high-level land development deals around Crimson.

Although some of the entries were recent, it was difficult

to tell if the books seemed so convoluted because of her unfamiliarity with ranching business or because the record keeping had been ignored or mismanaged since Tyson's death.

Eventually she'd walked away from the computer, wandering to the window to gaze at the lone figure on horseback far out in the pasture. Her attraction to Caden made her feel like a lovesick schoolgirl, so she'd pushed away from the window and made her way downstairs, hoping to find something to distract her from thoughts of the handsome rancher.

Which was what had led her to switching out her mother's tacky holiday decorations for the ones that clearly belonged in the cozy farmhouse. Normally Lucy didn't mess with Christmas. She'd worked retail since she was sixteen, which meant she'd seen the best and the worst of the holiday spirit. She also knew the words to every corny seasonal song ever written and had put up and taken down more plastic trees than she cared to count.

But she'd long ago given up hope of being the recipient of any Christmas miracles. The holiday season was for working—waiting on impatient customers and helping others choose the perfect gifts for friends and loved ones while she preferred to spend her Christmas watching old movies and eating take-out Chinese from the carton.

Yet here she was walking toward Caden and what looked like the mountain version of a golf cart with a metal trailer hooked to the back. And those damn butterflies went crazy once more, both at the sight of Caden in his fitted jeans and Stetson and the thought of an adventure in the woods.

"You'll appreciate the warmth when we get going," he said, moving aside and opening the vehicle's door for her. "It's a perfect day and the UTV has heat but since the top's open, the wind can get chilly when the sun starts to set."

"UTV?" She arched a brow. "That sounds like something I'd make a doctor's appointment to handle."

Caden chuckled and shook his head. "Utility terrain vehicle," he explained. "The path into the forest is too narrow for the truck."

"Got it." She climbed in and immediately the heat from the vents under the dashboard warmed her feet. A moment later Caden spread a heavy blanket over her legs. Lucy resisted the urge to sigh as he tucked it firmly under her thighs.

"It's no fun out there if you're half-frozen," he told her.

"Thanks," she whispered. She tried to ignore the scent of him, shampoo and spearmint gum, even as it tangled through her senses. He hadn't mentioned the kiss or shown any sign that he even remembered pulling her into his arms. Maybe he'd stayed away from the house last night because he'd feared she'd try to seduce him.

He'd made no secret of the fact that he believed her mom to be a gold digger and Lucy to be cut from the same cloth.

She had to keep that in mind. Her mother wanted her to convince Caden that having Maureen as a stepmom was a good thing. That was Lucy's only purpose in Colorado. It definitely wasn't in anyone's best interest to lose a piece of her heart to this man.

Caden threw her a sidelong glance as he climbed behind the wheel. "Everything okay?"

"Yep. Let's find a Christmas tree."

Caden looked like he wanted to call her out on her lie, but instead he shifted the UTV and they rumbled out of the driveway and down the snow-packed trail that led toward the forest.

Lucy had never been one for nature outings. A chair on the beach and her toes in the water were about as adventurous as she got. But riding in the off-road vehicle was exhilarating. They raced across the landscape, bumping slightly as the trail dipped and pitched. Soon they were in the trees, and her breath caught at the beauty surrounding her.

The pine tree needles were laced with snow, and icicles hung suspended from some of the longer branches. The forest was dappled in sunlight, although she definitely felt a drop in temperature as they made their way up the trail and left the open fields behind them.

Caden seemed to know the area well and maneuvered the UTV around corners and across a frozen creek bed. The trail grew narrow in some spots and Lucy laughed as the roll bar on the UTV brushed a low-hanging branch and they were dusted with snow.

Eventually they drove into a clearing, and Caden abruptly cut the engine.

"What's wrong?" she asked, grabbing his arm. Although there was no doubt Caden knew his way around the forest, the city girl in her didn't like the thought of being stuck out in the woods in the middle of December.

Caden leaned close and used one finger to turn her head to the side. "Look over there," he whispered, pointing with his other hand to the far edge of the meadow.

Lucy's breath caught in her throat as her gaze tracked to the massive animal staring at her through big black eyes. "Reindeer," she whispered.

Caden's soft chuckle was warm against her jaw. "Elk," he corrected her. "You know the herd bull because he has the antlers. Six points."

The elk's antlers were massive but she had no experience with wildlife in the...well...the wild. "Unless you're talking basketball, six points means nothing to me."

"Count the tips sticking out on each antler. He's called a six by six."

"And the rest are girls?"

"Cows," Caden clarified.

"Does that one bull service all the ladies?"

Caden laughed again. "Yeah. During the spring and summer, the cows and young elk are often on their own. But there are usually one or two bulls with the herd through the winter."

"So he's a busy guy."

"I doubt it's a problem for him."

Lucy couldn't help but smile. "Right."

The elk made a noise and the females who were nosing in the snow looked up. A few pawed at the ground and snuffled. Then the herd moved forward and disappeared into the trees.

"That was amazing." Lucy turned to Caden, surprised to find that he hadn't moved away from her. Her nose grazed his cheek and he sat back like she'd burned him. "I didn't realize elk were so beautiful."

"They're majestic," he agreed. "That herd stays on the ranch most of the year."

She looked around. "Is this still your property? I thought we were on public land here."

"A few miles up the trail it becomes forest-service land," he told her, pointing to the other side of the clearing. "Garrett has almost two thousand acres. He inherited a lot from his dad but has added acreage as land became available over the years."

"You don't work the whole thing, do you?"

"A lot of it is natural prairie or forest. The cattle are free-range so in the summer they spread out pretty far. But Crimson has grown quite a bit even since I was a kid. Garrett wants to make sure some of the open spaces are preserved."

"You do that a lot," she murmured.

He cocked a brow.

"You refer to him as Garrett and not Dad."

A muscle ticked in Caden's jaw. "He's my dad."

"I know that." But she got the distinct impression that Caden didn't quite believe it even after almost twenty years of living on the ranch.

"Let's find a tree before the weather turns."

"What are you talking about?" Lucy pointed a finger toward the sky. "It's a perfect day."

"There were storm clouds gathering on the peak as we left the ranch. They should get to us within the hour."

"Um...okay." Lucy had always gotten her weather forecasts from the local news, but she wasn't going to argue. Instead, she hopped out of the UTV. "What tree do you want?"

"Whichever one makes you happy." Caden pulled an ax from the trailer and came to stand next to her.

She crossed her arms over her chest. "I can't pick. I don't know what makes a good Christmas tree."

He gave her an incredulous look. "You've celebrated Christmas before, right?"

"Well, yes. But never with a real tree. Or even a fake one that's full-size." She tugged on the hem of her pink parka. "Except at some of the stores where I worked. But I didn't pay much attention as we were putting them up."

"You've never had a real tree?"

She waved a hand in the air. "Too much trouble."

"Not even when you were a kid?"

"Definitely not," she admitted. "My mom didn't like the mess of pine needles on the carpet."

He studied her for a moment as if weighing an important decision. Then he handed her the small ax he held. "Let's go find the biggest, most beautiful Christmas tree that will fit in the house. We have a lot of years to make up for."

Without waiting for an answer, he turned and started into the forest. Lucy stared after him, blinking away unbidden tears. She'd told herself for so many years that there was no such thing as Christmas spirit—it was just a materialistic holiday that produced fake cheer and the need for people to spend money they didn't have.

Although working retail did that to a person, even before endless hours spent at a cash register, she'd given up on Christmas. Year after year of having her mom care about the holiday only when there was a man around to impress had worn on Lucy. Some years there was an abundance of over-the-top gifts and some years, when depression had its claws dug deep, Maureen could barely rouse herself out of bed. Lucy didn't trust Christmas. It had shown itself to be a fickle friend.

The idea that Caden wanted to make up for that overwhelmed her. She hadn't even admitted to him her pathetic history, yet he still knew just what to do to give her the happiest holiday moment she could remember.

Maybe it was silly, but the thought of a real Christmas tree made Lucy feel like a little girl again. Anticipation bubbled up inside her and she didn't bother to tamp it down. This afternoon had nothing to do with her mother or convincing Caden that the marriage was a good idea.

This moment was all about Lucy's happiness. It was long past time she made herself a priority in her own life.

Caden paused and looked over his shoulder. "Are we doing this?"

She quickly swiped at her eyes and held up the ax. "Call me Paula Bunyan," she said and hurried to join him.

Chapter 6

Lucy stopped so suddenly that Caden almost ran into her. "That's it," she whispered.

He followed her line of sight and frowned. "What's it?"

"The perfect Christmas tree." She moved forward awkwardly, her boots crunching as she sank into the snow.

They'd been walking through the woods for almost forty-five minutes. As Caden predicted, clouds had rolled in and the temperature had dropped. Snow flurries whirled through the air, and Caden was slowly losing sensation in his toes. He hadn't realized how long the outing would take and regretted not wearing insulated boots.

Despite her years as a Floridian, Lucy seemed strangely undeterred by the cold or snow or waning daylight. It was like he'd unleashed a kid in a Christmas tree candy store. She'd vetoed at least a dozen beautiful trees that would have fit perfectly on Sharpe Ranch. But the one she was proudly standing in front of now…

"Are you going for the *A Charlie Brown Christmas* look?" he asked, rubbing his gloved hands together.

"This is a beautiful tree," she argued. "Not too big and not too small."

"You sure about that, Goldilocks? It looks a little scraggly from where I'm standing."

She rolled her eyes and turned to the tree, holding up her palms to each side of the branches like she was covering its ears. "Don't listen to him. I see your potential. You are perfect just the way you are."

The words were like a fist to Caden's gut. They were eerily similar to what Garrett had said when he'd first spoken to him about adoption. Ironically, the conversation had taken place after Caden purposely knocked over a big bag of horse feed in the barn. Garrett had sent Tyson to the house and ordered Caden to sit down on a bale of hay so they could "talk."

From what Caden had then deduced from both his mother and his more recent foster parents, on good days a "talk" meant the back side of an adult's hand or on bad days, the sharp sting of a belt on his bare skin. Instead Garrett had reached behind the hay bale and picked up a squirming kitten from the litter the resident barn cat had given birth to weeks before.

He'd dropped the ball of fluff into Caden's arms and waited. Caden had tried to stay still and withhold any emotion, but the sweet kitten was too much—even for a surly kid. He'd lifted the kitten and cuddled it to his chest, all the while muttering about how much the animal annoyed him.

Garrett had smiled and said, "You've got potential." Then he'd asked Caden how he'd feel about coming to live on Sharpe Ranch permanently.

Sometimes Caden wondered if he'd ever live up to the potential his adoptive father had first seen in him.

"Let's bring it home, then," he told Lucy now.

"Really?" Her cheeks were pink from either cold or excitement. He couldn't tell which. Snowflakes clung to her gaudy pink hat, and her hair looked even darker as she swung it over her shoulder. "I thought you didn't like this one."

"It's your tree. Plus I'm freezing. I want to get the hell out of the woods."

"Come on, baby," she crooned to the tree, and unwanted heat pooled in Caden's belly at her voice's sultry cadence. "You're mine now."

It was a miracle Caden's tongue didn't loll out of his mouth. For a moment he suspected she was talking to the tree in that tone just to mess with him. Then she lifted the ax and waved it around with so much disregard for her own safety that he forgot all his lustful thoughts and concentrated on keeping her from chopping off her own head.

"This isn't *The Walking Dead*," he warned. "You don't have to mutilate it." He strode forward and turned her so her back was to him. "I'll show you." He adjusted her grip on the ax and demonstrated the proper technique for felling a tree.

The Douglas fir was barely taller than a shrub. He watched as she bent low and swung forward, the ax's sharp blade thunking into the trunk.

"You do the rest," she said, leaving the ax stuck in the tree. "I feel like I'm hurting him."

He gave her a long look. "It's a tree."

"Trees are living things," she countered.

"Right." He'd never met anyone like Lucy, a mind-boggling blend of sophistication and innocence. But despite his frozen toes, Caden couldn't remember the last time he'd had so much fun.

He pulled the ax from the tree and chopped it down with several well-placed swings. The good thing about Lucy's scraggly tree was that the size made it easy to haul back to the UTV.

Although they'd walked through the woods longer than he expected, Lucy had actually circled back toward the main path, so it didn't take long to reach the vehicle.

"The snow is really coming down," Lucy said as he hefted the tree into the trailer.

"We're supposed to get six inches overnight."

He turned on the UTV and climbed in next to Lucy. The blanket covered her lap, but he could see the shivers passing through her.

She turned to him and made a face. "I didn't notice the cold when I was searching for the perfect tree, but now..."

"Come here," he told her, and she scooted toward him on the bench seat. She smelled like flowery shampoo and the cold, and he wrapped an arm around her waist, pulling her even closer. His body tightened when she snuggled against him.

The ride back to the ranch was slower than he would have liked with visibility lowered because of the blowing snow.

He finally pulled to a stop in front of the house and turned to Lucy. "I'll bring in the tree, and then I need to check on the animals in the barn. You should go inside and warm up."

"Do you need help?" she asked through chattering teeth.

"I need you to not turn into a Popsicle on my watch," he answered and pulled the blanket from around her.

"I think I can manage that." She got out of the UTV and walked up the porch steps and into the house.

He got the tree onto the porch and dusted it off, then covered it with the tarp he had in the UTV's trailer. He headed to the barn next and made sure all of his animals were warm and dry.

Chad came in just as Caden was about to head to the house. "There's a problem with the propane heater near the trough in the west pasture."

Caden cursed under his breath. With the temperatures dropping and snow in the forecast, he couldn't afford for the herd's drinking water to freeze.

"I need to put on my other boots and I'll be ready to go."

Chad eyed his feet then raised a brow. "You're liable to lose a toe to frostbite wearing those in this weather."

"Don't be a drama queen," Caden muttered. "I'm fine. I didn't expect to be out so long."

"I saw you and Lucy heading for the woods earlier. Hot date?"

"No date at all. We went to get a Christmas tree."

"How romantic," Chad said in a singsong voice.

"Shut it," Caden told him.

"It's okay to admit you're human," Chad shot back. "Any man with two eyes and half a heartbeat would be into her. She's hot as hell. I mean, if Jessica and I don't work out, I could give you some competition."

Caden leveled a look at his young ranch hand. "Lucy is off-limits for you."

He expected an argument or some kind of smart comeback, but Chad only grinned. "I figured as much."

Caden finished pulling on his heavy work boots and stood. "Let's take care of the heater before we lose all our daylight."

It was almost six that evening when Lucy heard the front door open and shut. She pushed away from the computer where she'd been working for the past hour and ran a hand through her hair.

She didn't want to admit, even to herself, that her feelings were hurt because Caden had ditched her at the house with the Christmas tree. It had been foolish to read so much into their jaunt to the forest.

She wanted it to mean something that he'd suggested she

pick out the Christmas tree for the house. Clearly, all it meant was that he didn't want to be bothered with the task.

As cold as she'd been on the ride home, it had felt amazing to press herself against Caden's strong body, the heat of him warming her. It embarrassed her now that she'd run into the house and changed into her best jeans and a red V-neck sweater, spritzing herself with perfume as she anticipated a late afternoon spent trimming the tree and cuddling in front of the fire.

She'd even made hot cocoa, which had long ago cooled in the pan on the stove. She'd finally realized he wasn't coming back to the house. Her stupid little fantasy about a picture-perfect holiday moment was just that. A fantasy. She should have known better. It's why Lucy didn't like Christmas to begin with—as soon as she allowed herself to have holiday expectations, she was disappointed when things didn't work out the way she wanted.

Just to prove that she wasn't waiting for him, she'd dragged the tree into the house, leaving a trail of pine needles in her wake. She'd found a tree stand in the bottom of one of the ornament boxes and managed to get the tree upright in one corner of the living room. Who needed a man, anyway?

Maybe Caden had been right about the size. It looked a little scraggly now that it wasn't surrounded by other trees, but she still loved it. Even though it had been cut down on Sharpe Ranch property and now stood in Garrett's house, the tree belonged to Lucy.

And she hadn't waited to decorate it because she was still hoping Caden would show up. Nope. She'd just wanted to put in some more time on the financials before she had her own private tree-trimming party.

She quickly turned back to the computer when footsteps

sounded on the stairs. Let him come to her, and she could blow him off just as easily.

"Hey, there."

She glanced up and pretended to be surprised to see him standing in the doorway, as if she'd been so engrossed in her work she hadn't heard him come in. She most certainly hadn't been waiting for him.

"Oh, hello," she said breezily, like she was greeting a casual acquaintance she hadn't seen in months. "I lost track of time. Did you have a nice afternoon?"

He reached out to grip either side of the door frame with his hands, making him look even broader than normal. He'd taken off his hat and his hair was rumpled and sticking up in several places, as if he'd been raking his hands through it. He still wore his heavy canvas jacket and his cheeks were bright pink, his eyes tired.

"No," he told her, moving toward the desk, "my afternoon sucked." He pressed his knuckles against the cherry top and leaned forward, the scent of winter and ranch work spilling off him. "I'd thought I was going to spend it with you, and instead I've been dealing with an emergency with one of the propane heaters."

"Oh," she breathed as relief rushed through her. He hadn't ditched her after all. There'd been a ranch emergency. He definitely looked exhausted and unhappy.

"You could have told me," she blurted even though he didn't owe her an explanation. He didn't owe her anything. But her feelings had been bruised, and it was hard to let that go.

He straightened, and she thought he might walk away. "You did good getting the tree in on your own. I would have helped."

"I wasn't sure you were coming back."

"I'm sorry," he said quietly.

She shrugged. "This is stupid. You don't want to hang out

with me. You don't even want me on the ranch. It's silly for us to try to be friends."

"Friends," he repeated, chewing on the word like it was something he'd never tasted before. "Are we friends, Lucy?"

"You tell me, Caden."

"I'd like to be your friend," he admitted after a moment, "but that doesn't change how I feel about your mother."

"Maybe we should leave my mom and your dad out of this," she suggested. "At least for a little while."

"Good idea." One side of his mouth quirked. "An even better idea would be a shower."

Lucy felt her mouth drop open, as those darned butterflies did their thing in her belly.

Caden chuckled. "Me in the shower," he clarified. "Alone."

She blew out a breath. "I knew that."

His slow grin widened. "I need to wash off this day and after that, I'd like to eat dinner and decorate the tree." He arched a brow. "The dinner and decorating part with you." He frowned when she didn't answer. "If you don't have other plans?"

She barked out a laugh. "No plans. But I don't cook."

"I do," he told her. "Give me ten minutes."

"You can shower and get changed in ten minutes?" Lucy wasn't high maintenance, but that seemed lightning fast.

"Want to watch?" he asked.

She felt color flood her cheeks. "Of course not."

"Liar," he whispered and walked out of the room.

She thought about throwing the stapler at his head, but the thought of someone cooking dinner for her was too appealing. Maureen was a fabulous cook, but she chose to use her culinary skills only when a man was involved. When her mother was in a relationship, they ate like kings.

But when it was just the two of them, Lucy had become adept at heating canned spaghetti and various frozen dinners.

As a result, she'd come to view cooking as another form of manipulation—a tool in her mother's arsenal for snaring whatever man she'd set her sights on in the moment.

Even when Lucy had moved out on her own, she'd refused to learn to cook. Her lack of culinary skills drove her mother crazy, and it had been a weak form of rebellion but one Lucy'd never outgrown.

When she heard the shower turn on in the hall bathroom, she jumped up from the chair and practically tripped her way down the stairs. It would be pure torture to sit there and imagine Caden stripping off his clothes and stepping under a steaming hot shower.

She'd been through plenty in her life, but torture wasn't high on her to-do list.

She stumbled toward the front door, trying hard to push the image of a naked Caden from her brain. She yanked open the door and stepped out onto the front porch, hoping the bracing air would cool the fire raging through her body.

Her breath came out in puffy clouds in front of her face, and she dug her toes into the ice-cold coir doormat.

"Everything okay, Lucy?" a deep voice called.

She glanced up to see Chad staring at her from across the driveway.

"Just enjoying December in Colorado," she shouted, giving him a wave.

He looked at her like she'd lost her mind, and maybe that was true. Never had she reacted to a man like she did to Caden. In fact, she'd always secretly judged her mother for having no willpower when it came to guys and falling so fast and hard whenever a handsome man crossed her path.

Now Lucy feared she'd inherited more from her mom than a decent complexion and a love for jelly donuts.

When Chad continued to stare, she waved again and backed

into the house. She made her way to the kitchen and opened the fridge, hoping to distract herself by finding something to start for dinner. There were various containers of cheese and meat and a whole drawer full of vegetables, but to Lucy it felt like trying to read a book in a foreign language.

Finally she pulled out a head of lettuce, a yellow bell pepper and a bag of baby carrots. At least she was fluent in salad.

She was chopping a handful of carrots when Caden walked into the room, and she promptly came close to cutting off the tip of her finger.

Usually he was handsome in his rancher gear of the ubiquitous denim shirt and Carhartt jacket, but tonight he wore a plain white T-shirt that stretched across his chest and low-slung jeans hugging his muscled legs in a way that made her mouth go dry. From under one sleeve she could just see the shadow of dark ink. Not surprising for a man like Caden, but the urge she had to trace her fingers and tongue across his skin was shocking.

She schooled her features and offered a smile she hoped came off as friendly and not predatory. The truth was that outside her outrageous desire for Caden, she actually liked him. If she discounted the fact that he pretty much despised her mother and wanted Lucy off the ranch and out of his life.

Conflicting goals when it came to their parents notwithstanding, she had fun with him. She respected his work ethic and his protective instinct when it came to Garrett.

Of course, her heart melted at what he was doing to rescue and rehome the animals in his care. He made her laugh and he got her humor. It wasn't natural for Lucy to feel comfortable hanging out with men. She'd been raised to see them as either conquests or not worth her time. But it was easy to be herself around Caden.

She figured nothing she did would change his opinion of

her or her mom, but the camaraderie was a nice break from the normal anxiety she felt with guys.

So she didn't want to mess up this chance for friendship, as fleeting as it might turn out to be.

"Feel better now?" she asked casually, and he nodded.

"When I was deployed, I used to dream about long, hot showers."

"How long were you in the army?"

He opened the refrigerator and grabbed an armload of food. "I did two tours in Afghanistan and one in Iraq."

"Did you like it?"

He shrugged. "I was a decent soldier, and I liked that. It made my dad laugh how quickly I took to the routine and discipline of military life when I'd chafed against every rule he ever set for me." He was quiet for a moment as he placed the containers and bags of food on the counter. Then he added softly, "I thought I'd be a lifer."

"But you got out to help on the ranch after your brother died."

"I owed it to Garrett."

"Why?"

His sharp gaze crashed into hers. "Sorry," she said quickly. "It's none of my business."

"Tyson died while I was on leave. It was on a rock climbing trip on the other side of the pass that I was supposed to take with him. If I'd been there…" He shook his head. "He was rappelling down the last pitch of a route he knew well, but he lost sight of the end of his rope and thought it would reach the ground. He fell from about thirty feet in the air. By the time the other climbers got to him, he was gone. I would have been the strongest one in the group. I could have—"

"You can't do that," Lucy interrupted, reaching for his arm.

She wrapped her fingers around his wrist and squeezed. "You weren't there. It wasn't your fault."

He stared at her hand like having someone touch his skin was unfamiliar to him. "We weren't speaking at the time," he said, his voice desperately hollow. "Tyson had moved to Denver for a job and only came back to Crimson once a month. I'd fallen hard for a woman I met on leave—a waitress here in town. Turns out she was his girlfriend, and she'd gone after me to punish him for not taking her with him when he left."

"What a bi—" Lucy stopped when Caden yanked his arm away from her.

"He tried to convince me she was using both of us, but I wouldn't listen. I accused him of being jealous because someone finally picked me over him. Things got heated and we both said things… I said things I didn't mean." He closed his eyes for a moment, and when he opened them again the stark pain in their green depths stunned Lucy.

"You loved him," she whispered. "I barely know you and I can see that in you. He knew it."

He gave a humorless laugh. "I can be a real prick when I set my mind to it."

She arched a brow. "I'm shocked."

The corners of his eyes crinkled but he didn't smile. "Tyson first brought me home when he realized my foster dad was taking out his temper on me. I know he's the one who convinced Garrett to adopt me."

"Your father is a grown man who makes his own decisions."

"Yeah, but he and Tyson were a team after Julia died. I owe everything I have to my brother, and I repaid him first by betraying him then by turning my back on him when he called me out on it."

He stepped closer, crowding her against the counter. "It

wasn't a joke when I said I'd hurt you, Lucy. I ruin everything good that comes into my life."

A part of her wanted to run. As much as she tried to be tough, Lucy knew she was close to losing her heart to this man. She'd never been much of a rescuer, but something about Caden pulled at her soul. She wanted more than anything to help him heal. But she was smart enough to believe what he told her. She could very easily end up hurt.

Right now it didn't matter.

"But I'm not good for you," she said, tipping up her chin to meet his intense gaze. "Remember, I'm the enemy. That should keep me safe."

"Safe," he repeated, but his shoulders lowered slightly. "That's funny." He lifted his thumb to her mouth, traced it over the seam of her lips, then tugged down on the lower one.

Lucy forced herself not to moan at the touch. Despite his warnings and the very real risk of being hurt, she felt safe with him. He lowered his head and all she wanted was his mouth on hers. Then her stomach gave a loud rumble, breaking the spell between them.

He stepped away and moved toward the refrigerator. "You need to eat."

"What are we making?" she asked, impressed that her voice didn't shake.

He took a beer from the refrigerator and glanced over his shoulder. "Want a drink? There's beer in the fridge. Garrett has wine downstairs."

"A beer is fine."

He handed her a bottle, and she traced a finger over the blue mountains on the label.

"Chicken tacos tonight," he told her. "You've got a good start on the salad."

"How else can I help?" She twisted the cap off the beer and

took a long drink. Despite the snow she could still see coming down outside the kitchen window, the cool liquid refreshed her overheated body.

"Grab the spices from the cabinet."

She laughed. "Can you be more specific? I wasn't joking when I said I don't cook."

He rattled off a list of spices and pointed to the cabinet next to the stove.

"Mind if I ask why you don't cook?" he asked as she began collecting the colorful jars on the counter. "One thing I'll say for your mom is that she knows her way around the kitchen."

Lucy's hand jerked, and a container of cumin clattered onto the counter. "She cooks to impress men," she answered honestly. "And she wanted me to learn for the same reason. It tainted cooking for me."

He gave her a small nod. "You're not your mother. You know that, right?"

"Of course," she whispered and turned back to the spice cabinet, blinking away tears. She wanted to believe that but she'd never trusted that she wouldn't turn into her mother if she weren't careful. Genetics was a powerful influencer.

They worked in mostly companionable silence for the next thirty minutes, Caden giving her only occasional directions. Soon the rich scent of spicy chicken and black beans filled the room. He showed her how to heat tortillas over the stove. Then she offered to grate a block of cheese, strangely proud to be helping with the meal.

Whenever her mom had given her tasks when cooking, it had felt like she was an indentured servant. But like everything with Caden, tonight felt new and real and like it belonged just to her.

Chapter 7

Caden didn't understand why a simple dinner of chicken tacos eaten at the farmhouse kitchen table felt like a five-star meal, but he couldn't stop the stupid smile that curved his mouth every moment he wasn't chewing.

He'd made a thousand meals in this kitchen, but tonight was different. Lucy made it different. They cleaned up the plates and moved to the living room, her enthusiasm trickling into his bones and making him truly excited at the prospect of decorating her scrawny Christmas tree.

"We start with lights, right?" she asked, and he nodded. She pulled the strands of colored lights from one of the boxes, and they strung them around the tree, working together like they were old friends.

Friends.

Tyson had been the first friend Caden had ever had, and every day he felt the loss of his friend and brother like there was a hole in his heart. It felt wrong that this woman was quickly filling it, as if his happiness was somehow disloyal to

Tyson. He'd had buddies in the army but had been remiss about staying in contact with them since he'd gotten out.

"These ornaments are so sweet," Lucy said, drawing his attention to where she knelt on the floor next to one of the boxes. She held up the wooden figures of a raccoon and deer, rough and rudimentary.

"I used to carve a new ornament for Garr—" he cleared his throat "—for my dad every year. It was the only thing he asked for each Christmas. They were pretty bad at the beginning, and I'm surprised he even trusted me with a knife."

"They deserve pride of place," she said, walking over to hang the small animals from branches at the front of the tree. The exact spot Garrett gave to his tiny creations every year. They hadn't bothered to put up a tree last year, and Caden hadn't realized how much he missed the tradition until now.

"These were from Tyson's mom," he said, handing her a box of vintage balls of all different colors. "I guess they hung on her family's tree when she was a girl. Maybe we don't mention that part to your mom."

"Maybe not," Lucy agreed as she took the box and hung the ornaments.

She looked so damn beautiful in the soft light from the Christmas tree. He continued to give her ornaments to hang, explaining the significance of each one. Pretty soon all that was left was the beaded star.

"You should do the star," she told him, crossing her arms over her chest. "I kind of took over trimming the tree."

"I liked watching you," he said honestly. Hell, he could watch her take out the trash and would probably find it fascinating.

He took the star and stretched up to place it on the top of the tree. As kids, he and Tyson had argued about who got to put the star on top until Garrett had grabbed it from their hands and announced he'd be in charge of the star every year.

"It's beautiful," she whispered when he stepped away. Her palms were pressed together and her eyes shone with delight.

"Beautiful," he repeated and moved toward her, wrapping his hand around hers and tugging her closer. He brushed his lips across hers, which he'd wanted to do all day. The tightness that had been clamped around his chest for so long loosened ever so slightly. To Caden the change felt like the slight shift of snow that could start an avalanche. He was scared as hell of being buried under the weight of it.

So when she leaned in, he pulled back, ignoring the shadow that crossed her eyes.

"I need to check on the animals one more time tonight. Thank you for a great evening."

As goodbyes went, it was pathetic. But he didn't know how to rein in his feelings for her. Without dinner to make or a tree to trim, there were no distractions. Nothing to keep him from putting his hands all over her. That was a terrible idea, even though his body shouted it would be the best way to end this evening.

"Can I help?" she asked, biting down on her bottom lip.

"It's cold and snowy out there. The barn is heated but it's not—"

"I think I can handle it," she said with a laugh, then frowned. "Unless this is you brushing me off?" She stared at him a moment. "Right. This is you brushing me off. I get it."

He shook his head. "You don't." How could he make her understand that he was trying to keep a distance between them because the alternative was that he'd want more than he should from her? More than he guessed she'd be willing to give. Keeping himself closed off was a defense mechanism he'd perfected long ago.

If he didn't care, he couldn't be hurt.

When he didn't care, he didn't hurt other people.

Lucy had already gotten under his skin, and he knew his willpower was no match for the way he wanted her.

"Then explain it to me."

"If you want to help," he said by way of an answer, "put on boots, a heavy coat and gloves. Grab a flashlight from the closet in the front hall and meet me in the barn." Then he walked past her, shoved his feet into his boots, grabbed his jacket from the hook in the entryway and headed out into the cold before he changed his mind.

He wasn't sure if she was going to follow him. He'd been purposely rude, striding to the barn like he was running away from the playground bully. Which was ridiculous and made him feel like a jerk.

He let the dogs out of their respective pens and opened the back door of the barn that led to an enclosed corral. The dogs barked and yipped, running around and doing their business, most of them oblivious to the cold. A few of the ones that were older or didn't have a heavy coat of fur went back to the barn.

As the dogs played, Caden grabbed a container of vegetables from the refrigerator in the office and let himself into the bunny room. Fritzi, the Holland Lop that was a permanent fixture in the barn and a certified therapy pet, hopped to the front of the hutch for her nightly nose rub and snack. The other rabbits followed her lead, and Caden smiled as he visited with each of them.

Once or twice he glanced over his shoulder, but when Lucy didn't appear, he figured his abrupt exit had made her want to keep her distance. He wasn't sure if he was disappointed or relieved.

Who was he fooling? It killed him to know he'd so quickly

ruined his chances with a woman who made him happier than he'd been in years.

He finished with the rabbits and went to check on the cats, but a short bark from one of the dog pens had him hurrying down the barn's main corridor.

Turning the corner around the converted horse stall, he stopped in his tracks. "What are you doing?" he whispered frantically.

Lucy looked up, clearly surprised at his tone. "Snuggling," she answered and dropped a kiss on the head of the dog pressed against her side.

"Cocoa's not friendly," he said. "She bites."

"This dog?" Lucy asked, glancing between the brindled shepherd–pit bull mix and Caden. "Are you sure?"

"She was abused by her owner," he explained, "and she's pregnant."

"Aww," Lucy murmured, running her hand down the dog's side and rubbing Cocoa's enlarged belly. "I wondered about that."

"Seriously, Lucy. I'm working with her, but she's not safe around people yet. I think she'll calm down once the puppies are born, but…"

He trailed off as the dog tipped up her chin and delicately licked Lucy's cheek.

"You're gonna be a mama," Lucy cooed.

Caden felt his mouth drop open. Cocoa would barely let him touch her, and she'd had to be muzzled and sedated when the vet first came to examine her.

Jase Crenshaw, an attorney in town, and one of the few people Caden had befriended in high school, had called him about the dog. Jase grew up in a trailer park on the outskirts of Crimson, and while moving his dad from there a month ago, he'd found Cocoa chained to a stump in below-freezing temperatures. Part of the dog's ear was missing and she had scars on her face and neck like she'd been used as a fighter.

Jase had called Caden along with the county humane society, and after animal enforcement had threatened the owner with charges, the owner had told Caden to go ahead and shoot the dog because she was so damn mean he'd never rehabilitate her.

The man was the only one in danger of being shot, but Jase had convinced Caden the guy wasn't worth the trouble.

Instead, Caden had managed to get near enough to the dog to unchain her, then lure her into a crate. She'd growled low under her breath the entire time but snapped only when Jase got too close. It was as if she'd recognized in Caden another spirit that knew what it was like to be truly unwanted.

Even the animal control officer had labeled the dog a lost cause, but Caden hadn't been willing to give up on her. He'd wanted to lash out at the world after his mom died and he was dumped in the foster-care system.

He'd given Garrett every reason to kick him out on multiple occasions, but his adoptive father had been consistent in his love, and eventually Caden had found a fragile kind of peace in his world. It never changed who he was at his core, but it made life more manageable.

He'd planned on taking as much time as needed to gain Cocoa's trust, but Lucy had accomplished the impossible in a matter of minutes.

What was it about her that made the nearly feral dog trust her so quickly?

He laughed under his breath. Hell, wasn't he just the same? As much as he knew she wasn't good for him, he'd been putty in her hands from the start.

"Please come out of her pen."

The dog turned her head as he spoke and gave him a baleful look.

"Don't worry," Lucy said gently as she straightened. "I'll come back and visit with you tomorrow."

Caden held his breath as Cocoa stood and pushed her big block head into Lucy's leg. He half expected the dog to become aggressive. His muscles remained tense, ready to intervene if things went south, as Lucy walked forward.

Cocoa let out a high-pitched whine, then walked to the corner of the pen, turned around twice and settled on the bed of fresh hay he'd given her earlier that morning.

He grabbed Lucy's arm and pulled her close as soon as she shut the door to the stall. "You scared the hell out of me."

She tipped up her head to look at him. "Caden, she's a sweetheart."

"I've never seen anything like that. Are you sure you don't have experience as an animal trainer?"

Lucy grinned. "I had a goldfish I won at a carnival in third grade. But he died after a week."

He laced his fingers with hers and headed toward the back of the barn. "How do you know it was a boy?"

"Because I named him Fernando," she said matter-of-factly.

"Of course you did. Want to help me feed the cats?"

"As long as none of them try to escape."

He reached up onto a high shelf and pulled down a plastic crate. "Not when it's dinnertime."

They walked into the room to a chorus of plaintive meows. He handed Lucy the container of food and pointed to the bowls. "You can put a scoop in each. They'll love you forever."

"I like the sound of that," she said, and his heart squeezed in a way that had him pressing his fingers to his chest.

She laughed as the cats and kittens tumbled around her. Caden was secretly relieved she seemed to enjoy his crazy menagerie of pets. He'd always had a thing for stray animals but sometimes felt embarrassed sharing that part of himself with other people.

It wasn't until Erin MacDonald had heard about the animals he used as therapy pets and asked him to bring them to visit her after-school program for at-risk kids that he went more public with his adoption efforts. Before that, it had mainly just been word of mouth leading him to match animals with good families.

"I'm glad you're helping with the adoption event," he told Lucy now.

She'd picked up one of the kittens and was snuggling it under her chin. "Really?"

She seemed as surprised by his words as he was saying them. "Yeah. I have a sense for where an animal belongs, but marketing isn't my thing."

"I never would have guessed." She placed the tiny cat back with his brothers and sisters and took a step away from the animals. "I wasn't sure you'd agree to my involvement, but I've already been working on some ideas. I have a Facebook page started for the event, and I'd like to take some pictures of the animals tomorrow for publicity. I read online that good photos are one of the things that can attract people to rescue animals. Erin and I have been texting. We're going to talk to local businesses about donating items for baskets to raffle. Katie Crawford at the bakery has agreed to provide cookies during the event."

"Is that all?" Caden asked with a stunned laugh.

Lucy frowned. "You're joking?"

He moved closer, smoothed her dark hair away from her face and placed a kiss on her forehead. "I'm joking. Thank you for taking care of all of that, especially after I was such an ass."

"I'm getting used to it," she said, poking him in the chest.

"Lucky for you, your skills in the kitchen make up for your surly personality."

"It's time to say good-night to the animals," he said, laughing. It felt odd to have a woman teasing him. Oddly wonderful.

Lucy made a point of petting each of the dozen cats in the room before leaving. Caden checked the barn's heater, then turned down the lights, and they walked in silence back to the house. Stars lit the night sky, and the waning moon reflected softly against the snow.

At one point, Lucy slipped on a patch of ice and he put a hand around her waist to steady her. The innocent touch made his body yearn for more. He wanted her out of her layers of clothes and in his bed.

Without the distraction of dinner or the animals, the desire that had pounded through him earlier came back in full force. He wanted Lucy in a million different ways, any way she would have him. But he had to stay strong and keep his need for her under control.

Tonight had been amazing and he didn't want to ruin the tenuous friendship they'd established by taking advantage of her.

So when he opened the door to the house and followed her in, he had every intention of retreating up the stairs and locking himself in his bedroom if that's what it took.

But as soon as the door shut behind him, Lucy turned and lifted up on tiptoe, pressing her mouth to his like she'd been waiting to do it all night.

How could he resist that sort of invitation?

For a moment, Lucy wasn't sure how Caden was going to react to her kiss. He went perfectly still, his mouth not moving against hers. Maybe she'd misread the connection between them.

Maybe it was one-sided.

Then he wrapped his arms around her and lifted her off her feet. His lips parted and his tongue met hers, pulling a low groan from her throat.

She held on as he moved forward, depositing her gently onto the couch. She tugged off her hat and gloves, then unzipped her heavy coat. Her mouth went dry as he shrugged out of his jacket, leaving him standing in front of her in just the white T-shirt and jeans.

Suddenly nothing in the world was more important than touching his body. She lifted to her knees and pulled the hem of his shirt up and over his head.

"Wow," she whispered as she took in his muscled body. His shoulders looked even broader now, and there was a faint sprinkling of hair across the planes of his chest. She could clearly see the tattoo on his biceps, an eagle holding a tattered American flag.

"Good wow?" he asked. "Or 'wow, you're weird looking'?"

She bit down on her lower lip as she stared into his green eyes. "Good wow."

"Right back at you."

She laughed. "I haven't done anything to wow you yet."

"You don't have to," he murmured. "You wow me every second without even trying."

Heat pooled low in her belly and, emboldened by his words, she lifted her palms to his bare skin. She ran them through the patch of hair on his chest, noticing that he sucked in a breath as she grazed his nipples.

He pulled her closer, kissing her like a man who'd been thinking about doing just that for a very long time. The kiss was an exploration, deep and soulful, and she lost herself in the sensation of it. His hands skimmed under her shirt, making goose bumps rise on her skin as his calloused fingers trailed up her spine. Then he moved them around to her front, skimming his thumbs across her nipples and making desire spike through her.

She wanted him so badly, but something inside her head warned her she was moving too fast.

Then a different voice told her to go for it. It felt like an ice-cold glass of water splashed in her face because that second voice sounded like her mother telling her this was exactly where she wanted Caden—wrapped around her finger.

She wrenched away, scrambling to the far side of the couch like she was a teenager caught making out with her boyfriend after prom.

Caden stared at her, his green eyes cloudy with lust.

"We can't," she whispered miserably.

He blinked and seemed to come back to himself, grabbing his shirt from the floor and putting it on again. Lucy wanted to cry out in protest, but she only straightened her clothes and stood up to face him.

"It's not that I don't want to—"

"I get it."

"You don't." How could he when she barely understood it herself? She couldn't be with him because somehow her mother would find a way to use their relationship to her own ends. Lucy couldn't do that to Caden.

Or herself.

"Thank you for a lovely evening," she said, feeling like a fool for sounding so formal. "I'll get to work on plans for the adoption event first thing tomorrow morning."

Better to keep things businesslike between them. As if that was even a possibility given how her heart ached watching the warmth and desire disappear from his eyes.

"Sure," he agreed, and she rushed past him and up the stairs to her bedroom. She moved to the connecting bathroom and washed her face, then brushed her teeth and put on her pajamas like this was a normal night.

Like her stomach wasn't pitching and swirling with regret and unfulfilled need.

She climbed into bed a few minutes later and heard the creak of floorboards as Caden made his way upstairs. Longing filled her as she imagined him in his bed. Did she dare to even consider what he wore to bed? No way.

She was glad he hadn't decided to spend another night in the barn but wondered how she'd ever fall asleep knowing he was across the hall.

Chapter 8

Lucy stumbled down the stairs and made a beeline for the coffeepot in the kitchen, as had become her habit at the ranch. Back in Florida, she didn't allow herself to drink a cup of coffee until ten o'clock, a little ritual she had to monitor her caffeine intake.

But sleep remained elusive in Colorado, and she had no doubt it was because she went on high alert every time Caden was nearby. Annoyingly, even when they weren't in the same room. She could tell where he was in the house just by the humming low in her belly and the prickling of her skin. Her mind remained committed to keeping her distance, but her body definitely hadn't gotten the memo.

She hadn't seen much of him since the night she'd run out of the living room like a big scaredy-cat, afraid of the things he made her feel and the cost for both of them if she acted on those feelings.

As if she had a sixth sense, Maureen called to check on whether Lucy had made any progress on convincing Caden that the marriage was a good idea. Much to her mother's irritation, Lucy hemmed and hawed when giving an answer.

"You should borrow one of my push-up bras," Maureen told her. "That would help attract his attention."

Lucy's face flamed hot, both at the thought that her mother was not so subtly pimping her out and at the memory of Caden's hands on her breasts. She was certain she didn't need a push-up bra for him to notice her.

"That's rude," she whispered to her mother, but Maureen only snorted.

"You have a lot to learn, Lucy-Goose. Garrett and I are having the most wonderful time." Her voice turned forlorn. "But I hate to have to worry about things back in Colorado."

"You wouldn't have to worry if he knew the full truth," Lucy countered.

"Room service is at the door," Maureen said instead of answering the accusation. "I'll call you in a few days."

Lucy tossed the phone to the counter, grabbed a mug from the cabinet and filled it to the brim with steaming coffee.

She was used to eating breakfast alone, with Caden out the door each morning long before sunrise. She'd gone on Pinterest the day after their meal together and filled a board with easy dinner recipes, then headed to the grocery store in Crimson with a mile-long list, resolved to finally learn to cook.

If her hot rancher could whip up a decent meal, surely she could put together some ingredients. And she was determined to spend time in the kitchen without any weird emotional trauma left over from her childhood.

She'd started with spaghetti sauce, which hadn't turned out half-bad. In fact, Caden had said it was the best he'd ever had, but she was pretty sure he was lying. Not that she didn't appreciate the compliment.

That was the routine they'd fallen into for the past couple

of days. He was off to work on the ranch before sunrise, generously making a fresh pot of coffee and timing it to brew at seven, which was exactly when she came downstairs. She didn't bother to ask how he knew her sleep schedule.

She worked on the adoption event in the mornings, then had lunch with Caden and Chad, who came in from whatever they were doing like clockwork every day at noon.

Chad continued to flirt, which never failed to amuse Lucy, but it was the discreet ways Caden found of nudging her or pressing a palm to the small of her back as he passed that kept her senses reeling.

She'd been embarrassed that first afternoon to invite him to have dinner with her, but he'd grinned and nodded, telling her she was the best way of motivating him to get his work done.

He hadn't kissed her again, but she knew he wanted to—and thoughts of his mouth on her body filled her mind at the most inconvenient times. Like this morning when she'd been making a pitch to the local feed-and-supply store to offer discounts on pet supplies to anyone who adopted at tomorrow's event.

After showering and changing into jeans and a sweatshirt, she grabbed the deep purple down jacket she'd bought in town. Although the wind blowing against her face as she crossed to the barn was brisk, the bright sun made the morning feel not as frigid. Or maybe she was getting used to the cold, or beginning to appreciate the concept of "dry" cold, as the women at the bakery referred to Colorado's climate.

She let herself into the barn and headed for Cocoa's pen, greeting many of the other animals along the way. The dog trotted over to the door, and Lucy let her out for a short walk up the driveway. Cocoa didn't like to interact with the other dogs, so Lucy tried to give her extra attention each day. It seemed like her belly was getting rounder each time Lucy visited the barn, and Caden had told her that the puppies were due the following week.

Lucy had never been around newborns of any kind and couldn't wait for the tiny pups to make their arrival into the world.

Cocoa sniffed at the snow, did her business near the edge of a snowbank, then turned for the barn.

"Getting tired, Mama?" Lucy asked, and the dog gazed up at her with those big chocolate eyes that melted Lucy's heart.

She'd taken photos of Cocoa along with the other animals, although Caden had assured her he wouldn't be adopting the dog out until after the puppies were weaned and she'd had some time to adjust to regular dog life.

"Every time I see you with her it makes me wonder if you were a dog trainer in a former life."

Lucy turned from latching Cocoa's pen to find Caden at the far end of the barn.

"Highly doubtful," she told him.

"This place looks great." He gestured to the strands of lights strung down the barn's center walkway and the pink garland and trimmings she'd hung on the door of each pen.

"I recycled my mom's decorations," she said, stating the obvious.

"I don't know why, but all the pink works in the barn."

"I'm glad you like it." She stepped closer. "Are you nervous?"

He stared at her for a long moment and she saw his throat bob as he swallowed. "About what?"

"The adoption fair is tomorrow. Do you worry that your babies won't find homes?"

"They've got a home," he said, his voice a low rumble, "for as long as they need one."

Lucy had never understood the phrase "ovaries clenching"

until this moment. She blinked away tears and willed her heart to stop stuttering. The craziest part was that Caden wasn't even trying to impress her with his sweetness.

She'd certainly had guys turn on the charm—men like Chad who made a game out of seduction. Lucy had fallen for her share of pretty lines when she'd been younger and desperate for someone to call her own. But she liked Caden best when he was simply being himself.

"Do you worry that they *will* find homes?" she asked when she trusted her voice enough to speak normally.

Caden lifted a brow.

"You'll have to let them go," she clarified, "and I know you love them."

He shrugged. "They don't truly belong to me, and if I know they'll be happy, that's enough."

Will you let me go so easily? she wanted to ask but was smart enough to keep her mouth shut. Even though they'd forged a tentative friendship and attraction simmered under the surface every time they were together, she didn't fool herself into thinking it was something lasting. Caden would not only let her go, he'd probably be relieved to escort her to the county line or whatever the equivalent of the ole heave-ho was here in Colorado.

"It's good to hear you say that," she lied, "because I have a feeling a lot of people are going to be bringing home new family members for Christmas this year."

"If they do, it's because of you."

She shook her head. "I only highlighted the work you've done with these animals."

He reached out and pulled her closer, dipping his head to press his mouth to hers. Her body tingled as she breathed him in and wound her arms around his neck. She loved that she could feel his heart beating wildly in his chest.

"It's you," he whispered, his breath tickling her skin. "All of it is you."

She knew it was the two of them together. How could she not believe in the magic of Christmas when everything she'd ever wished for seemed to be coming true?

Lucy had never been one for delayed gratification, but her years of loneliness and disappointment almost felt worth it if they'd led her to Caden.

"I have to run into town," she said, breaking the embrace before she did something stupid like whip off all her clothes in the middle of the barn. "I'm picking up coupons for a free initial vet visit from Dr. Johnson's office."

"Megan donated vet visits?" Caden rubbed a hand over his jaw, the sound of it making Lucy want to moan. Who knew stubble was such a turn-on? "I'll remember to thank her."

Lucy crossed her arms over her chest, thinking of the petite blonde veterinarian she'd met yesterday and how the woman had been so effusive in her praise of Caden's work with unwanted animals in the area. "Thank her from a polite distance."

"Are you jealous?" Caden asked, laughing softly.

"No," she muttered. "You are free to frolic with whomever you choose." She flipped her hair over her shoulder and pretended to adjust the wreath hanging from one of the stall doors. "There's nothing between us."

"I disagree." Caden came up behind her, nuzzling his face into the side of her neck. "There's way too much between us." He nipped at her earlobe and her knees went weak. "Although I wish there was nothing."

She turned her head to glance at him as disappointment coursed through her. "You do?"

"No jackets, no shirts or jeans." He trailed kisses along the side of her neck. "Nothing but skin on skin and you in my bed."

"Oh," she breathed and sagged against him. If she'd been

wondering how Caden felt about her, that pretty much summed it up. Every inch of Lucy's body felt like it was on fire and she stumbled a step when he moved away.

"You're the only woman," he told her, tapping a finger to her nose, "with whom I want to do any frolicking. Remember that, Lucy."

A moment later Chad called to him from the barn's entrance and Caden walked away.

Lucy turned back around, gripping the wooden posts on the door of Cocoa's pen. The dog whined and gave her an almost-sympathetic look.

"I know," Lucy whispered. "Men. Canine or human, they're trouble. Every one."

Despite what he'd told Lucy, nerves skittered through Caden's stomach as the first cars pulled up the driveway and parked in front of the barn the following morning.

"It's like a caravan of adopters," Erin said next to him. Lucy had recruited Erin, David, Katie Crawford from the bakery, her husband, Noah, and a few other women she'd met in town in the past couple of days to volunteer at the event. Some of them had dogs on leashes while others were tasked with introducing the cats and bunnies to prospective families. "I can't believe she put all of this together in a week."

"It's amazing," he agreed.

Erin nudged him. "You mean *she's* amazing."

He glanced down at the grinning schoolteacher. "Yeah," he admitted, "that's what I mean." There was no use denying it. He was falling for Lucy. After their interlude in the barn yesterday, he'd seriously contemplated lifting the self-imposed ban he had on kissing her in the house.

He'd told himself that if he kept things platonic when they were together anywhere near a bed, that would keep both of them safer. But Caden didn't want to be safe with Lucy. He wanted to claim her and make her his, and he was pretty certain his heart had leaped eons ahead of his body on that count.

She'd managed to find her way past all the walls and defenses he'd erected. He wasn't sure how long he could continue to resist the attraction that drew him to her like a magnet against steel.

Then his phone rang, his dad calling from New York City. Garrett sounded like a lovestruck schoolboy as he'd told Caden about the trip. Caden wanted his dad to be happy, but he still didn't believe that was possible with Maureen. The fallout of another blow so soon after he'd started to recover from Tyson's death could be devastating for Garrett.

As much as Caden wanted Lucy, his needs were nothing compared to protecting his father. He owed everything to Garrett. How could he put that aside because of his own desires?

"You look about as welcoming as a nest of wasps."

Lucy's voice broke into his thoughts and he realized she'd taken Erin's place next to him. "I know they're your babies," she said, "but it's time to find them good homes. Put a smile on that handsome face, cowboy, and dust off your charm. It's showtime."

He watched her walk forward and greet the families emerging from cars. She was a natural with people, but he felt the old fear about being judged a punk kid who'd only cause trouble rise to the surface. What if he scared people off or they didn't appreciate the animals he'd rescued?

His gaze snagged on a couple climbing out of a minivan at the end of the row of cars. The woman, who looked to be in her midthirties, opened the back door and took the hand of a small girl in a pair of rainbow-patterned leggings, a fur-lined puffy pink coat and long braids. The girl seemed reluctant to move forward, eyeing the barn like it was some kind of medieval torture chamber.

Something shifted in Caden's chest, and all his nerves disappeared as he remembered the old Border collie mix that had come to greet him the first time he'd visited the ranch.

The ancient ranch dog had ambled up to him, sniffed at his skinned knee, then nudged his hand with a wet nose until Caden bent to pet him. "If Otis likes you, you're in," Tyson had said, already having decided that Caden was meant to be his brother.

Having never been "in" before, Caden didn't realize what that meant, but the dog's unequivocal acceptance had actually allowed him to believe he might be worth choosing.

"Mind if I borrow this one?" he asked David, grabbing the leash of the rescue dog David was holding instead of waiting for an answer. The pale yellow Lab at the end of it walked at his side as he approached the small family.

"Welcome," he called. The girl moved behind her mother's legs and the dad gave him a tight smile.

"Great setup you've got here," the man said.

"Y'all looking to add a furry friend to your household?"

The couple exchanged a look. "I'd like a dog," the man said after a moment. "I've always had one, but my wife isn't so sure."

"I got bitten when I was a child," the woman said tightly. "Dogs aren't my thing, and Macy is afraid of them."

"Because you've taught her to be," the man said under his breath.

The woman's shoulders stiffened and the little girl gripped her leg. "I don't know why I let you talk me into this."

"Because, Jen, a kid needs a dog," the man insisted.

"Does she look like she wants a dog?" Jen shot back.

"Dogs aren't for everyone," Caden agreed easily. "But sometimes all it takes is the right animal for the right family."

He bent and gave the Lab next to him a gentle head scratch. "Sage here is a great example. She's hoping to find a good home today, but she's a special dog."

"I really don't want a big dog," the woman offered.

"I do," her husband shot back.

"Why is she special?" the girl asked, peeking around her mother's legs.

"Well, now," Caden said conversationally, "she wasn't exactly taken care of properly at her last home. Sage likes to get in water, but her owner didn't dry out her ears and she got a real bad infection in them. She can't hear anymore."

"That's sad," the woman murmured, her attention on the Lab.

Caden lowered himself to kneel next to the dog. "She doesn't mind much, but she'll need a fenced-in yard and to be on a leash when she's outside so she doesn't get lost."

"We've got a fenced-in yard," Macy offered.

"Do you, now?" Caden rubbed the dog's side and Sage immediately flopped onto her back to expose her belly. "Sage also likes to be petted. Some dogs have a lot of energy, but not her. She's only three, but sometimes I call her the breathing footstool. She likes a slow walk around the block or a short hike, but mainly she wants to be loved."

"I love her," the little girl whispered and crouched down to pet the dog.

"Macy," her mother said in an exasperated tone, "this is the first dog you've seen. I haven't even agreed to adopting one."

As if sensing the trio needed to be won over, Sage rolled to her feet. She licked the little girl's face, then moved to the woman, plopping down on her butt and gazing up with a look of pure canine adoration.

"She likes you," the husband said.

Jen looked unconvinced but tentatively lowered a hand to give the dog an awkward head pat.

"She's been certified as a therapy dog," Caden told them. "Her temperament is perfect for kids."

Sage lowered her front paws and basically draped herself across the woman's feet. "She's pretty sweet," Jen murmured.

"Can we adopt her, Mommy?" Macy asked.

Jen shared a look with her husband. "I don't know…" She broke off as the dog let out a loud fart.

"She smells like Daddy," Macy shouted, earning a laugh from her mother and an eye roll from her dad.

"Of course," Caden said, "there are other dogs available. And we have cats and bunnies if a dog isn't right for your family."

"What do you think, honey?" the man asked.

The woman shrugged. "She smells like you. If that isn't a sign…"

Macy gave a loud whoop of delight. Jen stared at Caden. "I can't believe we've been here less than five minutes and now I'm adopting a dog. I don't know anything about dogs."

"I know plenty," her husband assured her.

The woman's eyes widened. "What happens when you're at work?" she asked her husband.

"She's well behaved, but I can recommend a great dog trainer if you want some extra help with her," Caden said, handing the leash to Macy. "It's important that you all feel comfortable handling her. Especially because she's deaf."

"I'd like that," Jen said, nodding.

"Sage is a very lucky dog," Lucy said from behind Caden. "If you all would just head inside, our volunteers can help you get checked out and start you off with a bag of supplies and Sage's records."

The husband clapped Caden on the shoulder as he walked by. "Thanks, man. I never thought she'd agree to this."

"Give me a call if there are any issues or you need help during the transition. We'll make sure everything goes smoothly." The man gestured to his wife and daughter. "It already has."

Caden had been so focused on Sage meeting the small family, he hadn't realized the driveway was quickly filling with more cars.

"You did it," he said, pulling Lucy in for a hug and dropping a kiss on the top of her head.

She grinned up at him. "I watched that whole exchange. How did you know Sage was the right dog for that family?"

"The woman looked terrified and her husband was like a kid on Christmas morning. I could tell he'd want a bigger dog, and Sage is about as gentle as they come. She's perfect for a mom without much experience, but Labs still have the 'cool' factor to make the man happy."

"You have a pretty awesome 'cool' factor going on yourself," she said but ducked away when he would have lowered his mouth to hers. "We're on the job, cowboy. Back to work. You've got a barn full of animals to match."

The rest of the day flew by in a blur. Caden knew that a big part of the reason the event was so successful was Lucy's marketing efforts. Her photos of the animals were intimate and personal, the total opposite of normal shelter mug shots. She'd made individual identification cards for each animal, highlighting what made them special.

She'd been at the ranch only a week but had managed to capture the spirit of what he wanted to accomplish through rescuing the unwanted pets and finding them new homes.

Of course, Caden was also scared as hell that she'd captured his heart, something he hadn't thought possible for himself.

But every moment he spent with her was a revelation, tiny scraps of his defenses peeling away with each smile she gave him.

By the end of the day, the only animals left were the ones that belonged to him—a couple of barn cats, Cocoa and Fritzi, the therapy rabbit, plus her bonded mate, Julius. In fact, he had a waiting list of prospective adopters looking for animals. He'd referred several families to the local humane society, but a few insisted that he be the one to match them with the right rescue animal.

It was a daunting task, but Caden had been getting calls about unwanted animals that needed to be rehabilitated and rehomed on almost a weekly basis. He didn't have room for all of them, but if he could develop a pipeline of families waiting to adopt, that would certainly help him continue to save more animals.

As the last of the volunteers left at the end of the day, he got ready to do his evening chores. He said his goodbyes, weirdly touched at how invested the people of Crimson were in his little rescue operation. He knew this community was special, although he'd kept himself at arm's length from most people after the fiasco of falling for his brother's girlfriend.

"If you feel like coming into town later," David told him, shaking his hand, "we'll be at Elevation. There's a cold beer and a huge plate of wings with your name on them."

"Thanks," Caden said, then stopped himself from refusing the invitation outright. It might be nice to take Lucy out on a real date, and hanging out with friends was as good a place as any to start. "Maybe we'll see you later."

Erin smiled. "I knew you liked her," she said quietly.

He rolled his eyes. "I'll admit it. You were right. Does that make you happy?"

"Ecstatic," she said with a laugh.

"You'll never hear the end of it," David warned him, then took Erin's hand. "Better bring earplugs to town tonight."

The truth was, Caden didn't even mind giving Erin credit for realizing what he'd been too stubborn to admit from the moment he met Lucy. She was amazing.

He glanced around and saw her in deep conversation with Katie Crawford. He left the barn and headed toward the pasture that bordered the forest to check on the herd. The sooner he finished, the sooner he could get back to Lucy.

The sun sank behind the snowcapped peak of Crimson Mountain as he drove his truck across the property. The cattle were lowing as he approached the field where they grazed on the hay Chad had put out for them. He climbed out of the truck and scratched one of the big cows between her ears, his chest tightening at the thought of the empty barn.

Lucy had been right when she'd said he loved each of the animals he rescued, even though he knew he was only a stop on their journey to a happily-ever-after.

But when the last cat had been boxed up in a carrier and put into the car with its new owner, Caden realized his life would be a little emptier until a new crop of animals came into his care.

He'd just turned back for the barn when Lucy came running across the field, her arms waving frantically.

He headed toward her, his heart stammering when she tripped and went down on all fours in the snow. The snow was packed down in some places but not others, and she could easily posthole through and twist an ankle.

"Stop," he called when she'd gotten up and begun running again.

"It's Cocoa," she shouted in response. She was close enough to him now that he could see the panic in her dark eyes. "Something's wrong. You have to help her."

He reached her, cupping her cold, tearstained cheeks in his gloved hands.

"Something's wrong, Caden. I think the babies are coming and she can't handle it. She has to be okay. The babies have to be okay."

"Shh, honey," Caden soothed as he took her hand and headed for the house. "I'll make sure she's fine." It was a promise he prayed he'd be able to keep.

Chapter 9

"Grab towels from the closet in the hallway upstairs, plus scissors from the first-aid kit, rubbing alcohol and dental floss in case I need to tie off any of the umbilical cords." Caden didn't turn around as he issued the order, all of his attention focused on the pregnant dog.

They'd moved Cocoa into the laundry room of the main house the night before, when Caden had finished the whelping box he'd built for her.

Although Caden assured her it was a normal part of the process, it had broken Lucy's heart that the animal didn't seem to know how to settle on the bed of blankets Lucy had given her. It was as if Cocoa didn't trust something so soft. Instead, she'd curled up next to the makeshift bed on the hardwood floor, letting out a heavy sigh.

When Lucy had come in the house after the volunteers went home, Cocoa finally climbed into the whelping box, pawing at the blankets and tearing apart the sheets of newspaper as if she was making a true nest.

Lucy had let the dog out back for a potty break, then scooped a bowl of kibble and put it on the floor next to the bed. She'd gone upstairs for a shower, but when she'd returned to check on Cocoa, she realized something wasn't right.

The dog was lying on her side on top of the newspaper, her chest rising and falling in shallow pants like she was having trouble getting air. She moaned softly when Lucy touched her but hadn't moved despite Lucy's gentle coaxing.

Then Lucy had noticed a black, tarry discharge on the blankets, and she'd thrown on boots and rushed out to find Caden.

Worry making her movements jerky, she gathered the supplies and returned to the laundry room.

"She's in labor," Caden said, running a gentle hand over Cocoa's belly.

"And it's all going like it should?" Lucy asked, dropping to her knees next to him just outside the whelping box.

"Maybe," he answered, but she could tell from his tone that there were complications.

"What is it?"

He shook his head. "It seems like the first pup should have come out by now. You can see the contractions rolling across her belly, and she's pushing, but this dark-green-and-black discharge isn't normal."

"So what do we do now?"

"We wait."

"Shouldn't we call Dr. Johnson or—"

"Megan's office is an hour's drive from the ranch, and she lives another twenty toward Aspen. That's when the roads are dry. By the time she gets out here, we won't need her. We have to believe Cocoa can do this on her own."

Lucy wasn't a big fan of having faith in anything, but now she smoothed a hand over the dog's head and whispered,

"You've got this, girl. We believe in you. You're so tough, and these puppies can't wait to meet their mama."

It wasn't until Caden pulled her against his side that she realized tears were dripping down her face as she spoke. She turned her head in to his shoulder and cried. He didn't try to give her false hope or tell her to pull it together. But the way he held her was far more comforting that she ever could have imagined.

"Take a look," he whispered after a minute.

Lucy sniffed and wiped at her cheeks, turning to the dog. She lifted one of her back legs as her vulva expanded and a dark sac appeared under her tail.

"It's happening," she said.

"Yeah," he agreed. "Let's give her a little space." They moved away slightly and watched as Cocoa lifted her head and began to lick at the puppy that had just been born. She gently broke the thin membrane that surrounded the pup with her teeth and chewed through the umbilical cord.

"I've never seen anything like this," Lucy whispered as the dog roughly licked at the puppy's face until it began to wriggle and cry. She nudged it with her nose and adjusted its position so that the baby could latch on and begin suckling.

The puppy continued to whimper and whine, much like any newborn crying after it came into the world. Cocoa licked the pup a few more times, as if comforting the tiny creature, then laid her head to rest on the blanket.

"Usually the puppies are born within around thirty minutes of each other," Caden explained, "but if Cocoa needs more rest between births, it could take longer."

Lucy lost track of time as they watched the dog and her growing brood of puppies. It could have been minutes or hours or days, but she couldn't take her eyes off the miracle taking place before them.

Between each puppy's arrival, Cocoa rested, then would begin to shift and stand, pacing the small space inside the whelping box as her labor intensified. During these times, Caden and Lucy put the pups in a laundry basket lined with blankets that had a heating pad underneath so Cocoa wouldn't inadvertently hurt them.

Finally there were six tiny, wet, squirming puppies, all latched onto their mother.

"She did it," Lucy murmured, a fresh round of tears flooding her eyes.

"She's not done yet," Caden said, his voice low and serious.

Cocoa had seemed almost relaxed as the first six puppies had been born, but now she moaned and strained as if she was in distress.

Lucy sucked in a breath. "She's in pain. Are there more? You have to do something."

A muscle ticked in Caden's jaw as he shifted forward to gently massage the dog's distended belly. He whispered soothing words to her and Lucy wondered whether she or Cocoa took more comfort in his strong, steady presence.

Finally another sac emerged partway from the birth canal, and it was clear the last pup was coming out feetfirst. Cocoa didn't seem to have the strength to push it out, so Caden carefully pulled the pup from her body. This one was the smallest of the litter and the only one that didn't move.

"What's wrong?" Lucy asked even though she already feared the answer she'd receive.

Cocoa gave the puppy a few licks, then turned her attention back to the others crowding around her belly. Caden ripped the membrane away from the pup's nose and mouth and used a towel to vigorously rub its body. After a minute, his movements stopped.

"Stillborn," he whispered, gently lifting the pup into his hands.

Lucy felt a sob rise up in her throat as she reached out a finger to touch the unmoving animal. "Not after all that."

Caden wrapped the pup in a towel and set it to the side. "Its eyes and ears aren't developed, so I'd guess the puppy has been dead for a while. She's got six to take care of now," he said quietly. "If she can..."

Cocoa had closed her eyes and her breaths were once again coming in shallow pants.

"But they're all out." Lucy could hear the panic in her own voice. "She's done."

"Give her some time," Caden urged. "Her body went through a lot."

"What if she doesn't have time?" Lucy demanded, squeezing her hands into tight fists. "The puppies need their mama. Can't we do something to help her?"

Caden wrapped his big hand around both of hers. "She's going into the third stage of labor. Her uterus will contract and she'll expel any remaining placenta, blood and fluid."

The puppies continued to nurse. "They're eating," Lucy whispered. "That's a good sign, right?"

"They're getting colostrum now." Caden's voice was calm but she could hear the worry threading through it. "Her milk should come in within a day or two."

"And if it doesn't?"

He took her hand and squeezed her fingers. "We'll take care of them."

Lucy swallowed around the lump of emotion in her throat. They'd already lost one puppy. She couldn't stand to think of the others not surviving. Even more, she needed Cocoa to be okay. There was something about the wayward dog's instinct for survival and the fact that she'd bonded with Lucy that made Lucy feel as if Cocoa belonged to her. She hadn't realized how badly she wanted something of her own until she was close to losing it.

Minutes passed, but finally Cocoa raised her head. Her body released a spurt of fluid and she shifted and turned, her pink tongue flicking out to lick the little pups once again.

"She's got it," Caden whispered.

"Keep going, Mama," Lucy told the dog in her gentlest tone. Cocoa blinked and her big chocolate gaze caught on Lucy's for a moment.

"You're doing great." Lucy spoke as though the dog could understand her, which was silly. Cocoa nudged the pups with her nose. The sounds of slurping and whimpering followed as the dogs piled on top of each other at her stomach, and Lucy finally breathed a sigh of relief.

"She needs space now." Caden picked up the towel with the stillborn puppy and stood.

"We have to bury this one." Lucy eyed the tiny bundle.

"That's going to be a challenge with the ground frozen." He met Lucy's gaze and nodded. "We'll figure it out tomorrow. I promise."

Lucy was quickly discovering that she liked being able to have faith in someone. She had no doubt that Caden's word was good.

"Thank you for being so calm during all of that. I'm sure you're used to stuff being born."

"Stuff," he repeated with a smile, setting the towel on the counter next to the washing machine.

"Animals," she clarified with an eye roll. "Baby cows and horses."

"Calves and foals," he corrected as they washed their hands.

"I know that," she said, pressing her fingers to her chest. "I can't think right now. I just..." To her embarrassment, a tremor snaked through her body and tears stung the back of her eyes. She turned away as her shoulders started to shake.

"It's okay, sweetheart," Caden murmured and pulled her close. She buried her face in his shirt, trying to regain control of herself. But with the adrenaline that had been buzzing through her now wearing off, all of her fear over Cocoa and her puppies set off an avalanche of emotions.

Caden scooped her into his arms and carried her through the house and up the stairs. She concentrated on pulling in air, trying desperately to make her heart beat a normal rhythm.

But when she opened her eyes, her heart stuttered for a different reason entirely. "This is your bedroom."

He pulled down the covers and set her on his big bed, one side of his mouth quirking. "I don't think you should be alone right now. This doesn't mean I'm expecting—"

"I don't want to be alone," she interrupted, and to hell with both of their expectations. But when she reached for him, he backed away a step.

"Give me five minutes," he instructed, lifting his hands, palms out. "Between the adoption event, the cattle and a litter of puppies, I stink like a barn. I need a shower and then—" he paused, his eyes going dark "—I'll be back."

She bit down on her bottom lip as he walked away, tugging his shirt over his head as he moved. A minute later she heard the water in the hall bathroom turn on, and her stomach dipped and whirled as it had every day for the past week as she listened to him shower and imagined...

Lucy had a vivid imagination.

She needed a shower as much as he did, but she kicked off her shoes then brought her knees to her chest and waited. For all of about thirty seconds. Then she got up and walked toward the bathroom, steam pouring out into the hallway as she let herself in. She could barely make out Caden's silhouette behind the frosted glass of the walk-in shower but stepped forward, anyway.

The shower door opened slightly and Caden's face appeared, droplets of water clinging to his skin. "You don't take direction well, do you?" he asked, his voice rumbly but laced with humor.

She shook her head. "I *really* don't want to be alone right now." She continued moving toward him, pushing open the door and walking into the shower. Her eyes drifted shut as the heat and scent of his shampoo surrounded her. "Don't mind me," she whispered. "You won't even know I'm here."

He gave a low chuckle and smoothed her wet hair away from her face. "Did you think about getting undressed first?"

"I'm done thinking for the day," she answered, earning another soft laugh.

"Works for me," he said, and she felt his fingers begin to undo the buttons of her soaking wet blouse. She dropped her head and watched his hands, big against the tiny buttons. The shirt clung to her body and she sucked in a breath when he peeled it off her shoulders.

He bent and unfastened her jeans, pushing them down over her hips and lower on her legs. She stepped out of them and felt a rush of cool air as he deposited both garments on the bathroom floor. He slid his palms up her calves, his calloused fingertips tickling the backs of her knees.

She felt him press an openmouthed kiss to her inner thigh. Heat shot through her body at the intimate caress. He straightened and cupped her cheeks in his hands.

"Look at me, Lucy," he commanded, and she opened her eyes. "This doesn't have to go anywhere right now."

"You're naked," she told him.

"I'm aware." He kissed the tip of her nose. "But you've had

a hell of a day. I get that you don't want to be alone, but I also understand that doesn't mean—"

"It does mean something," she argued and leaned in to lick the base of his throat.

His groan heated all the cold places inside her as much as the hot water. He wrapped his arms around her and undid her bra with one deft movement. She let the straps fall down her arms and the bra to drop the floor, then hooked her thumbs in the waistband of her panties and pushed them over her hips.

"That's better," she whispered with a saucy smile.

"Much," he agreed and lifted his hands to cup her breasts. She whimpered when his thumbs grazed over her nipples. He bent his head to cover one tight peak, and she might have melted to a puddle on the shower floor if he hadn't been holding an arm around her waist.

As his attention switched to the other breast, Lucy threaded her fingers through his wet hair. Then he moved lower, kneeling in front of her, and sparks lit up her body like she was a firework on the Fourth of July.

Her back pressed to the cool tile as his mouth worked its magic. And when pleasure exploded through her, she cried out his name. She felt her knees start to give way again as the last bits of pleasure pulsed through her.

"Stay with me," Caden said, flattening his open hand on her belly as if to hold her up while he turned off the water.

Oh, she was with him. Too far gone to let go now.

He stepped out of the shower, grabbed a towel and wrapped it around her, not bothering to cover himself, much to Lucy's delight. His body was perfection from head to toe and everywhere in between. He scooped her into his arms, edging around the doorway so she didn't bump her head.

She scraped her fingers gently along his chest, then touched one flat nipple with the tip of her tongue. He sucked in a breath and stumbled a step.

"I'm going to end up taking you in the hall if you do that," he said, his voice hoarse.

"We should start with the bed," she answered, and a moment later they were in his bedroom again. He set her on her feet, the backs of her legs bumping the mattress.

"You're so damn beautiful," he whispered, and she knew the words should have thrilled her. What woman didn't want to receive a compliment from a handsome man who'd just given her the greatest orgasm of her life?

But a part of Lucy wanted to believe Caden saw her for more than just what she looked like. Her beauty was genetic, inherited from a mother who'd wielded her looks like a weapon. Even though Lucy knew she wasn't cut from that same cloth, she hated being judged on her looks alone.

As if reading her mind, Caden pressed a hand to her chest where her heart beat against his palm. "In here," he whispered. "Your spirit is beautiful, Lucy. You have a huge heart, and you're smart and talented. There's so much more to you than you even know."

Do you really think so?

She wanted to ask the question out loud, but that would make her needy and pathetic. And right now she didn't feel either of those things. She felt strong and cherished and truly seen by this man.

It was everything.

She laced her fingers with his and moved onto the bed, Caden following until his body covered hers. He kissed her until she was practically senseless, her body humming with need. "I want you," she whispered. "Now."

He reached to the nightstand, pulled out a condom packet, and tugged it open with his teeth.

"Let me," she told him, and rolled the condom down his length. He entered her in one thrust, and Lucy had never felt so complete as she did with Caden filling her.

"So good," he whispered. "You feel so good."

"It's not me," she answered, meeting his gaze. "It's us."

His eyes went dark at her words, and when he kissed her it was like a promise between them. They moved together as if they'd known each other for ages. Brilliant pressure built in her body as Caden both took her out of herself and kept her tethered to reality with the sweet words he whispered against her skin.

It wasn't long before Lucy broke apart again, an explosion of light and color surging through her body. A moment later she felt Caden tremble, and he let out a low groan and dropped his head into the crook of her neck.

He lifted his head a moment later and gave her a goofy half smile. "I like everything about you, Lucy. Especially having you come apart in my arms."

"I like you, too," she whispered and pretended her mind didn't want to substitute a different *l* word entirely to describe her feelings for this man. She'd settle for *like*. After all, settling was something she did quite well.

Caden watched the light turn from gray to pink as he held Lucy in his arms. Her breathing was slow and rhythmic, her body warm and pliant tucked into his.

He'd always been an early riser, convenient when living on a ranch, but this morning he wished he could stay in bed all day. He figured maybe then he could gain some kind of control around this woman. Or not, if last night was any indication.

After that first time, they'd dressed and gone back downstairs to check on Cocoa and her puppies. The dog and the six little pups already seemed bigger. Caden had attached a different-colored piece of rickrack around each of their necks to tell them apart, and it was funny to already see distinct personalities emerging.

He knew it still bothered Lucy that Cocoa had lost one of the puppies, but Caden realized how lucky they were that the others were healthy. He and Lucy had shared a simple meal of sandwiches and salads as they watched the animals. He'd worried that the intimacy that had rocked his world might have comprised their tentative friendship, but instead he felt even more connected to Lucy.

When Cocoa and the pups were settled again, Lucy had taken his hand and led him back upstairs. They'd undressed each other slowly, hands and mouths exploring. He wanted to know every part of her, and for the first time he was willing to share pieces of himself he'd kept hidden.

Even when she'd run a hand over the tiny scars below his shoulder blade, he hadn't tensed.

"They look like..." she'd whispered, her voice trailing off. He understood from her tone that she'd realized exactly what had made the marks.

"Cigarette burns." He'd supplied the words she couldn't seem to form. It was the first time he'd named the scars to anyone other than Tyson. "Such a cliché, but my foster dad had a thing for that movie *The Breakfast Club*. There's a scene where one of the kids in detention talks about his father putting out a cigar on his body as punishment for a spilled can of paint. It was twisted, but he wanted to recreate—"

"Stop." Lucy had placed her hands over his back like she could erase the truth of what had happened to Caden after his mom died and he got sucked into the foster-care system.

"Don't be sad for me." He'd flipped her onto her back and wiped away the tears that slipped from the corners of her eyes. "Tyson lost his mind when he first saw the scars. I think he went home to Garrett that night and made the case for me coming to live on Sharpe Ranch."

He smiled, trying to take the edge off the horror of what he'd shared with her. Lucy's mom might be a gold digger, but from what he could tell she hadn't exposed her daughter to anything like what he'd experienced.

Lucy thought she understood him, but she had no idea how broken Caden was on the inside. "In some ways that bastard did me a favor. It got me out of there and gave me Garrett and Tyson."

Her mouth pressed into a thin line. "It never should have come to that. You were a kid."

"Bad things happen," he said simply, the only truth that had remained indisputable for his entire life.

"Good things can happen, too," she countered. "You deserve the good things, Caden."

He sucked in a breath as his heart leapt. The feeling was a strange mix of hope and caution because he'd found happiness to be all too fleeting. Besides, he wasn't sure he agreed with that statement, but he didn't bother to argue. Not when Lucy was staring at him like she could see all the way into his soul.

He dropped a kiss on her shoulder now, but she didn't stir. Her breathing changed to a soft snore that made him smile. It was difficult to believe how badly he'd misjudged her. Lucy was a light in the darkness of his lonely life. He could far too easily come to depend on her radiant brightness.

He climbed out of bed, grabbing his clothes and taking them downstairs to dress so he wouldn't disturb her. He couldn't help but think that if he'd gotten her personality and intentions so wrong, maybe he needed to give Maureen a chance.

Caden had thought he'd found love with Becca, until he'd realized she was only using him to hurt Tyson. Although it was too soon to put a name on what he felt for Lucy, his heart told him this was the real deal.

He couldn't remember a time when he'd felt so damn happy. Even more than the happiness—not to mention the afterglow from the best sex of his life—there was a peace inside him. It was as if all the jumbled parts of himself that had been clamoring around inside for years had finally found a home. He fit together now because Lucy was the piece he'd been missing.

Was it possible that Maureen did that for Garrett? They'd all lived in the halcyon shadow of Tyson's mother for so many years, it was difficult to believe Garrett could find happiness with another woman, especially someone like Maureen Renner.

But no one deserved happiness more than Garrett. If he had it with Lucy's mother, maybe Caden needed to have a little faith in his father's judgment.

Chapter 10

After finishing his chores the next morning, Caden drove into Crimson. He knew Lucy would want to spend the day watching over Cocoa, so he planned to pick up breakfast, lunch and something easy to make for dinner.

To his surprise, he was greeted with hugs and a chorus of excited congratulations about the weekend's adoption event from the ladies behind the counter at Life Is Sweet.

One of the baristas took great pride in showing him photos on her phone of the cat she'd taken home on Saturday and immediately dressed in a superhero costume.

"I named him Wayne," she confided with a goofy grin. "He's the best."

"He looks good in a cape," Caden agreed, not sure what else to say.

The young woman scurried back around the counter to take an order as Katie and Noah Crawford walked out from the back of the store along with their toddler daughter, Ryan. Noah wore his olive green forest-service uniform. He'd been managing the local ranger district since he moved back to town a couple of years ago.

Katie wore a striped apron with Ask about My Sticky Buns embroidered across the front. He'd known both of them since middle school and would never have expected the soft-spoken baker to make a match with Noah, who before Katie had quite the reputation as a ladies' man. But contentment was written across both their faces and a little pang of envy shot through him at the sight of it.

"You're toast," Noah told him. "Everyone in town has seen your soft underbelly now. There's no going back to scowling, scary rancher man."

"I don't have a soft underbelly," Caden argued. "And I wasn't trying to scare anyone." That wasn't exactly true. He liked keeping people at a distance. It worked for him. At least, until Lucy had blown his defensive walls to smithereens.

Katie laughed. "You didn't have to try." The little girl perched on her hip stretched out her arms and dived toward Caden.

"Ryan," Katie cried. "Where do you think you're going?"

He scooped up the girl, with her riot of soft blond curls and a smudge of blueberry on her cheek. She poked at his Stetson. "Hat," she told him.

"My hat," he agreed and, balancing her in one arm, took the hat off his head and perched it on hers. She giggled as it covered her eyes.

"Ryan's hat," she shouted.

Noah glanced behind him to the coffee bar. "Now you're good with kids, too. Dude, you're going to be swarmed by single women."

Caden followed Noah's gaze and saw the three women behind the counter staring at him with looks that ranged from mildly interested to positively predatory. Uh-oh.

"I'm not on the market," he said quickly, placing the hat back on his head and handing Ryan back to Katie.

"Perhaps because you're already off the market?" Katie asked, one brow raised.

"I don't know... I mean, I'm not..." Caden blew out a breath. "I just want a bag of muffins," he said helplessly.

"I like Lucy," Katie said, leaning forward. "She's a good fit for Crimson."

"I'm not sure about that," Caden said. "She's used to living in Florida. Colorado winters might not be her thing."

Katie shook her head. "I mean she's a good fit for the community. For you."

He felt his mouth drop open and quickly snapped it shut. "She's too good for me," he muttered.

Noah dropped a smacking kiss on the top of his wife's head. "Those are the best kind," he offered.

"I'll get the muffins," Katie said with a laugh.

"You know," Noah said quietly, leaning in closer, "guys finding a woman better than we deserve is sort of a thing around here."

"I get that," Caden agreed, thinking of the men he knew and the women who loved them. "But there's not being good enough and there's being emotional napalm."

"Which are you?"

"Everyone knows what happened between Tyson and me," Caden said through his teeth, hating to discuss the rift with his brother but at the same time needing someone to understand. "I made some really stupid choices. People got hurt. My brother died."

Noah took a step back. "You can't blame yourself for that. I was on duty out at Cherokee Ridge when the call came in from his buddies. The search-and-rescue captain told me it was a freak accident."

Caden's heart, which had been so full after last night, went cold at the reminder of the circumstances of Tyson's death. "If I'd been there—"

"Nothing would have changed," Noah interrupted. "You couldn't have saved him."

"I could have tried." Caden met Noah's blue gaze, daring the other man to argue.

Noah only inclined his head. "Guilt and I are old friends," he said quietly. "I can tell you she's not worth the trouble."

"Here you go," Katie said, approaching with a pink bag that had the bakery's logo on the front. "I threw in a chocolate croissant because that's what Lucy always orders."

"Thanks," Caden told her, reaching for his wallet.

Katie held up her hands. "No charge today. We had several new customers come in yesterday from the adoption event. Think of the muffins as a referral fee."

Caden wanted to argue. He didn't like to be indebted to anyone, but Noah was staring at him like he wasn't done with the conversation about Tyson.

Caden was done.

He leaned in and gave Katie and Ryan a quick hug. "Thanks again," he said and walked out of the bakery.

He was halfway down the street when a man called his name. He thought about ignoring the greeting. This morning had already been too much.

But he turned and held out a hand when Derek Lawson approached. "Morning, Derek. How are things?"

Derek ran a hand through his thinning hair, looking more agitated than Caden had ever seen him. "You tell me, Sharpe. I got a call from some chick I'd never met playing twenty questions about the way I keep your dad's books. What the hell is that about?"

Caden felt a muscle tick in his jaw but forced a casual shrug.

He took a calming breath and glanced down the street toward the park that spread across an entire city block in the middle of town. There was an enormous Christmas tree decorated with handmade ornaments from kids at the elementary school and a big star on top.

A few feet from the tree was an ice-skating rink, several families were already twirling on the ice. Maybe he'd bring Lucy into town for an afternoon of holiday fun. He'd never been much for the town festivities. Never had a reason before now.

"The daughter of my dad's fiancée," he explained, keeping his voice steady.

"The one you think is after your dad's money?" Derek asked, his eyes narrowing.

"He's happy," Caden answered noncommittally. When Garrett first brought Maureen home, Caden had confessed his fear over her intentions to Derek. In specifically unflattering terms. Terms that would light up Lucy's temper like a powder keg if she ever knew. Although still not a fan of Maureen, he now regretted opening his big mouth.

"Lucy is staying at the ranch while Garrett and her mom are in New York City. She has a background in finance and he asked her to take a look at things just to give her something to do." The truth was, Caden had forgotten that his dad had given Lucy access to the business accounts. She'd done so much last week for the adoption event, he hadn't realized she was also reviewing the books.

"I didn't like the way she was talking to me," Derek told him, falling into step with him as they neared the truck. "Seemed like just as much trouble as her mom."

"Lucy's not—"

Derek stepped closer, lowered his voice. "Did you ever consider that this was the plan all along? I mean, what sort of financial background are we talking about?"

"I don't really know," Caden admitted.

"Exactly." Derek shot a finger in the air like Caden had just proven some kind of important point. "Could be this Lucy chick is casing the books for her mom to see how much the old man's truly got in the accounts. I wouldn't be surprised if she tried to act like things aren't right."

He crossed his thin arms over his chest. Derek had been a friend of Tyson's from high school. His family owned the hardware store in town and he'd gotten an accounting degree, then come back to run the business when his father had a stroke.

He'd offered to help with the Sharpe Ranch finances in the aftermath of Tyson's accident. "Wouldn't be surprised if she tried to throw me under the bus. That'd be convenient, right? She could make up issues with what I've been doing so that they can get their hands on the money."

If Derek had made his accusation against Lucy a week ago, Caden would have jumped all over it. But things had changed. He'd changed...because of her.

Yet a sliver of doubt snaked through his veins. He'd been a fool for a woman before with grave consequences. Could Lucy actually be orchestrating a con while he played right into her deception?

"She has no reason to—"

"Come on, man," Derek urged. "Don't let some woman lead you around by your junk. How many times has the mom been married?"

Caden swallowed. "This would be number four."

"Your dad hasn't been himself since Tyson died. We both know that. It could have been different if you'd been on the trip with him, but you weren't. Now we both need to look out for Garrett's best interests. It's what Tyson would have wanted."

Derek's careless words were like a punch to the gut. As much as Caden appreciated Noah Crawford's claim that there wasn't anything that could have been done differently to save Tyson, everyone knew it wasn't true. Derek had just proved it. Caden also knew that he had to protect his father against any more pain.

His feelings for Lucy had made him lose sight of his purpose for a moment, but he had to refocus on what was important in his life.

Unfortunately, his own happiness didn't count for crap.

"I appreciate everything you've done to help," he said, placing a hand on Derek's shoulder and squeezing. "Dad and I both do. I'll make sure Lucy doesn't overstep her bounds. You've got nothing to worry about."

"I hope not, man." Derek nodded. "I've got my hands full already with the store. I'm happy to help with the ranch's accounting. Anything for Tyson. But not if it means some stranger busting my—"

"I'll handle it," Caden told him. He tightened his grip on the bakery bag, placing it on the floor on the truck's back seat. Acid burned in his gut and a stale metallic taste filled his mouth. The thought of taking a bite of one of Katie's sweet baked goods made his stomach lurch. Had he really been a fool for…? Not love. It couldn't be love that he felt for Lucy.

He ignored the rest of the errands he'd planned and headed back to the ranch. The snow was creamy white under the gentle sun of early morning. He drummed his fingers on the steering wheel and concentrated on pulling air in and out of his lungs.

He didn't want to give any credence to the insinuations Derek made toward Lucy and her mother. He wanted to go back to last night and the sweetness of holding Lucy in his arms.

She was in the mudroom, cross-legged on the floor in a pair

of black yoga pants and a stretchy top, when he walked in. She grinned up at him, a mug of coffee cradled in her hands. His heart stammered at the tenderness in her eyes. "Cocoa is such a sweet mama," she whispered, "and the puppies are already developing their own personalities." She pointed to the darkest of the pups. "This one is the leader, but the one with the purple rickrack gives him a run for his money."

"We need to move them back out to the barn," he said coolly. "Garrett doesn't allow pets in the house."

"I bet he'd make an exception for puppies," she murmured, then uncrossed her legs and stood. "I talked to my mom this morning. They got tickets to *Hamilton*, so they're going to stay in New York for an extra couple of days."

Caden bit back a curse as he pulled his phone from his jacket pocket. He'd missed a call from his dad while he was in town and there was a text message shining up at him from the home screen.

This old cowboy likes the big city. Changed flights to come home on December 22. Take care of Lucy.

"Garrett never takes vacations like this," he muttered.

"I guess it's nice they're having so much fun together," Lucy suggested quietly. "Mom sounded really happy on the phone."

"I bet she did." Caden saw Lucy's shoulders stiffen at the insinuation in his tone. "Your mom must be pretty damn good between the..." He drew in a breath, stopping the flow of ugly words before he said something he couldn't take back. "They'll return soon enough."

"What's wrong?" Lucy placed a hand on his arm, and it felt like his skin was on fire under the fabric of his work shirt.

He shrugged off her touch. "It's fine for my dad to take a break, but I've got work to do."

What he needed was to get away from Lucy and the spell she wove around him. Even now, as frustrated as he was at not being able to figure out what the hell was going on with her, he wanted to pull her close and breathe her in. To forget everything except the way she made him feel.

But he understood the price he could pay for losing himself to a woman. Nothing was worth risking that again.

"I stopped at the bakery." He thrust the pink bag into her hands. "I'll make up a place for Cocoa and her puppies in the barn when I have a break later."

Lucy frowned at him. "Caden, what's—"

He held up a hand. "I've got to get going on the day." Then he turned and walked away.

Snow flurries started coming down around lunchtime as Lucy sat in front of the computer. The house remained quiet for the next several hours as she worked on deciphering the tangled spiderweb of financial records from Garrett's various properties and business ventures.

She didn't bother making another call to the family friend who was supposedly handling the books for Sharpe Ranch. Derek Lawson had been outright rude to her when they'd spoken a few days earlier. Besides, the more she uncovered, the more certain she was that Derek was at the heart of many of the discrepancies she found.

It was good to have something to keep her busy so she wouldn't spend the whole day ruminating over Caden's bizarre behavior. Her emotions ranged from anger to shock to disappointment. Not heartbreak, of course. She couldn't have her heart in the mix after one night together, no matter how amazing that night had been.

When Erin texted and invited her to go caroling through downtown with a group of women meeting at the Crimson

Community Center that night, Lucy accepted right away. She might as well put all her useless holiday song lyric knowledge to good use. Not to mention that she couldn't stand the thought of spending an awkward evening in the house with Caden either ignoring her or acting like a jerk.

She checked on the puppies, made sure Cocoa went out for a potty break and had fresh water, then dressed and drove into town. The snow was still coming down, and she had no idea where on the property Caden and Chad were working today. She didn't bother to leave a note. Based on his behavior this morning, Caden would be happy to have an evening alone in the house.

Her little rental car slid on the snow-covered roads a couple of times, and by the time she parked around the corner from the community center, Lucy's knuckles were white from gripping the steering wheel so tightly.

The group was gathered in front of the historic brick building, and Erin waved as she approached.

"I'm so glad you could make it," Erin said, giving her a warm hug. "Let me introduce you to everyone."

Katie Crawford also hugged her. "Lucy is the publicity genius behind the success of Caden's adoption event. We're hoping she decides to stay in Crimson so I can tap her to help with the bakery's marketing plan for the summer season."

"Then I'd like to talk to her about the new campaign for the community center." A delicately beautiful woman with dark hair and pale hazel eyes stepped forward. "I can always use a fresh set of eyes. I'm Olivia Travers. Nice to meet you, Lucy."

Lucy shook Olivia's hand. "I don't really have an official background in marketing."

"But you're so good at it," Katie countered.

There were two other women in the group. Millie Travers, Olivia's sister, happened to be married to the brother of Olivia's husband. She also met Julia Crenshaw, who was the sister of Katie's husband. They were clearly a tight-knit group, and Lucy suddenly felt like the outsider she was in this town.

"Okay, Olivia," Julia said after introductions were made. "Caroling was your idea." She leaned in closer to Lucy. "My plan was to hit the Mexican restaurant for enchiladas and margaritas."

"We can do that anytime," Olivia answered. "Christmas is special and the chamber of commerce has asked certain businesses to coordinate these little caroling outings to add a bit more spirit to downtown during the holiday season."

Julia rolled her eyes. "I know. Jase told me all about it. He's very proud of what a do-gooder I've become."

Lucy tried to cover her snort, but Julia turned with a grin. "My husband heads up the chamber along with Olivia. They're the official Crimson cheerleading squad. I come along kicking and screaming."

"Or singing," Millie added, nudging her sister. "Even though Olivia can't carry a tune to save her life."

Olivia sniffed. "Jasper thinks I have a beautiful voice."

Millie laughed. "He's two," she explained to Lucy. "Can you sing?"

"Actually, yes," Lucy answered, surprised to find herself admitting the talent to these women. "I used to sing all the time when I was younger. It sounds silly now, but my mom nicknamed me Songbird." She gave a small laugh. "For a while she was convinced I could become America's next pop princess."

"No pressure," Julia said quietly.

"Exactly," Lucy agreed, recognizing sarcasm. "I didn't do well under pressure. She entered me in a few competitions at malls but it turned out that while I had the voice of an angel at home, I also suffered from horrible stage fright." She made a face. "The end of my short-lived career was the day I puked up my nervous stomach all over a panel of judges."

"Alright, then," Olivia said, linking her arm with Lucy's. "There will be no puking this evening. How about I stand in front and lip-synch and you can hide in the back and belt out the songs?"

Lucy felt warmth infuse her veins at the ease with which these women made her part of the group without judgment. No forcing her to play a part or be someone different than who she was. Being Lucy seemed to be enough for them.

They made their way to the center of downtown Crimson. Most of the shops were still open, and they stopped on the corner across from the ice-skating rink. Olivia turned to the group, pulling small booklets out of her tote bag.

Julia groaned. "We have songbooks? This is so official."

"Jase's idea," Olivia answered with a grin. "He said you have a habit of making up your own lyrics and they're not always appropriate."

Julia stuck out her tongue. "But they're fun."

"What song do we start with?" Erin asked, paging through the sheets.

"'Santa Claus Is Coming to Town,'" Millie suggested. "Everyone knows that one."

"What do you think, Lucy?" Julia asked.

"I worked retail for so many holiday seasons that I know all of them."

"Brilliant," Olivia said with a bright smile. "You're going to make us sound amazing."

"Tall order," Julia muttered, and Lucy smiled.

"Why am I suddenly so nervous?" Erin asked. "We should have stopped at Elevation first for some liquid courage."

"Not too late," Millie offered.

Olivia narrowed her eyes at her sister. "Are we ready?"

The women nodded, each focused on her own small songbook. After a moment it was obvious no one wanted to start, so Lucy cleared her throat and began singing, "You'd better watch out…"

Erin, Millie and Julia added their voices to the mix while Olivia stepped forward and motioned to the people standing nearby to join them. By the time they got to the chorus, Lucy forgot to be nervous.

Instead she remembered how much she loved to sing. She sang the words, not even embarrassed when Julia turned and flashed a grin, her eyes wide with surprise. A few of the people on the street began singing and by the last verse, a crowd had gathered around their small group like they were buskers in some Victorian Christmas pageant.

Applause erupted as they finished and one of the men watching shouted, "'Joy to the World' next."

Olivia turned to Lucy with a questioning glance, and Lucy nodded. "You're so good," Erin whispered, squeezing her fingers.

"Thanks." Unfamiliar pride bubbled up in Lucy. It had been a long time since she'd been recognized for having talent at anything except being a pretty face. She did her best to believe in herself but sometimes it was hard to remember why she should.

She launched into a cheery rendition of "Hark! The Herald Angels Sing," then transitioned to "Rudolph the Red-Nosed Reindeer" and led the women in "Silent Night" and "Deck the Halls."

The crowd continued to sing with them, and by the time they'd finished close to a dozen carols, Lucy realized the group had slowly pushed her to the front.

She felt her palms grow sweaty as the final song came to an end and all eyes remained on her.

Olivia threw her arms around Lucy. "That was so much fun." With Lucy hugged tight to her side, she faced the crowd. "Can we get another round of applause for the most amazing Lucy Renner?"

Lucy shook her head, but cheering and whistles from the people gathered in front of them drowned out any protest she might have offered.

"I think we have time for one more song," Olivia said, glancing at Lucy. "Is that okay with you?"

"Sure," Lucy said. The truth was she could have spent the entire evening singing.

"How about 'O Holy Night'?" a deep voice called, and Lucy's entire body went still.

She looked wildly around the faces in front of her until her gaze landed on Caden, who stood near the back of the crowd near the edge of the ice-skating rink, David and Noah flanking him.

"Good choice," Olivia called.

"It's not in the book," Erin said from behind Lucy. "I only know the 'fall on your knees' part."

"Me, too," Millie agreed.

"I'm not sure I know that much," Julia added.

Olivia frowned. "Maybe another—"

"I can do it," Lucy told her and took a step forward. "'O Holy Night' is one of my favorites. Anyone who knows it is welcome to join in."

She closed her eyes when nerves tingled down her skin, and took a deep breath to calm herself. She wasn't a scared ten-year-old girl in front of a row of jaded judges. She was helping people get into the Christmas spirit, and for once, she appreciated how magical coming together as a community during the holiday season could be.

She sang the words softly at first, feeling joy rush through her as a few people sang with her. It was one of her favorite songs, and she wondered how Caden knew to request it.

By the time she sang about hearing angel voices, Lucy could feel tears pricking the back of her eyes. Yes, she knew the words to so many holiday songs, but on this December night, surrounded by new friends and strangers, the meaning of Christmas felt real for the first time.

As the song's final note ended, a hush fell over the people gathered around their little caroling group.

"Merry Christmas, everyone," Olivia called after a moment. "Enjoy your time here in Crimson."

There was more enthusiastic clapping and then the crowd began to disperse. Millie, Julia, Erin, Katie and Olivia surrounded Lucy in one big group hug.

"Best Christmas activity ever," Millie shouted.

Julia wiped at her cheeks. "You made even a grinch like me cry, girl. Where did you learn to sing like that?"

Lucy bit down on her lip and shrugged. "I just like to sing."

Katie grinned. "The best way to spread Christmas cheer—"

"No quoting *Elf*," Julia interrupted, winding a hand around Katie's neck and clapping a hand over her mouth. "Katie and my brother love Will Ferrell. It's a problem."

"Will Ferrell is never a problem." Noah untangled his wife from Julia and kissed the top of Katie's head. "Lucy, you've got some pipes."

"Major pipes," David agreed, coming to join them. Erin pressed herself to his side. "Are you ladies in need of a thirst quencher after all that singing?"

"Absolutely," Millie told him, glancing at her phone, then to her sister. "Logan and Jake are going to meet us there. Claire is coming to the house to babysit Jasper and Brooke."

Lucy's heart fluttered as the women—her new friends— paired up with their respective men, and she tried not to look for Caden. It all seemed so easy and effortless, although she imagined each of the couples had their own story to tell.

She'd never had an expectation of getting her own happily-ever-after, so envying the people in love around her had never been an issue. But since she'd come to Crimson, so much had changed...and a lot of it had to do with her feelings for Caden.

The flutter morphed into a full-fledged racing gallop, and she didn't have to glance up to know who stood in front of her.

"How did you know that's my favorite Christmas song?" she asked, clasping her hands tight in front of her to keep from reaching for him.

They'd had one amazing night together, but that didn't mean she had any claim on him. Based on his behavior today, it didn't mean anything at all.

His mouth curved into a smile. "I didn't know, but it was the one I wanted to hear you sing. Your voice is..." He reached out and traced a finger along her cheek. "You have the most beautiful voice I've ever heard."

"I can carry a tune," she said, loving the feel of his calloused fingertip on her skin. "It's not a big deal."

"You love to sing."

"I used to," she agreed.

"But..."

"But I don't love to perform."

"You could have fooled me. You held the entire town captive with your talent tonight."

She laughed. "I don't know about the entire town."

"Admit it. You wowed the crowd."

She tried to play it off, to stay cool and unmoved, but it was a losing battle. She felt a goofy smile split her face and did a little victory dance like a wide receiver who'd just caught a touchdown pass in the Super Bowl.

"I really did," she whispered. "Who knew all those years

of listening to canned Christmas music would have prepared me for this?"

"You took my breath away," he told her, his eyes once again shining with tenderness.

"What happened this morning, Caden? I don't understand why, but it felt like we were right back where we started with you hating me."

"I never hated you."

"It certainly felt that way."

"I'm sorry," he said softly. "About how we began and how I acted this morning. Last night was amazing." He ran a hand across his jaw. "It's difficult for me to trust amazing."

"Are you two going to join us?" Erin called from across the street. "First round's on my hottie fiancé."

"We'll catch up," Lucy answered, waving the group on without them.

She studied Caden for another long moment, trying to figure out what it was he wasn't saying. "Why did you come to town tonight?"

He leaned in, brushed his mouth across hers. "For you, Lucy. I came for you."

Chapter 11

"You should record an album."

"Seriously, I'd pay money to hear you sing."

Caden watched as color crept into Lucy's cheeks once again. The two guys who stood in front of her were the latest in a long line of patrons at Elevation who wanted to talk to her about her voice.

She seemed flattered but uncomfortable with the attention, and his desire to take care of her intensified as she shifted closer.

"Thank you," she said with an unassuming smile and gripped the back of his shirt tighter.

He moved so he was partially blocking her from view. "Nice talking to you," he told the two guys, both of whom were staring at Lucy like she was an angel straight out of heaven.

He could appreciate the sentiment, but he wanted to be the only one free to gaze at her like that. The men seemed to understand his tone because they moved on after a minute.

Lucy let out a strained laugh. "It's weird to be the center of attention."

He took a long pull on his beer and kissed her forehead. "You deserve it, sweetheart. These are your adoring fans."

She stared at him, searching his face like she was trying to figure out if he meant those words. "You're not angry that people keep interrupting us to talk to me?"

He shook his head. "Are you kidding? I'm thanking my lucky stars I get to be the guy at your side tonight. I'll play second fiddle to you anytime I have the chance."

She gave him a slow smile. "I can't ever imagine you as a second fiddle, but I'm glad you followed me tonight."

He was, too. He'd spent the whole damn day thinking about her and cursing himself for how he'd acted. Of course she was looking at the ranch's finances. It's what his father had asked her to do. Derek must have misread the situation. After all, Lucy hadn't mentioned any concerns about the books to Caden. He had no reason not to trust her, despite his problems with her mother.

She gestured to the corner of the bar where her group of carolers had retreated with their men. "Should we join them?"

"It's your night, Lucy. Whatever you want."

She bit down on her lower lip as her eyes darkened, telling him without words exactly what she wanted. Heat curled through his body in response.

"I want to go home," she told him, reaching up to press her hand to the back of his neck and draw him down to her for a slow, heated kiss. "Back to the ranch," she clarified.

"Sounds like a perfect plan to me. It's still coming down hard out there, so I'll drive us back and we can get your car tomorrow once they've plowed the roads."

She nodded. "I realized on the way into town that a two-wheel drive compact isn't exactly made for winter driving."

They said goodbye to their friends and walked out into the snowy night. "Does it always snow this much in Colorado?"

she asked, pulling her hat down around her ears and snuggling against Caden's side as they walked.

"Not always so consistently this early in the season," he answered, catching a few of the fluffy flakes on his gloved hand. "It's good for the ski resorts, though, and it explains why downtown Crimson has been so busy. People hear the snow is great out here, and they make plans to spend the holidays on the slopes."

"Do you ski?"

Caden nodded. "Tyson taught me the first winter I came to live with them. He was so damn fast on the mountain. I never could keep up with him."

"I'm sure you tried."

"I ate so much snow my first ski season from all the face-planting I did." He laughed softly, surprised at the fondness of his memories. Everything about his relationship with his brother had been tainted by Tyson's death. It had forced Caden to refocus his past through the lens of how he'd failed Tyson. But tonight the guilt seemed to fade away to leave nothing but happy thoughts.

Another gift Lucy gave him.

"Tyson's idea of lessons was taking me to the top of the highest peak and racing down."

"That must have been terrifying."

"We were both adrenaline junkies."

"Is that why you joined the army?"

He shrugged, no longer shocked at how easily she could read him. "Partly, I think. At that point, I also wanted something that belonged to just me."

"I understand that," she said softly.

When they got to where he'd parked the truck, he opened the passenger-side door for her, then came around and turned on the ignition.

"Do you want to learn to ski while you're here?"

She laughed. "No, thanks. The thought of strapping sticks to my feet and hurtling down a mountain is enough to make me queasy. There are plenty of other ways to get my heart racing."

"I can think of a few," he told her and leaned over the console for a kiss. He'd meant it to be only a brief embrace, a prelude for what was to come.

But when his mouth met hers, it was as if someone lit a match to a bonfire inside him. He flamed to life, and Lucy was the oxygen his fire needed to keep it raging.

She hadn't yet buckled her seat belt, so he lifted her up and over the console, into his lap.

She seemed as engulfed in incendiary need as he felt. She reached inside his coat and tugged at the shirt he'd tucked into jeans. Her clever fingers skimmed along his skin, and all he could think about was getting closer.

So much for the belief that one night would satisfy his need. He kissed her like his life depended on it, because maybe it did. He slanted his head, tangling his tongue with hers as he pressed his palms into the small of her back. Even in the crowded truck cab, she fit perfectly against him.

Hot air blasted from the dashboard vents as he took hold of her hips, pulling her even tighter against him. She moaned low in her throat, a sound that drove him wild.

Suddenly he was a teenager again, parked with a girl and wondering if there was anything more perfect than the feel of soft curves against his hard body.

A firm knock on the window made Lucy jerk away from him. Her back slammed into the steering wheel, and the blare of the horn split the quiet. She scrambled back into her seat as a light flashed in the fogged-up front window.

Caden drew in a breath and hit the button to roll down the window on the truck's driver's side.

"Howdy, folks," Marcus Pike, one of Crimson's deputy sheriffs, drawled.

"Hey, Marcus." Caden squinted and held up a hand. "Mind turning off the flashlight?"

"Sure thing, Sharpe," the older man said with a knowing smile. "I noticed your truck was running but you weren't going anywhere. It's a cold night and a lot of people are doing some preholiday celebrating. Thought I'd check and make sure everything's okay."

"Just letting her warm up before heading back to the ranch," Caden explained, patting the dashboard.

"I bet." Marcus leaned in closer and waved at Lucy. "I heard a bit of your caroling tonight, ma'am. You have a lovely voice."

She cleared her throat. "Thank you."

"It's been a few years," he said to Caden, "since you and I have found ourselves in this kind of situation, Sharpe." Marcus let his gaze slide from Caden to Lucy. "Our boy here dated my daughter when they were in high school."

Caden stifled a groan. He hadn't exactly "dated" Britney Pike, but he'd been caught with her on the ridge where local teens hung out on weekend nights.

"I heard Britney got married a couple of years ago. Living in Golden now, right?"

Marcus nodded. "About to give Jana and me our first grandbaby."

"Congratulations." Caden forced a smile. "If there's nothing else, I guess we'll be on our way."

"That work for you, ma'am?" Marcus asked Lucy, and the implication that she might not be fine with Caden made him want to roar in protest.

He'd been adopted by Garrett almost twenty years ago, but some people in Crimson refused to see him as anything but the troubled kid with the mom who'd overdosed and no other family to step in and help raise him.

Lucy didn't seem to realize there might be an underlying meaning in the deputy's question, or if she did, she pretended to ignore it. She reached across the console and laced her fingers with Caden's. "I'm exactly where I want to be. Thanks for checking on us, Officer."

Some of the tension gripping Caden's chest loosened. "Tell your dad I said hello," Marcus said, then turned and headed back to his cruiser.

Caden shifted to face Lucy as he rolled up the window, ready to apologize for putting her in that sort of situation.

Only to find her dissolving into a fit of giggles. "That was hilarious," she said, her shoulders shaking. "I feel like I'm fifteen except that never happened to me when I was a teenager. We actually got caught making out."

She pointed at Caden. "And you once had a thing with the sheriff's daughter?"

"Marcus Pike is a deputy sheriff. Cole Bennett took over the department a couple of years ago when the old sheriff retired. Cole is about—"

"Stop changing the subject." Lucy threw back her head and laughed more. "Did you have some kind of death wish as a teenager?"

"Maybe," he admitted and found himself grinning back at her. He'd had plenty of run-ins with law enforcement as a surly kid and rowdy teenager, and even though he'd done well in the army, back in Crimson his feelings about authority were mired in and convoluted by the mistakes he'd made as a youth.

As she seemed to do with every aspect of his life, Lucy changed his normal dynamic. She changed who he was and who he wanted to be. Her fingers were still intertwined with his, and he lifted her hand, turning it over to place a kiss on the inside of her wrist.

He continued to hold her hand as he drove, the truck's headlights illuminating the whirling snow and limiting his vision to only three feet in front of them.

Her phone chimed and he released her so she could pull it from her jacket pocket. "Mom says their flight out of JFK got canceled."

"I thought it wasn't scheduled until tomorrow?" he asked.

"The East Coast is getting hit with a big storm, too, so flights are already being affected. They're coming home a day later now."

"Not much time for her to plan a Christmas wedding," he muttered, wondering if Maureen had somehow orchestrated the delay to keep him away from his father until right before the big event. Realistically he knew she couldn't control the weather, but it seemed awfully convenient.

"Oh, she sent me a list of things to do so that everything's ready to go when they return."

I'm not ready, he wanted to shout but kept his mouth shut. He'd been a jerk this morning and wasn't going to be stupid enough to ruin tonight, too. It wasn't Lucy's fault his dad and her mom were stuck on the East Coast. He also couldn't make himself believe that she had any corrupt intentions where his father was concerned. In fact, it seemed as though her mother's various machinations with men had been difficult for Lucy.

She was as much a pawn in Maureen's schemes as any of them. Caden needed Garrett back on the ranch so he could truly determine if his dad's heart was in jeopardy. Garrett could say what he wanted about making his own decisions, but Caden couldn't afford to let him be hurt again.

Not that he minded a few extra days with Lucy. They hadn't talked about her plans for after the holidays, but he assumed she'd be returning to Florida. He wanted to make the most of every moment he had with her.

The thought pinged through his mind that he should ask her to stay, but he pushed it aside before it had a chance to take root. Lucy deserved a man who could love her with his whole heart, and Caden's had been too damaged over the years to be much use to anyone.

"You're still hoping your dad will call off the wedding," Lucy said quietly.

Garrett took the turn that led to the ranch, gripping the steering wheel with both hands. "I'd be happier if they didn't rush into anything."

He held his breath as he waited for her response.

"That would probably be wise, given..." She stopped, her body going stiff as if she was about to say something she shouldn't.

"Given what?" he demanded.

She turned to him and smiled, but it didn't reach her eyes. "It's been a whirlwind courtship, and your dad seems like an old-fashioned kind of guy. Mom is all about instant gratification, but sometimes waiting only makes the outcome sweeter in the end." She raised a brow. "Know what I mean?"

He actually had no idea what the hell she was talking about. But he was damn sure it wasn't what she'd meant to say in the first place.

They could deal with the reality of her mother and his father when they returned from New York. Tonight all he wanted was to hold Lucy in his arms again.

"You snore," he said instead of answering her.

He watched her mouth drop open as he parked his truck in the oversize garage bay.

"I d-do not," she stammered. "I can't believe you'd say that to me. That's like telling a woman a pair of jeans makes her butt look big."

He hopped out of the truck, walked around to her side and opened the door. "Good news. The jeans you wear make your butt look amazing." He gave her an exaggerated leer. "I'd say your butt is perfect no matter what you're wearing, but I better double-check to make sure. Climb down and turn around for me."

She got out of the truck and promptly shoved him in the chest. He took a step back, smiling at how flustered she appeared. "Are you trying to *not* get lucky tonight?" she demanded, flipping her long hair over one shoulder. "Because that's where you're headed pretty darn quickly."

Lucky. Wasn't that just the right word to describe how he felt with Lucy? Lucky to have his heart filled with happiness. Lucky to be the man she'd chosen, if even for a short time. "I think it's cute," he said, reaching for her.

"It's embarrassing." She sidestepped him and stalked out of the garage and toward the house. The floodlight that hung above the garage illuminated the driveway now that the snow had finally slowed.

"Be careful," he called as he hit the button to close the garage door, then followed her. "The ground will be slick in spots."

As she got close to the porch, she bent forward and grabbed a handful of snow. Before he realized what she was doing, she hurled a snowball toward him. It landed with a thunk against his chest, snow splattering everywhere.

"Nice aim," he said with a chuckle.

She gave him an arch look. "I was going for your head." She bent and formed another snowball. He ducked as it went whizzing by him, then gathered enough snow to make one of his own.

"You're in trouble now, sweetheart."

He expected her to declare game over, but as always, Lucy surprised him. "I'm going to take you down, cowboy," she shouted and ran behind the edge of the porch rail for cover.

The next few minutes were filled with shouts and laughter as they engaged in an epic snowball fight, the kind of fun Caden hadn't had since he and Tyson were kids.

He landed a few good ones, but Lucy proved to have the aim of a major-league pitcher. By the time she called a truce, he had icy water dripping down his front and back.

He held up his hands, palms forward as he moved toward her. "You win," he called.

"I don't snore," she insisted.

"Whatever you say."

She reached out a hand and brushed snow from his shoulder. Her cheeks were flushed and her eyes sparkled. She was so damn beautiful it took his breath away. "I got you good."

"You have no idea," he murmured and leaned in to kiss her.

"I like winter," she said against his mouth. "It's kind of fun."

"Everything is fun with you, Lucy."

She wound her arms around his neck. "But now I'm ready to warm up."

"I can help with that," he told her and lifted her into his arms. She wrapped her legs around his hips, and he carried her up the porch steps and into the house.

A shiver passed through her as his fingers moved under her clothes to press into her back. He walked up the stairs, careful not to bump her into a wall, and carried her down the hallway, into his bedroom.

By the time he gently put her down on the bed, her whole body trembled. "I'd like to think that's a reaction to me," he said, straightening to tug off her boots, "but you're freezing."

"May-maybe winter and I," she said through chattering teeth, "don't ge-get along so well af-after all."

"I'll be your personal space heater."

She smiled at the simple jest and something shifted in his heart. More like an unfurling, all the tender bits that he'd hidden for years advancing into the light that seemed to emanate from Lucy like a beacon. He was falling for her, fast and hard and unable or unwilling to stop the descent.

He quickly helped her undress, then shucked off his clothes, hissing out a breath as her ice-cold hands flattened on his chest. Within minutes, her shivers had subsided and they were both heated from the inside out, a tangle of limbs and sweet caresses.

It was difficult to know where he ended and Lucy began, and he'd never imagined he could feel so unfettered in joining himself to another person. He wasn't sure how he'd stand it when this finally ended. Or how to make sure it never did.

Chapter 12

Lucy stood in front of the Christmas tree the following afternoon, reaching out a hand to touch the tip of one of the colorful lights Caden had strung. The scent of pine filled the room, and each of the decorations she'd placed made her heart happy.

She realized she'd never appreciated the holidays at the various retail shops where she'd worked because the lights and trimmings held no meaning for her. And her mother's vacillating relationship with Christmas, going all out when she was with a man, then ignoring the holidays completely when it was just her and Lucy, had also tainted the season.

Her time in Crimson made Lucy understand how special Christmas could be. She understood that the decorations represented years of tradition, of the love between a husband and wife, a mother and son, and later the family Garrett had created with Tyson and Caden.

For the first time, Lucy wanted to create her own traditions. Caroling on a downtown corner with friends…a raucous snowball fight breaking the quiet of a December night. She pressed her fingers to her chest as her breath caught at the thought of little boys with Caden's tousled hair and mischievous smile romping through the snow.

Could that sort of life be possible for her? She'd learned the best way to avoid disappointment and heartache was to keep her expectations low. But Caden made her want a life she believed could make her happy.

She knew it wouldn't be easy. Even if her mother truly loved Garrett, Maureen had a tendency to sabotage the good things in their lives. Lucy would have to trust Caden enough to explain fully her mother's history and hope that he'd understand and allow his father to make his own decisions about his life.

But she couldn't go forward until they were both on the same page about her past, the choices Maureen had made and Lucy's role in protecting her mother when reality got to be too much for Maureen to handle.

There was another truth she had to make Caden see first, and nerves skittered through her as she heard the front door of the house open and shut.

He appeared in the doorway a moment later, his color high from the cold. "How fast can you get ready?"

"For what?"

A small smile played at the corner of his mouth. "A date."

"With you?"

His grin widened. "Unless you have someone else in mind."

She shook her head. "Of course not. I just wasn't expecting... I hadn't planned..."

"New plan." He stepped forward, lifted her hand to his mouth. "I'd like to take you out on a real date, Lucy. Something special. Will you go with me?"

"Yes," she whispered, the weight of the conversation she'd planned to have with him lifting momentarily. They had time to discuss the serious bits later.

She wanted to believe what she had to tell him wouldn't change things between them, but there was no doubt it would cast a shadow on their night. Now that she'd become accustomed to basking in the light of her feelings for him, she wasn't ready to risk giving the darkness an opening.

She took a quick shower and got ready, borrowing a dark green sweater dress from her mother's closet. It had long sleeves and fell almost to her knees, so it would be appropriate for December, but the deep V of both the neckline and back added a pinch of sexiness to the outfit.

She'd packed one pair of high heels, black and strappy, and slipped her feet into them, loving the tiny bows at the ankles. After curling her hair and adding a bit of mascara and lip gloss, she spritzed herself with perfume and turned to the full-length mirror that hung on the closet door.

The dress was gorgeous, but was it appropriate for whatever Caden had planned? They were still in Colorado in December. He'd said "special," but for all Lucy knew, that meant a hoedown at the local lodge.

"You're the most beautiful thing I've ever seen."

She whirled around at the sound of Caden's deep voice. He stood in the doorway, wearing a dark sports jacket with a crisp white shirt, burgundy tie and pair of navy trousers. A wide-brimmed Western hat was perched on his head, and she'd never seen her high-mountain cowboy look more handsome.

"Thank you," she said, "but I think you need to get out more."

He shook his head. "I've been all over the world. You're it for me."

It felt as though her heart skipped a beat. She knew he was talking about how she looked, but she had trouble not reading more into the words. The way he said them, his tone filled with awe, made her feel like he was choosing her, and nothing had ever meant so much.

"You look quite handsome yourself," she said, making her voice light. No sense in letting him see how far gone she was. Not until she was certain he felt the same way. "Cowboy couture suits you."

"Cowboy couture," he repeated with a chuckle. "Is that official retail lingo?"

She moved toward him. "That's officially me giving you a compliment." She tipped up her chin and kissed him. With the heels on, she didn't need to go up on her toes, although he was still a couple of inches taller than her. He took her hand and led her down the stairs to the front of the house.

"I'm going to pull the truck to the front porch so you don't twist an ankle in those shoes walking across the snow."

She made a face. "I forgot about the snow. I could change into—"

"Hell, no," he interrupted. "Your shoes are the stuff of my wildest fantasies. You can keep them on all night." He leaned in and nipped at her earlobe. "Maybe later we'll negotiate you wearing the shoes and nothing else."

She sighed. "What do I get in the deal?"

"Whatever you want."

You, she wanted to shout. *I want you.*

Her heart pitched at the thought, and she pushed away. "I need to check on Cocoa and the puppies. I'll be out in a minute."

The dog wagged her tail and looked up at Lucy when she came into the laundry room. Thankfully, there'd been no more talk about moving Cocoa to the barn. The puppies were tiny but they were beginning to gain weight and size. "I've got a date with a hot cowboy tonight, Cocoa. Wish me luck."

The dog yawned and turned to lick the smallest pup. Lucy

still hated that they hadn't been able to save the last puppy, but Cocoa didn't seem to feel the loss. She had her hands full with her six wriggling bundles.

"You've got more important things to worry about than my love life. I'll see you when we get back, sweet girl."

She slipped into her coat and opened the front door. A gust of frigid air whipped across her bare legs, and for a moment she rethought her decision to wear the dress with no tights. But then she remembered the look in Caden's eyes when his gaze had swept over her. A minute of cold was definitely worth his reaction.

He was waiting on the porch, and took her hand as she walked out. "I can make it to the truck," she told him with a laugh.

"Give me some credit." He placed his other hand on the small of her back. "I'm trying to be a gentleman. It's new for me."

She laughed and allowed him to lead her down the steps and help her into the truck.

"Where are we going?" she asked when he turned out of the driveway in the opposite direction of downtown Crimson.

"Aspen."

Of course Lucy had heard of the ritzy ski town, but she'd never imagined going on a date there. When she'd first come to Crimson, her only purpose had been to protect her mother's relationship with Garrett.

In the course of almost two weeks, the town had become her home. She had more of a life here than she'd made in a decade living in Florida. She was so grateful for everything she'd experienced and couldn't wait to have a night out with Caden. In some strange way, it felt as though this night made what was between them official.

"You know you don't have to try to impress me," she said

quietly, keeping her gaze trained on the guardrail at the edge of the highway. "I'm a sure thing."

"Don't make yourself less than who you are, Lucy."

The words were spoken gently, but they felt like a slap to the face.

"I'm not," she insisted.

"Yes, you are." He reached for her hand, but she pulled away, embarrassed that he could read her so easily. "Even though we started off unconventionally—"

"Because you hated me," she muttered.

"I didn't trust you," he clarified. "But now I know who you are, and I want you to see yourself the way I do. I want to woo you. I want you to understand you deserve every good thing. You deserve to be cherished."

I deserve to be loved.

She clasped a hand over her mouth and turned to Caden, afraid she'd spoken out loud her most secret desire.

"You don't have to agree with me," he said, and she could tell by his relaxed manner that she'd only thought that last bit. Thank goodness. "But I hope you can allow yourself to enjoy the night. I know I plan to have a hell of a time."

"I can't wait for whatever you have planned," she said honestly.

What he had planned turned out to be dinner at one of the fanciest restaurants in Aspen. La Bonne Maison was an elegant, French-inspired bistro she'd seen mentioned in the tabloids because of its popularity with the celebrities who flocked to Aspen during the ski season.

"This place is famous," she whispered as he pulled to a stop at the curb and a uniformed valet immediately opened her door.

She climbed out of the truck and almost gasped as one of her favorite actresses walked past her and into the restaurant.

Caden took her hand, squeezing gently.

She knew she was gaping but couldn't stop herself. "That was—"

"I know," he said quietly. "Aspen is full of Hollywood types, especially during the holidays."

"You don't seem impressed."

He shrugged. "You impress me. I bet Ms. A-List Actress couldn't assist a cantankerous dog through a difficult birth without freaking out."

"Cocoa is not cantankerous," Lucy countered as Caden led her forward. A doorman opened the heavy wooden front door and they walked into the space, with its dark paneled walls and oversize fireplace that took up one whole wall. The lighting of the restaurant was soft, giving it an intimate feel. A woman greeted Caden at the hostess stand, air-kissing each of his cheeks before turning to Lucy.

"Welcome to La Bonne Maison," she said in a heavy French accent. "I'm so happy Caden finally had a reason to accept my offer."

"I'm excited to be here. As far as your offer…" Lucy threw a questioning glance toward Caden.

"Louisa owns La Bonne Maison. I helped match her with her dog," he explained almost sheepishly.

"Jacques is the best companion I've ever had," the woman said with a nod. "Far more agreeable than my ex-husband. I've wanted to thank Caden with a special dinner, but apparently he's never had a reason to dine with us until you."

Caden cleared his throat, appearing uncomfortable at the restaurant owner's comments. "The ranch keeps me busy," he muttered.

"*Oui, mon chéri.* But you must make time for the joie de vivre." She took Lucy's hand. "This one has finally helped you to see that."

"*Oui,*" Caden agreed in an exaggerated accent, making Lucy smile.

Louisa led them to a small booth that afforded both privacy and a view of the rest of the patrons. "Our best table," Louisa explained. "Mariah was not pleased..." She shrugged. "But c'est la vie."

When she walked away, Lucy leaned across the table. "That must be one incredible dog."

Caden grinned. "He's a good fit for her."

"Thank you for taking me here," Lucy said after a waiter had brought a bottle of wine and poured two glasses.

He arched a brow. "My father isn't the only one who can wine and dine a woman."

A tendril of unease snaked along Lucy's spine. "I don't want you to think I need to be wined and dined. I'm not my mother."

Caden set his wineglass on the table and took her hand. "I know that, but I wanted to share this night with you. It's about us, Lucy. No one else."

As was his way, Caden seemed to know exactly what to say to put her mind at ease. Her body relaxed and she smiled at him. "Then let's have the most amazing evening. Just us."

"Don't even tell me my snoring woke you up."

Caden smiled as he crawled back under the covers the next morning. "Working a ranch woke me up," he said, dropping a kiss on her bare shoulder. "But all I could think about was the image of you warm and naked in my bed."

She gave a little yelp as his cold fingers brushed the curve of her waist. "You've already been out?"

"It's almost eight, sleepyhead."

She turned to him, wrapping a leg around his hip and making his body pound with need. As beautiful as she'd looked last night in her fancy dress and heels, she was even lovelier with no makeup and her hair tumbling over the pillow. "Someone kept me awake all night. I was catching up on sleep. Are you playing hooky this morning?"

"For an hour or so," he answered. "Chad is going to work on the fence line near the edge of the west pasture. I'll catch up with him later."

"Then we'd better make the most of this hour," she whispered and snuggled closer.

They both laughed as her stomach gave a low growl. "You've been in bed too long," he said, kissing her hair. "It's time for breakfast."

"I can make something easy," she told him, keeping the sheet tucked around her gorgeous breasts. "If you need to get back to work…"

"No sense playing hooky if I don't make the most of it." He pulled a navy Henley over his head. "How do you like your eggs?"

"However you make them."

"Butter or jelly on the toast?"

She smiled. "Butter *and* jelly."

"Got it." He smoothed a strand of hair away from her face and kissed her again. "Breakfast in fifteen minutes."

"I could grow accustomed to the service around here," she told him.

He winked. "I sure hope so." He moved toward the kitchen, passing his father's bedroom near the top of the staircase. He'd gotten a text early this morning that Garrett and Maureen were rebooked on a flight that would arrive in Denver tomorrow morning. Caden wasn't sure what that would mean for his relationship with Lucy, but he knew he couldn't imagine saying goodbye to her now.

He had no doubt they'd have to get creative with their time together. Caden thought about how he might fix up the small guesthouse situated to the south of the barn. Would Lucy want to get her own apartment in town if she was going to stay in Crimson?

Could he ask her to stay beyond the holidays? Garrett had always told him Christmas was the time for new beginnings, but Caden never had a reason to believe it since he'd first come to live on Sharpe Ranch, until Lucy.

He started frying bacon in a pan on the stove, then chopped vegetables and cracked eggs into a mixing bowl to make omelets.

By the time Lucy appeared in the kitchen, her hair damp and in a loose bun at the back of her neck, he was plating the food. She sat a stack of files on the table and slipped into a seat.

"You're an amazing cook," she said around a bite of omelet. "How am I ever going to go back to cold cereal for breakfast?"

"Don't," he replied immediately and wasn't sure which one of them was more shocked by the word. "Stay in Crimson," he said before he lost his nerve. "Stay with me."

She studied his face, as if searching for something to help her know how to answer. "Caden, I want to say yes."

He sat down across from her. "Then say yes."

"I need to talk to you about something before we go any further." She pushed her plate to the side and grabbed one of the file folders.

"That sounds ominous," he said with a smile that she didn't return. His stomach clenched when she opened the folder to reveal the spreadsheets and ledgers he recognized from the ranch's finances.

"Derek Lawson is stealing from you," she said, then swallowed hard. "I know he was your brother's friend—"

"Tyson's best friend," Caden clarified, shock and disbelief coursing through him. "Like one of the family."

Her chest rose and fell like she couldn't draw in enough air, but her gaze never left his. "He's skimming money from Garrett's accounts, Caden. I can prove—"

He stood up so suddenly his chair upended, landing on the floor with a clatter. "He warned me you'd do this."

Lucy's dark eyes widened. "He *warned* you?"

"He told me you called him and made some veiled accusations that—"

"I called him to see if he could explain the way he'd been keeping the books. Of course he got defensive because he's taking advantage of Sharpe Ranch and your dad's other businesses."

Caden paced to the counter, unable to look at her a moment longer. He gripped the edge of the granite until his knuckles turned white. "I bet you have a plan for getting things back on track," he said through clenched teeth.

"I have a few ideas," she agreed. "But first you need to confront Derek. He needs to admit—"

"No." Caden whirled around and stalked to the table. He couldn't allow himself to consider that Derek had betrayed him. Caden had been the one to recommend Tyson's old friend when Garrett needed help with the finances. If Derek was the villain here, it was once again Caden's fault for allowing him into their lives. He had to believe Lucy was lying.

She got out of her seat as he came toward her, not backing down for a moment. "You need to admit that this was your end game the entire time," he said.

He grabbed her arms and pulled her close enough that he could clearly see the flecks of gold around the edges of her brown eyes. "You and your mother planned the whole thing."

"Take your hands off me," she whispered, and he immediately let her go. Guilt warred with frustration inside him as she rubbed her hands against her skin where he'd held her.

Even now he wanted to put aside all of his anger and draw

her to him, continue to pretend that neither of them had a history that would make what was between them impossible. "How would I have planned for someone to steal from you? I didn't even know about Derek when I came to Crimson."

"But you knew that my dad had lots of money. Your mom knows how to pick the ones with deep pockets, right?"

Lucy narrowed her eyes but didn't contradict him, only fueling his temper.

"Derek warned me you were scheming to get your hands on Garrett's money. His guess was that your mom set you up to review the books and find fault with his methods."

"I find fault with him ripping you off," she insisted.

"You're lying. This is a con."

The color drained from her face at his accusation. "How can you believe that after everything that's happened between us?"

He crossed his arms over his chest and lifted a brow. "What's really happened, Lucy? Great sex? A couple of canned Christmas adventures? Did you stage the whole thing?"

She opened her mouth to argue, but the doorbell rang at that moment. Caden wanted to ignore it, but Sharpe Ranch didn't get many unannounced visitors. It could be something important. "We're not done here," he said as he turned away and moved toward the front of the house.

"Oh, yes, we are," she shouted after him.

He opened the door to reveal a tall beach-bum-type man, probably in his midfifties, with sandy blond hair and blue eyes framed by deeply tanned skin. He wore board shorts and a bulky down coat.

"You lost?"

"I'm looking for Reenie," the man said, trying to peer over Caden's shoulder. "She's not returning my calls."

"There's no one—"

"Bobby?" Lucy asked from behind him. "What are you doing here?"

"Your mom won't let up with the divorce papers, Luce. She flew me out to Colorado in the middle of winter, and now she's blowing me off."

Caden was so shocked at the man's words, he automatically took a step back.

Bobby used the opportunity to blow past Caden, heading straight for Lucy, who was now white as a ghost. "I told her the last time she can't get rid of me that easily." He wagged an angry finger in her face. "I'm not some old toy to be thrown in the trash."

"She doesn't love you, Bobby. Let her go."

"Not until she makes it worth my while. Her new man might think he can scare me off, but we both know better than that." He grabbed Lucy by the shoulders. "Talk to her, Luce."

She tried to shift away but the man held tight. "Don't touch her," Caden said.

"Dude, stay out of this. Lucy and I have got some business. Then I'll be on my way."

"You'll be on your way now." Caden grabbed the man's arm and twisted it behind his back.

Bobby let out a grunt, but his reflexes were slow, and Caden had him out into the cold morning before he could put up a decent fight.

He slammed shut the door and turned to Lucy. "I suppose you have an explanation for that, too?"

"You have to understand." She shook her head. "Mom told me she'd handle Bobby."

"So you knew she was ready to commit bigamy with my father?" The duplicity of that cut deep.

A tear tracked down Lucy's cheek as she squeezed her eyes shut. "She wouldn't have let it get that far."

"Right. It's all becoming clear now. I'm guessing Bobby is what ruined things with your mom's last boyfriend. Your mother and her not-so-ex-husband?"

"You have to believe me, Caden. She really loves your dad. I can hear it in her voice. She's different this time."

"Give me a break. The only thing that's different is that I ignored my gut when I should have trusted it. I knew you were trouble from the start. She brought you here to target me."

"No." She swiped a hand across her cheek. "She asked me to talk to you, but that was it."

"The sex was your idea of clinching the deal, then. Should I be flattered?"

"Stop making what we have into something ugly."

"We don't have *anything*."

She bit down on her lip, then whispered, "I love you, Caden. I know you feel—"

"No more." He reached her in two long strides but didn't touch her. Couldn't touch her without fear he'd lose his mind. Like he'd already lost his heart. "You know nothing about me or how I feel, so let me enlighten you."

He leaned in and she stumbled back a step. "I don't feel anything but disgust for you and your mother. You can damn well bet I'm going to do everything in my power to make sure my father sees your mother for the gold-digging grifter she truly is. There will be *no* marriage. I can promise you that."

"They're happy together."

"Until she breaks his heart."

"She won't," Lucy argued, but there was no heat behind it. "I'll make sure she doesn't."

"And I'm going to make sure you both are out of our lives. For good."

She closed her eyes as if it was too painful to look at him and, once again, Caden wanted to pull her to him. Instead he stalked out of the house toward the barn, welcoming the cold as it matched his frozen heart. He'd forgotten to grab a coat, so he pulled one from the office and climbed in his truck to check the fence line at the edge of the property.

He wasn't sure how his life had gone to hell so quickly, but right now he needed to get away from Lucy and the thought of her betrayal.

Even though he'd known better than to open his heart, he'd done it for her. Now his chest ached like it had been cut open. He wished he could remove the throbbing organ and get rid of it forever because he knew it would never mend from this pain.

Chapter 13

"You can stay here as long as you want."

Lucy sniffed as Erin handed her a bowl of ice cream later that night. She tried to force a smile but the corners of her mouth refused to pull up.

"I don't want to be in the way, especially during the holidays." She gestured to the Christmas tree set up in one corner of the cozy family room. "I must be ruining whatever plans you and David had for tonight."

After the argument with Caden that morning, Lucy had packed her bags and left Sharpe Ranch. How could she possibly face him again knowing what he believed about her?

Maybe she understood his initial reaction to what she'd told him, especially if Derek Lawson had already planted the seeds of doubt in his mind. Lucy often had misgivings about her mother's motivations regarding men, but there was something about the way she talked about Garrett that made Lucy believe this time it was different. Real.

It had been real for Lucy. That's why it hurt so badly when

Caden hadn't been willing to even hear her out. Now all she had was a heart that was truly broken.

"The bar is crazy busy with people in town for the holidays, so David and I don't have plans." Erin dropped onto the couch next to Lucy. "Today was the last day of school before winter break, so all I want to do is relax and watch sappy Christmas movies. It's good to have company for the night."

Lucy let out a watery laugh. "I'm terrible company right now."

"He'll come to his senses," Erin said quietly.

Lucy had wandered in and out of the shops in downtown Crimson most of the afternoon, watching people select last-minute Christmas presents for family and friends. She'd gotten more depressed with each passing minute, hating the fact that she'd opened herself to Caden and actually believed she might finally have a chance at love.

She'd tried calling and texting her mom, but Maureen hadn't responded to any of her messages. Her makeshift plan had been to check in to one of the local hotels until she'd run into Erin coming out of Life Is Sweet.

Erin had asked the innocuous question "How's it going," prompting Lucy to burst into fat, messy tears. Without missing a beat, Erin had wrapped her in a tight hug, then led her through the front of the bakery to the commercial kitchen, where Katie Crawford was just taking a pan of muffins out of one of the big ovens.

The two women had comforted Lucy, plying her with muffins and hot tea until she'd felt marginally better. She'd been through plenty of disappointment in her life and never realized how much having friends to support her could help make the pain more manageable.

"I think he's already made his decision." Lucy wiped her nose on her sleeve, not caring that she must look like a total wreck. "I feel like he's been waiting for a reason to prove to both of us that we could never work." She took a big bite of ice cream but missed her mouth. The spoonful of chocolate ice cream landed in the middle of her chest then rolled down the front of her gray sweatshirt. "I'm a mess," she whispered as fresh tears streamed down her cheeks.

"Oh, sweetie." Erin hurried to the kitchen, grabbed a paper towel from the roll hanging under the counter, then returned and picked the glob of chocolate off Lucy's stomach. "You're not a..." She paused, a pained look on her face. "We've all been where you are right now."

Lucy shook her head. "You've been red faced and blotchy with no place to go and chocolate all over your shirtfront?"

Katie gave a small laugh. "I didn't actually mean literally. I was talking about heartbroken."

"I should have known not to fall for him." Lucy placed the dish of ice cream on the coffee table, unable to stomach any more sugar. She'd never been much of a drinker, but she could make a career as a professional emotional eater. "He told me the first time we met that he'd hurt me." She hugged her arms around her waist.

"Caden doesn't have much experience letting down his defenses. He really cares about you, Lucy."

"Not anymore."

"You can't just turn off emotions like that."

"He did."

"I don't believe it. He's upset. He blamed himself for Tyson's death and became too focused on protecting Garrett after the accident. I think he was terrified of losing the only other person who really loves him."

"I loved him," Lucy whispered.

Erin arched a brow. "Past tense?"

"I still love him, because I'm the biggest fool on the planet. It doesn't matter, anyway."

"Of course it does. Give him time. To admit that Derek is stealing from Sharpe Ranch would mean that Caden failed to protect his dad. I'm not sure he could stand that."

"But it isn't his fault."

"I know that and you know that, but it's how his mind works. Why do you think he takes in all those unwanted animals? He's a rescuer. And Garrett is important because of how he once rescued Caden from that horrible foster care situation."

"You know him well," Lucy murmured.

Erin shrugged. "I was a shy kid so I did a lot of watching the people around me. I notice things." She smiled softly. "Caden was always so big and scary in school. I think he liked the reputation he had as a bad boy. He liked people being afraid of him. But when I was a freshman and he was a sophomore, I saw him sneaking behind the bleachers of the football field by himself every day during his lunch period and after school. I might have been shy, but I was always too curious for my own good."

A laugh bubbled up in Lucy's throat. "There's curious and there's having a death wish. Weren't you scared of what you'd find?"

Erin leaned in closer. "It was a nest of baby squirrels. I think the mom had died or deserted them, and Caden was hand-feeding them."

"Why didn't he just take them home to the ranch?"

"Maybe he thought Garrett wouldn't let him keep them. But after that, I knew his rough exterior hid a soft heart. I'm sure he thought I was crazy because I smiled and waved at him every chance I got from then on. He's built a lot of walls around his heart over the years, but the goodness inside him hasn't changed."

"The fact that I love him isn't enough. He doesn't trust me, and he doesn't trust my mom." Lucy shrugged. "Half the time I don't trust her, so I should have known better than to get involved with him. My mom always manages to land on her feet no matter what life throws at her. I'm more a face-plant-on-the-ground sort of girl."

She stood and walked to the window, looking out at the quaint neighborhood of historic bungalows decorated with colored lights. This Christmas was supposed to be different, but here she was, alone again.

"He'll be back to the house by now," she said, more to herself than Erin. "He must realize I'm gone."

"Did you leave a note?" Erin asked.

"No. A clean break is better for both of us."

"It doesn't have to be a break," Erin insisted, conviction lacing her gentle tone.

"Yes, it does." Lucy blinked away another round of tears. *No more crying.* "Caden made that quite clear, and I'm not going to beg anyone for a second chance."

If there was one thing she knew how to do, it was move on with her life.

"Are you drunk?"

"Go away, Chad. What I do on my time is none of your damn business." Caden went to slam the door in the young ranch hand's face, but his hand didn't connect with the wood, so instead he lost his balance and stumbled into the wall.

Chad stepped into the house, shutting the door behind him. "You drink over half that?" he asked, pointing to the bottle of whiskey on the coffee table.

Caden righted himself and tried to focus, but the edges of his vision remained blurry. "Maybe," he muttered, narrowing his eyes. "You want a glass?"

"Where's Lucy?" Suspicion laced Chad's tone.

"You're asking a crap ton of questions tonight." Caden walked toward his empty glass of whiskey, cursing under his breath as his shin hit the edge of the table.

"Are you going to answer any of them?"

"Another question." Caden pointed to the overstuffed leather chair on the opposite side of the coffee table. "Have a seat and a drink."

Chad whistled under his breath but moved to the wet bar, pulling a shot glass out of the cabinet. Caden handed him the whiskey bottle but made a noise of reproach when Chad poured only a finger of amber liquid into the glass.

"Who's the party pooper now?" Caden demanded.

"It's called pacing myself, buddy." Chad lifted his drink in mock salute. "You should try it."

Caden grabbed the whiskey bottle and tipped it up to his lips, not bothering with his glass. "I'm celebrating tonight."

"I can't wait to hear about the occasion."

"I dodged a bullet today." Caden smiled even though it felt like his insides were ripping apart as he said the lie out loud.

"Care to elaborate?"

"I got duped by the wrong kind of woman once already and paid dearly for my mistake. We all did. It cost Tyson his life."

Chad dropped into the leather chair and ran a hand through his blond hair. "Not this again."

"You're right." Caden pointed a finger at Chad but had a hard time zeroing in on him since the young ranch hand appeared to have two heads. Maybe Chad was right and Caden should stop drinking. Instead, he took another long pull on the whiskey bottle. "Never again will I allow myself to be led around by the—"

"Where's Lucy?" Chad asked, sitting forward. "I have a bad feeling you were an idiot today."

"I've been an idiot." Caden shook his head, then stopped abruptly when the room began to spin. "Today Lucy Renner revealed her true nature to me."

Chad rolled his eyes. "And how'd she do that?"

"I'm glad you asked." He rubbed a hand across his jaw but couldn't exactly feel his face at the moment. "She accused Derek of stealing from Sharpe Ranch."

He studied Chad for a reaction, but the cowboy just stared at him.

"Did you hear me?"

"I did." Chad nodded. "I have to say it doesn't surprise me."

"Are you joking?" Caden tried to lurch to his feet but landed back on the couch with a thump. "Derek was Tyson's best friend. My dad trusted him to help with the finances because he's like family. He'd never take advantage of us that way."

"Derek was jealous of Tyson. Always had been."

"Not true," Caden argued.

"My sister dated Derek in high school. I was a few years younger but I remember her complaining that he was obsessed with beating Tyson at everything."

"Your sister also dated Tyson," Caden said quietly.

"Yeah," he agreed. "After she broke up with Derek. I don't think that went over too well, either."

Caden narrowed his eyes. "Are you saying you believe Lucy?"

"Did she have proof?"

"I don't know," Caden admitted. "I shut her down before she had a chance to explain much to me."

"I have an even worse feeling now." Chad took a deep breath and asked, "How'd you shut her down?"

"I accused her of framing Derek so she and her mother could get to Garrett's money."

Chad let out a long groan. "Dude."

"What?" Caden demanded, suddenly feeling far more sober than he should have based on the amount of alcohol he'd consumed tonight. "Her mother has a history."

He stabbed at the air with one finger. "Hell, Maureen isn't even divorced from her last husband, who showed up here in the middle of my argument with Lucy. How do you like that little twist? Maureen Renner is willing to do anything to get what she wants. And Lucy knew about the husband. She doesn't—"

"Have you talked to your dad?"

Caden opened his mouth to answer then shut it again.

"Seriously?" Chad asked. "Don't you think you should figure out what Garrett knows before you make assumptions about the situation?"

"Of course he doesn't know," Caden said, blinking.

"He's not stupid, Caden. He was a wreck after Tyson died, but you weren't much better. He's got things under control. He met Maureen and fell in love with her, but he can take care of himself. If she has skeletons in her closet, I bet he knows they're there."

Caden shook his head. "He's not the same man as he was before the accident."

"Are you?"

"I don't matter."

"Tell that to your dad." Chad lifted his glass to his lips and drained it, then set it back on the table with a thunk. "Tell that to Lucy."

But Caden couldn't tell Lucy anything because...

"She's gone."

"Gone where?"

Caden lifted a brow. "She packed her bags and took off."

"Did you call her?"

"Why would I call her?"

Chad held out his hands, palms up. "To apologize for being an idiot?"

"You don't know that she's right about Derek."

"You don't know that she's wrong."

"I do..." Caden stopped midsentence as his stomach filled with bitter acid. The truth was, he didn't know anything. He'd made assumptions about Lucy and her mother based on what had happened to him—the way he'd been deceived and hurt. He should have known better than anyone that people's pasts didn't define them.

If that were the case, Garrett and Tyson would have never invited him into their home. He never would have had a family of his own. He'd made so many damned mistakes in his life, and there was a good chance the biggest one had been this morning when he'd hurt Lucy.

"It's actually good to know," Chad said as he stood, "that you're as human as the rest of us."

Caden glanced up, trying to focus on Chad's words over the pounding in his head. "What the hell is that supposed to mean?"

"Around here you're superhuman. You get up earlier than anyone else and work later. Hell, you even rescue unwanted animals. As far as Garrett is concerned, you can do no wrong."

Chad held up a hand when Caden was about to argue. "It sucked that Tyson died. There's no two ways about it. But it wasn't your fault, and everyone seems to know that except you. Your dad lost one son. Don't you think you owe it to him to let go of your guilt and be happy? That's all he wants, Caden."

"I'm happy," Caden lied.

"Lucy made you happy," Chad said. "I'm not a rocket scientist, but I'm smart enough to know that if a woman like her chose me, I'd do anything in my power to make sure I didn't screw it up."

He walked toward the front door, then turned back to Caden. "I get that loyalty is a big deal to you, but take another look at Derek. He might not be the friend you believe he is. And Lucy definitely isn't the enemy here, Caden."

Caden sat back against the couch cushions as the front door opened and closed. He swallowed against the bitterness rising in his throat. Was Chad right? Had he made a mistake in doubting Lucy? He'd been so sure he had a handle on things.

But the truth was his feelings for her scared the hell out of him, and in some ways having an excuse to push her away had been easier than really giving what was between the two of them a shot. She'd left him, but as much as that hurt, he could only imagine how much worse it would be if he'd admitted he loved her.

Oh, hell. He loved her.

He tipped back his head and the room started to spin again, matching the emotions swirling inside him. He closed his eyes, hoping to make everything go away, especially the mess he'd created for himself and the pain he'd caused the woman he loved.

Lucy slammed the trunk of her rental car shut the next afternoon and then turned to Erin.

"Have a wonderful Christmas," she said cheerily, pasting on a bright smile.

Erin's eyes gentled and Lucy knew she wasn't fooling her friend with her chipper tone.

"You should stay," Erin told her gently.

Lucy shook her head. "It's time for me to leave Crimson. My mom doesn't need me like she thinks she does. Garrett clearly loves her. As much as I'll miss you and the other ladies, this isn't my place. I can't go back to the ranch, and without that…"

"I'm still shocked that Caden hasn't come to his senses and reached out to you."

"Clearly Caden said everything he needed to me the other morning."

"But you can't spend Christmas alone," Erin insisted.

Lucy shrugged. "It won't be the first time, and at this point I just need to get home." Her voice cracked on the last word, and she pressed her lips together. During her short time in Crimson, this town had started to feel like home. Sharpe Ranch felt like home. Caden had become her home.

But that had all been an illusion, wishful thinking on her part.

"My plan is to stay the night in Albuquerque. If I make good time on the drive, I should reach Memphis by tomorrow. Maybe I'll spend Christmas at Graceland this year."

Erin looked past Lucy to the clouds gathering over Crimson Mountain. "The snow is going to get worse. You should at least wait until the storm passes."

Lucy glanced at her watch. "I don't know what's going on with my mom's phone, but Garrett texted that they made it to Denver and are on their way home. I want to be far enough away when they get to Crimson that she can't expect me to come back to the ranch. It's too difficult to think about facing Caden again."

"I'm going to have some words with that man," Erin told her.

"No." Lucy gave Erin a quick hug. "He's just trying to protect his dad."

"You're not the bad guy."

"I hope he realizes that someday."

Erin grabbed her hand and squeezed. "Are you sure you won't stay?"

"He hasn't given me a reason to," she said, pulling away.

"Be safe on the drive. Cell service is spotty until you get over the pass. Text or call when you're on the other side."

"I will." After a final hug, Lucy started on her way. As if on cue, the snow fell heavier as she turned onto the highway that led out of town. She patted the tiny car's dashboard, saying a silent prayer that the roads remained drivable until she was over Crimson Mountain.

Her initial plan had been to wait and leave after the forecast storm, but she had a vague premonition of being stranded in Crimson and her mother forcing another confrontation with Caden.

As much as she loved her mom and wanted to believe her feelings for Garrett were true, Caden hadn't been wrong in his assessment of Maureen's romantic history. The fact that Bobby Santino had shown up at the ranch and was probably still hanging around town didn't help matters.

No, she had to get out now.

There was only so much rejection she could withstand at one time. She needed to begin the difficult process of rebuilding her life and mending her broken heart. What other choice did she have?

Chapter 14

Caden pulled out his cell and punched in Lucy's number, then hit Cancel before placing the call. He'd done the same thing so many times throughout the day, he was surprised he hadn't worn an indentation into the phone's touch screen.

But not once had he actually let the call go through. He didn't know what the hell he'd say if she actually picked up. He'd woken early with a Rocky Mountain–sized headache. After a morning spent in one of the far pastures, he'd come into the house and flipped open the files Lucy had left on the kitchen table.

The accounting side of the business had never been his responsibility, but he looked for discrepancies or ledger entries that would give him some clue as to the truth of what was happening with the Sharpe Ranch finances.

When he heard the front door open late in the afternoon, he sprang up, hope blooming that Lucy had returned and they could work things out.

Instead, he found his dad and Maureen in the farmhouse's entry, both hauling in giant suitcases.

"You didn't leave with that much stuff," he said by way of greeting.

Garrett gave a hearty laugh. "We had to buy new luggage in the city just to manage our haul for the way home."

"Your father is quite the shopper," Maureen said, grinning at him.

"Right," Caden muttered, then felt his mouth drop open as Garrett's eyes lit with excitement.

"Those salespeople couldn't keep up with me," he said with a laugh. "We're going to have one helluva Christmas this year, son." He turned to Maureen and gave her a smacking kiss on the lips. "I can't remember when I had so damn much fun."

Maybe he hadn't realized it before, but Caden was suddenly struck by how happy his dad looked. Color was high on his cheeks and his blue eyes sparkled with joy.

"Where's Lucy?" Maureen asked, pulling a small paper bag out of her purse. "I found something for her in the airport. She used to collect snow globes, so I—"

"She's gone," Caden said tightly.

Erin MacDonald had texted him last night with the message that Lucy was staying in town with her. At least he knew she was safe and with a friend, but he wasn't ready to share that with Maureen. If Lucy had wanted her mother to know where she was, he figured she would have called her.

Garrett took off his canvas jacket and hung it on the coat hook next to the door. "When will she be back? The four of us should go into town for dinner tonight."

Caden's stomach clenched at the question he had no idea how to answer. "I don't think she's coming back."

Maureen's finely arched brows drew together. "What happened?" She took a step toward Caden. "What did you do?"

"Let him explain, darlin'." Garrett placed a hand on Maureen's arm.

"I think *you* need to explain," Caden told Maureen, letting yesterday's anger surge back into his veins. "Maybe you want to explain to my father why your not-so-ex-husband paid a visit to the ranch and Lucy accused a longtime family friend of stealing from the ranch."

Maureen's mouth dropped open. "Bobby was here?"

"I told you I didn't think my message to him went through on the plane," Garrett said, shaking his head. "I hope he didn't give you and Lucy any trouble, Caden."

"What message?" Caden demanded.

"I told him I need to reschedule our meeting for today."

Caden pointed between his father and Maureen. "You already know she's still married?"

"I wanted to keep it a secret and try to handle Bobby myself," Maureen admitted. "But that didn't work out so well in the past. Lucy convinced me to share the truth with your father."

Garrett took a step forward, and Caden was reminded of all the times he'd been lectured for making stupid decisions as a teenager. "You knew I asked Lucy to review the finances. I needed someone unbiased to confirm my suspicions about Derek."

Caden ran a hand through his hair, a sick pit opening in his stomach. "Suspicions?"

"I could tell something wasn't right with the way he was handling the books. His monthly reports had discrepancies that made no sense. But he was a supposed friend of your brother's and you seemed to trust him implicitly. I didn't want to accuse him without having proof."

"Lucy truly is a whiz with numbers. They trusted her with everything at the store in Florida—at least, until I got involved." Maureen shook her head, obviously regretting the difficulties she'd caused her daughter.

Caden cursed under his breath. "Derek convinced me that Lucy and Maureen were trying to frame him so they could get access to your money."

Garrett's eyes narrowed. "That son of a—"

"I love your father," Maureen said, taking Garrett's hand in hers. "I understand you had your doubts when I came to Crimson, and I hoped spending time with Lucy would show you I couldn't be the woman you first thought. Not with Lucy in my corner. She's truly the best part of me."

"I said awful things to her," Caden said quietly, hating himself for what an ass he'd been. But not half as much as he imagined Lucy hated him right now.

"I raised you better than that," Garrett said sharply.

"Damn it, I was trying to protect you. I've failed everyone I ever loved, and I wasn't going to fail you again."

Caden couldn't stand the sorrow in his father's eyes. He couldn't help but believe he'd put it there.

"You've never failed me," Garrett whispered.

Caden wanted to run away, like he had as a boy after his mother had died. Like he had from the first foster home social services had dropped him into. And the second. And the third. But it was time both he and Garrett faced the truth of what he'd done. It was the only way he'd ever move forward. "I let Tyson die."

Garrett took a step back, as if Caden had slapped him. "You don't believe that. You can't."

"Why not?" Caden threw up his hands. "It's the truth. If I'd been there, I might have reached him in time."

Garrett squeezed his eyes shut, his barrel chest rising and falling. Caden noticed that he never let go of Maureen's hand.

In fact, Garrett pulled her closer as if drawing strength from having her next to him.

Caden realized that's how he'd felt about Lucy when they were together, and another wave of regret washed over him.

"Tyson was killed on impact," his dad said in a dull tone. "You talked to the search-and-rescue commander. We both read the report."

"But I—"

"It was an accident, Caden. A horrible, tragic accident. The only thing that kept me from going crazy was that I still had you. The fact that you put your career—your whole life—on hold to come back here meant everything to me. But it tears me apart to know you're still blaming yourself. You've let your entire world shrink to this ranch because of some misplaced sense of duty."

"It's not misplaced. You're my father," Caden said, clearing his throat when his voice cracked. "You saved me."

"It was an honor to raise you." Garrett moved forward and placed a gentle hand on Caden's shoulder. "I'm proud of the man you've become despite everything you've been through. But for you to hurt Lucy—"

"Why didn't you say something to me about Derek?"

Garrett's smile was sad. "You're protective and loyal to a fault. Derek was supposed to be your brother's best friend. I wanted to be certain before I took action."

"I've screwed up so badly."

"Where's Lucy?" Maureen interrupted. "I lost my phone yesterday when we were walking through Central Park. Garrett texted Lucy to keep her updated on our arrival home, but she didn't call back or message him."

She took a shuddery breath. "She doesn't know that Garrett had flown Bobby to Colorado to force him to sign the divorce papers. She probably thinks I didn't handle anything and left her out here to deal with the fallout from my mistakes."

"Lucy is staying with a friend in Crimson. But from what I understand, she has good reason to believe that about you."

"Caden." Garrett's tone had that telltale angry-dad edge.

"He's right," Maureen admitted. "I haven't always been the best mom. I'm selfish and immature."

"Darlin', no," Garrett murmured.

"I'm trying to be a better person." She swiped under her eyes and looked straight at Caden. "Your father has a lot to do with that. But so does Lucy. She deserves better."

Caden sighed, scrubbed a hand across his jaw. "If she gives me another chance, I'm going to be the man she deserves."

Maureen turned to Garrett. "Give me your phone, hon. I have to reach her."

"Let me call," Caden said, pulling his phone from his back pocket.

Maureen lifted a brow. "Do you really think she'll want to talk to you right now?"

Caden wanted to argue, but she was right.

Maureen paced to the edge of the room as she punched in the number. "Pick up," she whispered, the phone pressed to her ear. "Pick up." She let out a little cry of relief. "Lucy-Goose, it's me. I just heard about your argument with Caden."

There was a pause, and Maureen's lips pressed into a thin line. "I know, sweetie. I'm sorry. Garrett flew him to Colorado so we could handle the divorce paperwork in person. He's agreed to sign. Garrett made sure of it. I took your advice and told him everything."

Another pause. "You were right about that, too. Caden knows we had no plan to take advantage of anyone." Her voice lowered. "He's really sorry, baby. I can tell how bad he feels about doubting you." She shook her head as she listened to something Lucy said. "You've got to drive back out to the ranch. We can work everything—" Her mouth formed a small

O. "What do you mean you're gone? Where in the world is Jackrabbit Pass?"

Caden took a step forward. "That's on the other side of Crimson Mountain," he told Maureen, then glanced to the window where snow blew in frenetic circles, dancing in the light from the porch lamp. "Usually they close it in this kind of weather."

Garrett nodded. "From the time we got off the interstate and drove into town, at least two inches of snow fell. I can only imagine the conditions on Jackrab—"

He broke off as Maureen let out a startled cry.

"Lucy!" she screamed into the phone. "Are you there?"

"What happened?" Caden rushed forward and snatched the device from her hand.

"She yelled something about sliding," Maureen said, her voice shaking. "Then there was a terrible sound. Metal on metal. Like a crash."

The screen had gone dark, and he immediately punched in Lucy's number again. The call went straight to voice mail.

Caden tossed the phone to his dad and grabbed his coat. "Get a hold of Cole Bennett. See if anyone from the sheriff's department is out that way. Then try the fire department and Jeremy. They should have plows running out that way. Someone has to be close to her. Call me if Lucy contacts you."

"Where are you going?" his father asked as he reached for his phone.

"Jackrabbit Pass," Caden answered, snow billowing into the house when he opened the door. "I'm going to bring Lucy home."

It took Caden almost an hour to reach the summit, although he drove like he was qualifying for the winter version of the Indy 500.

The plows had taken care of the main highway, but as soon as he turned onto the winding, two-lane road that led up Crimson Mountain and south toward Jackrabbit Pass, conditions worsened with every passing minute.

His rear wheels lost traction several times even though his truck had studded snow tires and sandbags weighing down the back end. He couldn't imagine Lucy's cracker-box rental car driving up and over the icy pass. Hell, she must have been desperate to put miles between the two of them to attempt it.

He'd seen a couple of big SUVs making their way slowly down the curvy road, but neither of them had stopped despite him flashing his brights to flag them down.

His cell phone remained maddeningly dark where it sat on the console next to him. He didn't put a lot of stock in prayer, but he'd offered up a litany of silent pleas, mainly addressed to his brother, begging to find Lucy safe.

With his heart thudding against his ribs and tension pounding through his bloodstream, it was difficult to remember why he'd been so angry with her. He quickly realized pride and fear had mingled together to drive his reaction. It was tough to admit he'd so misjudged a man he thought was a family friend, especially after the deception by his lying, cheating ex-girlfriend had caused the rift with Tyson.

But he'd allowed his anger toward one woman to make him wrongfully mistrust another. Lucy's mother did truly love his father. He'd been so convinced that he couldn't trust any woman again, but part of that had been fear of being hurt overshadowing what his heart felt.

He loved Lucy in a way he'd never imagined himself capable of feeling. That scared the hell out of him. Love meant being hurt. But nothing could hurt as much as the thought of losing her.

He had to find her and convince her to give him another chance—to make sure she was safe.

He couldn't lose her, too.

Snow swirled in the light of the truck's lights as he started down the other side of Jackrabbit Pass. The storm raged so fast and hard that there were no other tire tracks on the road, and he was forced to slow down and pay close attention to the snow markers along the shoulder. The side of the mountain dropped off sharply on his right, with the tops of snow-covered pine trees forming a blanket across the landscape.

Although he was used to winter driving in the mountains, his whole body was rigid with tension. How the hell could Lucy handle this?

As if in answer to his question, his lights picked up the flash of taillights about a hundred yards ahead of him around the bend of a sharp switchback.

He swallowed back a rush of terror when he inched closer and recognized Lucy's car. It had crashed into the guardrail and the front quarter of the vehicle was hanging over the shoulder. He pulled off and bolted from the truck, racing through the snow and darkness toward the small car.

"Lucy," he shouted, but the only answer was the wind whistling around him.

The car looked stable, but as he got closer he noticed the driver's-side door was slightly ajar. Panic almost brought him to his knees as a hundred terrifying scenarios ran through his head.

"Lucy," he called again, shining the flashlight from his phone toward the interior of the car. A thick layer of fresh snow covered the windows, and he dusted it off, praying to find her uninjured.

"Caden?"

He whirled around at the sound of her voice behind him. Suddenly headlights from a truck he hadn't noticed when he pulled up illuminated her. Terror changed to relief but the power of what he felt still threatened to bring him to his knees.

He moved toward her, hardly believing she was real.

"How did you get here?" she asked. "The snowplow driver told me—"

He crushed his mouth against hers, needing to feel her for himself. He needed to inhale her breath into his lungs, trying to regain his footing from the emotional abyss on which he still teetered.

"You scared the hell out of me," he whispered against her skin, trailing kisses across her cheeks and over her eyelids. "You're okay?" He pulled back, cupping her face between his palms. "Tell me you're fine, Lucy."

"A little shaken up," she admitted. "And the car is in bad shape."

"Tell me—"

"I'm okay," she said, putting a finger to his lips. "I was going really slow and I know I should have pulled off, but I was—"

"Leaving me," he finished.

Her brow furrowed. "You made it clear that we had no future. You didn't trust me. You accused me of... How could you think those things? How can we ever have a chance when you're willing to believe the worst?"

Lucy was proud her voice remained steady as she asked the questions that had been plaguing her since she'd driven away from Sharpe Ranch.

She wanted to lean into Caden, to let his strength melt away the lingering terror from the drive up the mountain and the rental car's slide across the icy road and into the guardrail.

But while her time in Crimson had been short, the town and the friends she'd made there had changed her. She'd always been satisfied with scraps of a life because she hadn't believed she deserved anything more.

Now she did, and even though she loved Caden, she wouldn't allow anyone to make her feel less than who she knew herself to be.

He studied her for several long moments, snowflakes clinging to his hair and his breath coming out in tiny clouds of air.

"I'm sorry," he said finally. "You have every reason to walk away from me, Lucy. I tend to make a mess of things with the people I love most."

She sucked in a breath, almost choking on the cold air. "You love me?"

The tips of his warm fingers melted the snowflakes that stuck to her cheeks. "I love you with everything I am, but I have a hard time believing that's enough." He closed his eyes for a moment and when he opened them again, she saw the scared little boy that had survived so much before coming to live on Sharpe Ranch. "I can't believe *I'm* enough, so it's easier to create a reason why things won't work out. Because if I end it first, the break will hurt less."

"Does it hurt less?" she asked quietly.

He shook his head. "It feels like I ripped out my own heart."

"Mine, too."

"I'm sorry I hurt you. You're everything to me, Lucy. My very own Christmas miracle, and I don't even believe in miracles. Not until you came into my life and turned it upside down. You're beautiful and smart and have the sweetest heart I could ever imagine. I know I don't deserve another chance but give me one, anyway. Please. I can do better. I will do better. I'll make you so happy."

"You already do," she told him, hope blooming warm and bright in her chest, like they were standing in a sunny field of flowers instead of on a remote mountain pass in the middle of a blizzard.

He leaned in and kissed her gently as if mending the pain he'd caused. "Will you take me on, Lucy? I promise I'll leave my idiot days in our past." The words were soft against her lips. "You're the only future I want. I can't imagine my life without you. Please say—"

"Yes," she whispered and wrapped her arms around his neck, sighing when he pulled her tight against him. "I'll give you a million chances. I love the man that you are, although we're definitely going to need to work on the idiot tendencies."

"Reformed idiot," he said with a smile. "You've reformed me."

"I wouldn't want that job to go to anyone else." She laughed as he lifted her and spun her around.

A loud whistle had them both turning to see the snowplow driver waving from the cab of his truck. "Y'all think you might want to take that lovey-dovey stuff indoors? If you haven't noticed, the snow's not letting up. We need to get off this mountain sooner than later."

"Let's go," Caden said, tucking Lucy against his side. They spoke to the driver for a few moments, and he suggested they follow him down the mountain in Caden's truck and come back for Lucy's car once the storm passed.

"I'm sorry you had to come out in this to find me," she said after they'd collected her things and climbed into the truck. Caden turned it around and pulled back onto the road.

"You never have to apologize," he answered. "There isn't anything I wouldn't do for you, Lucy. I'd drive through a thousand storms to bring you home. I love you."

"Home," she repeated, cherishing the thought of finally having a place she belonged. And knowing without a doubt that her place was with Caden. Forever.

Epilogue

"It's almost midnight," Lucy told Caden one week later as she glanced at her watch.

"Time for a New Year's Eve break," he said, plucking the paint roller from her hand.

"But we're so close." She stepped back to survey her progress. As Caden worked on installing new trim and crown molding throughout the cozy family room, Lucy had been busy painting the decades-old pine paneling a fresh shade of creamy white.

Although they'd been invited to ring in the New Year with friends in Crimson, Lucy and Caden had chosen to stay on the ranch and continue renovations on the little guesthouse behind the barn. Garrett and Maureen weren't scheduled to return from their honeymoon for another week, and Lucy wanted to make sure Caden was settled in the guesthouse before they got back. They wanted to give the newlyweds privacy and also retain some for themselves where they could.

She'd moved in with Erin MacDonald and planned to sublet

her new friend's apartment once Erin and David were married over Valentine's Day weekend. As much as she loved Caden and her time with him, she felt strangely old-fashioned about living with him at the start of their relationship. Everything felt so fresh and new, and she wanted them both to have time to adjust to the changes in their lives before they moved in together.

"Can't we just count down later?" she asked. "I'm so close to finishing this wall."

"Maybe you want to rethink the business degree," Caden said with a laugh, gently taking her wrist and tugging her toward the door, "and go for your contractor's license. I've never met someone who wants to work like you, and I grew up on a ranch."

"I might consider that," she said. "Some of the online programs I'm looking at have specializations in construction management." The truth was, she loved everything about renovating the old space and turning it into something new. Although just a month ago, she would have dismissed the idea of trying a new focus for her career, she'd come to see that she had way more to offer than she'd ever realized.

"You'd be a natural," he said, pulling a coat from the rack and draping it over her shoulders. "But I believe you'd be a success at anything you set your mind to."

"I like the thought of that," she said, slipping her hand into his. They walked out into the cold, clear night and Caden led her behind the house, to the edge of the field where they had an unobstructed view of Crimson Mountain.

"It's pretty in the moonlight," she said.

"Just wait."

As if on cue, there was a loud whistling in the distance, and a bright light shot into the air from the base of the mountain. A moment later, a booming sound reverberated through the night, and fireworks exploded above the peak.

Lucy gasped with delight. "It's amazing."

Caden shifted so that he was standing behind her, and she leaned back against his chest as his arms came around her. "Happy New Year," he whispered against her ear. "I love you."

"I love you, too," she said and turned her head to kiss him, letting the happiness she'd discovered this holiday season light her heart until she flared as bright as the fireworks on Crimson Mountain. "Always and forever."

* * * * *

BRING ME A MAVERICK FOR CHRISTMAS!

BRENDA HARLEN

This book is dedicated to Ryan. I know you stopped writing letters to Santa a lot of years ago, but as you finish up your first term at university, I'm making three wishes for you this season:

1. that you eternally believe in the magic of Christmas;

2. that you always know how proud I am of you; and

3. that you forever remember how much I love you. XO

Chapter 1

"No way in ho-ho-hell," Bailey Stockton said, his response to his brother's request firm and definitive.

"Hear me out," Dan urged.

"No," he said again. He'd been conscripted to help with far too much Christmas stuff already. Such as helping Luke decorate Sunshine Farm for the holidays and sampling a new Christmas cookie recipe that Eva was trying out (okay, that one hadn't been much of a hardship—the cookies, like everything she made, were delicious). His youngest brother, Jamie, had even asked him to babysit—yes, babysit!—so that he could take his wife into Kalispell to do some shopping for their triplets and enjoy a holiday show.

In fact, Bailey had been enlisted for so many tasks, he'd begun to suspect that his siblings had collectively made it their personal mission to revive his holiday spirit. Because he couldn't seem to make them understand that his holiday spirit was too far gone to be resurrected. They'd have better luck planning the burial and just letting him pretend the holidays didn't exist.

"But it's for Janie's scout troop," Dan implored.

Janie was Dan and Annie's daughter—the child his brother had only found out about when he returned to Rust Creek Falls not quite eighteen months earlier. Since then, his brother had been doing everything he could to make up for lost time. Which Bailey absolutely understood and respected; he just didn't want to be conscripted toward the effort.

"Then *you* do it," he said.

"I was planning to do it," Dan told him. "And I was looking forward to it, but I'm in bed now with some kind of bug."

"Is that a pet name for Annie?"

"Ha ha," his brother said, not sounding amused.

"Well, you don't sound very sick to me," Bailey noted.

"That's because you haven't heard me puking."

"And I don't mind missing out on that," he assured his brother.

"I need your help," Dan said again.

"I'm sorry you're not up to putting on the red suit, but there's got to be someone else who can do it."

"You don't think I tried to find someone else?" Dan asked. "I mean, no offense, big brother, but when I think of Christmas spirit, yours is not the first name that springs to mind."

Bailey took no offense to his brother speaking the truth. But he was curious: "Who else did you ask?"

"Luke, Jamie, Dallas Traub, Russ Campbell, Anderson Dalton, even Old Gene. No one else is available. You're my last resort, Bailey, and if you don't come through—"

"Don't worry," Annie interrupted, obviously having taken the phone from her husband. "He'll come through. Won't you, Bailey?"

He hated to let them down, but what they were asking was

beyond his abilities. And way outside his comfort zone. "I wish I could, but—"

That was as far as he got in formulating a response before his sister-in-law interjected again.

"You can," she said. "You just need to stop being such a Grooge."

"A *what*?"

"A Grooge," she said again. "Since you have even less Christmas spirit than either the Grinch or Scrooge, I've decided you're a Grooge."

"Definitely not Santa Claus material," he felt compelled to point out.

"Under normal circumstances, I'd agree," Annie said. "But these aren't normal circumstances and your brother needs you to step up and help out, because that's what families do. And that's why I know you're going to do this."

Chastened by his sister-in-law's brief but pointed lecture, how could he do anything else?

But he had no intention of giving in graciously. "Bah, humbug."

"I'll take that as a yes," Annie said.

Bailey could only sigh. "What time and where?"

"I'll meet you at the Grace Traub Community Center in an hour."

And so, an hour later, Bailey found himself at the community center, in one of the small activity rooms that had been repurposed as a dressing room for the event. Annie bustled around, helping him dress.

"Is this really necessary?" he asked, as she secured the padded belly.

"Of course, it's necessary. Santa's not a lean mean rancher—he's a toy maker with a milk-and-cookies belly."

He slid his arms into the big red coat and fastened the wide belt around his expanded middle.

"Now sit so that I can put on your beard and wig and fix your face," Annie said.

He sat. Then scowled. "What do you mean—fix my face?"

"Relax and let me do my thing."

"'Do my thing' are not words that inspire me to relax," he told her.

But he clenched his jaw and didn't say anything else as she unzipped a pouch and pulled out a tube that looked suspiciously like makeup. She brushed whatever it was onto his eyebrows, then took out a pot and another brush that she used on his cheeks.

"I can't believe I let you talk me into this," he grumbled.

"I know this isn't your idea of fun, but it means a lot to Dan that you stepped up."

"I didn't step," he reminded her. "I was pushed."

Her lips curved as she recapped the pot and put it back in the bag. "Now the beard," she said, and hooked the elastic over his ears.

"No one's going to thank me for this when I screw it up," he warned her.

"You're not going to screw it up."

"Beyond *ho ho ho*, I don't have a clue what to say."

"This might be a first for you, but it's not for the kids," she told him. "And if you really get stuck, I have no doubt that your wife will be able to help you out."

Wife? "Who? What?"

"Mrs. Claus," she clarified.

"You didn't say anything about a Mrs. Claus."

And he didn't know if the revelation now made things better or worse. On the one hand, he was relieved that he wouldn't have to face a group of kids on his own. On the other, he was skeptical enough about his ability to play a jolly elf, but a jolly elf with a wife?

"I didn't think any kind of warning was necessary," Annie said now. "It was supposed to be me—I was going to be the missus to Dan's Santa, but when he got sick, well, I couldn't leave him to suffer at home alone, so I asked a friend to fill in. But you don't have to worry. Mrs. Claus will be here to hand out candy canes and keep the line moving—no romantic overtures are required."

"Thanks, I feel so much better now," he said dryly.

"Good," she said, ignoring his sarcasm. "And speaking of spouses—I should get home to my husband, who isn't feeling better but is feeling grateful."

"Do you want me to drop off this costume later?"

"No, I'll come back and get it," she said.

When she'd gone, Bailey chanced a hesitant glance in the mirror. He was afraid he'd look as stupid as he felt—like a kid playing dress-up—and was surprised to realize that he looked like Santa.

There was a brisk knock at the door. "Are you just about ready, Santa?" The scout leader poked his head in the doorway. "Wow, you look great."

"Ho ho ho," Bailey said, testing it out.

The scout leader grinned and gave him two thumbs-up. "The kids are getting restless."

"Mrs. Claus isn't here yet," he said. Although he hadn't originally known there was supposed to be a Mrs. Claus, he now felt at a loss on his own.

"Maybe she got caught up baking cookies at the North Pole," the other man joked.

Whatever she was doing, wherever she was, his missus was nowhere to be found, reminding Bailey of the foolishness of depending on a spouse—even a fictional one.

"Okay, then." He exited the makeshift dressing room and followed the scout leader backstage. Though the curtains were closed, he could hear the excited chatter of what sounded like hundreds, maybe thousands, of children. All of them there to see Santa—and getting stuck with a poor imitation instead.

He felt perspiration bead on his brow and his hands were clammy inside his white cotton gloves. The leader handed him a big sack filled with candy canes and nodded encouragingly.

It was now or never, and although Bailey would have preferred to go with the never option, he suspected his brother would never forgive him if he chickened out.

Just as he was reaching for the curtain, he heard footsteps rushing up the stage stairs behind him.

Mrs. Claus had arrived.

He didn't have time to give her much more than a cursory glance, noting the floor-length red dress with faux fur trim at the collar and cuffs, and a white apron tied around her waist. Despite the white wig and granny glasses, he could tell that she was young. Her skin was smooth and unwrinkled, her lips plump and exquisitely shaped, and her eyes were as bright and blue as the Montana sky.

"Good, I'm not late." She was breathless, obviously having run some distance, and paused now with her hand on her heart as she drew air into her lungs.

Of course, the action succeeded in drawing his attention to her chest—and the rise and fall of nicely rounded breasts.

"Are you ready to do this?" she asked.

He nodded. *Yes. Please.*

She sent him a conspiratorial wink, and suddenly he felt warm all over. Or maybe it was the bulky costume and the overhead lights that were responsible for the sudden increase in his body temperature.

Then she stepped through the break in the curtains and began to speak to the children.

"Well, we ran into a little bit of rough weather on our way from the North Pole, but we finally made it," she said.

The crowd of children cheered.

Bailey listened to her talk, enjoying the melodic tone of her voice as she set the scene for their audience. He didn't know who she was—he hadn't thought to ask his sister-in-law—but it was immediately apparent to Bailey that Annie had cast a better Mrs. Claus than her husband had a Santa.

"I know you've all been incredibly patient waiting for Santa to arrive and everyone wants to be first in line to whisper Christmas wishes in his ear, but I promise you, it doesn't matter if you're first or last or somewhere in the middle, everyone will have a turn."

They had a wide armchair set up on the stage, beside a decorated Christmas tree surrounded by a pile of fake presents. All he had to do was walk through the curtain and settle into the chair. But his feet were suddenly glued to the floor.

"While Santa finishes settling the reindeer," she said, offering another explanation for the delay of his appearance, "why don't we sing his favorite Christmas song?" She looked out at the audience. "Who knows what Santa's favorite Christmas song is?"

Through the narrow gap between the curtains, he could see hands immediately thrust into the air.

Mrs. Claus listened to several random guesses as the children called for "Jingle Bells," "Let It Snow" and "All I Want for Christmas," shaking her head after each response.

"Okay, I'm going to give you a clue," she said. Then, in a singing voice, she asked, *"Who's got a beard that's long and white?"*

The children responded as a chorus: *"Santa's got a beard that's long and white."*

It was an upbeat and catchy tune with call-and-response lyrics that made it easy for the kids who didn't know the words to sing along anyway, and Bailey found his booted foot tapping against the floor along with the music.

The young audience was completely caught up in the song, and he was reluctant to interrupt. But when Mrs. Claus asked, *"Who very soon will come our way?"* it seemed like an appropriate time to step out from behind the curtain.

"Santa very soon will..."

The response of the chorus faded away as the singers noticed that Santa was, in fact, here now. Several clapped, others pointed and many whispered excitedly to their neighbors.

"And here he is," Mrs. Claus said, then smiled warmly at him and gestured for him to take a seat.

Bailey nodded as he made his way to the chair. He was too nervous to smile back, although she probably couldn't tell if he was or wasn't smiling behind the bushy mustache that hung over his mouth anyway.

He settled into his seat as the leader announced that the young Tiger Scouts would get to visit with Santa first. There were craft tables at the far end of the room for groups waiting to be called and refreshments available.

Bailey felt his palms grow clammy again as the kids lined up, but it didn't take him long to realize that his sister-in-law had been right: the kids knew what they were doing. In fact, most of them didn't expect much from him beyond listening to their wishes and offering them a "Merry Christmas."

There were a lot of requests for specific toys and new video games. A couple of requests for puppies and kittens, building blocks and board games, hockey skates or ballerina slippers. Some of the kids asked questions, wanting to know such random facts as "who's your favorite reindeer?" or "how old is Rudolph?"

He gave vague responses, so as not to contradict anything else they might have been told by their parents, and he was careful not to make any promises, assuring each child only that he would do his best to make their wishes come true.

And if he was a little stiff and unnatural, his supposed wife was the complete opposite—warm and kind and totally believable. She did more than move the line along and hand out candy canes. She seemed to instinctively know what to say and do to put the little ones at ease.

He was about halfway through the Bear Scouts and finally starting to relax into his role when a scowling boy climbed into his lap.

Bailey, anticipating one of the usual requests, was taken aback when the boy said, "Christmas sucks."

"Yeah," Bailey agreed. "Sometimes it does."

Mrs. Claus gasped and the boy's eyes immediately filled with tears.

"You're not s'posed to agree," the child protested. "You're s'posed to tell me that it's gonna be okay."

Since Bailey didn't know what *it* was, he didn't feel he should make any such promises. But he belatedly acknowledged that he shouldn't have responded the way he did, either. Being called out by the child was only further proof that taking his brother's place as Santa had been a bad idea.

"Now, Santa," Mrs. Claus chided. "I told you not to take your grumpy mood out on the children or I'll have to put *you* on the naughty list."

This threat served to both distract and intrigue the little boy, who eyed her with rapt fascination.

"I'm sorry, Owen," she continued, speaking directly to the child now. "Santa's a little out of sorts today because I warned him that he has to cut down on the cookies if he wants to fit down the chimneys on Christmas Eve."

Then she sent Bailey a pointed look that had him nodding in acknowledgment of her claim as he rubbed his padded belly. "I really like gingerbread," he said, in a conspiratorial whisper to the boy his "wife" had called Owen. "But I definitely don't want to end up on the naughty list."

"Can she do that?" Owen asked.

He nodded again, almost afraid to do otherwise. "So tell me, Owen, is there anything Santa can do to help make the holidays happier for you?"

"Can you make Riley not move to Bozeman?" he asked hopefully.

This time Bailey did shake his head. "I'm sorry."

The child's gaze shifted toward Mrs. Claus again. "Can *she* do it?" Because apparently the boy believed Mrs. Claus not only had authority over her husband but greater magical powers, too.

"I'm sorry," he said again.

Owen sighed. "Then maybe you could leave a PKT-79 under my tree at Christmas and I can give it to Riley, so that he'll have something to remember me by."

It wasn't the first request for a PKT-79, and though Bailey still had no idea what it was, he was touched by the child's request for the gift to give to someone else.

"I'll see what I can do," Santa told him. "Merry Christmas."

"Yeah," Owen said, his tone slightly less glum. "Merry Christmas."

Mrs. Claus held out a candy cane to the boy.

Owen paused to ask her, "You'll make sure Santa can get down my chimney, won't you?"

"You bet I will," she promised, with a wink and a smile for the boy.

Bailey paid more attention after that, to avoid another slipup. When all the children had expressed their wishes to Santa, he and his wife wished everyone a Merry Christmas and headed backstage again.

By the time he made it to the dressing room, Bailey was more than ready to shed the red coat and everything it represented, but Mrs. Claus walked into the room right behind him.

Closing the door firmly at her back, she faced him with her hands on her hips. "I don't know why anyone would ask someone with such an obviously lousy disposition to play Santa, but you have no right to ruin Christmas for the kids who actually look forward to celebrating the holiday."

Bailey already felt guilty enough for his unthinking response to Owen, but he didn't appreciate being taken to task—*again*—by a stranger, and instinctively lashed out. "A lecture from my loving wife? Now I really do feel like we're married."

"I'd pity any woman who married you," she shot back.

His ready retort stuck in his throat when she took off the granny glasses and removed the wig, causing her long blond hair to tumble over her shoulders, effecting an instant and stunning transformation.

Mrs. Claus was a definite hottie.

Too bad she was also bossy and annoying. And...vaguely familiar looking, he realized.

She twisted her arm up behind her back, trying to reach the top of the zipper, but her fingertips fell short of their target.

While she struggled, Bailey removed his own hat, wig and beard.

She brought her arm around to her front again and tried to reach the back of the dress from over her shoulder, still without success.

He should offer to help. That would be the polite and gentlemanly thing to do. But as his sister-in-law had noted, he was a Grooge and, still stinging from Mrs. Claus's sharp rebuke, not in a very charitable or helpful mood. Instead, he unbuckled his wide belt, removed the heavy jacket and padded belly, eager to shed the external trappings of his own role.

Finally, she huffed out a breath. "You could offer to help, you know?"

"If you need help, you could ask," he countered.

"Would you *please* help me unzip my dress?" she finally said.

"Usually I buy a woman dinner before I try to get her out of her clothes." He couldn't resist teasing. "But since you asked…"

Chapter 2

She turned her back to give Bailey access to the zipper, but not before he saw her roll her eyes in response to his comment. "Do you have to work at being offensive or is it a natural talent?"

"It's a defense mechanism," he said, surprising them both with his honesty. "I screwed up in there—I know I did. I knew I would. That's why I didn't want to put on the stupid suit and pretend to be jolly."

"You ever try actually *being* jolly instead of just pretending?" she asked, as he tugged on the zipper pull.

"Yeah, but it didn't work out so well."

"I'm sorry." She pulled her arms out of the sleeves and let the bodice fall forward, then stepped out of the skirt to reveal her own clothes: a snug-fitting scoop neck sweater in Christmas red over a pair of skinny jeans tucked into knee-high boots.

A definite hottie with curves that should have warning signs. He looked away from the danger zone, pushing the suspenders off his shoulders and stepping out of Santa's oversize pants, leaving him clad in a long-sleeve Henley and well-worn jeans. He picked up the flannel shirt he'd shed before donning the Santa coat and put it on over the Henley.

She neatly folded her dress and tucked it into a shopping bag. He watched her out of the corner of his eye, unable to shake the feeling that, though he couldn't think of her name, he was certain he knew her from somewhere.

Before he could ask her if they'd met before, there was a knock at the door.

"Come in."

They both said it at the same time, then she smiled at him, and that easy curve of her lips only increased her hotness factor.

The door opened and Annie poked her head in.

"Oh, Serena, I'm so glad to see that you made it."

"I did. Sorry I was almost late. There was some excitement at the clinic this morning."

Serena.

Clinic.

The pieces finally clicked into place and Bailey realized why the substitute Mrs. Claus looked familiar. She was Serena Langley, a vet tech at the same clinic where his sister-in-law was the receptionist.

"What kind of excitement?" Annie asked, immediately concerned.

"Alistair Warren brought in a fat stray that he found under his porch. The cat turned out not to be fat but pregnant and gave birth to nine kittens."

"Nine?" Annie echoed.

Serena nodded. "Exam Room Three is going to be out of commission for a while, because Brooks doesn't want to disturb the new mom or her babies."

"I can't wait to see them," Annie enthused. "But right now, I want to hear about the substitute Santa's visit with the local scout troop so that I can report back to his more-sick-than-jolly brother."

Bailey turned to Serena again. Truthfully, his gaze had hardly shifted away from her since they'd entered the dressing room. He'd thought it was because he was trying to figure out where they might have crossed paths before, but even with that question now answered, he found his attention riveted on her.

He waited for Serena to say that the substitute Santa had sucked and that the event had been a disaster—although maybe not in terms quite so blunt and harsh. At the very least, he anticipated her telling his sister-in-law that Bailey had screwed up and almost made a kid cry. And he couldn't have disputed either of those points, because they were both true.

But Serena seemed content to let him respond to the inquiry, and he did so, only saying, "It was…an experience."

His sister-in-law's brows lifted. "I'm not sure how to interpret that."

Bailey looked at Mrs. Claus again.

"Everything went well," Serena assured her friend.

Annie exhaled, obviously relieved. "Of course, I knew the two of you would be able to pull it off."

"If you were so confident, you wouldn't have rushed over here to interrogate us," he pointed out. "Although I suspect your concerns were really about Santa and not Mrs. Claus."

"Well, you were the more reluctant substitute," she told him. "Serena didn't hesitate when I asked her to fill in."

"I'm always happy to help a friend," Serena said. "But now I should be on my way."

"What's your hurry?" Annie asked.

"I'm not in a hurry," she denied. "It's just that I left early this morning and...well, you know that Marvin doesn't like it when I'm gone all day."

She seemed a little embarrassed by this admission, or so he guessed by the way her gaze dropped away.

Bailey frowned, wondering about this Marvin and the nature of his relationship with Serena. Was he her husband? Boyfriend? How did he express his disapproval of her absence? Did he give her the cold shoulder when she got home? Or did he have a hot temper?

The possibility roused his ire. Lord knew he wasn't without faults of his own and tried not to judge others by their shortcomings, but he had no tolerance for men who bullied women or children.

"You worry too much about Marvin," Annie chided.

"You know I can't stand it when he looks at me with those big sad eyes."

"I know you let him use those big sad eyes to manipulate you," Annie said. "You need to stand firm and let him know he's not the boss of you."

Bailey didn't think his sister-in-law should be so quick to disregard her friend's concerns. No one knew what went on behind closed doors of a relationship.

"Is Marvin your...husband?" Bailey asked Serena.

In response to his question, Annie snickered—inappropriately, he thought—and Serena's cheeks flushed with color as she shook her head.

"No, he's my, uh, bulldog."

"Your bulldog," he echoed.

She nodded, the color in her cheeks deepening.

Well, the *big sad eyes* comment made a lot more sense to him now. As the humor of the situation became apparent, he felt his own lips curve.

"He's a rescue," she explained. "And very...needy."

"Only because you let him be," Annie said. "Not to mention that you have a doggy door, so he can go in and out as required."

"Well, yes," Serena admitted. "But he still doesn't like to be alone for too long."

Which led Bailey to believe that there wasn't anyone else at home—husband or boyfriend—to put the dog out or deal with his neediness.

Not that it mattered, because he wasn't interested in any kind of romantic relationship with his sister-in-law's friend and colleague.

Was he?

"I hope Danny is feeling a lot better before Tuesday," Annie said as she picked up the bags containing the costumes.

The worry was evident in her friend's voice, compelling Serena to ask, "What's happening on Tuesday?"

"We're supposed to play Santa and Mrs. Claus for a visit to the elementary school."

Which gave Annie's husband only two days to recuperate from whatever had laid him up.

"I'd be happy to fill in again," Serena immediately offered.

"Oh, that would be wonderful," Annie said. "And such a weight off my shoulders to not have to worry about finding a replacement at the last minute again. Thank you both so much."

"Both?" Bailey echoed. "Wait! I never—"

But his sister-in-law didn't pause long enough to allow him to voice any protest. "In that case, I'll leave the costumes with you and just pop over to Daisy's to pick up some soup for Danny. Fingers crossed, he'll be able to keep it down."

"—agreed to anything," he continued.

Of course, Annie was already gone, leaving Serena and Bailey alone again.

She wasn't surprised when he turned toward her, a deep furrow between his brows. "I never agreed to anything," he said again.

"I know, but Annie probably couldn't imagine you'd object to doing a favor for your brother," she said reasonably.

"*Another* favor, you mean."

"Was today really so horrible?"

"That's not the point," he said. "But you're the type of person who's always the first to volunteer for any task, aren't you?"

She shrugged.

It was true that she hadn't hesitated when Annie asked her to fill in as Mrs. Claus. Although she generally preferred the company of animals to people, she was always happy to help a friend. And when she'd acceded to the request, it had never occurred to her to ask or even wonder about the identity of the man playing Santa Claus.

But even if Annie had told her that it was Bailey Stockton, Serena wouldn't have balked. Because how could she know that she'd have such an unexpected visceral reaction to her friend's brother-in-law?

After all, this was hardly their first meeting. She'd seen him at the clinic—and even once or twice around town, at Crawford's General Store or Daisy's Donut Shop. He was an undeniably handsome man. Of course, as far as she could tell, all the Stocktons had been genetically blessed, but there was something about Bailey that set him apart.

Maybe it was the vulnerability she'd glimpsed in his eyes. It was the same look of a puppy who'd torn up the newspaper and only realized after the fact that he'd done something wrong. Not that she was really comparing Bailey Stockton to a puppy, but she could tell that Bailey had felt remorseful as soon as he'd agreed with Owen's assessment that the holidays sucked.

Serena knew as well as anyone that Christmas wasn't all gingerbread and jingle bells, but over the years, she'd learned to focus on happy memories and embrace the spirit of the season.

But now that she and Bailey were no longer surrounded by kids pumped up on sugar and excitement about seeing Santa, now that it was just the two of them, he didn't seem vulnerable at all. He was all man. And every womanly part of her responded to his nearness.

When he'd unzipped her dress, he'd been doing her a favor. There had certainly been nothing seductive about the action. But she'd been aware of his lean hard body behind her, and his closeness had made her heart pound and her knees tremble. And although she was wearing a long-sleeved sweater and jeans beneath the costume, she'd felt the warmth of his breath on the nape of her neck as the zipper inched downward, and a shiver had snaked down her spine.

While she was wearing the costume, she could be Mrs. Claus and play the role she needed to play. But now that the costume had been packed away, she was just Serena Langley again—a woman who didn't know how to chat and flirt with men. In fact, she was completely awkward when it came to interacting with males of the human species, so she decided to do what she always did in uncomfortable situations: flee.

But before she could find the right words to extricate herself, Bailey spoke again.

"And what if I have plans for Tuesday afternoon?" he grumbled. "Not that Annie even considered that possibility."

"If you have plans, then I'll find somebody else to fill in," she said.

In fact, that might be preferable, because being in close proximity to Bailey was stirring feelings...desires...that she didn't want stirred. And while she liked the idea of a boyfriend who might someday turn into a husband, her track record with men was a bunch of false starts and incomplete finishes.

Well, not really a bunch. Barely even a handful. But the number wasn't as important as the fact that, at the end of the day, she was alone.

"Do you have other plans?" she asked.

"No," he reluctantly admitted. "But that's not the point."

"If you don't want to help out, say so," she told him.

"I just don't think I'm the best choice to fill the big guy's boots," he said.

"You managed okay today."

"I'm not sure Owen would agree," he remarked dryly.

"A bump in the road," she acknowledged. "But I'm confident you won't make the same mistake again."

"You're expressing a lot of faith in a guy you don't even know," he warned.

"I'm a pretty good judge of character."

Except that wasn't really true with respect to men. Canines and felines, yes. Even birds and rodents and fish. And while most people would doubt that fish had much character, she'd had a dwarf puffer for four years that had been a true diva in every sense of the word.

"But if you really don't want to do it, that's fine," she said to him now. "I'm sure I can find someone else to play Santa."

And that would probably be a better solution all around, because he was clearly a reluctant Santa and she was reluctant to spend any more time in close proximity to a male who reminded her that she was a woman without a man in her life.

Most of the time, she was perfectly happy with the status quo. But every now and again, she found herself thinking that it might be nice to share her life with someone who could contribute something other than woofs and meows to a conversation. And then she'd force herself to go out and try to meet new people. And her hopes and expectations would be dashed by reality. Again.

But Bailey surprised her by not immediately accepting this offer. "Well, I'm not sure that what I want really matters, since Annie will tell Dan that I agreed to do it and then, if I don't, I'll have to explain why and how I wriggled my way out of it."

"Are you saying that you *will* do it?" she asked, half hopeful, half wary.

"I guess I am," he agreed.

"Then I guess, unless Dan makes a miraculous recovery, I'll see you at the school on Tuesday."

"Or maybe now," Bailey said, as Serena moved toward the door. Because for reasons he couldn't begin to fathom, he was reluctant to watch her walk away. Or maybe he was just hungry.

She looked at him blankly. "Maybe now what?"

"Maybe I'll see you now—which sounded much better in my head than it did aloud," he acknowledged ruefully. "And which was supposed to be a segue into asking if you wanted to get something to eat."

"Oh." She seemed as uncertain about how to answer the question as he'd been to ask it.

"I was so nervous about the Santa gig that I didn't eat lunch before, and now I'm starving."

Serena offered him a leftover candy cane.

"I think I'm going to want something more than that," he said. "How about you? Are you hungry?"

"Not really."

Her stomach rumbled, calling her out on the fib.

His lips curved. "You want to reconsider your answer?"

"Apparently I am hungry," she acknowledged, one side of her mouth turning up in a half-smile.

"Do you want to grab a bite at the Gold Rush Diner?"

She hesitated.

"It's a simple yes or no question," he told her.

"Like...a date?" she asked cautiously.

"No." His knee-jerk response was as vehement as it was immediate.

Thankfully, Serena laughed, apparently more relieved than insulted by his hasty rejection of the idea.

"In that case, yes," she told him.

Since nothing was too far from anything else in the downtown area of Rust Creek Falls, they decided to leave their vehicles parked at the community center and walk over to the diner. Even on the short walk, the air was brisk with the promise of more snow in the forecast.

The name of the restaurant was painted on the plate-glass front window of the brick building. When Bailey opened the door for Serena, a cowbell overhead announced their arrival.

Though the diner did a steady business, the usual lunch crowd had already cleared out and he gestured for her to choose from the row of vacant booths. She slid across a red vinyl bench and he took a seat opposite her.

After a quick review of the menu, Bailey decided on the steak sub and Serena opted for a house salad.

"Your stomach was audibly rumbling," he reminded her. "I don't think it's going to be satisfied with salad."

"I'm supposed to be going to a dinner and dance at Sawmill Station tonight. The salad will tide me over until then."

"The Presents for Patriots fund-raiser," he guessed. "I've been working with Brendan Tanner on that this year."

"Dr. Smith bought a table and gave the tickets out to his staff."

"Then I'll see you there."

"Unless I decide to stay home with Marvin, Molly and Max."

"I know that Marvin's your dog," he said. "But Molly and Max?"

"Cat and bunny," she admitted.

"You have a lot of pets," he noted.

"Animals are usually better company than people."

"Present company excluded?" he suggested dryly.

Her cheeks flushed. "Maybe it would be more accurate to say that I'm better with animals than with people."

"You were great with the kids today," he assured her.

"Thanks, but kids are generally accepting and easy to please. Especially kids who are focused on something else—such as seeing Santa Claus."

"That reminds me," he said. "What do you know about this PKT-79 all the kids were asking about?"

"It's an upgrade of the 78 that came out in the spring."

"The 78 *what*?"

"An interactive pocket toy that communicates with other similar toys," she explained.

"And where would I find one?" he asked.

"You won't," she told him. "They're sold out everywhere."

"They can't be sold out everywhere," he protested, nodding his thanks to the waitress when she set his plate in front of him.

"It was a headline on my news feed last week—'Must-Have Toy of the Year Sold Out Everywhere.'"

He shook salt over his fries as he considered this setback to his plan.

"Of course, you could always ask Santa for one," she said, tongue in cheek, as she stabbed her fork into a tomato wedge.

"Do Santa's elves have a production line of PKT-79s at the North Pole?"

"They might," she allowed. "The only other option is an aftermarket retailer."

"Like eBay?" he guessed.

She nodded. "But you won't find one reasonably priced," she warned. "Supply and demand."

"I was hoping to get one for Owen," he confided. "To give him a reason to believe that Christmas doesn't suck."

"And because you feel guilty?" she guessed.

"Yeah," he admitted.

"Well, it's a really nice idea," she said. "But I promise you, he'll have a good Christmas even without a PKT-79 under his tree."

"How do you know?"

"Because I know his family, and yes, it's going to suck that his best friend is leaving town after the holidays, but he'll be okay."

"I guess I'll have to take your word for it," Bailey decided. "And since I'm apparently going to do this Santa thing again, I could use some pointers on how to interact with the kids."

"Just try to remember what it was like when you were a kid yourself," she suggested. "Remember the anticipation you felt in those days and weeks leading up to the holiday? All of it finally culminating in the thrill of Christmas morning and the discovery of what Santa left for you under the tree?"

But he didn't want to think about the anticipation leading up to Christmas. He didn't want to think about the holidays at all. Because thinking about the past inevitably brought to mind memories of his parents and all the ways that they'd made the holidays special for their family.

With seven kids to feed and clothe, Christmases were never extravagant, but there were always gifts under the tree—usually something that was needed, such as new work gloves or thermal underwear, and something that was wanted, such as a board game or favorite movie on DVD.

He was so lost in these thoughts—of what he was trying

not to think about—that he almost forgot he wasn't alone until Serena reached across the table to touch his hand.

The contact gave him a jolt, not just because it was unexpected but because it was somehow both gentle and strong—a woman's touch. And it had been a long time since he'd been touched by a woman.

He deliberately drew his hand away to reach for his soda, sipped. "Remembering those Christmases only serves to remind me of everything I've lost," he told her. "Not that I expect someone like you to understand."

Serena sat back. "What do you mean…someone like me?"

There was a slight edge to her voice that he might have heard if he hadn't been so caught up in his own misery. But because he was and he didn't, he responded without thinking, "Someone who can't know that happiness and joy can turn to grief and despair in an instant."

She reached for her own glass, sipping her soda before she responded. "You should be careful about making assumptions about other people." Then she meticulously folded her napkin and set it beside her plate. "Thanks for lunch, but I really do need to get home to my pets."

And then, before he could figure out what he'd said or done to put her back up, she was gone.

Chapter 3

By the time she got home, Serena had decided to skip the Presents for Patriots Dinner, Dance & Silent Auction. Though it was barely four o'clock, she'd had a full day already and had no desire to get dressed up and go out. Or it could be that she was looking for an excuse to stay home and avoid seeing Bailey Stockton again.

As she climbed the stairs to her apartment above an accountant's office, the urge to put on a pair of warm fuzzy pajamas and snuggle on the sofa with her pets was strong. And made even stronger when she opened the door and was greeted with so much affection and enthusiasm from Marvin that she couldn't imagine leaving him again.

After giving Marvin lots of ear scratches and an enthusiastic belly rub, she made her way to the bedroom—and found Molly curled up in the center of the bed. She sighed, the exasperated sound alerting the calico to her presence. The cat blinked sleepily.

Serena tried to establish boundaries for her pets—the primary one being that they weren't allowed on her bed unless and until specifically invited. Marvin mostly respected her rules; Max was usually content in his cardboard castle; but Molly roamed freely over the premises.

"Off," she said firmly, gesturing from Molly to the floor.

The calico slowly uncurled herself, yawning as she stretched out, unashamed to have been caught breaking the rules and unwilling to be hurried.

Marvin, having followed Serena into the room, finally noticed Molly on the bed and barked. Molly hissed, as if chastising him for being a tattletale. The dog plopped onto his butt beside Serena and looked up at her with adoring eyes.

"Yes, you're a good boy," she told him.

His tongue fell out of his mouth and he panted happily.

"And you—" She wagged her finger at Molly, then let her hand drop to her side, acknowledging that there was no point in reprimanding an animal who wasn't motivated to do anything but whatever she wanted. As much as the attitude frustrated Serena at times, she couldn't deny that she admired Molly's spirit.

The cat, having made her point, nimbly jumped down off the bed and sauntered toward the door. Marvin started to follow, then turned back to Serena again, obviously torn.

She chuckled softly. "You can go with Molly. I'll be out as soon as I put my jammies on."

But when she opened the closet to put her sweater in the hamper, her gaze was snagged by the dress hanging in front of her.

The dress she'd planned to wear to the Presents for Patriots Dinner, Dance & Silent Auction tonight had been hanging in her closet for eleven months. She'd bought it on sale early in the new year—an after-holiday bargain that she'd been unable to resist—and she'd been excited for the opportunity to finally wear it. Because as much as she usually preferred the company of her animals over that of people, she also enjoyed getting dressed up every once in a while.

She lifted a hand to stroke the crushed velvet fabric. It was the color of rich red wine with a scoop neck, long sleeves and short skirt. She sighed, silently acknowledging that if she skipped the dinner and dance tonight, it might be another year—or more—before she had the opportunity to wear the dress.

Not to mention that Dr. Brooks Smith's table would already be short two people, as Annie, the clinic receptionist, was at home caring for her sick husband. Which meant that if Serena didn't show, a third meal would go to waste.

But while Annie and Dan would miss the event, Dan's brother would be there—and she wasn't sure if Bailey's attendance was a factor in favor of going or staying home.

When Bailey Stockton left Rust Creek Falls thirteen years ago, he'd thought it was forever. His life and family were gone—torn apart by *his* actions—and he hadn't imagined he would ever want to return. He'd tried to move on with his own life—first in various parts of Wyoming, then in New Mexico—certain he could find a new path. After a few years, he'd even let himself hope that he might make a new family.

That hadn't worked out so well. Though he'd had the best of intentions when he'd exchanged vows with Emily, it turned out that they were just too different—and too stubborn to compromise—which pretty much doomed their marriage from the start.

And then, last December, he'd heard that his brother Luke had made his way back to Rust Creek Falls, and he'd impulsively decided to head in the same direction. He'd arrived in town just in time to witness their brother Danny exchange vows with his high school sweetheart. At the wedding, Bailey had reconnected with most of his siblings, who had persuaded him to stay—at least for a while.

Eleven and a half months later, Bailey was still there. He was living in one of the cabins at Sunshine Farm now and filling most of his waking hours with chores around the ranch. Still, every few weeks he felt compelled to remind himself that he was going to head out again, but the truth was, he had nowhere else to go. And while he'd been certain that he wouldn't ever want to return to the family ranch that held so many memories of the parents they'd lost and the siblings who'd scattered—he'd been wrong about that, too.

When Bailey, Luke and Dan left town, they'd believed the property would be sold by the bank to pay off the mortgages it secured. They'd been shocked to discover that Rob and Lauren Stockton had insurance that satisfied the debts upon their deaths—and even more so to discover that their maternal grandfather had kept up with the property taxes over the years. And while they would all have gladly given up the farm to have their parents back, they were now determined to hold on to the land that was their legacy.

Of course, holding on to the land required a lot of work—and his brothers had started with the barn, because that was the venue where Dan and Annie had promised to love, honor and cherish one another.

The simple but heartfelt ceremony Bailey had witnessed was very different from the formal church service and elaborate ballroom reception that had marked his own wedding day, but he was confident now that his brother's marriage was destined for a happier fate.

On the day Dan and Annie exchanged their vows, though, Bailey had been much less optimistic about their prospects. Still smarting from the failure of his own union, he'd felt compelled to caution another brother when he saw the stars in Luke's eyes as he'd looked at his date.

Luke and Eva had gone their separate ways for a short while after that. Bailey didn't know if his advice had played a part in that temporary breakup, but he was glad that his brother and new sister-in-law had found their way back to one another. Luke and Eva had gotten engaged last New Year's Eve and married seven months later.

In addition to being committed to one another, they were committed to using Sunshine Farm to spread happiness to others. In fact, Eva's childhood friend Amy Wainwright had recently been reunited with her former—and future—husband, Derek Dalton, at the farm, resulting in the property gaining the nickname Lonelyhearts Ranch.

Bailey couldn't deny that a lot of people were finding love in Rust Creek Falls, including four of his six siblings. But he had no illusions about happily-ever-after for himself. He'd already been there, done that and bought the T-shirt—then lost the T-shirt in his divorce.

But he was happy to help out with Presents for Patriots. He would even acknowledge that he enjoyed working with Brendan Tanner—because the retired marine didn't try to get into his head or want to talk about his feelings, which was more than he could say about his siblings.

Bailey believed wholeheartedly in the work of Presents for Patriots. He had the greatest respect for the sacrifices made by enlisted men and women and was proud to participate in the community's efforts to let the troops know they were valued and appreciated. Maybe sending Christmas gifts was a small thing, but at least it was something, and Bailey was pleased to be part of it.

He was less convinced of the value of this dinner and dance. Sure, it was a fund-raiser for a good cause, but Bailey suspected that most of the guests would be couples, and—as the only single one of his siblings currently living in Rust Creek Falls—he was already tired of feeling like a third wheel.

Not that he wanted to change his status. No, he'd learned the hard way that he was better off on his own. No one to depend on and no one depending on him. But it was still awkward to be a single man in a social gathering that was primarily made up of couples.

He looked around the crowd gathered at Sawmill Station, hoping to see Serena in attendance. She'd said that she had a ticket for the event, but considering the abruptness with which she'd left the restaurant after lunch, he had to wonder if she'd changed her mind about coming.

Her plans shouldn't matter to him. After all, he barely knew her. But he couldn't deny there was something about her— even when she was admonishing him for his admittedly inappropriate behavior—that appealed to him.

In fact, while she'd been scolding him, he'd had trouble understanding her words because his attention had been focused on the movements of her mouth. And he'd found himself wondering if those sweetly curved lips would stop moving if he covered them with his own—or if they'd respond with a matching passion.

Yeah, he barely knew the woman, but he knew that he wanted to kiss her—and that realization made him wary. It had been a lot of years since he'd felt such an immediate and instinctive attraction to a woman, and he would have happily lived out the rest of his days without experiencing that feeling again. Because he knew now that the euphoric feeling didn't last—and when it was gone, his heart might suffer more dings and dents.

So it was probably for the best that she'd walked out of the diner before he'd had a chance to ask her to be his date tonight.

Because while he wasn't entirely comfortable being a single man surrounded by couples, at least he didn't have to worry about the stirring of unexpected desires—and the even more dangerous yearnings of his heart.

Just when he'd managed to convince himself that was true, he turned away from the bar with a drink in hand and saw her. And his foolish heart actually skipped a beat.

The silky blond hair that had spilled over her shoulders when she'd removed the Mrs. Claus wig was gathered up on top of her head now. Not in a tight knot or a formal twist, but a messy—and very sexy—arrangement of curls. Several loose strands escaped the knot to frame her face.

She was wearing a dress. The color was richer and deeper than red, and the fabric clung to her mouthwatering curves. The skirt of the dress ended just above her knees, and she wore pointy-toed high-heeled shoes on her feet.

He took a few steps toward her and noticed that there were sparkles in her hair. Crystal snowflakes, he realized, as he drew nearer. She'd made up her face, too. Not that she needed any artificial enhancement, but the long lashes that surrounded her deep blue eyes were now thicker and darker, and her temptingly curved lips were slicked with pink gloss.

"You look... Wow," he said, because he couldn't find any other words that seemed adequate.

Her cheeks flushed prettily. "Back atcha."

He knew his basic suit and bolero tie were nothing special, particularly in this crowd, but he smiled, grateful that she didn't seem to be holding a grudge. "I wasn't sure you were going to come."

"Neither was I," she admitted.

"I'm glad you did," he told her. "And I hope you brought your checkbook—there's a lot of great stuff on the auction table."

"As soon as I figure out where I'm sitting for dinner, I'll take a look," she promised.

"You can sit with me," he invited.

"I think I'm supposed to be at Dr. Smith's table."

He shook his head. "There are no assigned tables."

She looked toward the dining area, where long wooden tables were set in rows on either side of the dance floor. The decor was festive but simple. Of course, Brendan and Bailey had left all those details in the hands of the event planners, who had adorned the tables with evergreen branches and holly berries, with tea lights in clear glass bowls at the center of each grouping of four place settings. The result was both festive and rustic, perfect for the venue and the occasion.

"I've never been here before," Serena confided. "But this place is fabulous. You and Brendan did a great job."

Bailey immediately shook his head. "This was all Caroline Ruth and her crew. The only thing me and Brendan can take credit for is putting her in charge," he said. "And picking the food."

"What will we be eating tonight?" she asked.

He plucked a menu off a nearby table and read aloud: "Country biscuits with whipped butter, mixed greens with poached pears, candied walnuts and a honey vinaigrette, grilled hand-carved flat iron steak, red-skin mashed potatoes and blackened corn, with huckleberry pie or chocolate mousse for dessert."

"And that's why I had salad for lunch," she told him.

He chuckled as he steered her toward the table where Luke and Eva were already seated, along with Brendan Tanner and his fiancée, Fiona O'Reilly, and Fiona's sister Brenna and her husband, Travis Dalton.

Conversation during dinner covered many and various topics—Presents for Patriots, of course, including the upcoming gift-wrapping at the community center—but Brendan and

Fiona's recent engagement was also a subject of much interest and discussion.

"So how long have you and Serena been dating?" Brenna asked, as she dipped her spoon into her chocolate mousse.

Bailey looked up, startled by the question. "What?"

Serena paused with her wineglass halfway to her lips, obviously taken aback, as well.

"I asked how long you've been dating," Brenna repeated.

"They're not dating," Eva responded to the question first. "But they're married."

"Really?" Brenna sounded delighted and intrigued by this revelation.

"Not really," Serena said firmly.

"I don't know." Eva spoke up again, winking at Bailey and Serena to let them know she was teasing. "There were a lot of people at the community center today who believe you are."

Serena rolled her eyes. "Only because we were dressed up as Santa and Mrs. Claus."

"There's nothing wrong with a little role-playing to spice things up in the bedroom," Brenna asserted.

Serena shook her head, her cheeks redder than the dress she'd worn during their role-playing that afternoon. "I should have stayed home tonight."

"I'm just teasing you," Brenna said, immediately contrite. "Although Travis and I fell in love for real while we were only pretending to be engaged."

"I cheered for both of you on *The Great Roundup*," Serena admitted.

"Then you saw me win the grand prize," Travis chimed in.

Bailey frowned. Though reality shows weren't his thing, it would have been impossible to be in Rust Creek Falls the previous year and not follow the events that played out when two local residents were vying for the big money on the television show. "It was Brenna who won the million dollars."

"That's true," Travis confirmed, sliding an arm across his wife's shoulders and drawing her into his embrace. "But I won Brenna."

She smiled up at him. "And I won you."

"And I need some air," Bailey decided.

"Me, too," Serena said, pushing back her chair.

They exited the main reception area but didn't venture much farther than that. Leaving the building would require collecting their coats and bundling up against the frigid Montana night.

"They don't mean to be obnoxious," Bailey said when he and Serena were alone. "At least, I don't think they do."

She laughed softly. "I didn't think they were obnoxious. I thought they were adorable."

"Really?"

"Yeah. I mean, I watched *The Great Roundup*, but you never know how much of those reality shows is real, how much is staged, how much is selectively edited. It's nice to see that they truly are head over heels in love with one another."

"For now," Bailey remarked.

Serena frowned. "You don't think they'll last?"

He shrugged. "I don't think the odds are in their favor."

"Love isn't about odds," she said. "It's a leap of faith."

"A leap that frequently ends with one or both parties hitting the ground with a splat."

"Spoken like someone who has some experience with the splat," she noted.

He nodded. "Because I do."

"Of course, most people don't make it through life without a few bumps and bruises."

"Bumps and bruises usually heal pretty easily," he said.

Bailey's matter-of-fact statement told Serena that the heartbreak he'd experienced had left some pretty significant scars. She also suspected that the romance gone wrong had reopened wounds caused by the loss of his parents and the separation from his family when he was barely more than a teenager.

"Usually," she agreed.

"I'm sorry," he said, after another moment had passed.

The spontaneous and unexpected apology surprised her. "Why are you sorry?"

"Because I obviously said something that upset you at lunch today."

"I can be overly sensitive at times," she admitted.

"Does that mean I'm forgiven?" he asked hopefully.

She nodded. "You're forgiven."

"That's a relief," he told her. "We wouldn't want the kids of Rust Creek Falls Elementary School to worry about any obvious tension between Santa and Mrs. Claus."

"I'm not sure they care about Santa's marital status so long as he delivers their presents on Christmas Eve."

"Which he wouldn't be able to do if the missus got possession of the sleigh and custody of the reindeer in the divorce," Bailey pointed out.

"Then he better do everything he can to keep her happy," she suggested.

"If Santa had a secret formula for keeping a woman happy, it would top every man's Christmas list," he said.

"Ha ha."

"I'm not joking," he assured her. "But in the interests of keeping you happy, can I buy you a drink?"

"No, thanks. I had a glass of wine with dinner and that's my limit."

"One glass?"

She nodded.

"Okay, how about a dance?"

"The words sound like an invitation," she remarked. "But the tone suggests that you're hoping the offer will be declined."

"Maybe, for your sake, I'm hoping it will," he said. "Because I'm not a very good dancer."

"Then why did you ask?"

He shrugged. "Because it might seem like everyone else is paired off, but I have noticed that there are a few single guys in attendance and I know they're just waiting for me to turn my back for a second so they can move in on you."

"Should I be flattered? Or should I get out my pepper spray?"

"Maybe you should just dance with me," he suggested.

So Serena took the hand he proffered and let him lead her to the dance floor. But the minute he took her in his arms, she knew that her acquiescence had been a mistake. Being close to him, she felt those unwanted feelings stir again.

She'd had a few boyfriends in her twenty-five years, and even a couple of lovers, but she'd never really been in love. And though she didn't know much about Bailey, the intensity of the attraction she felt for him warned her that he might be the man she finally and completely fell for.

But she also knew that he didn't want to be that man, and his brief and blunt comments about his marriage gone wrong should serve as a warning to her. Which was too bad, because she really liked being in his arms. And notwithstanding his claim that he wasn't a good dancer, he moved well.

As the last notes of the song trailed away, she tipped her head back to look at him.

The heels she wore added three inches to her height, so that if he lowered his head just a little, his mouth would brush against hers.

She really wanted him to kiss her.

But they were barely more than strangers and in a very

public setting. And yet, in that moment, everyone and everything else faded into the background so that there was only the two of them.

Then he did tip his head, so that his mouth hovered a fraction of an inch above hers. And she held her breath, waiting...

A guitar riff blasted through the air—an abrupt change of tempo for the couples on the dance floor—and the moment was lost.

Serena stepped back. "I—I'm going to check out the auction items."

So Bailey returned to the table without her.

"Watching you and Serena on the dance floor, I could see why Brenna thought that you guys were together," Luke commented.

"Why were you watching us instead of dancing with your wife?" Bailey asked his brother.

"Because I was working at Daisy's at 4:00 a.m.," Eva responded to the question. "And my feet are very happy to *not* be dancing right now. But he's right," she continued. "You and Serena look good together."

"Except that we're not together," he reminded his brother and sister-in-law.

They exchanged a glance.

"Denial," Eva said.

Luke nodded.

"Look, it's great that the two of you found one another and happiness together, but not everyone else in the world wants the same thing," Bailey told them.

"You mean they're not ready to admit that they want the same thing," Eva said.

Bailey just shook his head.

"A year ago, I was a skeptic, too," Luke said. "And then I met Eva."

The smile she gave her husband was filled with love and affection. And maybe it did warm Bailey's heart to see Luke and Eva so happy. And Danny and Annie. And Jamie and Fallon. And his sister Bella and Hudson. And maybe he was just the tiniest bit envious.

But only the tiniest bit—not nearly enough to be willing to risk putting his own heart on the line again.

Thankfully, he was saved from responding by the sound of—

"Is that dogs barking the tune of 'Jingle Bells'?" Eva asked.

"That's gotta be Serena's phone," Bailey noted.

Luke picked it up from the table, his brows lifting when he looked at the case. Then he turned it around so Eva and Bailey could see the image of a bulldog wearing a Santa hat.

Bailey wasn't going to judge her for loving Christmas as much as she loved her dog, especially when the call had provided a timely interruption to an increasingly awkward conversation. He took the phone from his brother and went to find Serena.

"This would send Marvin into a frenzy of joy," she told him, gesturing with the pen in her hand to a Canine Christmas basket filled with toys and treats that had been donated by Brooks Smith and his wife, Jazzy.

Bailey glanced at the bid sheet. "Looks like there's already a bidding war between Paige Traub and Lissa Christensen."

"And now me, too," she said, as she scrawled her offer on the page.

He lifted his brows at the number she'd written. "You doubled the last bid."

"It's for a good cause," she reminded him.

"So it is," he agreed.

"Is there anything here that's caught your eye?" she asked.

He knew she was referring to the auction table, but the truth was, he hadn't been able to take his eyes off *her* since she'd arrived.

"I'm still looking," he told her. But as he'd very recently reminded his brother and sister-in-law, he wasn't looking for happily-ever-after.

"There's a lot to look at," she said. "Everything from kids' toys and knitted baskets to a weekend getaway at Maverick Manor." She sighed. "Unfortunately, the bids on that are already out of my price range."

And yet she was willing to overpay for some dog toys to support a good cause and make Marvin happy.

"Is this Marvin?" he asked, holding up her phone.

She smiled. "No, it's a stock photo, but I bought the case because it looks a lot like him."

"Well, you might want to check your messages," he said. "Because you missed a call."

Serena finished writing her contact information on the bid sheet, then took her phone from him. "I can't imagine who might be calling me. Almost everyone I know is here tonight," she told him, as she unlocked the screen with her thumbprint.

He was surprised to see her expression change as she scanned the message. The light in her eyes dimmed, her lips thinned. She texted a quick response, then said, "I have to go."

"Now? Why?"

"My mom's at the Ace in the Hole."

"And?"

She just shook her head. "Long story."

"Do you want me to come with you?" he asked.

She seemed surprised that he would offer. "No," she said, but softened the rejection with a smile. "I appreciate the offer, but it's not necessary."

He took her phone from her again, then added his name and number to her list of contacts. "Just in case you change your mind."

"Thanks," she said, and even managed another smile. But he could tell that her mind was already at the bar and grill down the street—and whatever trouble he suspected was waiting for her there.

Chapter 4

Serena found a vacant spot in the crowded lot outside the Ace in the Hole and shifted into Park. She pocketed the keys as she exited her vehicle, the sick feeling in the pit of her stomach increasing with every step she took closer to the oversize ace of hearts playing card that blinked in neon red over the front door. She could hear the music from the jukebox inside as she climbed the two rough-hewn wooden steps. The price of beer was subject to regular increases, but the ancient Wurlitzer still played three songs for a quarter.

There were a few cowboys hanging around outside, cigarettes dangling from their fingers or pursed between their lips. She held her breath as she walked through their cloud of smoke and ignored the whistles and crude remarks tossed in her direction as she reached for the handle of the old screen door with its rusty hinges.

Once inside, her gaze immediately went to the bar that ran the length of one wall with stools lined up along it. Booths hugged the other walls, with additional tables and chairs crowded around the perimeter of the dance floor.

She made a cursory scan of the bodies perched on the stools at the bar. The mirrored wall behind the rows of glass bottles allowed her to see their faces. She recognized many, but none belonged to her mother.

Rosey Traven, the owner of the Ace, was pouring drinks behind the bar. Catching Serena's eye, she tipped her head toward the back. Serena forced her reluctant feet to move in that direction.

She found her mother seated across from a man that Serena didn't recognize. A friend? A date? A stranger?

Amanda Langley mostly kept to herself. For the past couple of years, she'd worked as an admin assistant at the mill, but outside of her job, she didn't have a lot of friends. And as far as Serena knew, she didn't date much, either.

She was an attractive woman, with the same blond hair and blue eyes as her daughter, but a more boyish figure and a raspy voice courtesy of a fifteen-year pack-a-day habit that she'd finally managed to kick a few years earlier.

The man seated across from her wasn't bad looking, either. He had broad shoulders, a shaven—or maybe bald—head, and a beard and moustache that were more salt than pepper.

Serena hesitated, trying to decide whether to advance or retreat, when her mother glanced up and saw her. Amanda looked surprised at first—and maybe a little guilty? Then she smiled and beckoned her daughter over.

Serena made her way through the crowd to the table.

"Rena—what are you doing here?"

She bent her head to kiss her mother's cheek. "I think the more important question is what are *you* doing here?"

"I'm having dinner with…a friend."

Serena looked again at the man seated across the table. Up

close, she could see that his twinkling eyes were blue and his good humor was further reflected in the easy curve of his lips. She added well-mannered to her assessment when he stood up and offered his hand. "Mark Kesler."

She took it automatically. "Serena Langley."

"It's a pleasure to finally meet you, Serena," he said. "Your mother's told me so much about you."

"That's interesting, because she's told me absolutely nothing about you."

"Serena." Her name was a sharp rebuke from her mother.

But Mark only chuckled. "It's okay, Amanda. In fact, it's nice to know that your daughter looks out for you."

"Is that what you're doing, Serena?" her mother asked.

"I can't seem to help myself," she admitted.

Because it was warm in the bar, she unwound the scarf from around her neck and unbuttoned her coat. Then she reached across the table to pick up her mother's glass and tipped it to her lips.

"If you want a drink, you can order your own soda," Amanda said dryly.

"I just wanted a sip," she said.

"And did that sip satisfy your…thirst?"

They both knew that what her mother really meant was *curiosity*, but Serena refused to feel guilty for needing to know what was in her mother's glass. And she wasn't going to apologize, either.

"As a matter of fact, it did," she said.

Amanda picked up a fry from her plate, nibbled on it. Then she said quietly, "Mark knows I'm an alcoholic."

The man in question reached into his jacket pocket and pulled out a coin, then slid it across the table for Serena to look at.

She immediately recognized it as a sobriety coin. Her

mother had recently earned one with the Roman numeral V on it, commemorating five years without a drink. The numerals inside the circle inside the triangle of this coin read XXV.

"I understand, more than most, that sobriety is a daily challenge for addicts," he told her.

"Then why would you bring her here?" she wanted to know.

"Because the Ace has the best burgers in town," Mark said.

Serena couldn't deny that, but she still worried about her mother's ability to resist the temptation that beckoned from the assortment of bottles lined up behind the bar. Gin had always been Amanda's preferred poison, but beggars weren't usually choosers, and for a lot of years, she drank anything she could get her hands on.

"But I forgot how much food they give you here," Amanda said now. "And while I managed to finish the burger, I barely touched my fries." She nudged the plate toward her daughter.

Serena shook her head, declining the silent offer. "I ate at the Presents for Patriots event."

"That's why you're all dressed up," her mother realized. "Did you go with a date?"

"No." But she thought about Bailey now—about how much she'd enjoyed chatting with him during the meal. And how much she'd savored the security of his strong arms around her on the dance floor, and the heat of his lean hard body close to hers, stirring long-dormant desires inside her.

But sitting at the same table and sharing a single dance didn't make a chance encounter a date. Maybe if he'd kissed her... And for a brief moment at the end of the song, she'd thought he might. But he didn't.

"Oh," Amanda said, obviously disappointed by her daughter's response. Then to *her* date, she said, "If Serena spent a little less time with animals and a little more with people, she might find a nice young man to settle down with."

"Maybe she doesn't want to settle down," Mark suggested.

"Thank you," Serena said, grateful for his acknowledgment of the possibility.

It wasn't the truth, of course. She *did* want to settle down—but she had no intention of settling. She wanted to fall in love with a man who loved her just as much, then get married and raise a couple of kids and grow old together.

"She wants a husband and a family," Amanda insisted, as if privy to her daughter's innermost thoughts. "But she has some trust issues that get in the way of her getting too close to anyone. Totally my fault," she acknowledged ruefully.

"Not totally," Serena said, because she couldn't deny that her childhood experiences continued to influence her expectations of adult relationships. "My father bears equal responsibility for walking out on both of us."

"And then I made things worse."

"I don't think there's anything to be gained by assigning blame," Mark protested, reaching across the table to cover Amanda's hand with his own, a tangible gesture of his support.

"Step Five—admitting the nature of our mistakes."

Mark started to say something else, but his attention was snagged by the vibration of his cell phone on the table. He glanced at the screen, then at Amanda. "I'm sorry but—"

"Go," she said. "You don't need to apologize, just go."

"Excuse me," he said to Serena, as he slid out of the booth, already connecting the call.

"Mark is an active AA sponsor," Amanda explained when the man in question had moved out of earshot.

"Is that how the two of you met?" Serena asked.

"We met at a meeting," her mother confirmed. "But he was never my sponsor."

"But he was an alcoholic," she noted.

"*Is* an alcoholic. Sober for more than twenty-five years, but still an alcoholic."

Serena nodded. Aside from her own experience with Amanda, she'd attended enough Al-Anon meetings as the daughter of an alcoholic to know that the battle against addiction was ongoing.

She also knew that her mother had worked hard to get and stay sober, and she deserved credit for that. "I'm sorry I overreacted," she said now.

"I'm sorry, too," Amanda said. "Because I know you have valid reasons to be concerned."

"Mark seems nice," she acknowledged.

"And you're worried that if I get emotionally involved and it doesn't work out, I'm going to lose myself in the bottle again?" her mother guessed.

Serena didn't—couldn't—deny it, so she remained silent.

"We both worried about the same thing," Amanda confided. "It's why we fought against our feelings for one another for so long."

"How long have you known him?" she asked curiously.

"Twelve years."

Her brows lifted. "How long have you been dating?"

"We've been spending more and more time together over the past few years, but tonight was our first official date," her mother told her.

"And your daughter crashed it."

Amanda smiled. "I'm always glad to see you."

It was a sincere statement, not a commentary on the scarcity of their visits, but she felt a twinge of guilt nevertheless. Over the past five years, her mother had made a lot of efforts and overtures that Serena had resisted—not as punishment or payback, but simply out of self-preservation.

She'd lost track of the number of times that she'd given her mother "one more chance" to be the mother that she wanted her to be, and somewhere along the line, she'd stopped believing that Amanda could ever be that person. Now, however, Serena acknowledged that she hadn't always been the daughter that her mother wanted her to be, and maybe it was time to work toward changing that.

When Mark finished his phone call and came back to the table, Serena wished them both a good-night and headed out. She caught Rosey's eye again as she passed the bar and gave the other woman a thumbs-up. Rosey nodded and continued to pour beer.

The time displayed on the Coors Light clock on the wall assured Serena that it wasn't too late to go back to the dinner and dance—and check on her bids—but her emotions were raw and she didn't think it was wise to seek out the company of a man whose mere presence churned her up inside.

No, the smart thing to do would be to go home to the animals who would shower her with unconditional love—or, in Molly's case, tolerant affection.

So resolved, she buttoned her coat up to her throat and braced herself for the slap of cold as she walked through the door and into the night. A different group of smokers huddled outside now—willingly braving the frigid air for a hit of nicotine.

Serena kept her head down and moved briskly toward her vehicle, parked at the far edge of the lot. As she drew nearer, she saw a tall broad-shouldered figure leaning against the tailgate of the truck in the slot beside her SUV.

She thought about the guys who'd been hanging around outside when she arrived and wondered—with more than a little bit of trepidation—if one of them had decided to wait by her vehicle until she came out again.

Her heart pounded against her ribs, and she considered

going back into the bar and asking Mark to escort her to her SUV. Instead, she drew in a steadying breath and slipped her hand into her pocket to retrieve her keys. She held them in her fist, so that the pointed ends protruded between her knuckles as her grandmother had taught her to do, and walked purposefully, projecting more confidence than she felt.

Though the figure was mostly in shadow, as she got closer, she sensed that there was something familiar about his shape.

"Bailey?"

He turned, and the light in the distance provided enough illumination of his profile to confirm that her guess was correct. Her heart continued to hammer against her ribs, though its frantic rhythm was no longer inspired by fear but relief—and pleasure.

"I know you didn't call, but I also know that the crowd here can get a little rowdy on weekends, and I wanted to make sure you were okay," he said, answering her unspoken question.

"I'm okay," she assured him.

"Do you want to talk?"

"No," she replied automatically, having grown accustomed to dealing with everything on her own since her grandmother had retired down to Arizona three years earlier. Then she reconsidered. "Maybe."

"We could go back inside to have a drink," he suggested.

She shook her head. "Definitely not."

His brows lifted.

"I wouldn't say no to hot cocoa at Daisy's, though."

"Hot cocoa at Daisy's it is," he agreed.

Daisy's Donut Shop was practically a landmark in Rust Creek Falls. Originally renowned for the best coffee—and the only donuts—in town, the owner had eventually responded to the demand for a wider range of food options. As a result,

Daisy's menu now included a rotating selection of soups and sandwiches, but it was the mouthwatering sweets on display in the glass-fronted cases that continued to draw and tempt the most customers.

There were several people lined up at the counter ahead of them when they arrived.

"I think we came in with the last of the movie crowd," Serena noted.

Bailey had almost forgotten that movies were shown at the high school on Friday and Saturday nights—but only so long as the Wildcats didn't have the gymnasium booked for a game, in which case the bleachers would be filled with residents cheering on the local team.

"Waiting in line gives us more time to check out the desserts Eva made today," he said, gesturing to the glass-fronted cases.

Of course, it was late, and the offerings that remained were limited—but still tempting.

"Just a regular hot cocoa for me," Serena said, stepping up to the counter.

Bailey looked dubious. "Just regular hot cocoa, like you could make for yourself at home?"

She shook her head. "I've tried all kinds of hot cocoa mixes. I've even tried making it from scratch, but it's never as good as Daisy's."

"Secret recipe," the server said with a wink.

"Coffee, decaf, for me," Bailey said. "And I've got to have one of those cheesecake-stuffed snickerdoodles."

"Didn't you already have dessert at Sawmill Station?" Serena asked him. "In fact, I'm pretty sure you ate your chocolate mousse and finished your sister-in-law's huckleberry pie."

"I did," he confirmed. "But that was more than two hours ago."

She smiled as she shook her head.

"Anything else for you?" the server asked.

"No, thanks," Serena said.

"Whipped cream and chocolate drizzle on your cocoa?"

"Mmm, yes," she agreed.

When they were seated with their hot beverages—and Bailey's enormous cookie—Serena wrapped her hands around her mug and announced, "My mother's an alcoholic."

"Ahh," he said, understanding now why she'd raced away from the silent auction when she learned that her mother was at the town's notorious drinking hole. "Was she…drunk?"

Serena shook her head. "She was drinking diet cola and eating a cheeseburger."

"Strange place to go for a diet cola," he noted. "Best place in town for a burger."

Now she nodded.

"So why are you all wound up?"

She couldn't deny that she was. Not when her hands were clutching her mug like it was a buoy keeping her afloat in stormy seas—but maybe that was an apt analogy for her life at the moment.

"I can't help it," she admitted. "I get a message like that, and the memories—years and years of horrible memories—play through my head like a horror movie on fast-forward."

"Who told you that she was there?"

"Rosey made the original call. Then Shelby sent a text when I was already on my way."

"I don't think I know a Shelby," he said.

"She used to be Shelby Jenkins, but she married Dean Pritchett a few years back," she told him. "She's worked at the Ace for a long time and has good instincts about people—and knows which customers to keep an eye on."

"Gives a whole new meaning to neighborhood watch," he remarked.

"Over the years, Rosey and Shelby have had a front-row seat to some of my mother's struggles—and mine," she explained. "And five years of sobriety hasn't helped me forget more than a decade of drinking."

His brows lifted.

She sighed. "And I guess two years of weekly therapy didn't quite succeed in helping me work through my anger and frustration and fear."

"That's why you wouldn't have more than one glass of wine tonight," he guessed.

She nodded. "Some scientists believe there's a genetic component to addiction, and I don't want to take any chances. Although—" she lifted her mug "—it wouldn't be wrong to say that I'm addicted to chocolate."

Then she sipped her cocoa, ending up with a whipped cream moustache that she swiped away with a stroke of her tongue.

The gesture drew Bailey's attention to the temptation of her mouth again, and he silently chided himself for not taking advantage of the opportunity he'd had to kiss her when they were on the dance floor.

But that opportunity had passed, and he owed her the courtesy of paying attention to what she was saying without being distracted by his own fantasies.

Except that a tiny bit of whipped cream clung to the indent at the center of her top lip, and it was driving him to distraction. He finally reached across the table and brushed his thumb over her lip, wiping away the cream.

He heard her sharp intake of breath, watched her eyes widen with awareness. And maybe...arousal?

Or maybe he was projecting.

"Whipped cream," he explained.

"Oh." She reached for her napkin and wiped her mouth. "I

probably should have skipped the whipped cream and chocolate sauce—they're messy."

"There's nothing wrong with messy," he told her, imagining that they could have a lot of fun getting messy together with whipped cream and chocolate sauce.

Serena blushed, making him wonder if her thoughts had gone in the same direction as his own.

There was definitely a zing in the air—a sizzle of attraction that ratcheted up the temperature about ten degrees whenever he was with her.

He'd been back in Rust Creek Falls for almost a year, and during that time, he'd crossed paths with any number of undeniably attractive women. Several had flirted with him, a few had offered more than a phone number, but he hadn't been tempted by any of them.

But after only a few hours with Serena Langley, he hadn't been able to get her out of his mind. When she'd left the Gold Rush Diner earlier that day, he'd counted the hours until the fund-raiser in anticipation of seeing her there. And when she'd excused herself from that event, he could tell she was upset about something. And because he'd worried about an attractive single woman walking into a place like the Ace alone, he'd followed her, just to make sure she was okay.

Now he was sitting across from her at Daisy's Donut Shop, watching her sip hot cocoa and trying to resist the temptation to imagine her naked. He was feeling better about life, the universe and everything than he'd felt in a very long time— maybe even since he'd left Rust Creek Falls following the deaths of his parents thirteen years earlier. Which confirmed a crucial fact: Serena Langley was a dangerous woman. And if he wasn't careful, her sparkling eyes, warm smile and open heart could pose a significant threat to the walls he'd deliberately built around his own damaged vessel.

So he would be careful, he resolved. He would take a step back—maybe several steps—to avoid the danger of another emotional splat. But those steps could wait until tomorrow, he decided, as he popped the last bite of snickerdoodle into his mouth.

Because tonight, he was really enjoying being with her.

Chapter 5

"I know, I know," Serena said, as she kicked off her shoes inside the door. "I promised I wouldn't be late, but I got caught up."

Marvin didn't move from the spot where he'd been sitting when she opened the door, his big sad eyes filled with silent reproach.

"I'm sorry," she said, crouching down to rub his ears.

He closed his eyes, savoring her touch.

Then she sighed. "Actually, that's a lie. I'm sorry you missed me, but I'm not sorry I'm late, because I had a really good time with Bailey tonight."

Marvin tilted his head.

"Am I forgiven?" she asked, continuing to scratch where he liked it best.

His licked her hand.

"Thank you," she said, and kissed the top of his head before rising to her feet again and moving toward the bedroom to change.

On the way, she checked on Max, who was sleeping soundly

in his bed. She found Molly curled up on *her* bed again, but Serena pretended she didn't see her there, because attempting to reprimand the stubborn calico only proved to both of them that the cat was the one calling the shots.

Instead, Serena hung her dress back up in the closet and finally donned the warm fuzzy pajamas that had beckoned to her hours earlier. After brushing her teeth, she wanted nothing more than to climb beneath the covers of her bed, but she felt guilty for neglecting Marvin through most of the day and night, so she returned to the living room. She played some tug-of-war with him and his favorite knotted rope, then a few minutes of fetch—he'd always been good at finding and retrieving the ball, but not so good at returning it to her.

When he finally tired of the game and crawled into her lap, she lifted her hand to his head to rub his ears, and he sighed contentedly and closed his eyes.

"I think I'm developing a serious crush," Serena confided to her pet.

He opened one eye, as if to assure her that he was listening.

She smiled as she continued to stroke his short glossy fur.

"I know it's crazy," she admitted. "I barely know the guy. And yet...there's just something about him.

"Or maybe it's just been so long since I've spent any time with a man that I'm making this into more than it is. I mean, it wasn't even a date—we just both happened to be at the same event. But it felt like a date. And it was so nice to talk to a guy who seemed to listen to what I was saying.

"Of course, you're a good listener, too, but sometimes it's nice to talk to someone who actually talks back."

Marvin responded with a low growl.

She laughed softly. "I'm not denying that you know how to communicate," she said, attempting to placate her pet. "But we really don't share a dialogue. And, if I'm being completely honest, I like to look at him, too. Because Bailey Stockton is hot. And the way he looks at me, I feel like I'm more than a vet tech or a pet owner or 'the girl who lives upstairs,' as Mr. Harrington calls me. I feel attractive and desirable, and I haven't felt that way in a long time."

Marvin tilted his head to lick her hand.

"I know you love me," she said. "And I love you. But as sweet as your doggy kisses are, they don't compare to real kisses. At least, I don't think they do. Of course, it's been so long since I've been kissed by a man, I can't be sure."

But there had been that almost-kiss moment, during which she'd experienced so much joyful anticipation she was certain that sharing a real kiss with Bailey Stockton would make her toes curl inside her shoes.

"And even though I was gone all night, I was thinking about you," Serena told Marvin. "And hopefully my bid on the— Well, I can't tell you what it was, because if my bid was successful, it will be your Christmas present and I wouldn't want to ruin the surprise. Anyway, tomorrow I will be home all day," she promised. "Maybe I'll even make some of your favorite treats."

Marvin's head lifted at the last word, and she laughed again.

"And, because you sometimes get too many *t-r-e-a-t-s*, we'll go for a nice long walk."

He immediately dropped his head again and closed his eyes, faking sleep so he could pretend he hadn't heard her.

"People told me to get a dog, they said I'd be more active. I swear, I got the only dog on the planet that's even lazier than me," Serena lamented. "But a walk will do both of us good— and I definitely need one because I had hot cocoa with whipped cream and chocolate sauce tonight."

And her lips tingled as she recalled the sensation of Bailey's thumb brushing over her lip to wipe away a remnant of the cream.

She pushed the tempting memory aside and refocused her attention on Marvin, who continued to fake sleep.

"I know you don't love to walk in the winter," she acknowledged. "But we'll put on your new Christmas sweater to keep you nice and warm."

Of course, Marvin hated wearing sweaters or coats, but it really was too cold to take him outside without one.

"And since you're obviously too tired to keep up your end of this conversation, I guess it's bedtime," Serena said.

Bedtime was another familiar word to him, and Marvin immediately hopped down off the sofa and raced over to the doggy door. But he sat obediently on his mat until she said "okay," then pushed through the flap and went outside to do his business.

A few minutes later, he was back, and immediately went to his bed in the corner.

Serena retreated to her bedroom—where Molly was still curled up in the middle of the mattress.

"You could at least move over and give me some room," she grumbled.

Of course, the cat didn't budge. Not until Serena had fluffed up her pillows and tucked herself in under the covers.

Then Molly crawled up to snuggle against Serena's chest, and purred contentedly.

Serena would never reject the calico's affection, but she couldn't deny that she longed for a different kind of company in her bed. As she drifted off to sleep, she was thinking of Bailey's strong arms around her, his heart beating in sync with her own.

Tuesday morning, Bailey spoke to Dan's wife on the phone. Annie had assured him that her husband was feeling better, but they agreed it wasn't worth the risk of exposing the kids to any remnants of the virus that might be lingering.

He should have dreaded the fact that he had to don the Santa suit again. Instead, Bailey found himself whistling as he drove to the elementary school, where he'd made arrangements to meet Mrs. Claus in the parking lot.

They walked into the school together and were directed to the teachers' lounge to change into their costumes. He zipped up Serena's dress and tied her apron; she secured his padding and whitened his brows. It was almost like they were a real married couple, helping one another get ready for a social engagement.

Only a few days earlier, he'd been sweaty and nervous and not at all looking forward to stepping out from behind the curtain and facing the group of children waiting in the community center. Today, there was no curtain. Today, they walked through the double doors of the gymnasium, but he felt much more comfortable and relaxed with Serena beside him.

He caught Janie's eye when he entered the gym, and the way her smile widened, she'd obviously recognized Uncle Bailey as the man behind Kris Kringle's white beard. But, of course, she didn't reveal his identity to anyone.

When the principal invited him to say a few words, he took advantage of the opportunity to explain that Christmas wasn't just about what they wanted to find under their trees the morning of December 25 but also about giving, and he encouraged them to talk to their parents about supporting Presents for Patriots in any way that they could.

As the afternoon progressed, he thought everything was going well. And then one of the kids—a little girl in second grade with reindeer antlers mounted onto a headband set in her curly red hair—climbed up onto his lap.

"Ho ho ho," Bailey said. "And what would you like for Christmas?"

Unlike most of the other kids who'd made a request for the usual variety of toys and games, she looked at him with big green eyes filled with worry and sadness and said, "I want my daddy to come home."

Which, of course, wasn't a wish that even the real Santa—if he existed—could grant.

Bailey was at a complete loss because he didn't have any idea where the child's father was or what could be preventing him from being with his family for the holiday. Maybe the little girl's parents were separated or even divorced. Maybe the father was traveling on business or serving overseas in the military. It was even possible that the child's father had passed away, ensuring that her wish was never going to come true.

He glanced, helplessly, hopelessly, at his missus.

And, once again, she came to his rescue and saved the day.

Crouching beside his chair, Serena spoke quietly to the child. "Your daddy's got an important job to do, Harley, and he can't come home until it's done. But I promise that he misses you and your mommy and your brothers as much as you miss him, and I know his wish for you would be that you have happy Christmas memories to share with him when he calls home."

The little girl nodded solemnly, eager to believe every word that Mrs. Claus said to her.

"So is there anything special you'd like to find under the tree on Christmas morning?" Santa asked her again.

This time, she responded without hesitation, confirming that although her first wish was to spend the holiday with her father, she was still a child. "A Stardust Stacie doll would be something good to tell daddy about."

"I'll see what I can do," Santa promised, even as he wondered if the doll would be more readily available than the pocket toys that Serena had told him were so popular this season.

Thankfully, Harley's request was the only snag in Santa's visit to the school. After all the children who wanted to share their wishes with Santa had done so, Mr. and Mrs. Claus retreated to the staff lounge to change out of their costumes and assume their real identities again.

"Who was the little girl who asked about her father coming home for Christmas?" Bailey asked Serena, as he rolled up his enormous red pants.

"Harley Williams," she said. "She's the youngest of three kids. Her mom works at the library and her dad is a marine, currently stationed in Syria."

"Do you know everything about everyone in this town?" he wondered aloud.

"Hardly," she told him. "But the family also has two cats—Bert and Ernie. You'd be amazed how much you learn about people when you help take care of their pets."

"So it would seem," he agreed, stuffing the pants and jacket into the costume bag. "And it seems that I owe you thanks for bailing me out—again."

"It was my pleasure."

"Actually, it was kind of fun today," he acknowledged.

She laughed at the surprise in his voice. "Yes, it was."

He wanted to say something else, something to prolong their conversation and give him an excuse to spend a few more minutes in her company.

It was strange to think that he'd only met her four days earlier, but between the Santa gigs and the Presents for Patriots event and the hot cocoa at Daisy's, they'd spent a lot of time together over those few days. And when he hadn't been with her, he'd been thinking about her.

He suspected that Serena was equally reluctant to part company with him, because after he'd stuffed the costumes in his truck, she asked, "Do you want to go for a ride with me? I'll bring you back here after."

"After what?"

She just smiled, and the sweet curve of her lips was like the sun breaking through the clouds on a gray day.

"Are you game to come with me or not?" she challenged.

Hmm...go back to Sunshine Farm and the chores that were always waiting? Or spend another hour—and maybe more—in the company of a bright and beautiful woman?

It was a no-brainer.

Because the more time he spent with Serena, the more he wanted to be with her. There was something warm and sincere about her that appealed to him. And okay, she was gorgeous and sexy, too, and he was far more attracted to her than he was ready to acknowledge—even to himself.

His romantic history wasn't particularly extensive or successful. Prior to meeting and falling in love with Emily, he'd only dated a few women. Growing up in Rust Creek Falls, he'd spent most of his waking hours at Sunshine Farm, doing any of the endless chores that filled the hours from sunup to sundown. And when those chores were finally done, he was usually too exhausted to go out and do anything else.

The one night he'd let Luke convince him that they deserved to have some fun had ended up being the worst night of his life.

He shook off the weight of those memories and focused his attention on the present—and the woman presently waiting for a response to her question.

"Why don't I drive and bring you back to your vehicle after?" he suggested. Because yeah, he was one of those guys who liked to be in the driver's seat—both literally and figuratively.

"After what?" she teasingly echoed his question.

He shrugged.

"And that's why I'm driving," she said. "Because I know where we're going." She thumbed the button on her key fob to unlock the doors.

He went to the driver's side first. She pulled back the hand that held her keys, as if she expected him to try to take them from her, but he only opened the door for her.

"Thank you," she said, appreciative of the gesture.

"You're welcome," he said, waiting until she'd slid into the driver's seat to close the door for her.

After he was buckled in, she turned her vehicle toward the highway, heading out of town.

After only a few minutes, Bailey figured out that they were making their way toward Falls Mountain and the actual Rust Creek Falls that gave the town its name. They passed a picnic area and signs that guided visitors to a viewing area for the falls. She continued to drive farther up the mountain, finally turning off the main road to park in a small gravel lot at the base of the trail that led to Owl Rock—the lookout point named for the large white boulder that resembled the bird and protruded out over the falls, as if keeping watch over them.

During the spring and summer months, vehicles would be packed closely together and the trails would be busy with hikers and families. But it was early December and too cold for most people, aside from the most hardy outdoor enthusiasts. Apparently Serena was one of those enthusiasts.

"Nice day for a hike," he commented, as he followed her up the trail.

And it was, because although the air was frigid, the sun was shining. Also, he had a spectacular view of her shapely butt, encased in snug-fitting denim.

"I haven't been up here since I was a teenager," he told her, as they arrived at the lookout point. "In fact, I'd almost forgotten this place existed."

"It's one of my favorite places in Rust Creek Falls," she confided, sitting down on a flat outcropping of rock with her legs crossed beneath her. "My grandmother brought me here when I first came to Rust Creek Falls, and whenever I'm feeling down, I find myself drawn back. Being close to nature always lifts my spirits."

"Why did you want to come here today?" he asked her.

She was silent for a minute before responding. "Because Harley's request about her dad brought back some painful memories."

As a man who carefully guarded his own secrets, he was reluctant to pry into hers. On the other hand, she'd invited him to come here with her today, which suggested that she wanted someone to talk to.

He lowered himself onto the rock beside her, sitting close enough that their shoulders were touching. "What kind of memories?"

"When I was just about Harley's age, I went to see Santa and asked him to bring my sister home from the hospital in time for Christmas."

"I didn't know you had a sister," Bailey admitted, surprised by her revelation.

"I don't." She unfolded her legs and drew her knees up to her chest, wrapping her arms around them. "Not anymore."

He didn't prompt her for more information. She would tell him more when she was ready.

"I was an only child for the first six years of my life," she began. "An only child who *begged* for a brother or sister. And when my parents finally told me that there was a baby in my mommy's tummy, I couldn't wait for her to be born.

"I don't know if my parents knew for sure that they were

having a girl, but I always thought of her as my sister. It was probably wishful thinking on my part, because I was seven, and I thought boys were mostly gross and dumb and I really wanted a sister."

She paused for a minute, gathering her thoughts—or maybe her composure.

"Then something went wrong, and my mom had to go into the hospital early. It must have been just before Halloween, because I was sucking on a lollipop that I'd stolen out of the bucket of candy my mom had bought for trick-or-treaters when Grams came into my room and told me that she was going to be staying with us for a few days.

"Miriam was born six weeks before her due date. I remember asking my grandmother why she didn't seem happy when she told me the news. She said it was because the baby was too small and that she might not make it.

"I didn't understand what she meant. The only information that registered with me was that I finally had a sister.

"So my grandmother bluntly told me that Miriam might die. I refused to believe it. Babies didn't die. Old people died. And I demanded to meet my sister.

"A few days later, Grams finally gave in and took me up to the hospital to see my parents and the baby. Miriam was in an incubator, though of course I didn't know what it was at the time. I only knew that she had tubes stuck in various parts of her body and she didn't look anything like a baby—at least nothing like Mr. and Mrs. Wakefield's baby, the focus of everyone's attention and well wishes at church earlier that morning.

"I think I started to cry, because my dad picked me up and tried to soothe me. And my mom got mad at Grams for bringing me to the hospital, but she argued that it was important for me to see my sister, in case anything happened.

"This made my mom cry and my dad told her to go. But I

got to stay for a while, snuggling with my mom while my dad told us that everything was going to be fine, because Mimi—that's what we called her—was strong, just like me. And he promised that we'd all be celebrating Christmas together in a few weeks.

"And he was right, although it wasn't really as simple or easy as that. Mimi had to stay in the hospital until she was a lot bigger and stronger, and the doctors warned that could take several weeks or even months.

"One night, in mid-December, my dad said that he had a surprise. Instead of going to the hospital, he took me to the local mall to see Santa." Serena nudged Bailey playfully with her shoulder. "Back then, it was what you did to see the big guy, because we didn't have a community center in town or any handsome cowboys willing to put on a padded red suit."

Taking his cue from her deliberate attempt to lighten the mood, Bailey lifted his brows. "You think I'm handsome?"

"To quote Ellie Traub, 'all those Stockton boys are handsome devils.'"

"Good to know," he said, equal parts flattered and embarrassed by the older woman's assessment. "But you were telling me about your visit to Santa."

"Right," she agreed. "My dad took me to see Santa and I thought of all the wishes I'd carefully printed on my Christmas list to decide which one I wanted most of all. That year, it was a toss-up between Mouse Trap, the board game, and a new pair of ballet slippers. But when it was finally my turn, all I could think was that I wanted my baby sister to come home from the hospital for Christmas."

"Did Santa deliver?" he asked gently.

She nodded. "Mimi came home the afternoon of December 24. It was as if we got our very own Christmas miracle. The next morning, I didn't even race downstairs to see if Santa had left any presents under the tree. Instead, I rushed across the hall to the nursery, to make sure she was still there.

"And she was. The Mouse Trap game and ballet slippers that I unwrapped later were bonuses—all I really wanted was my sister. Of course, she needed a lot of attention," Serena continued. "And I was happy to give it to her. Happy to finally have the sister I'd always wanted.

"If she cried, I wanted to be the one to pick her up. If she was hungry, I wanted to give her a bottle. Even when she was content to sit in her high chair or play swing, I was there, reading to her or singing the songs I'd learned at school. Long before she could talk, she would clap her hands and kick her feet whenever she listened to music."

She smiled at the memory. "And Christmas carols were her favorite. Maybe not that first Christmas," she acknowledged. "That year she mostly seemed fascinated by the colored lights and sparkly ornaments on the tree. But by the following year, when she was thirteen months old, she was munching on sugar cookies and tearing the bows and paper off presents. The year after that, she shook colored sugar onto the cookies before she ate them and even helped hang some sparkly ornaments on the tree."

Serena dropped her chin to her bent knees, her gaze focused on something in the distance—or maybe something in the past. "And then, just a few weeks after her third birthday, she disappeared."

Chapter 6

*D*isappeared?

Just when Bailey started to think he knew where the story was leading, it took a major detour. He caught the sheen of moisture in Serena's eyes, noted the tension in the arms that hugged her legs tight. He shifted on the rock so that he was sitting behind her, his legs splayed to bracket her hips, his arms wrapped around her.

"My parents had planned a special trip for all of us," she continued. "We went to Missoula to participate in the Parade of Lights and enjoy a performance of *The Nutcracker*. Of course, Mimi was too young to understand the show and she fidgeted through the whole thing, but I'd been dancing for five years by then, and I was completely entranced. Next to Mimi, that was the best Christmas present I'd ever received.

"The morning of our planned return to Rust Creek Falls, we stopped at the Holiday Made Fair so that my parents could do some last-minute shopping. It was crowded with booths and toys and goodies and lots of people. I was under strict instructions to hold tight to Mimi's hand, and I did." She swallowed. "Until I didn't."

He hugged her a little tighter, a wordless offer of comfort and encouragement.

"She saw the doll first," Serena said, resuming her narrative. "It was a replica of the Sugar Plum Fairy and she pulled me to it. There was a whole bin of them, and Mimi tugged her hand from mine so that she could pick one up. And I picked up another one, admiring the intricate details of her costume, and I turned to show Mimi something, but she wasn't there anymore.

"It happened that fast," she said, her voice hollow. "She was right beside me...and then she was gone. My parents were, of course, frantic. We didn't celebrate the holidays—we were too busy looking for Mimi. But she'd disappeared without a trace. The police got all kinds of tips and followed countless leads, but nothing ever panned out. As days turned into weeks and weeks into months, we began to lose hope that she would ever come home again.

"I know she's out there somewhere," Serena insisted. "And I believe with my whole heart that she's alive...just lost to us.

"By the summer, my mother was self-medicating with alcohol. I didn't know what that meant, except that I heard my dad say it to my grandmother. I did know that my mom stumbled around a lot, ran her words together so that sometimes I couldn't understand what she was saying, and slept a lot. And, of course, my parents fought. All the time. Several months later, before Christmas the following year, my dad took off."

And only a few days earlier, Bailey had accused Serena of not understanding that happiness was a fickle emotion that could be snatched away without warning. No wonder she'd cautioned him about making assumptions, because she did understand. Because she'd experienced a loss as profound as his own.

"He left a note," she continued. "It wasn't like when Mimi disappeared. But the note didn't say much more than that he felt as if he'd failed his family, and every day with us—without Mimi—was a reminder of that."

"I'm so sorry, Serena." The words sounded so meaningless, even to his own ears, but they were all he had to offer.

"There wasn't anything joyful about Christmas that year, either," she said.

"I can only imagine how difficult it would be to celebrate anything after losing a child," he acknowledged.

"Mimi's disappearance was devastating for all of us," Serena agreed. "But my parents had two children—and they didn't lose both of them."

But Serena had effectively lost both of her parents after the disappearance of her sister. And Bailey suspected that she'd been deeply scarred by it.

"Of course, my mom's drinking got even worse after my dad left. And Child Protective Services got involved in the New Year after my teacher called to report that I frequently wore the same clothes to school several days in a row and sometimes didn't have any food in my lunch box.

"That's when my grandmother came to stay with us again. She tried to get my mother back on track—and Amanda tried to stop drinking. But inevitably, after a few weeks—or sometimes not more than a few days—she'd decide that she needed 'just one drink' to take the edge off her pain and emptiness. Of course, one drink always turned into two and then three, until eventually she'd end up passed out on the sofa."

Bailey had been there—alone in that dark place where it seemed that nothing could take the edge off his aching emptiness and the only recourse was to drown his sorrows. He didn't do that anymore, but he could appreciate that it was a slippery slope and he was grateful that he'd managed to find his footing before he'd slipped too far.

"After a few such incidents, my grandmother talked her into going to rehab. She completed a thirty-day inpatient program and, when she came home, assured us that she'd turned a corner. A few days later, on what would have been her thirteenth wedding anniversary, she got drunk again."

"Significant dates and special occasions are triggers for a lot of people," he observed.

Serena nodded. "But as much as my grandmother was worried about her daughter's downward spiral, she was even more worried about me. So she packed up all my stuff and brought me to Rust Creek Falls to live with her. And she told my mother that, when she was ready to prove that her daughter was more important than the contents of a bottle, she would be welcome to stay with her, too."

"Sounds like a strong dose of tough love," Bailey remarked.

"It was tough on Grams, too. She wanted to make everything right, but she couldn't fight Amanda's addiction. So she focused her attention and efforts on me. I had sporadic contact with Amanda over the next few years," she confided. "I still feel guilty saying this out loud, but those were some of the most normal—and best—years of my childhood. Maybe it was a little strange that I lived with my grandmother rather than my mother or father, but I had no cause for complaint. I had regular meals and clean clothes, willing help with homework and even a chaperone for occasional school trips."

"I'm glad you had her," Bailey said.

"I was lucky," Serena acknowledged.

He hadn't had the same fortune when he lost his parents. In fact, Matthew and Agnes Baldwin had essentially told their three oldest grandsons to fend for themselves—and allowed their two youngest granddaughters to be adopted, forcing the split of seven children grieving the deaths of their parents.

"Does your grandmother still live in Rust Creek Falls?" he asked Serena now.

She shook her head. "A few years ago, after I'd graduated from college and she was sure my mother's life was back on track, she decided her old bones couldn't handle the cold any longer, and she moved to Arizona." She smiled a little. "It's been good for her. She's taken up golf, plays bridge and does water aerobics—and she's got a new beau."

"You can be happy for her and still miss her," Bailey assured her.

"I do miss her," she admitted. "But I've also realized that I maybe relied on her too much. I don't think the warmer climate was her only reason for leaving Rust Creek Falls. I think she wanted me to stand on my own two feet—not to see *if* I could, but to show me *that* I could. Because she always had a lot more confidence in me than I had in myself."

"I'd say her faith was well-founded."

"My grandmother's a wise woman," she acknowledged. "She's the one who taught me to focus on my happy memories of the holidays."

"That couldn't have been easy," he noted. In fact, considering how much heartache she'd endured—and so much of it focused around this time of year—he might have found the task impossible.

"It took me a while to look past all the bad stuff and remember the good stuff," she confided to him. "Although we only celebrated three Christmases together with Mimi, those were the happiest Christmases of my life. Every memory of my sister is a happy memory, and she loved everything about Christmas."

"You're an amazing woman, Serena Langley."

"I'm not sure about that," she said. "But focusing on the happy memories is the one thing—the only thing—I can do that helps me get through. And in remembering Mimi's holiday joy, I've rediscovered my own."

Her outgoing and optimistic demeanor had led him to make certain assumptions about her, but those assumptions couldn't have been more wrong. Not knowing what to say to her now, certain there were no words to express his regrets and sympathy, he merely pulled her closer.

Serena dropped her head back against his shoulder, and when her lips curved a little as she looked up at him, he knew that he was forgiven for what he'd said the other day.

And then his head tipped forward...and his lips brushed against hers.

He hadn't consciously decided to kiss her. Sure, he'd given the idea more than a passing thought. And yeah, he'd wondered if her lips would be as soft as they looked or taste as sweet as he imagined. And maybe, when they'd been dancing at the Presents for Patriots fund-raiser, he'd considered breaching the scant distance that separated their mouths.

But he'd resisted the impulse, because he knew that kissing her was a bad idea for a lot of reasons. First, after the breakdown of his marriage, he was wary of any kind of romantic involvement. Second, even if he was looking to get involved, it would be a mistake to hook up with a woman who was both a colleague and friend of his sister-in-law. Third—

He abandoned his mental list in favor of focusing on the moment—and the fact that Serena was kissing him back. And her lips were as soft as they looked, and their taste was even sweeter than he'd imagined.

And he realized that sitting on Owl Rock and kissing Serena was the absolute highlight of his day. His week. His month. Possibly even his whole year.

He lifted a hand to cup the back of her head, his fingers diving through silky strands of hair, tilting her head so that he could deepen the kiss. She didn't protest when his tongue slid between her lips but met it with her own.

He wrapped his other arm around her middle and dragged her onto his lap. Her arms lifted to his shoulders. Her legs wrapped around his waist. He wanted to touch her; he wanted his hands on her bare skin. But they were outside in Montana in December, which meant there were at least a half dozen layers of clothing and outerwear between them.

After a while—two minutes? Ten? He didn't know, he'd lost all track of time while he was kissing her—she drew her mouth away from his.

"Maybe we should…slow things down," she suggested a little breathlessly.

He took a moment to draw the sharp cold air into his own lungs. "That would probably be the smart thing to do," he agreed. "But it's not what I want to do."

"Right now, it's not what I want, either," she admitted. "But I haven't had much success with romantic relationships and I don't want to jeopardize our fledgling friendship by trying to turn it into something more."

"I suck at relationships, too," he told her. "I'm not sure I'm much better at friendships."

"You seem to be doing okay so far."

He appreciated the vote of confidence, but he remained dubious. "You think we're friends?"

"I think we could be," she said.

"Hmm," he said, considering.

"Unless you have so many friends that you don't want another one?"

He chuckled softly. "Before I came back to Rust Creek Falls

last year, I'd been gone for a dozen years and lost touch with not just my family but my friends."

"It was after your parents were killed that you left town, wasn't it?"

The surprise he felt must have been reflected in his expression, because she explained, "I've worked with Annie for almost three years, and when Dan came back—just a few months before you did—it sent her whole life into a tailspin. And sometimes, if we were on break together, she'd talk to me about it."

"So how much of the story do you know?" he wondered.

"I don't know all the details—and most of those that I do know are from her perspective. Essentially that you, Luke and Dan were of legal age, and your grandparents decided that you were able to take care of yourselves so they didn't have to."

He nodded. "That about sums it up," he agreed. "What really sucks is that we all assumed that Sunshine Farm would be lost. Our parents struggled for a lot of years and without my dad around to run the ranch, we couldn't imagine making a go of it. If we'd known that the mortgage was insured, we might have stayed." Then he shook his head. "Who am I kidding? We wouldn't have stayed. We couldn't have. Not after that night."

That night was the night both of his parents had been killed by a drunk driver. And the events of that night continued to haunt him and would undoubtedly do so forever.

"Look," Serena said, holding out a hand to catch a delicate flake on her palm. "It's snowing."

"So it is," he agreed, noting the fluffy flakes falling from the sky. "It's also getting colder by the minute."

"I know. I can't feel my butt anymore."

"I could feel it for you," he suggested, in an obvious effort to lighten the mood.

"I appreciate the offer, but maybe another time," she said, as she untangled her legs and rose to her feet. "We should be heading back now, anyway."

"You're probably right," he agreed, understanding only too well that driving conditions on the mountain roads could turn hazardous quickly.

But as they turned back toward the trail, he asked, "Did Owl Rock work its magic for you today?"

She nodded. "It's always so peaceful up here. But even better today was having someone to talk to."

"Glad to be of service," he told her.

At the top of the narrow trail, Bailey insisted on taking the lead so that he could check for slippery patches on the descent. But he also took her hand, to ensure she didn't fall behind.

The weather in Montana wasn't just unpredictable, it could change fast—and had done so while they were up at Owl Rock. By the time they got back to her vehicle, she had to pull her snow brush out to clear off her windows.

"You get in," Bailey instructed. "I'll take care of this."

She didn't object to that but handed him the brush and slid in behind the wheel, turning on the engine and cranking up the heat.

A few minutes later, Bailey put the brush away and took his seat on the passenger side.

"I'm happy to drive, if you want," he told her.

Her only response was to shift into Drive and pull out of the gravel lot.

At the midway point of their return journey, Bailey said, "Since we almost go right past Wings To Go on our way back to the school, why don't we stop in there to grab some dinner?"

"I can't," Serena said regretfully. "I've got animals waiting to be fed at home."

"Do you have dinner waiting, too?"

She shook her head. "I wasn't thinking that far ahead when I left home this morning."

"Do you like wings?"

"Who doesn't?"

"Well, here's an interesting fact about Wings To Go," he said. "Customers can actually place an order...and then take it away from the restaurant."

"No kidding," she said, sounding bemused. "I'll bet that's what the To Go part of the name refers to."

"And with that in mind, here's plan B," he said. "After you take me back to my truck and go home to feed your animals, I'll pick up wings and bring them over to feed us. What do you think of that plan?"

"I think I like that plan," she agreed. "Especially if it includes honey-barbecue wings."

After dropping Bailey off at his truck in the elementary school parking lot, Serena hurried home. Not just because she knew Marvin, Molly and Max would be waiting for her, but because she wanted to tidy up a little before Bailey showed up. She didn't think her apartment was a mess, but earlier in the day she'd been so focused on the anticipation of seeing Bailey that she honestly couldn't remember if she'd left her lunch dishes in the sink or her pajamas on the floor in the bathroom.

As she raced around the apartment, tidying a stack of mail on the counter, wiping crumbs—and a smudge of something sticky—off the table and pushing the Swiffer around, Marvin chased after her, delighted with what he assumed was a new game.

"It's not a game, it's housework," she told him. "And I do this at least once a week."

But she didn't usually clean at such a frantic pace, and Marvin refused to believe she wasn't playing with him.

She gave him his dinner, hoping the food would take his attention away from the Swiffer. The diversion worked—for the whole two minutes that it took him to empty his bowl. But she finished putting her apartment in order—and even managed to run a brush through her hair and dab on some lip gloss before she saw Bailey's truck pull into one of the designated visitor parking spots at the back of the building.

Marvin raced toward the door a full half minute before the bell rang, having been alerted to the presence of a visitor by the sound of feet climbing the stairs. Though he could easily have gone through the doggy door to greet the newcomer, Serena had been strict in his training to ensure his safety and that of her guests. So now he waited in eager anticipation, his entire back end wagging.

"No jumping," she admonished firmly as she opened the door.

Bailey's eyes skimmed over her, a slow perusal from the top of her head to the thick wool socks on her feet. "I wasn't planning on jumping," he drawled. "But I can't deny that the idea is intriguing."

"Ha ha," she said, taking the bag from his hands so that he could remove his boots.

As he reached down to unfasten the laces, Marvin whimpered.

"You must be Marvin," Bailey said, and offered his hand for the dog to sniff.

Marvin sniffed, then licked, then shoved his snout into the visitor's palm. Bailey chuckled and scratched the dog's chin.

Serena set plates and napkins on the table. "What can I get you to drink? I've got cola, root beer, real beer, milk or water."

"Cola sounds good," he said.

"Glass or can?"

"Can works."

She retrieved two cans from the fridge and set them on the table, then glanced back at the entranceway to discover that Bailey was sitting on the tile floor with Marvin sprawled across his lap. The dog's belly was exposed and his tongue lolled out of his mouth as his new best friend gave him a vigorous belly rub.

She shook her head. "Such an attention whore."

"I am not," Bailey denied.

"I was referring to the dog."

"Oh." He gave Marvin a couple more rubs, then carefully heaved the dog off his lap and stood up. He made his way into the kitchen and washed his hands at the sink. Marvin kept pace with him, practically glued to his shin.

"I'm the one who feeds you," Serena felt compelled to remind her canine companion.

Marvin wagged his whole body, but he didn't move away from Bailey.

And when Bailey took a seat at the table, Marvin settled at his feet.

"I feel like I talked your ear off when we were up at Owl Rock today," Serena said as she used the tongs to transfer several wings from the box to her plate. "But the truth is, I don't often talk about my sister or her disappearance. In fact, I doubt if more than a handful of people in this town even know what happened before I came to live with my grandmother all those years ago."

"Your secrets are safe with me," he promised.

"I'm not worried," she said. "But I'm thinking that it's your turn to tell me your life story."

"There's not much to tell." He took the tongs she offered, then proceeded to pick out half a dozen wings. "And you already know the highlights."

"I know why you went away, but I don't know anything

about where you went or what you did when you left Rust Creek Falls."

"Me, Luke and Danny headed to Wyoming together and found work on a big spread in Cheyenne. We stayed there for about six months together before we parted ways."

"Why?" she wondered aloud.

He shrugged. "Maybe because we had different goals and ambitions. Or maybe because we shared the same guilt and regrets."

She picked a piece of meat off the bone. "Where did you go after Cheyenne?"

"Jackson Hole for a while, then Newcastle and Douglas."

"So you stayed in Wyoming?"

"For a few years," he acknowledged. "Then I made my way to New Mexico."

"That was quite a move," she remarked.

He licked honey-barbecue sauce off his thumb. "There was a girl," he admitted.

"Ahh, I should have guessed."

He shook his head. "I promise you, I'm not in the habit of chasing women halfway across the country. That was the first—and absolute last—time."

"Putting aside the fact that New Mexico isn't really across the county but directly south of Wyoming, she must have been someone really special."

"Actually, she was my wife."

Chapter 7

*W*ife?

Serena nearly choked on a mouthful of cola.

Bailey watched her cough and sputter, his brow furrowed with concern. "Are you okay?"

"Yeah." She coughed again. "I'm fine." She took a careful sip of her soda. "I didn't realize you'd been married."

"Only because I was young and foolish enough to believe that love conquers all."

"I'm sorry it didn't work out," she said. "But at least you were willing to take a chance on love."

"I was young and foolish," he said again.

"And now you're old and wise?" she teased.

"Older and wiser, anyway. No way am I ever going to make that mistake again."

"You don't believe in love anymore?"

"I don't know," he said. "I mean, each of my brothers and even my sister Bella seems to have found a forever match, so maybe it's just me. Maybe I'm not capable of loving somebody that way."

"You must have loved your wife."

"I thought I did," he acknowledged. "But in the end, whatever I felt for her wasn't enough."

"It takes two people to make a relationship work," she pointed out. "Or allow it to fail."

"So it would seem," he agreed.

"Then again—" she picked up another wing "—what do I know?"

"You've never been in love?"

She shook her head. "The longest relationship I've ever had is with Molly."

His brows lifted. "Molly?"

"My cat," she reminded him.

"That's right. You've got Marvin, Molly and..."

"Max," she supplied.

"So where are Molly and Max?"

"Hiding," she admitted. "They're both leery of strangers. And—" she glanced at the bulldog under the table "—*not* attention whores."

"Why all the animals?" he wondered aloud.

She shrugged. "I've always loved animals."

"That would explain why you became a vet tech," he commented. "Not why you've turned your home into a mini animal shelter."

"And...they love me back. Unconditionally."

"That's something a lot of human beings have a problem with," he said.

"Yeah. Sometimes even the ones who are supposed to love you."

"Like your dad," he guessed. "And my grandparents."

She nodded. "All my animals want from me is a roof over

their heads, food in their bowls, some interaction and playtime, and the occasional lazy Sunday morning snuggle in bed."

"They sleep with you?"

"No. They have their own beds, but sometimes, if I'm feeling lazy and slip back between the covers after feeding them their breakfast, they'll follow me into the bedroom and want to cuddle with me."

"Even the cat?"

She nodded. "Molly is a surprisingly affectionate feline at times—at least with me," she clarified. "And Max. She absolutely adores the bunny. She's less fond of strangers."

"Marvin doesn't consider me a stranger," he noted.

"Marvin is forever devoted to anyone who gives him an ear scratch or belly rub. Or *t-r-e-a-t-s*," she said, purposely spelling the word so that the dog wouldn't get excited about the possibility of getting one. "Which reminds me—I guess my bid didn't win the Canine Christmas basket at the silent auction?"

Bailey shook his head. "You were outbid by Lissa Christensen."

"That's good for Presents for Patriots, but sad for Marvin," she said.

"And then Lissa Christensen was outbid by me."

"*You* bought the basket?"

He nodded.

"Why?"

"Because I know how much you wanted it," he said.

"You bought it for me?"

"Well, for Marvin, actually."

"That was really sweet," she said, then laughed when he winced. "How much do I owe you? I don't know how much cash I have, but I could write you a check."

"You're not writing me a check," he protested.

"Worried it might bounce?"

He shook his head. "I mean you're not paying for the basket."

"But you bought it for my dog."

"That's right," he said. "*I* bought it for you to give to him."

"Then I'll say thank you, and check Marvin's name off my shopping list."

"Yeah, I guess I should probably get started on mine," he acknowledged.

"You haven't even started your shopping yet?"

"It's only December 4," he pointed out.

"No," she denied. "It's *already* December 4."

"To-may-to, to-mah-to," he said.

"You'll be saying something different when you're fighting the frantic and desperate masses of last-minute shoppers at the mall on Christmas Eve."

"I won't wait until Christmas Eve. Probably."

She shook her head despairingly. "I'm planning to go into Kalispell to do some shopping on Saturday," she told him. "You're welcome to come with me, if you want."

"I guess it wouldn't hurt to get a head start this year."

"You'll be one of the early birds," she said dryly.

Bailey just grinned. Then he said, "Seriously though, I appreciate your offer to let me tag along."

"It's not a problem," she assured him. "But you're not allowed to complain if we're gone most of the day."

"I can't make any promises there," he said.

"Then I can't promise that you'll get a ride back home again."

When all the wing bones had been picked clean and the dishes cleared away, Bailey thanked Serena for her hospitality and made his way to the door.

He could have come up with an excuse to linger; he could

have requested a cup of coffee before he hit the road or offered to take Marvin for a walk or asked her to turn on the TV to check the score of the game—because there was always a game of some sort playing—and then allowed himself to get caught up in the action on the screen for a while. But when he realized that he was searching for a reason to stay, he knew it was time to go. Because the more time he spent with Serena, the more he wanted to be with her, and that was a dangerous desire.

Besides, he was going to see her again on Saturday.

Yeah, Saturday was four days away, but maybe a little space and time was what he needed to give himself some perspective and remember that he wasn't going to get involved.

Not with Serena. Not with anyone. Not ever again.

But when she walked him to the door, he was more than a little tempted to kiss her goodbye.

But she'd asked him to slow things down. She wanted to be *friends*. He had his doubts about that possibility—mostly because he really wanted to get her naked, and in his experience, lust tended to get in the way of friendship—but he decided to try it her way for a while.

So he didn't kiss her goodbye, but the memory of the kiss they'd shared at Owl Rock teased his mind and heated his body as he climbed into his cold truck and drove away.

But before he could head back to Sunshine Farm, he had one more stop to make. He'd promised to return the costumes to Annie after the visit to the elementary school—a promise he'd nearly forgotten until he spotted the bulky bags in the back seat.

"There he is," Annie said when she responded to his knock on the door.

"Who is it?" Janie asked from somewhere inside the house.

"Uncle Grooge," her mother responded.

"Bah, humbug," Bailey said, playing along as he held out the costume bags, and heard Janie giggle.

"Hmm..." Annie took the bags and stepped away from the door so he could enter. "That doesn't sound quite as cynical as it did a few days ago. Maybe this suit has magic powers."

He ignored her comment to focus on his niece, seated at the table with her schoolbooks open in front of her. "Homework?" he guessed.

She nodded. "Science," she said, her expression and her tone reflecting displeasure. "Dad was helping me, but Mom ordered him to go rest when you showed up."

"I ordered him to rest because he's still recuperating," Annie said in a no-nonsense mom voice.

"Oh, right."

The exchange struck Bailey as a little odd, but his sister-in-law didn't pause long enough for him to ponder it.

"Considering that school let out almost five hours ago, I hope you're not just getting back from the Santa gig now," she remarked.

"Of course not. Me and Serena went for a drive afterward," he admitted. "And then we decided to get some dinner."

"Like a date?" Janie asked.

"No," he immediately replied.

"Sounds like a date to me," his niece insisted.

"What do you know about dating?" he asked her.

"Nothing," she said with a sigh. "Nothing at all."

"Homework," Annie said, in an effort to redirect her daughter's attention. Then to Bailey, "But your non-date with Serena is interesting."

"What's so interesting about it?" he challenged.

"Just that, as far as I know, you haven't dated anyone since you came back to Rust Creek Falls."

"And I'm not dating anyone now," he said firmly.

His sister-in-law sighed. "Well, thank you again for filling in for your brother today."

"How's he doing?"

"Much better. In fact, he's in the living room watching TV if you want to say hi."

So Bailey went through to the living room, where his brother was stretched out on the sofa. Shifting his gaze to the screen, he saw that, sure enough, there was a game on.

"Hey," Dan said, clicking the mute button on the remote. "How'd it go today?"

"Pretty good," Bailey allowed.

"Janie said you were a very believable Santa Claus."

"Ho ho ho," he said, affecting the persona.

Dan nodded. "Not bad for a Grooge."

Bailey just shook his head.

"Seriously though, I appreciate you filling in for me again," his brother said.

"It wasn't really that big a deal," Bailey said.

"It was to me. For too many years, when I was living on my own, I forgot what it meant to be part of a family, to know there were people I could count on to help me out."

"I'm sorry I bailed on you all those years ago."

Dan shook his head. "That's not what I'm saying."

"I'm sorry anyway."

"We all made mistakes. And it really did mean the world to me that you found your way back to Rust Creek Falls for my wedding."

"That was just unfortunate timing on my part," Bailey said, not entirely joking.

"So you've said—on more than one occasion," his brother acknowledged dryly.

"But you and Annie…you really do work," he said. "Not just as a couple but a family."

"Coming home was the best thing I ever did," Dan said. "I only wish I'd found the courage to do so a lot sooner—then maybe I wouldn't have missed the first eleven years of Janie's life."

Yeah, it sucked that his brother had lost so much time with his daughter. And though Bailey didn't doubt that they'd hit some rough spots as they got to know one another, they were growing closer every day.

If Dan held on to any resentment because his daughter also continued to be close to Hank Harlow, who'd raised her as his own for the first decade of her life—even after divorcing Annie—he was smart enough not to show it. And if Bailey could believe his brother, Dan was sincerely grateful that Hank had been there for Janie during those years that her biological father wasn't.

"I'm hoping that it won't take too much longer for you to figure out that coming home was the best thing you ever did, too," Dan said.

Bailey shrugged, deliberately noncommittal.

When he'd shown up in Rust Creek Falls the previous December, he'd had no intention of staying for any length of time. He only wanted to touch base with his siblings before he moved on again. Almost twelve months later, he was still in town, still trying to figure out a plan for his own life.

He should be on his way, but things felt...unfinished. Though he'd reconnected with all of his brothers and two of his sisters, he knew that there would be a void in all their lives until Liza was found.

Bella's husband, Hudson Jones, had willingly bankrolled the search for his wife's missing siblings. Of course, Hudson had all kinds of money to throw around and there was no doubt the multimillionaire would do anything for Bella. In fact, it was the bigshot PI he'd hired—David Bradford—who'd managed to track down their brother Luke in Cheyenne, notwithstanding the fact that a payroll glitch had caused him to be working under the name Lee Stanton at the time.

Bailey had come back to Rust Creek Falls of his own volition a few weeks after Luke. But while the PI continued to look for their youngest sister, he'd yet to make any significant progress in that search.

"Anyway," Bailey said, not wanting to dwell on past mistakes or current problems, "I'm glad you've finally kicked back at that virus or flu or whatever knocked you down."

"Not as glad as I am," Dan said. "I don't mind staying in bed all day if my beautiful wife is there with me, but fever and chills sure can put a damper on a man's enjoyment between the sheets."

Bailey held up a hand. "I really don't want to hear about your bedroom activities."

"You're just jealous that I have a love life," Dan teased.

Maybe he was envious—not so much of his brother's bedroom activities, but the obvious and deep connection he shared with both his wife and newfound daughter. Dan was part of a family again, and thriving in the roles of husband and father.

Dan and Annie had fallen in love when they were teenagers, and somehow their love had survived not only a dozen years apart but Annie's marriage to another man during that time. Bailey knew there had been issues for them to work through when Dan finally returned to Rust Creek Falls—and a lot of hurts to be forgiven—and he wondered what it would be like to share that kind of relationship with someone.

Bailey had thought he was in love with Emily and wanted to build a life with her, but it quickly became apparent that he and his wife had very different ideas for their future together. He'd taken a chance and he'd blown it. He had no desire to open up his heart and let it be kicked around again.

But even as he reminded himself of that fact, he found his thoughts drifting again, and an image of Serena formed in his mind, tugged at his heart. She was obviously a lot stronger and braver than he was. She'd suffered the loss of her sister and subsequent breakup of her family, and somehow she still managed to greet each day with a smile on her face. Not only that, but she actually looked forward to celebrating the Christmas season and sharing her joy with others—including him.

"So you didn't mind partnering with Serena Langley?" Dan asked, breaking into Bailey's thoughts.

"No, it was fine," he said cautiously.

"Just fine?"

"What do you want me to say?"

His brother shrugged. "I just wondered what's going on with the two of you."

"*You* wondered what's going on?"

"Okay, Annie was wondering," Dan admitted. "You know she and Serena are friends as well as coworkers."

"I do know," Bailey confirmed. "And if your wife wants to know what's going on, maybe she should ask her friend and coworker."

"Believe me, I wouldn't be hassling you if Annie had had any success with her inquiries."

"Maybe Serena hasn't told her anything because there's nothing to tell," Bailey suggested.

"Luke said you danced with her at the fund-raiser—and that sparks were flying."

"Maybe between him and Eva," he countered. "But it's nice to know that my brothers have nothing better to do than gossip about me."

"Since you don't tell us anything, it's the only way we can keep up with what's going on in your life."

He wanted to protest that there was nothing to share, but

then he remembered the kiss. That kiss had definitely been something, and it made him want more. A lot more.

But that wasn't something he had any intention of sharing with his brother for Dan to then share with the rest of the family.

Even if it was kind of nice to be reunited with his siblings and to know that they cared.

Serena was waiting for Bailey to pick her up for their shopping trip Saturday morning when her phone rang. She intended to let the call go to voice mail, but a quick glance at the display identified the caller as Janet Carswell, causing her to snatch up the receiver.

"Hi, Grams."

"I got your Christmas card in the mail yesterday," her grandmother said. "The pretty winter scene on the front didn't make me miss the snow, but I do miss you."

"I miss you, too," Serena told her.

"How is everything in Rust Creek Falls?"

"Cold and snowy," she said.

"Nothing new?" her grandmother prompted.

"Well, I saw my mom last week."

"How is she?" Grams asked cautiously.

"Good," Serena said, and proceeded to fill her grandmother in on the conversation she'd had with her mother—and on Amanda's new boyfriend.

"I'm glad to hear that my daughter's doing well," Grams said. "But I really want to know what's been going on with my granddaughter and her new man."

"You've been talking to Melba Strickland," she guessed.

"Well, someone needs to keep me up to date with the happenings in Rust Creek Falls."

"I talk to you every week," Serena reminded her grandmother.

"But you always censor the good stuff."

She chuckled. "You only think I do. The truth is, there isn't any good stuff to censor."

"Maybe that's why I worry about you, Rena."

"You don't need to worry about me—I'm doing just fine," she assured her.

"You're alone," Grams said in a gentle tone.

"Hardly."

"Your pets don't count."

"Don't tell them that," Serena cautioned.

Grams sighed. "You've got so much love to give, but you're afraid to give it."

"I'm not afraid."

"It's understandable." Her grandmother forged ahead as if Serena hadn't spoken. "You've been hurt, and deeply, by so many people who were supposed to love you."

"You're the one who always said that whatever doesn't kill us makes us stronger."

"I was paraphrasing Nietzsche," Grams confessed.

"Still, I think there's a lot of truth in that statement."

"And I think you're one of the strongest women I know," her grandmother said. "With one of the softest hearts. But you don't let many people into your heart."

"I let plenty of people into my heart."

"You know what I mean," Grams chided. "You've hardly dated anyone since you broke up with Bobby Ray."

It was true. It was also true that she never should have let herself fall for a man who everyone knew was still carrying a torch for his high school girlfriend—notwithstanding the fact that she'd moved on and moved away and was now married to someone else.

But Serena had a habit of falling for men who were emotionally unavailable. Before Bobby Ray Ellis, she'd dated Howard Shelton, a widower with a gorgeous labradoodle. Before Howard, she'd gone out with Kevin Nolan, an attorney from Kalispell who'd been so focused on his billable hours he'd rarely had any time left for her.

And since she was thinking about time, she glanced at the clock and realized she didn't have much before Bailey was due to arrive.

"I've gotta go, Grams, but I'll call you next week," she promised.

As she hung up the phone, she couldn't help but wonder if she was making the same mistake with Bailey that she'd made so many times previously.

She knew that he had an ex-wife, but she didn't know any other details about his marriage or why it had ended. Was he still in love with the woman he'd married? Was her growing infatuation with the sexy cowboy going to end with more heartache?

Possibly...and yet, she couldn't stop her heart from doing a happy little dance when she saw Bailey's truck pull up in front of her building now.

Chapter 8

Bailey had called Serena on Friday night to confirm their plans for shopping the next day—and to offer to drive. She'd teasingly accused him of being worried that she might actually leave him at the mall, but she didn't oppose his plan. She did, however, request a slight detour when he picked her up Saturday morning.

"I have to stop at Crawford's before we head out," she told him, as she buckled her seat belt.

"You don't think that whatever you need from the general store could be picked up in Kalispell?"

"No, because what I need is a tag from the Tree of Hope."

He looked at her blankly. "The what?"

"The Tree of Hope," she said again. "It was Nina's idea," she said, referring to the woman who'd been born a Crawford but was now married to Dallas Traub, with whom she was raising his three sons and her daughter. "It started about five years ago, when families were struggling to recover from the catastrophic flooding that summer, and so many people had nothing left to put presents under a Christmas tree—if they even had a Christmas tree."

She went on to explain that gift tags marked with the age and gender of the intended recipient were hung on the branches of a decorated tree inside Crawford's General Store. Customers would choose one or more of the tags, purchase appropriate gifts and return them to the store with the tags. Then Nina—and any other volunteers that she managed to recruit—would wrap and deliver the gifts.

"Rust Creek Falls really does take care of its own," Bailey noted, pulling into a parking spot near the General Store.

"Sometimes we need a little help from our neighbors," Serena acknowledged, unbuckling her belt. "After the flood, we were fortunate that a lot of folks from Thunder Canyon came to town to help with the cleanup and rebuild."

"That's the second time you've mentioned a flood," he observed as he opened her door for her.

"I guess the news didn't make its way down to New Mexico."

"I guess not," he confirmed.

"It was five years ago, around the Fourth of July. There were torrential rains in the area, and a lot of homes were ruined by the floods. Several public buildings were destroyed, the Commercial Street Bridge was washed away, the Main Street Bridge was impassable, and Hunter McGee, the former mayor, died of a heart attack after a tree crushed the front of his car. That led to a battle between Collin Traub and Nate Crawford to fill the vacant office which, you could probably guess, Collin won, as he's still the mayor today."

"I had no idea about any of this," Bailey confessed.

"The devastation was unlike anything I've ever seen," she told him. "Afterward everyone pitched in to help with the cleanup and rebuild, but it still took months. And that," she said, passing through the door he held open for her and entering the store, "is the not-so-short story about the floods that led to the creation of the Tree of Hope."

Bailey followed Serena to the holiday display and the tree that appeared to be empty of tags. On closer inspection, he found two. "There are only a couple of tags left."

"It is only a couple of weeks until Christmas," she pointed out.

He reached for the nearest tag and removed it from the branch to read the information on the back. "Male, seventy-two-years, diabetic, shoe size ten."

"There are some older residents in town who don't have any family around to celebrate with, so Nina added them to the Tree of Hope to ensure they aren't forgotten during the holidays."

"Do you think you can help me find a gift for a seventy-two-year-old diabetic man who wears a size ten?"

"Sugar-free candy and warm slippers," she immediately suggested.

He nodded and held on to the tag.

Serena took the last one from the tree.

"What did you get?" he asked.

"Seven-year-old boy." She approached Natalie Crawford, who was organizing a display of building block sets nearby. "Did Nina happen to put a tag from the Tree of Hope aside for me?"

"Oh, hi, Serena," Natalie said. "And yes, she did." She finished stacking the boxes in her hand, then moved toward the cash register. Opening a drawer beneath the counter, she retrieved a tag that had been stored there for safekeeping. "Here you go."

"Thanks." Serena slid both tags into the side pocket of her handbag, then turned back to Bailey. "Now we can go."

* * *

"Are you going to tell me what that was about?" Bailey asked, when they were back in his truck and en route to Kalispell.

"You mean the tag that Natalie gave me?" Serena guessed.

He nodded.

"If there's a three-year-old girl who needs a gift, Nina will put that tag aside for me," she confided. "I know it's silly, but—"

"No," he interjected. "It's not silly at all. It's a good way to remember your sister at the holidays, at least until you find her again."

She was grateful for his understanding—and his confident assertion that she would one day be reunited with her sister. But she'd been hoping for exactly that for so long, she knew she had to accept the possibility that it might never happen. "*If* I ever do," she clarified.

"I didn't think I'd ever come back to Rust Creek Falls," he reminded her. "But here I am."

"And your family's thrilled to have you home," she said.

"I don't know about that, but it has been good to reconnect with most of my siblings. I haven't been able to spend much time with Dana, of course, because she's still living in Oregon with her adoptive family," he noted. "And we still don't know where Liza is, though Hudson's private investigator insists he's making progress."

"You don't believe him?"

He shrugged. "I think if I were a PI with a client whose pockets were as deep as Bella's husband's, I'd want to stay on his payroll, too."

"I don't think Hudson Jones is foolish enough to pay someone without results," she told him.

"You're probably right," he acknowledged. "But I know

Bella would feel a lot better if she actually saw results, preferably in the form of our youngest sister."

"I'm sure you'll *all* feel better when you find Liza," she said, as he pulled into the parking lot of the shopping mall. "But right now, you need to focus on finding an empty parking spot."

"I hate Christmas shopping," Bailey announced several hours later as he followed Serena up to her apartment, his arms heavy with the weight of the bags he carried.

"What is it that you hate?" she asked, as she slid her key into the lock. "The festive decorations? The seasonal music? The shopkeepers wishing you happy holidays?"

"The crazy drivers racing for limited parking spots, the desperate shoppers pawing through boxes of toys and piles of clothes, then pressing toward the cash registers like teenage girls rushing the stage at a Justin Bieber concert."

She smiled at the image painted by his words as she carefully sidestepped an excited Marvin, who seemed determined to get tangled up in her feet.

"The key," she told him, "is not to let yourself get caught up in the chaos."

"Easy to say, not so easy to do when the chaos is all around."

"But you can't deny it was a successful day."

He unloaded his shopping bags on the floor, then dropped to his knees to give Marvin some of the attention he was begging for. "Except that apparently I now have to wrap all that stuff."

"Yes, you do," she confirmed. "But you'll see that I already have a wrapping station set up on the table, so you can get started while I heat up the sauce and put a pot of water on to boil for the pasta."

"Or I could make the spaghetti and you could do the wrapping?" he suggested as an alternative.

She shook her head. "I'll help you *after* dinner."

Marvin, even in a fog of canine euphoria induced by Bailey's belly rub, recognized that last word and immediately scrambled to his feet and raced over to his bowl.

Bailey chuckled.

"Yes, it's almost time for your dinner, too," she assured the eager bulldog. "Although I doubt you've worked up much of an appetite, hanging around inside the apartment all day."

"He could probably use some exercise," Bailey decided. "Do you want me to take him out for a walk before dinner?"

Poor Marvin didn't know whether to lie down and feign exhaustion—his usual response to hearing the word *walk*—or remain seated by his bowl in anticipation of his *dinner*.

Serena shook her head. "If you'd really rather *w-a-l-k* the dog than wrap presents, his leash and sweater are on the hook by the door."

"Sweater?" he echoed dubiously.

"It's December, and his short hair doesn't do much to keep him warm."

Of course, Marvin hated the idea of the sweater as much as Bailey did, but with Serena's help, they managed to get it over the dog's head and his front legs through the appropriate holes.

When Serena returned to the kitchen to stir the sauce, Bailey clipped the leash onto his collar and said, "Let's go."

But Marvin did not want to go. In fact, he sat stubbornly on his butt and refused to move, even with Bailey tugging on the leash.

"I think your dog's broken," he said to Serena.

"He's not broken, he just hates the snow."

"You could have told me that when I first offered to take him out," he noted.

"I could have," she agreed, making no effort to hide her amusement. "But he really does need the exercise."

"Did you hear that, Marvin? You need the exercise."

Marvin dropped his head, as if ashamed, but his butt remained firmly planted on the floor.

So Bailey bent down and picked him up.

"Jeez, he's gotta weigh at least fifty pounds."

"Fifty-five at his last checkup," Serena told him.

"Well, at least I'll get some exercise hauling him down the stairs." Then to Marvin, he said, "But when we hit street level, your paws are on the ground."

Whether or not Marvin understood any of that, Bailey had no idea, but for now, the dog snuggled into the crook of his arm to enjoy the ride.

Serena held up her end of the bargain.

After Bailey and Marvin returned from their walk and the humans and animals had eaten, she helped him wrap the presents he'd bought.

Their efforts were occasionally impeded by her pets. Molly's curiosity about Bailey finally proved stronger than her wariness of strangers, and she ventured out from hiding to jump from chair to chair—and occasionally even onto the table—and knock various items onto the ground. Max somehow got tangled up in a length of curling ribbon, but after Serena untangled him, he mostly stayed out of the way, content to nibble on an empty wrapping paper tube. Marvin was the worst offender. Despite his pre-dinner walk with Bailey—who assured her that yes, he did make the dog walk—he remained full of energy and determined to cause mischief.

When Bailey folded the sweater he'd chosen for Bella and positioned it in the center of the paper he'd already cut, Serena shook her head.

"What?" he asked.

"You need a box."

"Why?"

"Because clothing should always go in a box—and because boxes are easier to wrap," she explained.

"You didn't make me put the pj's I bought for the triplets in boxes."

"Because you want kids' presents to be easy to open," she explained.

"There seem to be an awful lot of rules about gift-wrapping," he noted. "Maybe you should write them down for me."

She selected an appropriate-size box from her stock, lined it with tissue, refolded the sweater—after removing the price tag—laid it inside the box, closed the lid and handed it back to him.

He wrapped the paper around the box and fastened it with a piece of tape.

Serena picked up the gift she'd finished wrapping and looked beneath it, then under the table. "Did you take that bow?"

"What bow?"

"I had a green bow that I was going to put on this one."

"You have a whole box of bows," he pointed out.

"And I picked a green one out of the box and set it on the table right here," she said, indicating the spot. Then a movement caught her eye and she sighed. "Molly."

Bailey glanced over to see the cat in the middle of the living room, batting the missing bow around the floor.

Serena stepped away from the table just as Marvin decided to race ahead of her, knocking her off balance. Bailey instinctively reached for her—his arms wrapping around her and hauling her against him.

"Sorry." Her cheeks burned with embarrassment over her clumsiness, and her breasts—crushed against his chest now—tingled with awareness and arousal.

"I'm not," he said huskily, his arms still around her.

Then he lowered his head and touched his lips to hers.

Maybe she should have resisted the seductive pressure and the intoxicating flavor of his kiss. But the moment his mouth made contact with hers, her only thoughts were:

Yes.

This.

And, *More.*

He gave her more.

Parting her lips with his tongue, he deepened the kiss. He slid his hands down her back, then beneath the hem of her sweater. She shivered as his callused palms moved over her bare skin, an instinctive reaction that caused her breasts to rub against his hard chest, sending arrows of pleasure from her peaked nipples to her core.

He nibbled playfully on her lips, teased her with strokes of his tongue that made her tremble and ache with want. Her whole body felt hot, so hot she was sure her bones would melt.

And then he abruptly tore his mouth from hers. "What the—"

She drew in a slow deep breath and willed her head to stop spinning. "What?"

He looked down at his feet, where Molly was innocently licking her paw and rubbing it over her face.

But Serena knew better. "Molly," she said reprovingly.

"I think she left her claws in my skin," Bailey said.

"She's not overly fond of strangers," she admitted. "And she is somewhat protective of me."

He reached down to rub his shin. "Well, it's going to take a bigger cat than that to scare me away," he promised.

"Maybe she did us a favor," Serena suggested.

"I'm not feeling grateful."

"But we agreed we weren't going to do this," she reminded him.

"Why was that again?"

"Because neither one of us has had much success with relationships."

"That's true," he acknowledged. "And while I know I'm not so good with the opening up and sharing my emotions part, I promise you that I can muddle through the naked physical activity part."

"You sure do know how to tempt a girl, don't you?"

"Are you saying that you're *not* tempted?"

"I'm more tempted than I should be," she confessed.

"Obviously not tempted enough or we'd be doing it instead of talking about it," he told her.

"You've still got presents to wrap," she reminded him.

"I'd rather unwrap *you*."

The words were accompanied by a heated look that made her knees weak—and her resolve even weaker. She consciously steeled both, picked up a roll of paper and pointed it at him. "Wrap."

Bailey took the paper—and the hint.

He was undeniably disappointed that she'd put on the brakes *again*, but he didn't really blame her. Although they'd spent a lot of time together over the past week, they'd really only known each other a week.

So while Serena went to retrieve the bow Molly had stolen, he tried to focus on measuring and cutting the paper—and not stare at the sexy curve of her butt.

"Tell me about your marriage," she suggested, as she affixed the bow to the wrapped gift.

"Well, that question effectively killed the mood," he noted.

"That wasn't my intention."

"Are you sure? Maybe you want to hear about all the reasons my marriage failed so that you can feel justified in pushing me away."

"I'm not pushing you away," she said. "But I'm also not in the habit of jumping into bed with a man I just met."

"I've told you more about me than a lot of other people know," he confided.

"So why won't you tell me about your marriage?"

He shrugged to indicate his surrender. "What do you want to know?"

"How long were you married?"

"Almost two years. And before you say, 'that's not very long,' believe me, it was long enough for both of us to know it wasn't working."

"I'm sorry. I didn't mean to pry. I didn't realize it was such a touchy subject."

He sighed. "It's not really. I just don't like admitting that I failed—and it was my failure. Because from the day we exchanged vows, I was waiting for everything to fall apart."

"Why were you so sure that it would?"

He shrugged. "Maybe because of what happened to my parents."

"They were killed by a drunk driver."

"Yeah," he acknowledged. "And before that, they were happy together, running the farm and raising a family. And then everything changed."

"Because of a tragic accident."

"Because of *me*," he said.

Serena frowned. "What are you talking about?"

"It was my fault they were on that particular road at that particular time on that particular night."

And he proceeded to tell her about the events of that fateful evening. How his older brother had invited him to go to an out-of-town bar. Although Bailey wasn't yet of legal drinking age, Luke assured him that he knew of a honky-tonk dive that didn't care if their customers had ID so long as they had cash to pay for their beer. Bailey was always happy to tag along with his brother, and when Danny heard they were going out, he refused to be left behind.

The bartender didn't blink when Luke ordered a pitcher of beer and three glasses, which he carried over to the table where his brothers waited. But Danny, always a rule follower, went back to the bar to get a soda.

When Bailey had emptied the pitcher into his glass, Danny suggested that they leave and asked for the keys. Bailey, who had driven, refused, unwilling to let his little brother call the shots. Besides, a trio of young women had just settled around the neighboring table and immediately began to chat up the three cowboys.

"But Danny—devoted to Annie—was even less interested in flirting than in drinking," Bailey continued his explanation. "And when me and Luke refused to heed his warnings and pleas, he went to the pay phone outside and called our parents."

Even after so many years, the memories were clear, the pain sharp. Everything had changed that night. Not just for Bailey, Luke and Danny, but their four younger siblings—and especially their parents.

"They were on their way to get you," Serena realized.

He nodded. "Because I was too stubborn, too arrogant, to let my little brother have the keys."

"And you've been carrying the guilt of that decision for more than a dozen years," she realized.

"Because it was *my* decision."

"It was your decision to hold on to the keys," she acknowledged. "And Danny's decision to call your parents. And their decision to come after you. But the only one responsible for their deaths is the drunk driver who hit them."

"So why can't I let go of the feeling that it's my fault?"

Chapter 9

Serena understood guilt. She'd carried her fair share of it for a lot of years, and though she'd managed to let go of most of it, there were still moments that she wondered *what if*, still occasions when she felt sharp pangs of regret. So she wasn't going to tell Bailey to "let it go" and expect that he'd be able to do so. She knew it wasn't that easy, but she also knew that holding dark and negative feelings inside only strengthened their hold.

"I don't know," she said. "But I do know that talking about it can sometimes help."

"Like I said, I'm not good with the sharing feelings thing," he reminded her.

"Like anything else, it gets easier with practice," she promised.

"I don't know that that's true," he said. "But I do know that I find it easy to talk to you."

"I'm glad."

"In fact, all that stuff I just told you, about the night my parents were killed... I never told Emily," he confided.

"Why not?" she wondered aloud.

"When she asked about my family, I told her that my parents were dead and my siblings were scattered—though even I didn't know how scattered at that point. And she didn't seem interested in knowing anything more." He shrugged. "Probably because she was so close to her family, and me not having a family simplified our life. There was never any question about where we would spend the holidays—always with her family."

"How were those holidays?" Serena asked carefully.

"Fine," he said.

"Why is it, whenever someone gives that answer, it usually means not fine?"

"No, it was fine," he insisted. "I mean, I never got into the celebrations, but that was my fault. I had disconnected from my family and I didn't know how—or maybe I didn't want—to connect with hers."

"Did that become a source of friction between you?"

He shook his head. "There really wasn't friction between us. There really wasn't much of anything. In fact, I'm not even sure she noticed that I didn't connect with her family."

Now it was Serena's turn to frown. "What do you mean, she didn't notice?"

"She was the youngest of three kids and the only girl, Daddy's little princess and her mother's best friend, doted on by her brothers, close with both of their wives and a favorite aunt to the kids. She was accustomed to being the center of attention and basked in that attention.

"It all came to a head when her youngest brother's wife had their first baby. We, of course, raced over to the hospital to celebrate the big event, and Emily immediately fell in love with her new niece. I braced myself for what I knew was coming next—or what I thought was coming next."

Serena nodded, undoubtedly anticipating the same response that he had.

"She looked at her brother and sister-in-law with their newborn and said, 'That's what I want.' A baby, I guessed, having resigned myself to that eventuality, because after marriage comes kids, right? Well, not always in that order," he acknowledged, responding to his own question. "But she surprised me by shaking her head. 'Yes, I want a baby,' she told me. 'But I want more than that.'

"Of course, I'm not very good at reading between the lines, so I said, 'You mean, two kids?' 'No, I mean the whole package,' she said. 'I want a husband who looks at me the way Matt looks at Tanya. A husband who wants to have a baby with me because he knows that child will be the best of both of us and a bond that ties us together forever.'

"Or words to that effect," Bailey said. "The point was, we both knew that husband wasn't ever going to be me. And that was the end."

"Are things better now?" Serena asked.

"If you consider being divorced better," he said dryly.

"I meant, are you both satisfied with the decision to end your marriage?" she clarified.

"I assume so," he said. "I haven't seen or spoken to her since I filed the divorce papers three years ago."

"You haven't had any contact with her in three *years*?"

"I thought a clean break would be best," he confided.

"I think you need to talk to her," Serena said. "And she probably needs to talk to you."

"Why?"

"For closure."

He scowled. "What does that even mean?"

"It means understanding how and why the relationship

ended, so that you can accept that it has ended and move on," she explained patiently.

"We're divorced," Bailey reminded her. "I don't think either of us is under any illusions that the relationship isn't over."

"But have you moved on?" she prompted gently.

"I'd say the fourteen hundred miles I moved proves that I have."

"Have you dated much since the divorce?"

"Not really," he admitted.

"That's a rather vague response."

"Do you want to know the specific number of dates?"

"A range would suffice," she said.

"Then I guess it would be...more than zero and less than two," he confided.

"Only one?" she asked, surprised.

"And only if we're counting this as a date."

"This is a date?"

"Well, it was prearranged, I picked you up, we shared a meal—and a kiss. Doesn't that tick all the boxes?"

"I guess it does," she said, though she still sounded dubious.

"Or we could say it's not a date."

"I don't have a problem with the label," she said. "I'm just not sure how I feel about being your rebound girl."

"It's been three years," he reminded her. "I'm not on the rebound."

"Three years of not dating suggests you might have been more heartbroken over the failure of your marriage than you wanted to admit."

"Or maybe I'd finally accepted that I was so damaged by the mistakes of my past that I had nothing left to offer a woman."

"So what's changed to make you want to start dating again now?" she wondered aloud.

"I met you."

* * *

Those three simple words melted Serena's heart.

She was still thinking about them the next day as she slid the last tray of sugar cookies into the oven. Marvin, who'd been snoring in the corner, suddenly picked his head up, his ears twitching.

"Do you hear something?" she asked him.

He responded by leaping off his bed and racing toward the door. Serena wiped her hands on a towel and followed the dog, pulling open the door before she heard a knock.

"This is a surprise," she said, when she saw Bailey standing there.

"I left a message on your voice mail and sent a couple of texts, but you didn't respond, so I thought I'd take a chance and swing by after I ran some errands," he explained.

She stepped away from the door so that he could enter. "That's strange—I didn't hear my phone ring at all." And then a thought occurred to her. "Of course, I didn't plug it in last night, so chances are, the battery's dead."

"Is it okay that I stopped by?"

"Well, Marvin's certainly happy to see you," she said, with a pointed glance at the dog who had rolled over to display his belly.

Bailey chuckled as he bent down to give her pet a one-handed belly scratch. His other hand held up a padded envelope. "When I got home last night, this was on my doorstep."

"What is it?" she asked him.

"Another Christmas present that I need to wrap—and that I'm hoping you'll deliver for me."

She took the envelope and peeked inside. "You got a PKT-79?"

"Two of them," he told her. "For Owen and his friend Riley."

"I can't believe you managed to get your hands on not just one but two of the most popular toys of the season," she said.

"I took your advice," he admitted.

"eBay?"

He nodded.

"I'm not going to ask what these cost you."

"Good, because I'm not going to tell you," he said.

"You do know this wasn't necessary, right?"

"I know," he confirmed. "But it was something I wanted to do."

"It will definitely restore Owen's faith in Santa Claus," Serena murmured.

"I hope so," Bailey said. "Because spending time with you seems to be restoring my faith in the spirit of the season."

She smiled at that. "All the wrapping stuff is still on the table—I haven't got around to putting it away yet."

"It looks like you've been busy with other things," he said, glancing around the kitchen. Then he lifted his head and sniffed the air. "Cookies?" he asked hopefully.

She nodded. "But nothing as fancy as your sister-in-law makes."

"Cookies don't need to be fancy to taste good," he noted, as he washed his hands at the sink.

She lifted one off the cooling rack and offered it to him.

He picked up a towel to dry his hands, but instead of taking the cookie from her, he lowered his head and bit a piece off.

"Mmm," he said around a mouthful of cookie. "That is good." Then he took another bite, and another, until he was nipping at her fingers, the teasing nibbles making her blood pulse and her knees weak.

She took a step back and wiped her hands down the front of her apron, brushing the crumbs away.

He grinned, no doubt aware of the effect he had on her.

"So," he said, moving over to the table and selecting a roll of wrapping paper, "what are your plans for the rest of the afternoon?"

"The afternoon's almost over," she pointed out to him.

"Okay, what are your plans for tonight?"

The oven timer buzzed and she slid her hands into the padded mitts and retrieved the hot tray of cookies.

"After I get the kitchen cleaned up, I'm going to pop a big bowl of popcorn and snuggle up on the sofa with Marvin, Molly and Max to watch one of my favorite holiday movies."

"I don't see Molly as a snuggler," he said. "Of course, that might be because I can still feel her claws digging into my leg."

"She really is a sweetheart, once you get to know her."

He snorted, a clear expression of disbelief.

Serena filled the sink with hot soapy water and began washing her dishes.

"You didn't mention any plans for dinner," Bailey commented as he finished taping his present.

"I figured I'd skip dinner, because I've been sampling cookies all day," she confided.

"Or I could go over to the Ace and pick up burgers."

"I really don't need a burger." But now that he'd put the idea in her head, her mouth was watering.

"But do you want one?" Bailey asked, his tone suggesting that he already knew the answer.

"Now I do," she admitted.

"Fries?"

"No," she said firmly.

He chuckled. "Okay, just a burger."

"Cheeseburger," she clarified.

"Anything else?"

She started to shake her head, then paused. "Yeah—why are you doing this?"

"Because I'm hungry?" he suggested.

"I don't just mean the food. I mean why are you here?"

He held up the package he'd finished wrapping.

"You expect me to believe that Eva didn't have wrapping paper?" she asked.

"Okay, so maybe that was just an excuse to see you."

"You shouldn't need an excuse to visit a friend," she told him.

He sighed. "You're still determined to stick me in that friend zone, aren't you?"

"I think friendship is always a good place to start."

To start what? Bailey wanted to know.

But he didn't ask the question. He had no right to demand answers from Serena about the status or direction of their relationship when he hadn't yet figured out what he wanted.

But he knew that he wanted *her*. And the more time he spent with her, the stronger the wanting grew.

A smart man would realize that the key to getting a woman out of his head—and his hormones back in check—would be to put some distance between them. A smart man would have ignored the impulse that drove him into town and then steered him toward her apartment.

Apparently he was not a smart man.

Instead, he picked up burgers—and fries for himself—from the Ace in the Hole. When he got back to Serena's apartment, Marvin went nuts all over again, as if Bailey had been gone for days rather than forty minutes.

Growing up, there had always been a dog or two at Sunshine Farm and several cats hanging around the barn, but Bailey hadn't had a pet since he'd left Rust Creek Falls thirteen years earlier. He hadn't wanted the responsibility. But he was beginning to see how much joy an animal companion could add to life—at least an animal like Marvin. He was still skeptical about Molly and undecided on Max, who mostly kept to himself.

While he was gone, Serena had cleared off the dining room table so they had somewhere to sit and eat. Then Bailey took Marvin outside while she made popcorn and set up the movie.

He hadn't asked what they would be watching—because it really didn't matter. He just wanted to hang out with her, and if that meant watching Bing Crosby and Danny Kaye sing and dance with Rosemary Clooney and Vera-Ellen, so be it.

He was admittedly surprised when, instead of the instrumental notes of a classic Irving Berlin song, the screen filled with an image of an airplane coming in for a landing against the backdrop of an orange sky.

"*Die Hard* is your favorite Christmas movie?" he asked. "*Really?*"

"It's a Christmas classic."

"I don't disagree."

"But you thought I'd want to watch *White Christmas*," she guessed.

"Maybe," he acknowledged, happy to be proven wrong.

He settled on the sofa, the bowl of popcorn in his lap. Marvin scrambled up onto the sofa beside Serena and promptly fell asleep. Max positioned himself by her feet, where he nibbled on a carrot-shaped pet chew. Molly was apparently in hiding, which didn't hurt Bailey's feelings at all and allowed him to focus on the woman seated beside him.

Because he sure as heck couldn't focus on the movie—not with Serena so close. Not when his fingers brushed against hers every time he reached into the bowl. Not when her hair tickled his chin when she tipped her head back. And definitely not when he inhaled her tantalizing scent with every breath he took.

But the woman who was the center of his attention seemed

oblivious, her gaze fixed on the movie. When only a few unpopped kernels remained in the bottom of the bowl and the first staccato bursts of gunfire erupted on the screen, Molly sauntered into the living room, the tip of her tail high in the air, flicking side to side.

The cat made her way toward the sofa, then froze, her pale green eyes narrowing to slits. Apparently Bailey was in her spot, and she wasn't happy about it, as evidenced by the way she hissed at him.

"Molly!" Serena scolded.

The cat continued to stare at him, unaffected by the reprimand.

"I'm sorry," Serena apologized. "She's never...okay, not never...but she rarely does that." Her brow furrowed as she considered. "And it's only ever been when I have male company—which isn't very often," she hastened to add.

"She's protective of you," he said, echoing her earlier remark.

She glanced at the snoring lump pressed against her thigh. "Unlike Marvin, who would sell me out for a belly rub."

Bailey chuckled at that.

Serena leaned over to scoop up the cat, holding her so that she was nose to nose with the feline.

"Bailey is our friend," she said, her tone firm but gentle. "And you need to be nice to our friends. No biting, no scratching, no growling, no hissing."

The demon cat gently bumped her nose against Serena's, then rubbed her face against her cheek—and actually purred.

"I told you she can be affectionate," she said.

"Is she really being affectionate?" he wondered aloud. "Or is she just gloating?"

"What?"

"She's cuddling up to you but looking at me, as if to rub it in that she's your favorite."

Serena laughed at that. "Do you feel as if you're in competition with my cat?"

"Well, I can't help but notice that she's a lot closer to you than you've let me get."

"Molly's been with me eleven years," she reminded him. "I've known you just over a week."

"I hope you're not suggesting that it's going to take me another ten years and fifty-one weeks to get to second base."

She shook her head, but a smile tugged at her lips. "I'm suggesting that we should watch the rest of the movie."

So they did. But it seemed all too soon that the credits were rolling on the screen, and Bailey knew it was time to say goodnight and head back to his cold empty cabin at Sunshine Farm. His reluctance was a little unnerving. He was accustomed to being on his own and had always been content that way. Now it seemed that he might prefer Serena's company—and possibly even that of her furry menagerie.

"Thanks for letting me hang out with you tonight," he said when she walked him to the door.

"It was fun," she agreed.

"Maybe we could do it again next weekend," he suggested. "But instead of staying in, we could go out for dinner and a movie."

"I'd like that," she said. "Although this time of year, movie nights at the high school generally feature holiday films."

"Or we could drive into Kalispell and see a new release in a real theater."

"That sounds a lot like a date," she mused.

"It does tick all the boxes," he confirmed. "What time do you finish work on Friday?"

"Four o'clock."

"I'll pick you up at six," he said, already counting the hours.

Amanda Langley was seated inside Daisy's Donut Shop when Serena arrived to meet her at noon on Friday. They'd chosen the restaurant because of its proximity to the veterinarian clinic as Serena only had an hour for lunch—and because the food was as good as the service was prompt.

"I'm glad you were available to meet me today," she said to her mom, as she slid into the seat across from her.

"I was grateful for the invitation," Amanda replied.

Serena set aside her menu. She ate at Daisy's often enough that she already knew what she wanted, and the waitress immediately appeared to take their orders.

"I wanted to apologize to you," Serena said when the server had gone.

"Apologize?" Amanda echoed, sounding surprised. "For what?"

"Interrupting your date last Saturday night."

Her mother waved a hand dismissively. "It was fine. And Mark was glad that he finally got to meet you."

"So you did tell him about me?"

"I've told him everything," Amanda assured her.

"You have?"

Her mother nodded. "I've learned that keeping things inside isn't good for me—and that I need to stop doing things that aren't good for me." Then she smiled. "Mark is very good for me."

Serena chose to ignore the obvious implication, saying only, "Well... I'm glad you have someone you can talk to."

"Do you? Have someone that you can talk to, I mean?"

"Sure," she said, because she knew it was true. It was also true that she didn't usually like to talk about the past.

And yet, for some reason, she'd had no trouble opening up to Bailey. In fact, she'd *wanted* to tell him about Mimi. But even more surprising was the realization that he was a good listener. Understanding and empathetic.

And a really great kisser.

Of course, that probably wasn't something she should be

thinking about right now. Not just because she was having lunch with her mother, but because she was the one who had told him that they should slow things down. Although she was admittedly a little disappointed that he hadn't tried to kiss her goodbye when he'd left her apartment the other night.

"It's still so hard, not knowing," Amanda said.

The softly spoken remark drew Serena back to the present. She nodded, understanding that her mother was thinking about Mimi and that tragic day when she'd gone missing.

"There are so many possibilities...most of them too horrible to think about," her mother noted.

"So don't think about them," she urged.

"I try not to," Amanda admitted. "I want to believe that she was taken by somebody—a woman or even a couple—who desperately wanted a child but couldn't have one of their own. And maybe it seemed unfair, that I had two beautiful little girls—" she lifted her napkin to dab at the tears that trembled on her lashes "—so they took one home."

It was the same scenario that Serena clung to—the one that allowed her to sleep at night. It couldn't change the fact that her sister had been cruelly ripped from the arms of her loving family, but she desperately needed to believe that, wherever she was now, Mimi was loved and cared for and didn't miss her real family at all.

She reached across the table and touched her mother's hand.

"She was such a sweet child," Amanda said, turning her palm over to clasp her daughter's hand.

Serena nodded, feeling as if their joined hands were squeezing her heart.

"I should have held on to her tighter," her mother said.

"I was—" Serena swallowed. "I was holding Mimi's hand," she reminded Amanda.

Her mother's brow furrowed, as if she was struggling to

remember, then she shook her head. "You were a child yourself. I never should have made you responsible for your sister."

"I thought you blamed me," she said. "I thought that's why..."

"Why I turned into an alcoholic?" Amanda guessed.

She nodded again.

"I hate knowing that you could ever believe such a thing," her mother said, her eyes bright with unshed tears. "That I ever let you believe such a thing."

"I blamed myself," Serena confided.

"It wasn't your fault. Please tell me you know that none of what happened was your fault," Amanda implored.

"I do know. Now," she said. "Most of the time, anyway."

Her mother gave Serena's hand a gentle squeeze before releasing it as the waitress approached with their plates.

"You were the only light in my darkest days," Amanda said when the server had gone. "You were never responsible for any of the wrong choices I made, but you were the biggest part of the reason why I was finally able to get sober."

"I didn't do anything," she said, and she'd always felt a little bit guilty about that.

"You always were, and still are, my sweet, beautiful daughter. And I want to earn the right to be your mother again, to be worthy of your love again."

"You always were, and still are, my mother. And I have always, and still do, love you," Serena told her.

Amanda's lips started to curve, then her smile wobbled. "Dammit," she said, and lifted her napkin to dab at the tears that trembled on her lashes. "I promised myself that I wasn't going to get weepy today."

Serena's own eyes were watery as she picked up her fork. "So tell me more about Mark," she said, suspecting they'd both appreciate a change in the topic of conversation.

"He's asked me to go with him tomorrow to cut down a Christmas tree," her mother said.

Serena sipped from her glass of water while she considered this information. For most people, it would be a traditional holiday event, but she knew that holiday events were often triggers for her mom.

"How do you feel about that?" she asked cautiously.

"Scared," Amanda admitted. "I find it's easier to get through the holidays if I pretend they don't exist."

"Not easy to do when the whole town is decked out in red and green," Serena noted.

"Well, apparently, the world does continue to turn through the whole month of December—at least for everyone else."

"You know, you can tell him no," she said. "If you're not ready."

"I've been saying no for the past three years," her mother confided. "I think it's time to say yes. I want you to know that I'm strong enough to say yes."

"Don't do this for me," Serena said. "Please."

"I'm not. I'm doing it for Mark, and for me. Okay, and maybe a little bit for you…and for Mimi."

Serena swallowed another sip of water—along with the lump in her throat. "Then you better get a huge tree and decorate it with hundreds of twinkling lights and tons of sparkly ornaments."

"We will," her mother promised.

And Serena trusted that they would.

Chapter 10

There'd been plenty of chores around Sunshine Farm to keep Bailey's hands busy throughout the week, but the physical labor hadn't stopped him from thinking about Serena, wondering what she was doing and wishing he was with her instead of fixing fence, moving hay or cleaning tack. But he knew that she was busy, too, with her responsibilities at the vet clinic, preparations for the holidays and, of course, her animals.

By Friday, he could hardly wait for their date that night. In the afternoon, he slipped away from the ranch for a few hours to meet Brendan Tanner at the community center.

"This town is truly amazing," Brendan remarked, after they'd sorted through the gifts that had been donated for Presents for Patriots.

"You must not get out much," Bailey said dryly.

The other man chuckled. "I've been to a lot of places—bigger cities, prettier towns." He sighed wistfully. "Places with pizza delivery."

"There is something to be said for the luxury of food brought to your door," Bailey agreed.

"On the other hand, people who don't have that option are forced to go out and interact with other people," Brendan noted. "Maybe that's why there's such a strong sense of community in Rust Creek Falls."

"I don't think pizza delivery would jeopardize the town's identity."

"It's something to think about, anyway," the retired marine said.

Bailey stood back and looked at the pile of gifts. "Where did all this stuff come from?"

"Rumor has it that Arthur Swinton donates the majority of these gifts every year," Brendan remarked.

"Since when do you put any stock in gossip?" Bailey asked.

His friend shrugged. "It seems to be a favorite pastime in this town."

"Because there's not much else to do."

"Well, it's a fact that Swinton bankrolled this whole place," Brendan told him, gesturing to their surroundings. "The Grace Traub Community Center was made possible by his generous support."

"Who is this Swinton guy?"

"The former mayor of Thunder Canyon who went to prison for embezzlement several years back."

"He built this place with stolen money?"

Brendan chuckled. "No, I'm pretty sure he paid that back."

Bailey was captivated by this tidbit, but he wasn't nearly as interested in history as he was the future. More specifically, his future plans with Serena. He surveyed all they'd accomplished. "Looks like we're done here. Is it okay if I take off?"

"Hot date tonight?" his friend teased.

"Just heading into Kalispell to grab a bite and catch a movie," he said, deliberately not answering the question.

"By yourself?"

"No," he admitted. "With...a friend."

"Serena Langley?" Brendan guessed.

"Yeah."

"I guess the rumor mill got that one right, too."

"I don't want to know," Bailey told him.

His friend chuckled again. "Well, have a good time tonight."

Bailey planned on it.

He'd made reservations at a popular steak and seafood restaurant in Kalispell and previewed the movie listings so they could discuss their options over dinner. He'd been looking forward to this date with Serena all week, and he hoped that she had been, too.

So he was understandably surprised when she opened the door in response to his knock and he saw that she was dressed in flannel pajamas with fuzzy slippers on her feet.

"I don't think the restaurant has a dress code, but considering that it's only twenty degrees outside, you might want to put on a pair of boots."

"Restaurant?" she echoed, then winced. "Oh, right. Dinner and a movie."

"You forgot our date," he realized, surprised and more than a little disappointed.

"I did. I'm sorry. It was just a really lousy day, and when I got home, all I wanted were my pj's. And ice cream," she admitted.

He looked closer, saw the puffiness lingering around her eyes. "You've been crying."

"I'm out of ice cream," she said, her eyes filling with fresh tears.

"You had lunch with your mom today," he suddenly remembered.

She nodded. "But that was fine. My mother's really doing well."

"So what happened after lunch?" he asked.

"Thelma McGee came in with Oreo," she said.

"I'm not yet seeing the connection between your tears and cookies," he confided.

She managed a smile as she shook her head. "Oreo is—*was*—Thelma's black-and-white cat."

The *was* finally clued him in to the cause of her distress. He drew her into his arms, a silent offer of comfort.

She choked on a sob. "I'm sorry."

"There's no need to apologize," he assured her.

"Believe it or not, I'm getting better at dealing with the loss of an animal," she told him. "But it's never easy. And Thelma had Oreo for seventeen years."

"That's a pretty good life span for a cat, isn't it?"

"It is," she confirmed.

But he understood that when you loved something—or someone—and your time together came to an end, it was never long enough.

"She was sitting with him in the exam room, waiting for the doctor to come in, holding Oreo close to her chest, silent tears falling. And Oreo lifted a paw to her cheek, as if to comfort her."

Listening to Serena recount the story now, even he felt as if his chest was being squeezed. He could only imagine how much more heart-wrenching it had been for her in the moment.

"I love my job," she told him.

Bailey continued to rub her back. "I know you do."

She sighed. "But sometimes… I really hate my job."

"That's understandable," he assured her.

She sniffled again. "I need a tissue."

He pulled one from the box on the sideboard, offered it to her.

"Thanks." She wiped her nose. "I can't believe I completely forgot about our plans for tonight."

"It's not too late, if you want to go put some clothes on."

"I'm sorry," she said again. "But I really don't feel up to going anywhere tonight."

"Do you feel up to company?" he asked.

"You want to stay?"

"Well, I know for a fact that you've got a decent movie collection. And popcorn."

"But no ice cream."

"Do you want me to go get you some ice cream?"

She nodded her head against his chest.

"What kind?"

"It doesn't matter, as long as it's real ice cream."

"I didn't know there was such a thing as fake ice cream," he told her.

"Low-fat ice cream, frozen yogurt, sorbet—they're all fake ice cream."

"I'll get the real stuff," he promised.

He wasn't gone long, and when he came back, he offered her a ribbon-tied paper bundle.

"I meant to pick up flowers for you earlier, but I forgot."

"At least you didn't forget our date," she said, as she unwrapped the bouquet of red carnations and white chrysanthemums with accents of red berries and seasonal greens. "And these are beautiful, thank you."

"My pleasure," he said.

"What else have you got there?" she asked, noting the two grocery bags he set on the counter.

"Ice cream."

"That's a lot of ice cream," she remarked.

"I picked up a couple frozen pizzas, too, in case you get hungry for food. That way, we won't have to go out." He opened the freezer and stowed the pizzas away, then unpacked the ice cream.

Four different flavors of ice cream: chocolate chip cookie dough, mint chocolate chip, black cherry and butterscotch ripple.

She took a couple bowls out of the cupboard, then retrieved spoons and a scoop from the utensil drawer.

"Why don't you scoop up the ice cream while I put these flowers in some water?" she suggested.

He took the scoop she handed to him. "What kind do you want?"

"How am I supposed to decide when there are so many options?"

"A scoop of each?" he suggested.

"That would probably be a little overindulgent." She found a vase under the sink, filled it with water. "Maybe a little bit of mint chocolate chip and a little chocolate chip cookie dough."

While he dished up the ice cream, she snipped the stems off the flowers, arranged them in the vase, then set the bouquet in the center of the dining room table.

He handed her a bowl of ice cream. She noted that he'd gone for the butterscotch.

"Die Hard 2?" she suggested.

"Sounds good to me."

So they sat down with their ice cream and prepared to watch Bruce Willis fight bad guys at Washington Dulles International Airport.

When the British jet crashed on the runway, Bailey caught a flickering motion in the corner of his eye and realized it was Molly's tail twitching from side to side. Apparently the cat had overcome her distrust of him, at least enough to climb up onto the table beside the sofa and lap the remnants of ice cream from his bowl.

"Is she allowed to have that?" he asked Serena.

"Do you want to take it away from her?" she countered.

"No," he admitted.

She smiled. "A little bit of ice cream isn't going to hurt her."

"But will it make her like me?"

"That remains to be seen."

"How about you?" he asked, sliding his arm across her shoulders. "Did I earn points for feeding you ice cream?"

"You did." Then she dropped her head back against his chest and turned her attention back to the movie.

Though he'd wanted to take her out on a "real date" tonight, he realized that he was more than content to be here with her now. He couldn't remember ever feeling so comfortable and relaxed with his ex-wife. Emily was a social creature who'd always wanted to be going somewhere and doing something, and Bailey had almost forgotten that it could be fun just to relax.

"I'm going to preheat the oven for pizza," he said, after the hero had ejected himself from the cockpit of a plane.

"Why does it seem like you're always feeding me?" Serena asked when Bailey had completed his task and returned to his seat beside her.

"It's just frozen pizza."

She shifted slightly to face him. "Which doesn't answer my question," she pointed out.

He shrugged. "We seem to hang out together around meal times. And you made dinner for me after our shopping trip last week," he pointed out.

"That was once."

"Are we keeping score?" he asked, sounding amused.

"No." Then she revised her response, "Maybe."

He chuckled. "If you're really concerned about balancing the scales, you could offer to cook for me again sometime."

Serena considered this idea in conjunction with other thoughts nudging at her mind—and desires humming in her veins. "How about breakfast?" she suggested impulsively.

"Breakfast?" Bailey echoed.

"You know—the meal generally served in the morning," she clarified, her deliberately casual tone a marked contrast to the frantic beating of her heart. "Maybe after you've spent the night."

Heat supplanted the humor in his gaze. "When were you thinking you might make me this breakfast?"

The kisses they'd already shared assured her that the attraction she felt was reciprocated and gave her the courage to boldly respond, "Tomorrow."

Then, because she wanted him more than she wanted to watch a movie she'd seen a dozen times before, she breached the scant distance between them and touched her mouth to his.

That first contact was all it took to have desire pour through her system like molten lava, heating every part of her. What she'd intended to be a quick and easy kiss quickly changed, their mutual desire growing stronger and more intense. When he eased her back onto the sofa, she lifted her arms to link them behind his head, drawing him down with her, welcoming the weight of his body pressing her into the cushions. Her lips parted willingly when he deepened the kiss; her tongue dipped and dallied with his.

His hands skimmed down her sides, scorching her skin even through the fabric of her pajama top. She wanted to strip away her clothes and feel his hands on her bare skin; she wanted to strip away his clothes and use her hands on his bare skin. She wanted—

Beep-beep-beep.

Bailey drew in a ragged breath and eased away from her. "I better get that pizza in the oven."

After taking a moment to catch her own breath, Serena opened her eyes and found all three animals sitting in a row, staring at her.

"You have no right to judge me," she told them, reaching for the remote to pause the movie.

"Especially you," she said, pointing the control at Marvin. "Because you'd show your private parts to anyone for a belly rub." He pressed his wet nose to her leg, an acknowledgment more than an apology.

"And you act like you don't like him," she said to Molly. "But that didn't stop you from licking his ice cream bowl." The calico lifted her butt in the air and extended her front paws out in front of her, stretching lazily.

Max looked at her, his nose twitching. She gently scratched behind his ears. "And you'll cuddle with anyone, in your own time and on your own terms."

"Were you talking to me?" Bailey asked, returning to the living room.

"No," she said.

Thankfully he didn't require more of an explanation as he settled beside her on the sofa again. And though the press of his thigh against hers was enough to jolt her pulse again, she hit the play button to resume the movie.

Twenty minutes later, they were eating pizza and the animals were cowering from the noise of the firefight playing out on the TV screen.

And then they were kissing again.

She wasn't sure how it happened, or even who made the first move this time, she only knew that she didn't want him to ever stop kissing her. Or touching her.

She drew her knees up so they bracketed his hips, then

lifted her pelvis to rub it against his. She could feel his erection straining against his jeans and gloried in the friction of the denim against her flannel pajama bottoms. He groaned softly as he ground into her, giving her a preview of what she wanted, what they both wanted.

She gasped with pleasure—then shock, as a wet doggy tongue swept across her cheek.

"Maybe we should move to the bedroom—and close the door," she suggested.

He stood up, as if eager to accept her invitation, and offered his hand to help her to her feet. But when she started to lead him down the hall, he paused.

"What's the matter?" she asked.

"You said you wanted to slow things down," he reminded her.

"That was last week. Ten days ago, in fact." She didn't want to slow down anymore. She wanted to move full speed ahead—with Bailey. She wanted his hands on her body. All over her body. And she wanted to explore every inch of his in return.

"I can't believe I'm saying this, but ten days isn't so long," he pointed out. "And if this happens tonight, I might worry afterward that it only happened because you were trying to balance the scales."

"If this happens tonight, it's because I want it to happen—not because you brought ice cream or pizza or even flowers," she assured him.

"You had a lousy day," he reminded her.

"I'm pretty sure getting naked with you would make me forget about the lousy day."

"I'm pretty sure getting naked with you would make me forget my name," he told her. "But it's not the answer."

But before he left, he kissed her goodbye.

It was a long, lingering kiss that assured her that he desired her as much as she desired him, despite his insistence on giving her time she no longer wanted or needed.

And when he finally drew away, she watched him go when she really wished she'd been able to convince him to stay.

Ten days before Christmas, volunteers gathered at the community center to wrap Presents for Patriots. The event was the culmination of many hours of work by many hands, and by seven o'clock, the room was bustling with activity and practically overflowing with volunteers.

For the residents of Rust Creek Falls, the annual gift-wrapping was very much a social occasion—a welcome opportunity to get together with their neighbors and catch up on what was going on. As Bailey looked around, he had to agree with Brendan's assessment: this was an amazing community.

More surprising to him was the number of people that he recognized from years ago and others whose acquaintance he'd made more recently. Mallory and Caleb Dalton were in attendance, as was Caleb's sister Paige with her husband, Sutter Traub. Will and Jordyn Clifton were working at a table alongside Will's brother Craig and his fiancée, Caroline Ruth. Claire and Levi Wyatt were at an adjacent table, Lani and Russ Campbell at another. Even the mayor and his wife had helped with the wrapping for a short while before they had to slip away to another holiday party.

At one point, Winona Cobbs popped in, and while the eccentric psychic was sipping some of the complimentary hot apple cider, she told Bailey that his life was going to change before the night was over—but only if he was willing to let it. Everyone in town knew the old woman was more than a little odd, so Bailey tried not to let her words unnerve him.

Throughout the evening, he overheard some snippets of conversation and learned that Thelma McGee had already offered to foster cats for the animal shelter. She wasn't ready to replace her beloved Oreo, but she was eager to help out.

There were also murmurs, but no confirmation, that Paige and Sutter were expecting their second child, and that Paige's sister Lani was expecting her first.

There were sighs of relief, and some chuckles, when it was revealed that the heart attack that caused Melba Strickland to rush her husband, Gene, to the hospital in Kalispell turned out to be indigestion.

Christmas music played softly in the background throughout, and there was a refreshment table that offered not only hot apple cider but coffee, tea and hot cocoa, plus an assortment of seasonal cookies and treats—all donated by the generous folks of Rust Creek Falls. There was certainly plenty going on to keep the volunteers busy, and Bailey mostly hovered in the background.

Although he'd been involved in the planning and organization of the event almost from the beginning, he still felt like an outsider in the community. Of course, that was his own fault. He'd mostly resisted getting involved because, as he'd been reminding his family for almost twelve months, he didn't intend to stay.

And yet, he'd still made no plans to go.

He restocked the tables as wrapping supplies dwindled, collected finished packages and cleared away debris, and regularly found his attention shifting to the door. He told himself that he wasn't looking for anyone in particular, but when his gaze zeroed in on Serena and his heart bumped against his ribs, he was forced to acknowledge the truth.

He'd been watching for her.

And he'd been thinking about her almost non-stop since he'd declined the invitation to her bed. All the way home, after he'd kissed her goodbye at her door last night, he'd cursed himself for being a fool. It was little consolation to his aching body to know that he'd done the right thing. And he couldn't help but wonder if she'd ever give him another chance to make a different choice.

"I didn't see your name on the volunteer list," he said, after he'd crossed the room to meet her.

"Did you look for it?" she asked, a teasing glint in her eye.

He had, because he'd wanted to see her. And now she was here, but he wasn't quite ready to put all his cards on the table. "I looked at all the names," he said.

"Then you know there were more than enough people signed up for the wrapping," she explained. "So I thought I'd come late to help with the cleaning."

"We had more than enough people sign up for that, too."

"I can see that," she acknowledged. "Are you going to send me away?"

"Of course not." Instead, he dipped his head and touched his mouth to hers. "I'm glad you're here."

The unexpected—and unexpectedly public—gesture surprised Serena. She'd wondered, after he'd left her apartment the night before, if she'd misinterpreted the situation. His kiss, in addition to making her lips tingle and spreading warmth through her veins, reassured her that she had not.

She smiled at him. "*That* made the walk over here totally worthwhile."

He drew back to look at her. "Why on earth would you walk over here in twenty-degree weather?"

"So that I could ask you for a ride home."

"I'd be happy to take you home," he assured her. "But I'm not sure how much longer I'm going to be stuck—"

"As of right now, you're unstuck," Brendan interjected, obviously having overheard at least part of their conversation.

"Fiona already agreed to stick around and, no offense, but she's much prettier than you."

Bailey chuckled. "No offense taken, and Serena's much prettier than you, too, so I guess we both win."

Brendan held out his hand. "Thanks for all your help."

"It was my pleasure," Bailey said, clasping his hand and grasping his other shoulder.

Not quite a man-hug, but a gesture that spoke of the friendship and camaraderie that Serena guessed had developed between them over the past few months.

"Have you been here all day?" she asked, as she and Bailey exited the community center together.

"No, just since two," he said.

"Still, that's a lot of hours."

"Yeah, but it was a good day," he told her. "Being away from Rust Creek Falls for so long, I almost forgot what it was like to be part of such a tight-knit community."

"Did you miss it?"

"I didn't let myself," he admitted, opening the passenger door of his truck for her. "Not the town. And definitely not my family."

"Why did you finally come back?" she asked, when he was settled behind the steering wheel.

He turned the key in the ignition, then cranked the defroster to clear the windshield and warm up the truck's cab. "After my marriage fell apart, I was kind of at loose ends. I could have stayed in New Mexico, but I didn't want to, so I decided to make my way back to Wyoming, to see if I could track down Luke and Danny again.

"Of course, they were both gone by then, but the foreman at the ranch where Luke had last been working told me that he'd gone to Rusty River."

"Rusty River?" she echoed, amused by the bastardization of the town's name.

He shrugged. "Not a lot of people outside of Montana have heard of Rust Creek Falls, and the Rusty part was at least close enough that I was able to figure out where he'd gone—although I couldn't imagine why he'd want to come back to the town we'd said goodbye to forever."

"Well, whatever his reasons, I'm glad he came home," she said, as Bailey pulled into a vacant parking spot behind her building. "Because then you came home, too."

She unbuckled her belt, and he did the same, then came around to help her out of the truck.

"I didn't plan on staying—in Rust Creek Falls," he clarified, as they started up the steps to her apartment. "Even as the days turned into weeks and then months, I was sure I'd pack up and head out again."

"But you're still here," she noted.

"And right now, I don't want to be anywhere else."

She unlocked her door, then turned to face him. "Did you want to come in for hot cocoa and cookies?"

"I don't know," he said. "I seem to recall you once telling me that I needed to cut back on the Christmas cookies."

"I seem to recall that was an attempt to cover for your ill-tempered comment to a little boy."

"You don't think I need to worry about staying in shape?"

She splayed her palms on his chest. Even through his sheepskin-lined leather jacket, she could feel the hard strength of his muscles. "I don't think a couple of cookies are any cause for concern."

"What about the cocoa?"

She slid her hands over his shoulders to link them behind his head. "Maybe we should skip the cocoa," she said, and drew his mouth down to hers.

Chapter 11

They bypassed the kitchen and headed straight to her bedroom. On the way, Serena almost tripped over Marvin, who had eagerly raced ahead and jumped on the bed.

She sighed. "He thinks it's playtime."

"I was hoping the same thing," Bailey said. "But just between me and you."

She smiled at that, then turned to Marvin and in a firm tone said, "Off."

His excitement leaked out of him like air escaping from a punctured balloon, and he dropped his head and crawled to the edge of the mattress. He paused then, as if giving her an opportunity to rescind her banishment. Serena pointed to the door. Marvin reluctantly jumped down off the bed and retreated from the room.

"This is a new feeling for me," Bailey said.

"What's a new feeling?"

"I'm torn between the anticipation of finally getting you naked and guilt that you sent the dog away."

"If it makes you feel any better, I promise that Marvin doesn't hold a grudge. In fact, he's probably curled up on Molly's pillow already."

"So you're telling me it's okay to focus on the getting you naked part?"

"I'm suggesting we focus on getting one another naked," she said.

He smiled and pulled her into his arms. "That works for me."

Then he kissed her again. His tongue slid between her lips, to tease and tangle with hers. His hands slid under her sweater, searching for skin, and found a soft cotton T-shirt instead.

"Damn Montana winters," he grumbled, as he yanked the shirt out of her jeans and finally put his hands on *her*. His callused palms moved over her skin, stroking her body, stoking her desire.

She fumbled with the buttons of his shirt, desperate to touch him as he was touching her, and discovered that he was wearing a thermal tee beneath. "Damn Montana winters," she echoed his complaint.

He chuckled as he yanked the shirt over his head and tossed it aside. The rest of their clothes quickly followed. Then he eased her down onto the mattress, covering her naked body with his own.

Her hands slid up his arms, tracing the muscular contours. Her palms stroked the shape of his bare shoulders, so broad, so strong. Then trailed over the hard planes of his chest and his stomach. He had the body of a rancher, lean and tough, and she wanted to lick every bit of it. But for now, she reached down and wrapped her fingers around him.

He sucked in a breath.

She immediately loosened her grip. "Did I hurt you?"

"Oh, yeah," he said. "But in the very best way."

She stroked his rigid length, slowly, from base to tip, then back again, and watched as his eyes darkened and a muscle in his jaw flexed as he clenched his teeth together. She stroked him again, and he caught her wrist as his breath shuddered out between his lips.

"I can't take much more of that," he warned.

"Then take me," she suggested. "I want you inside me."

"I want to be inside you," he assured her, but he lowered his head to nibble on her earlobe, kiss her throat.

"So why aren't you there?"

"Because it's been a while for me," he admitted. "And I want to make sure that it's good for you."

"It's been a while for me, too," she told him. "And I don't want to wait another minute to have you inside me."

"In that case, give me fifty-five seconds," he suggested.

"What?"

"It's less than a minute," he pointed out, as his hands leisurely traced her curves.

He continued the exploration with his mouth, kissing her breasts, her belly. He parted the soft folds of flesh at the apex of her thighs, opening her to him. Then he lowered his head and touched the sensitive nub at her center with his tongue, a slow, deliberate lick that made everything inside her tighten in glorious anticipation.

"Bailey...you don't have to—"

"Shh," he whispered against her slick flesh. "I've only got another forty seconds."

She might have smiled at that, but his mouth was already on her again, licking and nibbling, tasting and teasing. Instead, she let her head fall back against the pillow, biting down on her bottom lip to prevent herself from crying out with shock and pleasure.

She tried to hold it together. She didn't want to come apart like this. She wanted to wait until he was inside her.

Her fingers curled, fisting the cover beneath her, and she closed her eyes and tried to count down the last thirty seconds. But the numbers blurred together in her mind, as the desires and demands of her body shoved aside everything else.

"Isn't—" her breath hitched "—your time up?"

"Not just yet," he said, and continued his intimate exploration.

She couldn't fight the onslaught of sensations any longer. The tension inside her had built to a breaking point, and she shattered into a million pieces.

When her body finally stopped shuddering with aftershocks, he sheathed himself with a condom and rose up over her, then buried himself inside her.

She gasped as he filled her. Deeply. Completely.

She braced her heels on the mattress and lifted her hips, taking him even deeper, drawing a low groan of satisfaction from his throat as her muscles clenched around him.

He began to move, slowly at first, a steady rhythm that stroked deep inside her. Then faster, harder, deeper. Her hips rose to meet him and her fingernails scraped down his back as he drove them both to the pinnacle of pleasure—and beyond.

Bailey had barely managed to catch his breath when he heard Marvin's plaintive whimper through the bedroom door.

"Does he need to go out?" he asked, mumbling the question into Serena's hair.

"He has a doggy door," she reminded him.

"So why is he whining?"

"He was probably a little confused by the noises we were making," she admitted.

"You mean the noises *you* were making," he teased.

"I'm gonna plead the Fifth on that one."

He turned his head to nibble on her ear. "You were pleading something very different twenty minutes ago."

She lifted a hand to shove at his shoulder, but she didn't put much force behind the motion. "A gentleman should never embarrass a lady."

"I'm not a gentleman, I'm a cowboy," he told her.

"Well, cowboys have a code, too," she pointed out.

"Uh-huh," he agreed. "A cowboy must never shoot first, hit a smaller man or leave a woman unsatisfied."

She choked on a laugh. "I think you made that last part up."

"But did I honor the code?"

"You know you honored the code."

"Good." He lifted his head to brush his lips over hers. "Because you totally rocked my world, too."

"Yeah?"

"Oh, yeah," he confirmed.

She smiled at that. "I'm glad I walked over to the community center tonight."

He kissed her again, softly, sweetly. "I'm glad you invited me up for cocoa and cookies."

"We never had the cocoa and cookies."

"I know." Another kiss, longer, lingering. "And I'm thinking we should not have cocoa and cookies again."

"Right now?"

"Right now," he agreed.

Bailey had known that sex with Serena would be good, and he hadn't been exaggerating when he'd told her that she'd rocked his world. Of course, she was the first woman he'd been with since he'd ended his marriage, so he suspected that the extended period of celibacy had something to do with the intensity of the experience.

Except that the second time with Serena had been even better than the first. And the third had exceeded all his expectations yet again. And even after three rounds of lovemaking, his desire for her had not abated in the least.

It was that realization that caused the first hint of panic to set in. His subconscious reference to their physical joining as *lovemaking* only exacerbated it.

He wasn't in love with Serena.

He wasn't foolish enough to go down that path again, especially not with someone he'd only known a few weeks.

Sure, she was an amazing woman. Beautiful. Smart. Sexy. Passionate. Compassionate. Resilient. Caring. He could go on and on enumerating her many wonderful qualities—qualities that proved she was too good for him.

And yet, by some stroke of luck, she'd chosen to be with him. And he was selfish enough to take whatever she was willing to give, for as long as she was willing to give it.

He fell asleep with her head nestled against his shoulder—and woke up with what felt like a ten-pound weight on his chest.

Turned out it was a ten-pound cat.

"I thought you said the animals don't sleep in your bed," he remarked, when Serena returned to the bedroom from the adjoining en suite bath.

"They don't," she confirmed.

"Well, don't look now, but there's a cat on my chest."

"A wide-awake cat who wants her breakfast."

"She's not the only one," he said. Then he looked at Molly and, utilizing the same command that Serena had used so effectively with Marvin the night before, said, "Off."

The cat just stared at him, those pale green eyes unblinking.

He pointed to the floor and tried again. "Off."

Molly continued to stare at him.

"Your cat doesn't listen very well."

"She's a cat," Serena said, sounding amused.

"I can practically hear the thoughts going through her head." Then he changed the tone and pitch of his voice to recite those imagined thoughts. "I'll move my tail when I feel like moving my tail."

Serena laughed as she tied the belt of her robe around her waist. "I admit that I talk to my animals, but I don't pretend they talk back."

"Look at her and tell me that's not what she's thinking," he demanded.

She tilted her head to look at the cat. "That's not what she's thinking."

"Then what's she thinking?" he wanted to know.

"She's hoping that Santa will leave a little catnip in her stocking this year."

"Catnip, huh?"

Serena headed toward the door. "Come on, Molly."

And the damn cat followed her.

Shaking his head, Bailey pushed back the covers and climbed out of bed.

"Do I smell coffee?" he asked, when he joined her in the kitchen after he'd showered and dressed again in last night's clothes.

She handed him a mug filled with the hot fragrant brew. "What would you like for breakfast?"

"You don't have to cook for me," he said. "Or is this about balancing those scales you're so worried about?"

She laughed softly. "It's about the fact that I'm hungry and I thought you might be, too."

"I am," he confirmed.

"Eggs okay?"

"Eggs are always okay."

"Bacon?"

He nodded emphatically. "The only thing I like more than eggs."

* * *

They cooked breakfast together and ate breakfast together, and it was all very nice and domestic. And maybe it did make Serena wish she had someone with whom to share not just a single morning but the rest of her life. And maybe, if she let herself, she could imagine Bailey being that someone.

But she didn't let herself because she knew that one night did not a relationship make. She was hopeful, however, that one night might lead to two, and maybe more.

She'd just gotten up from the table for a coffee refill when the landline phone rang. A glance at the display made her pause.

"Are you going to answer that?" Bailey asked when the phone rang again and she only continued to stare at it.

"I don't know who it is," she confessed, carrying the coffeepot to the table to top up his mug. "The area code is Arizona, which is where my grandmother lives, but the number isn't familiar."

So she let the machine answer. And because she had an old-fashioned answering machine hooked up to her landline, the message transmitted clearly through the speaker.

"Hi, Rena, it's Grams. I know you said you'd call next week when I talked to you last week, but, well, I'm not actually home right now." Then her voice dropped to a loud whisper. "I'm at George's place."

Bailey's brows lifted.

"We had the best time last night," Grams continued, and then she giggled. "And this morning."

Serena buried her face in her hands.

"Honestly, the therapeutic effects of orgasm cannot be overrated, and I know you're under a lot of stress, which is why you need to grab hold of that Stockton boy and—"

She leaped from her chair and snatched up the receiver, cutting off the recording.

"Grams, hi." She turned her back to Bailey, so that he wouldn't see that her cheeks were flaming. "I, uh, just got out of the shower."

Which wasn't technically the truth, since she'd showered when she woke up, but it wasn't exactly a lie, either.

"Do you have one of those massaging shower heads?" her grandmother asked. "I'm not saying they can replace a man's touch, but desperate times and all that."

Serena groaned inwardly. "So...tell me what's going on in your life," she said, desperate to change the subject.

For the next several minutes, her grandmother proceeded to do precisely that—in great and unnecessary detail—while Serena silently prayed that the ground would open up and swallow her. But of course that didn't happen.

"Just remember your own last rule," Serena said, when Grams paused to take a breath.

"I remember all my rules," her grandmother assured her.

"But do you follow them?"

"Oh, I've gotta run," Grams said. "George is signaling that breakfast is ready."

And before Serena could reply, she'd disconnected.

"That was your grandmother, huh?" Bailey said, amusement evident in his tone.

"That was my grandmother," she confirmed.

"And 'that Stockton boy'...that would be me?"

"So much for hoping you might pretend you hadn't heard that part," she muttered.

"Sorry," he said, not sounding sorry at all. "But now I'm wondering what you told your grandmother about me."

"Nothing," she immediately and emphatically replied.

"And yet, she apparently wants you to grab hold of me and... What exactly was it she suggested you should do?"

"You're enjoying this a little too much."

"Not as much as I enjoyed last night," he assured her. "But that phone call certainly added something to the morning after."

"Can you please just forget about the phone call?"

"Okay," he agreed. "But tell me about your grandmother."

"What do you want to know?" she asked warily.

"It's obvious the two of you are close."

"I lived with her growing up," Serena reminded him.

"And has she always offered such interesting advice?"

She nodded. "Grams has often been exasperating and opinionated, but she loves wholeheartedly and unconditionally. She also had some pretty strict rules for anyone living under her roof."

"Like what?"

She ticked them off on her fingers as she recited: "Tell where I'm going and who I'm going with. Call when I get there. Be home by midnight. Never leave a drink unattended. Never drink and drive. Never share naked pictures. And never have sex without a condom."

"Those sound like some pretty smart and savvy rules," he remarked.

"Grams is a pretty smart and savvy lady."

"So is her granddaughter," he said.

"You think so?"

"Well, she gave me some pretty good advice."

"What advice was that?" she wondered aloud.

"About talking to Emily," he confided.

"You called her?"

He nodded. "I did."

"Was she surprised to hear from you?"

"Yeah, she was surprised to hear from me. And then she shared some surprising news."

"What was that?"

"She got married again. Six months ago."

"That's big news," Serena noted.

"And the even bigger news—she's pregnant."

"Wow."

He nodded again.

"How do you feel about that?" she asked him.

"It has nothing to do with me."

"Your ex-wife is expecting a baby with her new husband—you have to feel something."

"I'm happy for her," he said. "Really. And…relieved."

"Why relieved?" she asked, curious.

"Because there was part of me that wondered if I'd ruined her life."

"Because you divorced her?"

He shook his head. "Because I married her."

"You loved her," she reminded him.

"Or thought I did, anyway," he acknowledged. "But in retrospect, I think my decision to marry Emily was also an attempt—and not a very successful one—to take back control of my life."

"What do you mean?"

"The night my parents were killed…in addition to the grief and the guilt, I felt such an overwhelming sense of helplessness. They were gone, and there was absolutely nothing I could do to change what had happened, to fill the empty space in all of our lives.

"And then our grandparents told us there was no way that they could take in seven kids, so my two brothers and I were essentially on our own. We had no choice about that, but we chose to leave Rust Creek Falls and make our own lives. Yeah, it was a hollow victory, but we needed to feel like we had control over something.

"Everywhere I went after that, every job I took, every decision I made, was an effort to prove to myself that I was in charge of my own destiny. Then I met Emily, and I decided that I wanted to get married. But was I motivated by my feelings for her or a desperate desire to be part of a family again?"

He shrugged, as if he still wasn't certain of the answer to that question. "And does it really matter? Because I never managed to fit in with her family. I never got what I wanted. My fault, I know. Because I never really tried. Because it didn't take me long to realize that I didn't want to be part of *a* family again, I wanted *my* family back. And that was never going to happen."

He was silent for a minute, no doubt pondering those revelations. "But the point of all of that is that you were right," he continued. "There were too many things left unsaid, and saying them will, I think, help both of us put that chapter of our lives behind us."

"I'm glad," she said sincerely.

He finished his coffee and carried his empty plate and mug to the kitchen. Setting the dishes on the counter, he pulled his cell phone out of his pocket and sighed. "Four text messages from Luke in the past hour."

"Is something wrong?" she asked, immediately concerned.

"Nah, he's just nagging me for not being there for morning chores."

"My fault," Serena realized. "Sorry."

He smiled. "I'm not." He kissed her then, softly, sweetly. "But I do have to go."

She nodded. "I know."

"I had a really good time last night."

"Me, too."

And though he'd said he had to go, he didn't move. "I'm not sure what else to say here," he confessed.

"You don't have to say anything else," she told him.

"I want to say something else."

"What do you want to say?"

"Well, I'd like to ask if I can see you again tonight, but I don't want you to think that I'm making any assumptions… or have any expectations…that we're going to do what we did last night. Again, I mean."

She took a moment to untangle his words. "So you're saying that last night was a one-night stand?"

"No," he immediately replied. "I mean, I hope not."

"That's good," she said. "Because I hope not, too."

"So…can I see you tonight?"

"I'll be decorating my Christmas tree tonight."

"I was surprised that you didn't have one yet," he admitted.

"Me and Grams always went to get one on December 16, so I carry on that tradition," she told him.

"Where do you go?"

"Just over to the tree lot in town."

"I've got a better idea," he suggested.

"What's your better idea?" she asked warily.

"Come to Sunshine Farm with me now and we'll cut one down together and bring it back here."

"You're already late for morning chores," she reminded him.

"They'll be done before I get back."

"And you figure that your brother will be less likely to yell at you if I'm there?" she guessed.

"Do you want to hassle me or get a Christmas tree?"

She gave him a cheeky smile. "Both. But I guess I need to put some clothes on for the latter."

He gave her a playful pat on the butt. "Be quick."

Chapter 12

"Are you still going to pretend that there's nothing going on between you and Serena Langley?" Dan asked Bailey.

It was Monday afternoon and the brothers had all been recruited to repair a section of downed fence at Sunshine Farm. The repair hadn't taken as long as they'd anticipated, and they were back at the barn now, attempting to warm their frozen hands with hot coffee.

"Why do you think I'm pretending?" he asked, not really denying the fact so much as wanting to know what his brother knew—or thought he did.

"Because your truck was parked outside her apartment overnight," Dan noted.

"Saturday *and* Sunday," Jamie chimed in.

"Only one of the things I forgot that I hate about small towns," Bailey grumbled.

"So what's the status of the relationship?" Luke asked.

"I don't know that I'd call it a relationship," he hedged.

"You're spending your nights in her bed," Dan said again.

"Two nights." So far. "And even in a small town, I don't think that's illegal."

"In a small town, people talk," Jamie reminded him. "And Serena's not that kind of girl."

Bailey felt a twinge of uneasiness—and not his first—as he silently acknowledged the truth of his brother's claim. Of course, he hadn't thought about the potential repercussions for her reputation when he'd accepted the invitation to go up to her apartment after the Presents for Patriots event Saturday night. He hadn't thought about anything but how much he wanted to be with her.

On the other hand, it's not as if he had a reputation for bed-hopping in town. In fact, he didn't have a reputation for much of anything, except being one of *those Stockton boys* who had returned to Rust Creek Falls after so many years away. And in the twelve months that he'd been back, Serena was the first woman he'd been with. In fact, she was the first woman he'd been with since his ex-wife—not that he had any intention of admitting as much to his brothers.

"I know you probably think this is none of our business," Luke began.

"Bingo," Bailey said.

"But it is," Dan insisted. "Not just because you're our brother, but because Serena is a friend—a good friend—of Annie's."

"I'm aware of that," he assured his brothers. "I'm also aware that she's an adult capable of making her own decisions."

Dan held up his hands in a universal gesture of surrender. "I'm not suggesting otherwise."

"Then this conversation is over," Bailey said, looking at each of his brothers in turn.

They exchanged glances, shrugs.

"Just…be careful," Luke urged.

"I always am," he said.

But their words and warnings continued to niggle at the back of his mind throughout the rest of the day. And even when he met Serena after work, as they'd planned, to take a reluctant Marvin for a walk, followed by dinner together again.

So maybe it wasn't surprising that Serena sensed his preoccupation. Or maybe he didn't do a very good job hiding it, because when she took his hand to lead him into the living room after the dishes had been cleared up, he balked.

"What's wrong?" she asked.

"I'm wondering if I should go," he admitted.

"Oh." She immediately released his hand. "If that's what you want."

"It's not," he assured her.

"Then why are you wondering about it?"

"Because people are already talking about the fact that my truck was parked outside your apartment last night," he said. "And the night before."

"Really?" She seemed surprised by this revelation—then surprised him by smiling again. "Good."

"Why is that good?"

"Because I've always been a good girl, never giving anyone reason to speculate or gossip."

"Well, they're speculating now," he told her.

"Grams will be so proud."

"Please tell me you're not going to tell your grandmother."

"I won't have to. She'll most likely hear it from Melba Strickland—if she hasn't already."

He winced at the thought. "And then she'll wonder, along with everyone else, what a nice girl like Serena Langley is doing with an aimless boy like Bailey Stockton?"

She lifted her arms and linked her hands behind his neck, her fingertips playing with the hair that curled over the collar of his shirt. "I don't think you're aimless," she said. "You're just taking some time to figure things out."

"So what are you doing with me?" he asked her.

"I know what I want to do." She rose up onto her toes to whisper her idea in his ear.

"Your wish is my command," he said, and scooped her into his arms to carry her to the bedroom.

After that first night with Bailey, Serena knew that she was well on her way to falling in love with him. When he'd invited her to cut down a Christmas tree at Sunshine Farm, where he'd undoubtedly participated in the same ritual with his parents and siblings for the first twenty years of his life, she felt the first glimmer of hope that maybe he was starting to feel the same way.

But she didn't want to get too far ahead of herself, because she knew that he'd put shields up around his badly damaged heart, and that he might never let them down enough to fall in love again. In the meantime, she tried to enjoy just being with him and making new memories with him as they participated in all the usual holiday rituals.

Unfortunately, she couldn't spend every minute of every day with him, because they both had jobs and responsibilities. In fact, she was clipping the nails of a Great Dane Wednesday afternoon when a knock sounded on the door, then Bailey stepped into the exam room.

"Annie said it was okay for me to come in," he explained.

"Sure," she agreed. "Tiny is always happy to meet new people." The Great Dane's tail thumped noisily against the surface of the metal table, but otherwise, the animal didn't move as she continued to work.

Bailey made a show of looking around the room. "Where's Tiny?"

She smiled. "*This* is Tiny."

"I doubt that animal was ever tiny, even as a puppy," he remarked.

"Norma Wilson has a fondness for irony," Serena explained. "Her other dog is a Chihuahua named Monster." She clipped the last nail. "All done."

Tiny nimbly hopped down off the table. Standing, his head was level with Serena's midriff. Then he dropped to his butt on the floor, sitting patiently, expectantly.

She retrieved a treat from the pocket of her lab coat and fed it to him. "Good boy," she said, and rubbed the top of his head.

"Do I get a treat?" Bailey asked.

She offered him a doggy cookie.

He lowered his head and kissed her instead.

"That's what I wanted," he told her.

"That was nice," she agreed. "But I suspect you didn't come into town just for a kiss."

"No," he agreed. "Not that one of your kisses wouldn't make the trip worthwhile, but Luke asked me to pick up some stuff at the feed store. And since I was here, I thought I'd check in to see if you wanted to reschedule the dinner and a movie that we missed last week. How's Friday night?"

"Actually, I already have plans for Friday night," she confided.

"Oh." He frowned. "What kind of plans?"

"The Candlelight Walk."

He looked at her blankly.

"Maybe you weren't back in town yet when it happened last year," she acknowledged. "It's exactly what the name implies—residents carry lit candles in a processional down Main Street."

"Yeah, I guess I missed that," he said.

"You don't sound too sorry," she noted.

He shrugged. "You know all that Christmassy stuff isn't really my thing."

"Which is why I didn't ask you to go with me."

"But if my only options are a Candlelight Walk with you or spending Friday night alone... Well, there's no contest."

"Really? You want to go with me?"

"I really want to go with you," he said.

She was used to feeling butterflies in her tummy.

The first time she'd ever met Bailey Stockton, a brief and impromptu introduction at the clinic one day when he'd stopped by to see Annie, Serena had felt flutters in her belly. And again, a few months later, when she'd crossed paths with him at Crawford's. And of course, the day that they'd played Santa and Mrs. Claus at the community center.

They'd spent a lot of time together since then, and yet, all it took was a look, a smile or a touch to have those butterflies swooping and spinning again.

As she got ready for the Candlelight Walk, she felt as if those familiar butterflies had multiplied tenfold—and then OD'd on caffeine. Because Serena knew that showing up at tonight's event with Bailey would make a statement about their relationship that would carry as much weight as a headline in the *Gazette*.

Even as she added a spritz of her favorite perfume, she wondered if this was a bad idea. If she was making their relationship into more than it really was. When she was with him, she was usually having too much fun to worry that she might be the only one emotionally invested in the relationship. It was only when she was on her own, with the holidays looming, that the doubts and insecurities raised their ugly heads.

Because each day that passed was a day closer to December 25, and Bailey had said nothing about his plans for Christmas—or asked about hers.

Not that she had any plans. While many residents of Rust Creek Falls were busy running here or there to spend time with family or friends, Serena was accustomed to being on her own with her pets. And that was okay. It was her own tradition—a day of quiet reflection and counting her blessings.

It was another tradition to spend the day after Christmas with her mother, *if* Amanda felt up to it. But her mother was spending the holidays with Mark this year, and although they were keeping their celebrations low-key, they'd invited Serena to join them. Of course, she'd declined. Not only because she didn't want to intrude on their first Christmas together, but because she was—perhaps foolishly—optimistic that she might be celebrating her own first Christmas with Bailey.

But she had accepted an invitation to Mark's house for lunch on Sunday, just two days before Christmas, and she'd ordered a Dutch apple pie—her mother's favorite—from Daisy's as her contribution to the meal. She'd told Bailey of her plans, emphasizing the fact that she didn't celebrate Christmas Day with her mom, but he hadn't taken the hint.

Of course, he'd only reunited with his family the previous year, so it was understandable that they'd be the focus of his plans. It was also possible that he planned to invite her to celebrate with him but hadn't yet done so.

Maybe tonight, she thought—fingers crossed—as she retrieved her hat and mittens from the closet. Then she reached for her boots, and Marvin immediately went to hide.

She laughed, then winced a little as she tightened the lace of her right boot. She'd had a little mishap at the clinic the day before and twisted her ankle. Although she'd iced and wrapped the joint, it was still a little sore—but not sore enough to keep her from participating in one of her favorite holiday events.

She'd just finished buttoning her coat when Bailey knocked at the door. He kissed her lightly, then looked at the floor by her feet. "Where's Marvin?"

"Hiding," she said.

"Why?"

"Because these are my *w-a-l-k-i-n-g* boots," she explained. "And not even the promise of a belly rub would entice him out for a second *w-a-l-k* in one day."

"That dog has issues," he told her.

"And his exercise phobia is only the tip of the iceberg," she admitted, as she closed and locked the door behind her. "He's also afraid of horses, cows and pigs."

"You're kidding."

"Nope." She shook her head as she descended the stairs beside him, trying not to put her full weight on her right foot. "One day when we were out, there were a couple of young girls riding horses on a trail, and he darted between my legs and would not move."

"Then that might be another reason he's hiding," Bailey suggested, as he led her around to the front of the building.

She halted in midstep. "What's this?"

"What does it look like?"

"It looks like a horse-drawn sleigh."

"Got it in one," he told her. "More specifically, it's a two-seat Albany sleigh."

And it was gorgeous, with gleaming bronze accents and tufted velvet seats and ribbon-wrapped pine boughs adding a festive touch.

"*Where* did you get it?" she asked him now.

"I borrowed it from Dallas Traub. And Trina—" he gestured to the gorgeous horse harnessed to the sleigh "—from his stables."

"Okay," she said. "But *why* did you borrow a horse-drawn sleigh for the Candlelight *Walk*?"

"Because Annie told me that you sprained your ankle at work—which you didn't mention to me," he said pointedly.

"Because it's fine," she assured him.

He just lifted a brow.

"And it's wrapped."

"But I don't imagine it will feel very good tomorrow if you're on it all night tonight."

"Probably not," she acknowledged. "But I didn't want to miss the walk."

"And now you don't have to," he said, taking her hand to help her climb into the seat.

"This is so…thoughtful."

"And romantic?" he suggested.

"Unbelievably romantic," she assured him.

And it was.

The walk started at the high end of Main Street, where volunteers from the city council handed out lighted candles in tall glass jars. Bailey left her in the sleigh while he went to get a candle for her, then they took their position at the rear of the crowd. Of course, night fell early in December, but the flicker of so many candles created a beautiful golden glow as the processional made its way slowly toward the park, where the bonfire would be lit.

Bailey held the reins in one gloved hand and Serena's free hand with his other.

"People are going to talk," she warned.

"People are already talking," he reminded her.

"And you just added fresh fuel to the fire."

"With this?" he scoffed, lifting their joined hands. "I doubt it. But maybe—" he tipped her chin up and brushed his lips over hers "—that will do the trick."

"If the trick is making me want to skip the bonfire and take you home to have my way with you, then yes."

"Participating in tonight's festivities was *your* idea," he reminded her.

"So it was," she confirmed.

And she was glad he'd agreed to come. Not only because he'd so thoughtfully provided transportation that allowed her to rest her sore ankle, but because she always enjoyed being with him.

At the end of the route, after the bonfire had been lit, eliciting gasps and cheers from the crowd, they caught sight of his brother Jamie with Fallon and the triplets, Henry, Jared and Katie.

The kids were excited to see "ho-zees," and after checking with Serena first, Bailey offered the reins to his brother so that he and his wife could take their kids for a little ride.

While they were gone, Bailey and Serena mingled with the crowd. And it was a crowd. The O'Reillys were in attendance en masse: Paddy and Maureen, their sons, Ronan and Keegan, and their daughters, Fallon, Fiona and Brenna, along with their respective partners. There were several representatives of each of the Crawford and Traub families, and even more Daltons.

They stopped to chat for a minute with Old Gene and Melba Strickland, the latter asking about Serena's grandmother. And though Serena was tempted to point out that Melba probably talked to Janet Carswell more than her granddaughter did, she managed to bite back the cheeky retort and simply assure the older woman that Janet was doing well.

Shortly after that, Jamie and Fallon returned and they traded places again, then Bailey directed Trina to take them back to Serena's place.

"Tonight was...amazing," Serena said, after he'd carried her up the stairs to her back door.

"I'm glad you had a good time."

"I suppose you have to get the horse and sleigh back to the Triple T," she said, naming the Traub ranch where Dallas and Nina lived with their four children.

"I do," Bailey confirmed.

"Do you want to come back here after you've done that?" she asked him.

He tightened his arms around her. "What horse and sleigh?"

She laughed softly. "I'm flattered. I know you wouldn't really neglect Trina after she dutifully escorted us around town all night, but I'm flattered."

"I'll be back as soon as I can," he promised.

"I'll be here," she assured him.

He kept his promise.

And when he made love to her that night, it was beautiful and magical and Serena finally acknowledged a truth she'd been trying to deny: she was in love with Bailey Stockton.

The realization filled her heart with joy—and her belly with trepidation. Because she knew that Bailey wasn't looking for a serious relationship. He'd been honest about that from the very beginning. But she'd fallen in love with him anyway.

She'd never felt like this before, and she was torn between wanting to tell him and worrying that if she did, the confession of her feelings would act as a wedge rather than a bridge between them. So for now, she resolved to keep the words to herself.

But as their bodies merged together in the darkness of the night, she knew that the truth and depth of her feelings were evident in every touch of her lips, pass of her hands and press of her body.

"You know, the first pie I ever made for Luke was an apple," Eva said conversationally, as she boxed up the dessert Serena had ordered.

"Proving that the way to a man's heart is through his stomach?" Serena guessed.

"Well, I can't argue with the results." The other woman grinned as she fluttered the fingers of her left hand, where a glittery diamond nestled against the wedding band on the third finger.

Serena smiled back as she passed her money across the counter.

"So are you going to tell me what this pie is for?" Eva prompted. "Or are you going to make me guess?"

"I'm going to lunch at my mother's boyfriend's house." It felt strange to say those words—*mother's boyfriend*—but Amanda and Mark seemed to have clearly defined their relationship, while Serena and Bailey had not.

"I would have guessed wrong," the baker said. "Is Bailey going with you?"

Serena shook her head. "No."

"Why not?"

"Because I didn't invite him."

"Why not?" Eva asked again.

"Because I'm not even sure *I* want to go," Serena admitted. "I certainly wouldn't drag anyone else into the center of my family drama."

"Every family has drama," Eva assured her. "And nothing shines twinkling lights on it like the holidays."

"Isn't that the truth?" she agreed.

"So…what are your plans for Christmas Eve?"

"Oh, the usual," Serena said, deliberately vague.

"What's the usual?"

"Hanging out with Marvin, Molly and Max," she confided.

The other woman's eyes narrowed. "Isn't Marvin your dog?"

Serena nodded. "My dog, my cat and my bunny."

"You don't spend Christmas Eve with your mom?"

"That would be too much drama even for me."

"In that case, you should come out to Sunshine Farm," Eva said.

"Oh." Serena was taken aback by the other woman's impulsive offer—and undeniably touched by the invitation. "Thanks, but I wouldn't want to intrude on your family celebrations."

"Don't be silly," the baker chided. "Everyone will be happy to see you."

"I don't know," she hedged. "Bailey hasn't said anything to me about his plans for the holidays." He certainly hadn't given any indication that he wanted to spend them with her.

"Because he's a man. He doesn't know how to make plans any more than twenty-four hours in advance of an event."

Serena smiled, but she wasn't convinced—especially since Christmas Eve was less than twenty-four hours away.

"Say you'll come," Eva urged. "It will be a lot more fun than hanging out with Marvin, Molly and Matt."

"Max," she corrected automatically. "And our holiday snuggles are something of a tradition."

"But I bet you'd rather snuggle with Bailey," his sister-in-law teased.

Serena couldn't deny it.

And Eva, confident that she'd made another sale, said, "Dinner will be on the table at six."

Two days before Christmas, Bailey wrapped the last of his gifts—this one for Serena.

It wasn't anything fancy or expensive, just a simple eight-by-ten enlargement of a photo of the animals that he'd snapped with his cell phone one day when he was at her apartment. In the picture, Marvin was sprawled out on his belly—his back end on his pillow, his shoulders and head on the floor; Max was stretched out beside him but facing the opposite direction;

and Molly was curled up with her face right beside Max's and one paw on his back. The candid shot attested to the camaraderie and affection between the animals, and he was confident Serena would love it.

He had yet to decide how and when he was going to give it to her. Because holding hands and stealing kisses in public was one thing, while sharing a major holiday took a relationship to the next level, and he wasn't sure they were ready to go there—or that they ever would be.

He always had a great time with Serena, and he thought of her often when they were apart, but that didn't mean he was ready to commit to a capital-*R* relationship. And spending Christmas together definitely implied Relationship, which was why he'd decided to fly solo over the holidays.

And why he was taken aback when Luke's wife told him what she'd done.

Chapter 13

"You did what?" Bailey said, certain he must have misunderstood or misinterpreted Eva's words.

"I invited Serena to come over on Christmas Eve," she repeated.

"Why?" he demanded to know.

She frowned, obviously not having anticipated his less-than-enthusiastic response to her announcement. "Because she came in to Daisy's and when I asked about her plans for the holidays, she admitted that—aside from hanging out at home with her pets—she didn't have any."

"She loves hanging out at home with her pets," he informed his sister-in-law. "It's kind of her thing."

"And because I thought you'd want her to be here," Eva added.

"You should have asked me before you asked her," he grumbled.

Her expression shifted from bafflement to concern. "Do you not want her here?"

"I just don't want her to think an invitation to spend Christmas Eve with my family means anything more than that."

"Serena doesn't strike me as the type of woman who would assume a casual invitation from her boyfriend's sister-in-law is a green light to start planning the seating chart for your wedding," she said dryly.

"I'm not her boyfriend," he said through gritted teeth.

"So what are you?" she challenged. "Just a guy who's bouncing on her bed for as long as it suits his purposes?"

That was all he'd wanted, but to hear his brother's wife put it in such blunt terms sounded harsh. And untrue.

"Why does everyone want to put a label on our relationship?" Because as much as he hadn't wanted a relationship, he couldn't deny that he was in one.

He cared about Serena. He enjoyed being with her. And yes, he enjoyed sex with her. But even he couldn't deny that their relationship was about more than sex. He liked talking to her, he appreciated the comfortable silences they shared, he even liked hanging out with her pets. Although Marvin was undeniably his favorite, he had no issues with Max and felt reasonably confident that he'd reached a détente with Molly.

But he wasn't ready for another Relationship. Or maybe he didn't trust himself not to mess up with Serena the way he'd messed up his marriage.

"Do you want me to uninvite her?" Eva asked him now.

"Is there any possible way to do that without an incredible amount of awkwardness?" he wondered aloud.

"Probably not," she admitted. "But I'd rather have an awkward conversation with Serena today than have her feel uncomfortable or unwelcome tomorrow."

"Don't bother," he said. "It's fine."

But Serena was right. Saying "it's fine" didn't make it so, and Bailey decided to go for a drive to clear his head.

Although he had no destination in mind when he set out, he wasn't really surprised when he found his truck slowing down as he approached the cemetery.

His heart was pounding hard against his ribs and his palms were clammy as he shifted into Park and turned off the ignition. He hadn't been here since that awful day his parents were put in the ground, and he was immediately swamped by a wave of memories and emotions. He pushed open the door and stepped out into the cold.

Someone had put an evergreen wreath decorated with holly berries and pinecones on an easel in the ground beside the headstone. Bella, he guessed. It was the type of thing she would think to do. He knew that she visited the cemetery regularly, and throughout the summer tended to the flowers she planted in the spring.

He took a couple steps forward and dropped to his knees in the snow, his watery gaze unable to focus on the names and dates etched in the stone. It didn't matter—the details were forever etched in his mind. The regrets forever heavy in his heart.

"I've screwed everything up," Bailey said, somehow managing to force the words through his closed-up throat. "Starting with that night in the bar, thirteen years ago." He shook his head. "I was so careless, so thoughtless. So stupid."

That long ago night, he'd ignored Danny's urgings to leave because there were pretty girls to dance with and beer to drink. And yeah, he'd actually thought it was funny that his little brother was such an uptight mother hen.

I've already got one mother. I don't need another one, he'd chided his brother.

Danny's expression had darkened, but Luke had laughed—sharing the joke, the good times.

Then the sheriff's deputy had walked into the bar, and the laughter had stopped.

"It was my fault," Bailey confessed to his parents as he stared at the headstone. "But they don't blame me. I don't know how or why, but Bella, Jamie, Dana…even Luke and Danny…don't blame me for what happened that night. But I know the truth. It was my fault. Serena thinks I'm still punishing myself. That I won't let myself be happy because I don't believe I deserve to be happy.

"She might be right," he acknowledged. "I never told Emily about that night, because I was afraid she'd look at me differently. At least, that was the justification I gave to myself. But maybe I wasn't ready to let go of any of my guilt and grief enough to share it."

It was a possibility he hadn't considered until right now. A truth that suddenly seemed unassailable.

"But somehow, I found myself telling Serena everything. Maybe because she's had to overcome devastating losses of her own. And yet, despite that, she is one of the most optimistic people I've ever met. Determined to find happiness in every day—and adding joy to mine whenever I'm with her.

"I really wish you could have met her—and that she'd had the chance to know you. She really is amazing. Beautiful and smart. Sexy and sweet." His smile was wry. "And undoubtedly too good for me."

Of course, there was no response to his monologue. But when Bailey finally rose to his feet again, his heart felt lighter. And for the first time in a long time, he felt hopeful about his future and willing to not just appreciate but embrace the joy that Serena brought to his life.

For a dozen years, Bailey hadn't thought he had any reason to celebrate the holidays. Last year, his first back in Rust Creek Falls after twelve away, he'd felt awkward and uncomfortable, like an imposter in his sister's home. Not that Bella had done or said anything to make him feel less than welcome. Just the opposite, in fact. She'd gone out of her way for him, even ensuring there were presents with his name on them under the tree Christmas morning.

But this year, being with his siblings again, along with their significant others and kids, he truly felt as if he was where he belonged. Even Dana had made the trip from Oregon—with the blessing of her adoptive parents—to spend the holiday with her brothers and sister.

Of course, the entire family wasn't there, but those who gathered together found pleasure in their renewed and strengthened childhood bonds and remembered those who weren't with them at Sunshine Farm. They all hoped that Liza would also be brought back into the fold someday, but for now, Bailey focused on being grateful for what he had—including the beautiful woman by his side.

"So tell me how you and Bailey met," Dana said to Serena.

"Well, I actually met him several months ago at the vet clinic where I work with Annie," she said. "But I didn't really get to know him until Dan went down with the flu. Bailey had to fill in for him playing Santa, and I did the same for Annie as Mrs. Claus, so she could take care of her sick husband."

"I guess it's lucky for both of you that Dan got the flu," Dana remarked.

Janie, only hearing the last part of her aunt's remark as she came into the living room from the kitchen, stopped in the entrance and looked worriedly toward the sofa, where her parents were seated. "Dad's got the flu?"

"Not now," her mother hastened to assure her. "He's fully recuperated now."

Janie looked puzzled. "When was he sick?" she wondered aloud.

"When Uncle Bailey had to fill in as Santa at the community center," Annie said.

"And your school," Dan chimed in.

"Oh, right." Janie chuckled, remembering. "Your fake flu."

Bailey frowned. "Fake flu?"

"Yeah," his niece confirmed, apparently oblivious to the can of worms she was opening. "Mom and Dad thought that forcing you to play Santa would help put you in the holiday spirit."

A heavy silence followed Janie's revelation, until Fallon spoke up. "Did you hear that?" she asked, though no one had heard anything. "I think the kids are starting to wake up. Janie, can you help me with them?"

"Sure," the tween agreed, always happy to lend a hand with her toddler cousins.

"I'll help, too," the triplets' father said. "Three sets of hands are always best with three kids," Jamie explained.

Bailey waited until they'd gone before he turned to Dan. "You *faked* being sick?"

"I did have a bit of a cold," Dan said defensively.

"You told me you were throwing up," Bailey reminded him. Then he turned to his brother's wife. "And you acted so concerned—going to Daisy's to get him soup. You even had Serena fill in for you because you couldn't risk leaving your oh-so-sick husband alone." He shook his head. "And now I find out it was all just part of the act."

"Or was it a romantic setup from the beginning?" Eva mused aloud. Head over heels in love with her husband, she wished for a happy ending for everyone.

The color that filled Annie's cheeks answered the question before she spoke. "I might have asked Serena to take my place because I hoped she and Bailey would hit it off."

"And she was right," Dana pointed out, obviously trying to ease the tensions between her siblings.

* * *

Serena could tell that Bailey wasn't in a mood to be appeased. Not that she could blame him for being angry and upset by the machinations of his brother and sister-in-law. She was none too happy herself—and more than a little embarrassed—to have been so completely caught up in the plot.

"Did you have any part in this?" he asked her now.

She immediately shook her head. "Of course not," she denied, shocked that Bailey could believe such a thing.

And maybe he didn't, but he was apparently too mad to think rationally right now.

He turned to his brother again. "You always think you know what's best for everyone else, don't you? Consequences be damned." Bailey didn't raise his voice, and his words were almost more lethal because of their quiet fury. "I would have thought you'd learned your lesson about sticking your nose into other people's business thirteen years ago."

When Dan's face drained of all color, Serena realized the brothers were arguing about something more than a feigned illness.

"That's enough," Luke said to his brothers.

But Dan refused to heed the warning. "Maybe I was, in a small way, trying to make up for mistakes I made in the past," he acknowledged. "Maybe I was trying to help you find the happiness you don't think you deserve."

"Contrary to what you think, I can manage my own life," Bailey said. "I don't need anyone's interference."

He turned on Eva now, as if having finally let his emotions loose, he couldn't stop. "And I certainly don't need anyone to set me up with a date on Christmas Eve. If I'd wanted a date, I would have got one myself—but I didn't."

The implication of his pointed words was unmistakable, and Serena flinched from the verbal blow. If she'd ever had any illusions that she belonged here, with Bailey, the vehemence of his response ripped that veil away.

Another, even heavier, silence fell around the room.

"Well," Serena said, clearing her throat to speak around the lump that was sitting there. "I think it's time for me to be on my way."

"But...we haven't eaten yet," Dana pointed out.

"And I've got animals at home that need to be fed," Serena said.

No one said anything else then. No one else tried to stop her. Certainly not Bailey.

She didn't look in his direction as she made her way out of the room. And she didn't hurry, keeping her chin up and her gaze focused ahead of her as she made her escape, so that no one would guess her heart was breaking into a million jagged little pieces.

She found her boots easily enough, but there were so many coats piled onto the hooks by the door, it took her a minute to uncover hers. Of course, her efforts were further thwarted by the tears that blurred her vision.

She'd been a fool to think that they were growing closer, maybe even building a relationship. She'd had reservations about accepting Eva's invitation to spend Christmas Eve with the Stocktons at Sunshine Farm, but Bailey's sister-in-law had assured her that he would want her there.

The silence in the living room had been broken. Voices were raised now, talking over one another so that she couldn't make out what anyone was saying—and she was grateful for it. Finally, she found her coat, shoved her arms into the sleeves, stuffed her feet into her boots and yanked open the door.

She blinked in surprise as she got a face full of snowflakes. An hour earlier, as she'd driven toward Sunshine Farm, she'd been enchanted by the pretty flakes dancing harmlessly in the sky. The wind had obviously picked up since then and the snow was falling heavily now—no longer appearing pretty or harmless.

Swiping at a tear that spilled onto her cheek, she inhaled a slow, deep breath. The icy air sliced like a sharply honed blade through her lungs, but that pain didn't compare to the ache in her heart.

She unlocked her SUV and climbed in. Shoving her key into the ignition, she cranked up the defroster and turned on the wipers. The snow that had accumulated on the windshield was swept away by the blades, and she shifted into Reverse, carefully backing around the other vehicles parked in the long drive. Cars and trucks that belonged to Bailey's brothers and sisters. Proof that he was surrounded by family. Proof that he didn't need her.

He'd referred to his family, with equal parts exasperation and affection, as nosy and interfering. And what Dan and Annie had done proved his description was apt. But Serena had no doubt that his brother and sister-in-law had acted with the best of intentions, wanting him to find the same kind of happiness they'd found together.

Still, Serena could understand why he was angry, if not the intensity of his anger. Or maybe she could. The day he'd told her about his long overdue conversation with his ex-wife, he'd also told her how much he'd hated feeling as if he didn't have any control over his life after his parents were killed. So maybe it was understandable that he'd be furious about the setup, because regardless of Dan and Annie's motivations, they'd taken control of the situation away from Bailey.

She believed the feelings they had for one another were real, but she could see why the manipulation of the situation might lead Bailey to question the legitimacy of his emotions. And that was something he needed to figure out on his own—if he even wanted to. Obviously the Stockton siblings had some other issues to work through, but she had no doubt that they would do so, because no matter their differences, they were a family who cared deeply about one another.

She thought of her own family—of herself, her mother and her grandmother. Three generations of women who had been through so much—and nearly let their trials tear them apart. But even the deepest wounds eventually healed, and for the first time in a lot of years, Serena felt optimistic about her mother's recovery and the relationship they were gradually beginning to rebuild.

Amanda was with Mark today. He understood that Christmas was a particularly difficult time for her and was happy to give her whatever support she needed to make it through the holidays without falling apart—or falling back into old habits.

Serena would celebrate this year the same way she'd done last year and the one before that—with Marvin, Molly and Max. She didn't need anyone else. Certainly not some stupid man who didn't know how lucky he was to have her.

And yeah, maybe she didn't need Bailey, but she couldn't deny that she loved him.

And it hurt to know that he didn't love her back.

Fresh tears filled her eyes, spilled onto her cheeks.

She didn't lift her hands from the wheel to wipe them away, because the snow was coming really fast and heavy now, and she felt her tires slip on patches of ice beneath the fresh snow. Her mechanic had warned her that she needed new snow tires, but she'd been certain that she could get one more winter out of them. She silently pleaded not to be proved wrong now.

"The Christmas Song" was playing on the local radio station she always listened to, and when Nat King Cole finished singing, the deejay's voice came through the speaker.

"I hope everyone's enjoying their Christmas Eve—and staying off the roads. Our local law enforcement has issued the following weather warning and travel advisory—heavy snow with significant blowing and drifting is imminent or occurring. Snowfall amounts up to eighteen inches with blizzard to near-blizzard conditions likely in many areas, making travel difficult or dangerous with road closures possible.

"So if you don't have to be out and about, pour yourself a glass of eggnog and sit back with your feet up by the fire and listen to the sounds of the season. I'm here to keep you company all night long."

It was good advice, and Serena vowed to do exactly as he suggested as soon as she got home.

But first she had to get home.

A flash of something caught the corner of her eye. She eased up on the gas and turned her head just in time to see a white-tailed deer leap up out of the ditch and onto the road ahead.

She instinctively hit the brakes to avoid hitting the majestic creature, but she braked a little too hard for the conditions. Her tires slid on the slick road, and the back end of her SUV fishtailed.

She immediately tried to steer into the skid, but her efforts had little effect. The vehicle continued to spin, as if in slow motion, then slid into the ditch. Because the point of impact was at the rear, the airbag didn't deploy, but she was thrown against her seat belt and then, when the SUV abruptly listed, she smacked her head against the driver's side window.

She winced at the explosion of pain and felt a trickle of something wet sliding down the side of her face. Had the window cracked? Was it snow?

She wiped it away, then saw the back of her hand was smeared with red.

Not snow.

Blood.

Merry frickin' Christmas to me.

Chapter 14

She didn't get out of the vehicle. There was no point. She could tell by the angle of the hood sticking in the air that she wasn't going to get out of the ditch without a tow cable. So she unclipped her seat belt to retrieve her purse, which had slid off the passenger seat to the floor. She winced a little, realizing that her shoulder was tender from the restraint. Thankfully, she hadn't been driving too fast, but she had no doubt she'd have plenty of bumps and bruises the next day.

She found her phone and swiped to unlock the screen. It remained blank.

Fresh tears burned her eyes. She was heartbroken, frustrated and angry. It was Christmas Eve and she just wanted to be home with Molly and Marvin and Max. Instead, she was stranded in a snowbank on the side of the road with a dead cell phone.

She never should have accepted Eva's invitation to spend Christmas Eve with the Stocktons at Sunshine Farm. She should have known that Bailey not asking her wasn't an oversight but an indication that he didn't want her there. She should have been satisfied with their friendship-with-benefits and not allowed herself to hope and believe the relationship could turn into anything more.

She dropped her forehead against the steering wheel as hot tears spilled onto her cheeks. She wasn't really hurt—not physically. But her heart was battered, her spirit beaten down. And because it was Christmas Eve and the whole town was experiencing blizzard conditions, she estimated the chances of another motorist passing by were slim to none.

Thankfully, she kept a spare charger in her center console. She also found a travel pack of tissues there. After plugging the charger into her phone, she pulled out a couple of tissues and pressed them to her temple to stanch the flow of blood.

Squinting through the window, she saw lights in the distance. Could it be…? Was that another vehicle coming her way?

Her bruised heart gave a joyful little jump.

Maybe her luck was turning around. Maybe something was finally going to go her way today.

She used the sleeve of her coat to wipe condensation off the side window—not that it helped much. She could barely see anything through the blowing snow, but she was almost certain now that there were headlights drawing nearer.

Apparently she wasn't the only resident of Rust Creek Falls who had disregarded the travel warning. Although, in her defense, she'd been unaware of the warning until she'd left Sunshine Farm and was already on her way toward home. Not that she would have stayed, even if she'd known about the road conditions. Not after Bailey had made it clear to everyone that she wasn't wanted.

She rubbed a hand over the ache in the center of her chest. Yeah, the truth hurt, but she would get over it—and him. It might take some time, she knew, but her heart had already proven its resilience, time and again.

As the vehicle drew closer, she saw that it was a blue pickup. Like Bailey's truck.

And her bruised heart gave another little jump.

She immediately chided herself for the reaction and dismissed the possibility. It couldn't be Bailey's truck. He'd made it clear that he didn't want her at Sunshine Farm, so there was no reason to suspect that he might have followed her when she'd gone.

Of course, it was possible that he'd left the ranch for another reason, although she couldn't imagine one that would compel him to venture out in such nasty weather.

But as the truck drew nearer, she realized that it *was* Bailey's truck.

So much for thinking this was a lucky break. She already felt like a fool. The absolute last thing she needed was for the man who'd callously broken her heart to ride to her rescue. Because of course he would stop, and then he would insist on driving her home. And every mile of the journey would be excruciating painful.

If I'd wanted a date, I would have got one myself.

She winced at the echo of his words in her head.

His vehicle slowed and carefully eased over to the side of the road behind her incapacitated SUV.

Serena swiped at the tears on her cheeks, not wanting him to know that she'd been crying. Not wanting him to think that she was crying over him.

Before she could catch her breath, her door was wrenched open from the outside and a blast of cold swept through the interior of the cab and stole her breath.

"Oh my God, Serena—what happened? Are you hurt?" He sounded genuinely concerned, maybe even a little panicked.

"You're bleeding," he said, then lifted a hand to her chin and gently turned her face so that he could inspect the gash above her eye.

"I braked to avoid hitting a deer," she confided.

"Of course, you did," he said, shaking his head. "Without thinking about the potential danger to yourself."

"It was an instinct," she said, a little defensively.

"Do you need a doctor? An ambulance?"

This time she shook her head, wincing as the movement escalated the throbbing inside her skull. "I'm okay. Just…stuck. I was going to call for a tow when I saw your headlights."

"It might take a tow truck driver a while to get out here, if you can find one willing to venture out in this storm. Everyone's being advised to avoid nonessential travel."

"I heard that on the radio…while I was driving," she admitted. "But why are *you* out on the roads?"

"Because I'm an idiot," he said. "And I'm sorry."

He reached into the cab to pull her into his arms and hold her close.

Serena remained perfectly still, not sure how she was supposed to respond to this unexpected show of concern. Not willing to let herself believe that anything had changed in the short time that had passed since she left Sunshine Farm.

"I'm so sorry, Serena." He whispered the words close to her ear, his tone thick with emotion.

"Why are you sorry?" she asked cautiously.

"Because I'm an idiot," he said again, his arms still wrapped tight around her, as if he couldn't bear to let her go. "I got mad at Danny for butting in, because I'd finally started to believe that I was back in control of my life, and finding out that he'd manipulated the situation… Well, it set me off," he admitted. "But obviously I do need someone to tell me what to do, because I just seem to screw everything up otherwise."

"You don't need to apologize for your feelings," she responded stiffly.

He loosened his hold enough to draw back to look at her—or maybe so that she could see the sincerity in his eyes. "I'm not apologizing for my feelings. I'm apologizing for *denying* my feelings—and for letting you get caught in the middle of an old dispute."

She shrugged, still reluctant to let herself hope. "I shouldn't have been where I obviously wasn't wanted."

"But I *did* want you there," he insisted. "And I was afraid to admit that I wanted you there. I was afraid to admit how much I want our relationship to work, so I sabotaged it instead. Because letting you go seemed easier than letting you into my heart."

"Then…why did you follow me?"

"Because the door had barely closed behind you when I realized that you're already in my heart, and I don't ever want to let you go." He lifted his hands to frame her face. "Maybe Dan and Annie manipulated the situation, but my feelings are real. I love you, Serena, and I want to spend not just this Christmas but all Christmases for the rest of my life with you."

His declaration—so unexpected and unexpectedly perfect—brought fresh tears to her eyes.

"Don't cry, Serena. I know I hurt you, but it can't be too late. Please tell me it's not too late."

"It's not too late," she assured him. "These are happy tears."

"Do they mean that you forgive me?" he asked hopefully.

"I forgive you. And I love you, too."

His lips curved. "Yeah?"

"Yeah," she confirmed. "For now and forever."

"Will you come back to celebrate Christmas with me and my noisy, nosy family?" he asked.

"Will you do me a favor?"

"Anything," he promised.

"Give me a ride," she said. "Because my vehicle isn't going anywhere anytime soon."

So they returned to Sunshine Farm, where the rest of the Stockton family was relieved to see her—although distressed by the sight of her injury. But after Annie and Eva had finished fussing and cleaning and bandaging her wound, they all *finally* sat down to dinner.

"I've already apologized to Serena," Bailey told his siblings, after the food had been passed around and everyone had loaded up their plates. "But I want to apologize to all of you, too, for my ill-mannered outburst."

"Since you apparently came to your senses and got back your girl, I guess we can forgive you," Jamie said.

Bailey smiled as he slid an arm around Serena's shoulders. "Did you hear that? You're my girl."

"I heard," she confirmed. "And I think that's a title I can live with."

"Good. Because I don't want to live without you." Then he glanced across the table at Dan and Annie. "And I guess I should thank both of you for introducing me to Mrs. Claus…" He paused then and turned back to Serena. "Or maybe…the future Mrs. Stockton?"

Serena stared at him, stunned. "Are you…" She let the words trail off, unwilling to complete the thought, in case she was wrong.

"I'm asking if you'll marry me, Serena."

She wasn't wrong. And with those words, her heart filled with so much happiness and love, she could barely breathe never mind respond to his question.

"Yay!" Janie immediately cheered. "There's going to be another wedding."

Henry, Jared and Katie—likely picking up on the excitement of their cousin's tone more than understanding her words—responded by clapping their hands.

"While I appreciate your enthusiastic support," Bailey said to his nieces and nephews, "Serena hasn't yet answered my question." Then he turned his gaze back to her. "What do you say?"

"I say yes," she told him. "Definitely yes."

A quick—and decidedly relieved—grin creased his face for an instant before he kissed her.

And then everyone was cheering and applauding.

"I know it's impolite to eat and run," Jamie noted, peering out the window as the table was being cleared a long while later. "But it's really snowing out there."

"It really is," Fallon agreed. "We should get the kids bundled up and make our escape while we still can."

"*If* you still can," Eva said, looking worried.

"Why don't you spend the night here?" Luke suggested as an alternative. "After all, we have plenty of cabins."

"Because Santa Claus is coming tonight," Fallon reminded them all.

"And we're not going far," Jamie pointed out. "Not to mention that Andy and Molly would be very unhappy to be left alone overnight," he said, referring to the puppies he'd adopted out of the litter of seven that he'd rescued two years earlier.

"What about Marvin?" Bailey suddenly asked Serena. "What if his doggy door gets blocked by the snow?"

"I already called Dee," she said, referring to the neighbor who occasionally checked in on her animals when Serena had to be away for any length of time. "She'll make sure the animals have everything they need."

"Does she know to give Max his apple wedge treat? And to fluff Molly's pillow?"

"She knows," Serena assured him.

But in that moment, she knew that if she hadn't already been head over heels in love with him, Bailey's concern for the welfare of her furry companions would have made her tumble.

"So they'll be okay if you stay here with me tonight?" he prompted.

"They might miss me, but they'll be okay" she assured him.

"Good," he said. "Because I'd miss you more if I had to spend the night without the woman I love."

"I've decided that Christmas is my favorite time of year," Bailey announced to Serena the next morning.

"And when did you arrive at this conclusion?" she asked.

"Just now, when I woke up and you were here, and I had the incomparable pleasure of making love with my beautiful fiancée on December 25."

"I've always loved Christmas," she reminded him. "But you've given me even more reasons to love it—and to look forward to all the Christmases we'll share together."

And as she snuggled in his arms and listened to the strong steady beat of his heart, she couldn't help but think of her sister and hope that wherever Mimi was—because with all of her heart and soul, Serena believed that her little sister was out there somewhere—she was also celebrating the holiday with someone she loved.

"I'm still not sure this is real," she said. "It seems like a dream."

"My dream come true," he told her.

"You really do want to marry me?"

"Why would you doubt it?"

"It just seems like everything happened so fast and—"

"Do *you* have doubts?" he interrupted to ask her.

"No," she immediately replied. "But I also never said that I'd never get married again."

"I did say that," he acknowledged. "Because I was sure it was true...and then I fell in love with you."

"So your proposal wasn't just an impulse?"

"The timing was a little impulsive," he admitted. "I probably should have waited to ask until I had a ring, but I promise as soon as stores open on December 26, I'll fix that oversight."

"I should probably say that I don't need a ring, but I want one. I want a visible symbol to show the world—or at least the rest of Rust Creek Falls—that I'm engaged to marry Bailey Stockton."

He shifted so that he was facing her, then lifted a hand to brush her hair away from her face and gently stroke her cheek. "I love you, Serena."

She smiled. "I love you, too."

They sealed their promises with another kiss, which might have led to more except that Bailey's cell phone buzzed on the bedside table. With obvious reluctance, he eased his lips from hers and picked up the offending instrument to read the text message on the screen.

"We're being summoned to the main house for breakfast and then gifts."

"Maybe I could borrow your truck and head back to my place to check on Marvin, Molly and Max," Serena suggested.

"If you're worried about them, we'll both go," he said.

"I'm not really worried," she admitted. "I just thought I should give you some time with your family."

"You're part of that family now, too," he reminded her.

So they got dressed and headed over to the main house, where everyone else was already gathered around the table overflowing with tasty offerings: platters of scrambled eggs, bacon and sausage, stacks of toast and bowls of fresh fruit.

"You're late," Jamie said when Bailey settled into a vacant chair beside him.

"I'd say I'm right on time," he countered, as Eva added a plate of sticky buns, fresh out of the oven, to the assortment of food already on the table.

"I want to know when it's nap time," Fallon confided. "We've been up for hours already with the triplets, and when we finish up here, we're heading over to my parents' place for Christmas Day—round three."

"I'm glad you were able to squeeze this into your schedule," Bella said sincerely.

"Are you kidding? This is the best part of the day," Fallon said to the woman who had been her friend long before she was her sister-in-law.

"It is special," Dana chimed in. "To be able to celebrate the holidays with all of you."

Of course, everyone was aware that the group was incomplete. Unless and until Liza was found, there would always be something missing. But for now, they focused on the joy of being together. And when everyone had eaten their fill, they retreated to the living room to disperse the presents that were piled under the tree.

"It's amazing, isn't it?" Annie said, nudging Bailey with her shoulder as the triplets attacked an enormous box that had all their names on it.

"What's amazing? The noise? The mess? The chaos?"

His sister-in-law laughed softly. "Well, all of that," she acknowledged. "Because it's all part and parcel of being a member of this family. But I was actually referring to the difference that a year can make."

"This time last year, you and Dan were newlyweds," Bailey noted.

"And you'd just returned to Rust Creek Falls, a bitter and cynical Grooge, certain you weren't going to stay."

He couldn't deny that was true—or that, until only a few weeks ago, he'd remained mostly bitter and cynical and unconvinced that there was a future for him in this town. And then his brother and sister-in-law had conned him into donning Santa's hat and coat.

He'd totally been faking it that first day. He'd had no Christmas spirit of his own to share with the kids. Serena had helped him find not just that Christmas spirit again but closure on his past and hope for his future.

She'd changed everything for him.

"It's true," he agreed. "A lot can change in a year—or when you finally find the one person you're meant to spend the rest of your life with."

"You're welcome," Annie said.

"Yeah, maybe I do owe you for that," he acknowledged.

"And I know just how you can pay me back."

"How?" he asked, a little warily.

She smiled. "Be happy." Then she kissed his cheek and moved away to find her husband.

But Bailey knew that he already was.

As he looked around the room, he was grateful and humbled to be part of this crazy family whose connection and affection had not only endured but grown stronger over distance and time. Of course, their family had grown in size, too, with so many of his siblings pairing up and having babies. Or, in Dan and Annie's case, an almost-teenager.

He found Serena in the crowd, and felt his heart swell to fill his whole chest. She was sitting on the floor by the fire with Jared—or was that Henry?—on her lap. The nephew had a gingerbread cookie in his hand, which he would gnaw on for a while and then offer to Serena, and she would gamely take a nibble of the soggy treat before the little guy shoved it back in his own mouth.

She fit so perfectly here. With his family. With him.

Annie was right—a single year could make a world of difference. And he hoped that by next Christmas, Serena would be his wife rather than his fiancée. And maybe, not too long after that, they'd have a child of their own to contribute to the mayhem.

That thought gave him a moment's pause.

Henry—or was it Jared?—toddled over to his brother with two chunky toy trucks clutched in his fists, obviously hoping to entice him away from his cookie to play. His brother was happy to abandon his snack, but he kissed Serena's cheek before sliding from her lap, and she smiled as she watched the brothers move away.

Bailey found a napkin on a nearby table and offered it to her. She wrapped the remnants of the soggy cookie, then wiped the crumbs from her hand.

"You looked deep in thought over there," she commented, as he sat down beside her.

"I was just wondering how long it takes to plan a wedding," he said, sliding his arm around her shoulders.

"You can't be talking about our wedding."

"Why not?"

"Because we only just got engaged."

"Do you know why I asked you to marry me?"

"Because you love me and want to spend the rest of your life with me?"

"All of that," he agreed. "And because I want to start our life together as soon as possible."

"I want that, too."

"So let's set a date," he urged.

"Okay," she agreed. "June 25."

"That's six months away."

"I figure it will probably take that long to plan a wedding."

"Unless we get someone to do it for us," he noted. "Caroline Ruth did a great job with the Presents for Patriots event."

"She did," Serena agreed. "And now that you mention it, Sawmill Station would be the perfect venue for a wedding."

"Then I suggest we reach out to her as soon as possible to get started with the planning."

"What's your hurry?" she wondered.

"Well, I was thinking—" he tipped his head toward hers, his expression filled with cautious hope "—the sooner we get married, the sooner we can get started making a baby."

Her heart fluttered, yearned. "In that case," she said, her eyes growing misty, "the sooner the better."

It was an almost perfect day.

Of course, spending Christmas morning with his siblings, it was natural that Bailey would think about the parents who were no longer with them. And while their absence tugged at his heart, he felt certain that Rob and Lauren Stockton were looking down on their children, happy to see them celebrating together.

Of course, they weren't all together. Not yet. But some of Serena's eternal optimism must have rubbed off on him, because he was starting to believe that the reunion of his siblings would soon be complete.

That thought had barely formed in his mind when the doorbell rang.

The sound didn't interrupt the festivities. Several of the adults exchanged curious glances, silently wondering who would be visiting on Christmas Day, then Luke went to discover the answer to that unspoken question.

A few minutes later, he returned with an unexpected but very welcome guest.

Bailey's heart hammered against his ribs as he reached for Serena's hand and linked their fingers together.

"Liza."

It was Bella who first ventured to whisper the name, and the younger woman's familiar blue eyes immediately filled with tears.

Then, more loudly for the benefit of those who hadn't realized that someone new had joined the party, Bella announced, "Liza's home."

The rest of her siblings all rushed forward to embrace the long-lost sister who had finally returned.

Serena decided it was an appropriate time to extricate herself from the family gathering. Though she was thrilled for Bailey and all his brothers and sisters, their impromptu family reunion was a painful reminder that her family was still in pieces. Yes, she was starting to rebuild a relationship with her mother, but she still felt the loss of the father who'd walked out of her life fifteen years earlier and, even more deeply, the absence of the sister who had disappeared without a trace a year previous to that.

But Serena's efforts to slip away were thwarted by her fiancé.

"Where are you going?" Bailey asked her.

"Home," she said. "I've already been gone longer than I intended to be."

"Your SUV is in a ditch," he reminded her.

She held up the keys in her hand. "Eva's letting me borrow her vehicle."

"That's not necessary," he said. "I can take you."

"I know you can, but you've been waiting for this reunion a long time."

"And you're still waiting for yours," he realized.

"I am," she admitted. "But seeing you with your siblings, knowing you found your way back to one another after so many years apart, gives me renewed hope that I'll find Mimi again."

"You will," he said confidently.

"But in the meantime, my pets are waiting for me," she told him.

"So we'll go get Marvin, Molly and Max and bring them back here," he decided.

"Don't you think that will be a little...chaotic?"

"No, I think it will be *a lot* chaotic," he acknowledged. "But it's Christmas, and family should be together on Christmas."

"You got more than you bargained for, didn't you?" Serena remarked later, after she and Bailey had returned to the relative quiet of his cabin following dinner with his family—and hers. Because Amanda and Mark had been at her apartment when they went to get her pets, and Bailey had persuaded them to join the festivities at Sunshine Farm.

"It was every bit as chaotic as you promised," he confirmed. "And I wouldn't have changed a minute of it."

Marvin, Molly and Max might have agreed with his assessment, but they were already snuggled up together and asleep in the dog's bed, exhausted from so much attention and excitement.

"Grams didn't even protest being dragged away from her celebration on the beach to hear the news of our engagement," Serena noted.

"Although she did request that we plan a summer wedding."

"June 25 is summer," she pointed out, referencing the date she'd originally suggested.

"And it's a long time to wait to make you my wife," he grumbled.

"I know you're eager to get started on a family of our own, but a June wedding ensures we'll have lots of time to practice our baby-making technique."

"Are you suggesting that I need practice?" he asked, his tone indignant.

"Of course not," she soothed. "I'm only suggesting that I would very much enjoy practicing with you."

"Okay, then," he relented.

"In fact… I was kind of hoping we might practice tonight."

And that's just what they did—all night long.

Epilogue

"Did you hear the news?" glowing newlywed Vivienne Shuster Dalton asked her recently engaged friend and colleague Caroline Ruth.

"If you're referring to the news that Bailey Stockton proposed to Serena Langley on Christmas Eve, then yes, I did," Caroline confirmed.

"That's six engagements in the past six months."

"Love is definitely in the air in Rust Creek Falls," Caroline agreed.

"Fingers crossed—" Vivienne demonstrated with her own "—we're going to be planning a lot of weddings in the upcoming year."

"But there are still a lot of single men and women in town," Caroline noted.

Vivienne clapped her hands together gleefully. "Which promises even more business in years to come."

Although Caroline shared her business partner's optimism,

she felt compelled to issue a word of caution. "Some of them might need a little nudge to set them on the right path."

"Oooh, you're right." Vivienne considered, then nodded. "That's a great idea."

Caroline wasn't sure how to respond to her colleague's unbridled enthusiasm. "What did I say? What's a great idea?"

"Adding matchmaking to our list of services."

"That wasn't my idea," she immediately protested.

But now that it was out there, the possibilities were undeniably intriguing...

* * * * *

IF YOU ENJOYED THIS BOOK WE THINK YOU WILL ALSO LOVE

HARLEQUIN SPECIAL EDITION

Believe in love. Overcome obstacles. Find happiness.

Relate to finding comfort and strength in the support of loved ones and enjoy the journey no matter what life throws your way.

6 NEW BOOKS AVAILABLE EVERY MONTH!

HSEXSERIES2020TRADE

SPECIAL EXCERPT FROM
HARLEQUIN SPECIAL EDITION

A single mom widowed after an unhappy marriage, Brynn Hale has finally returned home to Starlight. She's ready for a fresh start for her son, and what better time for it than Christmas? But Nick Dunlap is the one connection to her past she can't let go of...

Read on for a sneak peek at the next book in the Welcome to Starlight miniseries,
His Last-Chance Christmas Family
by Michelle Major.

"You sound like a counselor." The barest glimmer of a smile played around the edges of Brynn's mouth. "When did you get so smart, Chief Dunlap?"

"I was born this way. You never noticed before now because you were too dazzled by my good looks."

Her eyes went wide for a moment, and he wondered if he'd overstepped with the teasing. "I was dazzled by you. That part is true." She rolled her eyes. "But I guarantee you didn't show this kind of insight when we were younger."

He should make some funny comment back to her, keep the moment light. Instead, he let his gaze lower to her mouth as he took the soft ends of her hair between his fingers. "I might not have messed things up so badly if I had."

She drew in a sharp breath and he stepped away. This was not the time to spook her. "Come on, Brynn," he coaxed. "We both know it's not going to be good for anyone if you stay with your mom."

"She doesn't even want to meet Remi," Brynn told him, her full lips pressing into a thin line.

"Her loss," he said quietly. "All along it's been her loss. Say yes. Please."

She shifted and looked to where Tyler had disappeared with Kel. Without turning back to Nick, she nodded. "Yes," she said finally. "Thank you for the offer. I appreciate it and promise we won't disrupt your life." Now she did turn to him. "Very much, anyway," she added with a smile.

"Easy as pie," he said, ignoring the fact that his heart was beating as fast as if he'd just finished running a marathon.

Don't miss
His Last-Chance Christmas Family
by Michelle Major,
available December 2020 wherever
Harlequin Special Edition books and ebooks are sold.

Harlequin.com

HARLEQUIN
SPECIAL EDITION

Believe in love. Overcome obstacles. Find happiness.

Save $1.00

on the purchase of ANY Harlequin Special Edition book.

Available wherever books are sold, including most bookstores, supermarkets, drugstores and discount stores.

His Last-Chance Christmas Family
MICHELLE MAJOR

Save $1.00

on the purchase of ANY Harlequin Special Edition book.

Coupon valid until October 31, 2021.
Redeemable at participating outlets in the US and Canada only.
Limit one coupon per customer.

Canadian Retailers: Harlequin Enterprises ULC will pay the face value of this coupon plus 10.25¢ if submitted by customer for this product only. Any other use constitutes fraud. Coupon is nonassignable. Void if taxed, prohibited or restricted by law. Consumer must pay any government taxes. Void if copied. Inmar Promotional Services ("IPS") customers submit coupons and proof of sales to Harlequin Enterprises ULC, P.O. Box 31000, Scarborough, ON M1R 0E7, Canada. Non-IPS retailer—for reimbursement submit coupons and proof of sales directly to Harlequin Enterprises ULC, Retail Marketing Department, Bay Adelaide Centre, East Tower, 22 Adelaide Street West, 40th Floor, Toronto, Ontario M5H 4E3, Canada.

52616903

U.S. Retailers: Harlequin Enterprises ULC will pay the face value of this coupon plus 8¢ if submitted by customer for this product only. Any other use constitutes fraud. Coupon is nonassignable. Void if taxed, prohibited or restricted by law. Consumer must pay any government taxes. Void if copied. For reimbursement submit coupons and proof of sales directly to Harlequin Enterprises ULC 482, NCH Marketing Services, P.O. Box 880001, El Paso, TX 88588-0001, U.S.A. Cash value 1/100 cents.

5 65373 00076 2   (8100)0 12477

© 2020 Harlequin Enterprises ULC

HSECOUP1120TRADE